"Damn! Remind me not to piss you off!"

"Too late for that," Tychus responded, as he got up off the corpse. "But at least you and your girlfriends know how to fight. . . . That's more than I expected. Come on! Let's head for the armory!"

The squad crossed a parkin[illegible]ed with a dozen dead m[illegible] in on a brightly lit [illegible] already halfway do[illegible]s in the process of p[illegible]e in the final stages o[illegible] offered the men momentary c[illegible].

"Damn it!" Raynor exclaimed, as two rippers opened fire from the shadows. "What's going on here?"

"They're stealing stuff, that's what's going on," Tychus replied knowingly, as spikes buried themselves in the plascrete and the noncom jerked Raynor back out of the line of fire. "Which is real interesting because you'd expect the KMs to blow the place up!"

Raynor's mind was racing. "That's right! How long since the first announcement? Fifteen minutes max? They must've been loading at least some of those trucks *before* the attack began!"

"Well, I'll be damned," Tychus replied in mock amazement, "you aren't as stupid as you look! So General, let's kill those fekkin' rippers and find out where those trucks are going."

HEAVEN'S DEVILS

WILLIAM C. DIETZ

POCKET STAR BOOKS
New York London Toronto Sydney

Pocket Star Books
A Division of Simon & Schuster, Inc.
1230 Avenue of the Americas
New York, NY 10020

First Pocket Star Books paperback edition January 2011

POCKET STAR BOOKS and colophon are registered trademarks of Simon & Schuster, Inc.

Cover design by Alan Dingman
Art by Glenn Rane
Interior art by Wei Wang, Steve Hui, and Luke Mancini of Blizzard Entertainment, Inc.

Manufactured in the United States of America

10 9 8 7 6 5 4 3 2 1

ISBN 978-1-4391-7270-4
ISBN 978-1-4391-6365-8 (ebook)

This book is dedicated to my editor, Jaime Costas,
who was incredibly supportive from beginning to end,
a tireless problem solver,
and the inspiration for some really great lines!

ACKNOWLEDGMENTS

I would like to thank the Blizzard team for creating wonderful games, three-dimensional characters, and allowing me to play in the StarCraft universe.

HEAVEN'S DEVILS

CHAPTER ONE

"With Kel-Morian attacks spread across three of the five contested zones in the Koprulu sector, Confederate forces have been hard-pressed to keep a consistent response to the mining guilds' recent hit-and-run guerilla tactics. The resultant increases in military spending have hurt other sectors of the economy, with some of the most significant drops in agricultural support in years. Hardest hit are the independent farmers, and bankruptcies on Confederate agrarian worlds are rising sharply."

Max Speer, *Evening Report* for UNN
November 2487

THE PLANET SHILOH,
THE CONFEDERACY OF MAN

The early morning sun was a blinding ball of fire in the sky, and the hot air shimmered as it rose off the long queue of fuel trucks that snaked the curve and disappeared over the rise beyond. Jim Raynor, squinting behind a pair of mirrorshades, brought the tanker to a stop, switched off the ignition, and leaned back. During the hour he'd already spent in the line, he'd memorized every scuff and speck of dirt on the back end of the truck in front of him.

Through the open window of the truck's cab, Raynor scanned the familiar landscape. The gently rolling farmland was parched, and had been for more than a month, with the hottest weather still ahead. After a brief interlude, winter would fall like a hammer and the land would be covered with a thick layer of white. "She blows hot, and she blows cold," Raynor's father liked to say. "But Shiloh is a bitch either way."

The tedious grind had been difficult for the restless eighteen-year-old to get used to, but he had suffered through the first few weeks of the vespene gas ration with no complaints. His parents had enough to worry about already.

The ongoing Guild Wars had diverted resources away from the planet and, according to his father, most of the other worlds, too. As a result, farmers like Jim's parents had to deal with fuel rationing, city residents had to cope with food shortages, and everybody had to pay higher taxes. But they all did what they had to do, knowing their sacrifice would afford them protection against the Kel-Morian Combine.

Sitting on the console next to him, Raynor's fone chimed and Tom Omer's face appeared. The other boy was at the wheel of his father's flatbed truck three rigs back. *"Check it out,"* Omer said, as his image disappeared and a hologram blossomed over the passenger seat. It consisted of floating puzzle pieces, at least a hundred of them, which, if assembled correctly, would create a 3-D picture. A picture that Omer had pulled up from somewhere and ordered his fone to chop, mix, and deliver. *"Your time starts now,"* Omer said. *"Go!"*

The puzzle pieces were small. None were more than an inch across and they came in all sorts of sizes and shapes. But Raynor thought he recognized some of the colors and reached out to "pick" and "place" them with quick jabs of his right index finger. He made some errors, but was quick to correct them, and it wasn't long before an image of Anna Harper in her cheerleading uniform began to piece together.

"Nice," Raynor said approvingly.

"More than nice. She's my future wife," Omer replied. *"Too bad she doesn't know I exist."*

"Eh, you're not missing anything. Anna doesn't really have any substance."

"Substance?" Omer called out. *"You know what, Jim? Only* you *would say something like that. Anyway, you finished in forty-six seconds. Not bad for a motorhead. . . . What you got for me?"*

Raynor flipped through a bunch of pictures in the fone's memory and chuckled when he found one of Omer dressed in a clown suit taken back in sixth grade. "This pic is so hot, you'll forget all about Anna," he said, smiling. Raynor ran the image through the fone's dicer app, and sent it off. "I'll give you half an hour, and you'll need every second of it." There was silence as Omer went to work.

Raynor returned his attention to the road, but his mind was adrift. Upper school graduation was looming, and he had been thinking more and more about his future. He had spent his entire life on the farm, and even though their land wasn't the best, it was going to be his someday—provided his parents weren't forced to sell it to pay their increasingly high taxes.

Raynor figured that if he worked hard to help his family pull through, and the Confederacy won the wars, things would improve and he'd be able to focus on his own goals for a while, whatever they turned out to be. This gas shortage certainly wasn't helping matters—his family's fuel allotment wasn't enough for their machines to yield a profitable harvest, so the outlook was grim.

The hollow coughs of a hundred truck ignitions firing in quick succession broke both the silence and Raynor's train of thought. He turned the key, the engine started, and he put the tanker in gear. Then, having allowed the rig to roll forward for a hundred feet or so, it was time to stop again. He turned the engine off to conserve fuel and waited.

"Real funny," Omer said, as he finished the

puzzle. *"I think I'll hack your fone and delete that file."*

Raynor laughed. "I'd better make a backup then. You never know when a little blackmail might come in handy."

"Hey, Jim, you still here?" a voice rang out over the speaker mounted above Raynor's head.

Jim reached for the mic. "Hey, Frank. Yeah, I got a while to go yet."

Frank Carver was Jim's teammate on Centerville's demolition team, a high-octane sport played in the less refined parts of the Koprulu sector that was much like the demolition derbies their ancestors had participated in. Vehicles were built and raced with the dual purpose of winning and destroying opponents' vehicles. Since the wars started, the game had petered out due to a shortage of fuel and other materials.

"Yeah, me too—it seems even slower than usual today. You going into town tonight?" Frank asked.

"Nope, I can't," Raynor replied, "we gotta get the wheat in."

Omer's voice crackled through the frequency. *"The harvest will be over by the time you get through this line."*

Raynor saw a puff of black vapor as the truck in front of him started up.

"Hey, Omer," a young man's voice popped onto the feed, *"I hear you're actually joining the Marine Corps, for real. I had no idea there was a fourth string in the military! Congrats, brother!"*

A chorus of guffaws rang out as the trucks shuddered off again.

"Very funny," Omer said. *"When I come back for the victory parade, you'll be kissing my boots for saving your sorry little asses!"*

Raynor laughed, but his smile quickly faded. Despite everything his family had been through, the wars had still seemed so distant. But ever since Raynor's classmates had begun enlisting, it had started to hit home for him. He'd heard the stories around town; many soldiers never made it home from combat. But Tom was right—he could come back a hero in the end, and Jim would still be driving his half-broken-down robo-harvester, dreaming of a break from the monotony of life. There had been moments during the past few weeks when Raynor actually envied the kid.

Raynor reached up to wipe the sweat from his face; his hand brushed past a new growth of stubble on his cheek! He craned his neck to see his reflection in the side mirror. For years Raynor had wanted to grow a beard like his father's, and now it was finally coming in. He twisted his face in one direction, then the other, examining his tanned, youthful face, when the sudden *roar* of a powerful engine blasted him out of his thoughts.

"Jim, look alive!" Omer yelled through the comm.

Raynor glanced at the right side mirror, and saw a big blunt-nosed fueler pulling up next to him, about to swerve in the gap in front of his truck, crowding in ahead of all the others. The tanker's door said HARNACK TRUCKING.

Raynor quickly put in the clutch and up-shifted but he was too late to fill the gap as the invading truck driver jerked in front of him and stomped on the brake. That forced Raynor and all the rest to do likewise, and within seconds, a percussive string of metal crunching metal resounded behind him.

"Damn it!" Raynor roared, joining the thunder of expletives that rattled the truck's speakers. The frustration that had built up over the last hour sent adrenaline surging into his bloodstream. Raynor turned the engine off, set the brake, and was out of the cab in a matter of seconds. His boots delivered a muted thump as they hit the hot pavement. He quickly strode the length of the trailer in front of him as other drivers piled out of their trucks.

"Get that sonofabitch!" one of Raynor's buddies yelled, and most of the gathering crowd echoed their support. One of the local farmers tried to get in his way, but Raynor pushed past and approached the driver's door, fire coursing through his veins. He was about to throw it open and pull the bastard out by his neck when the door suddenly swung out.

A red-haired youth dressed in tattered shorts and a T-shirt hopped onto the truck's drop step, grinning wickedly and cracking his chewing gum. Raynor recognized him immediately as the star of the Bronsonville demolition team. It all came rushing back to him—the explosive match in which Harnack intentionally flipped his own vehicle on top of Raynor's as they went around a curve, nearly decapitating him in the process. The crowd went completely mad, and Harnack became an instant legend.

"What the hell is your error?" Raynor yelled over the clangor of loud, thrashing music that spilled out from inside the truck.

"My error? I'm lookin' at him."

"You're such a moron. You're gonna pay for all that damage back there!"

"Okay, farm boy, I'll pay you with some fresh manure. Cup your hands."

Furious, Raynor latched onto the Harnack kid's legs, attempting to pull them out from under him, but the youth held tight onto the door frame. Raynor jumped back to avoid a kick in the face, but then Harnack launched himself out of the cab, clearly intending to land on top of Jim and ride him to the ground.

But Raynor anticipated the move, sidestepped his opponent, and had the pleasure of seeing him land spread-eagled on the pavement. "Stomp him!" someone shouted, but Raynor shook his head and waited for the other driver to get up.

The Harnack kid had game, Raynor had to admit, as his foe bounced up off the road with fists raised. His forehead was bleeding, as was his right forearm, but he appeared to be in no way intimidated. "Come on, sissy boy," the other teenager said. "Show me what you got other than a funny looking face!"

"What are you, five years old?" His hands were up by then, held just the way his father had taught him, as both circled, looking for an opening.

"Knock his block off!" Omer shouted from the crowd. "Kick his ass!"

Raynor could tell it wasn't going to be that easy, as Harnack threw a couple of quick jabs and drove him backward. He responded in kind, landed a blow that glanced off the other driver's left cheekbone, and took a fist to the stomach in return.

Raynor knew that people were yelling things, rooting for him mostly, but the sound of it merged into an indecipherable roar. The first flush of anger had disappeared by then and his brain had kicked in. *Think,* he told himself, *look for some sort of weakness, so you can land some good punches and end this thing quickly.*

Harnack pressed forward and threw a succession of jabs, which Raynor easily avoided. Then, out of nowhere, as he dodged his opponent's fist, Raynor took a skull-splitting wallop to the back of the head. *What the hell?* He instantly reached back to confront his new attacker, finding instead a sizzling hot metal bar. He glanced behind him. Harnack had backed him into the truck's side mirror!

As Raynor turned again toward his foe, the kid flashed a gleeful smile before delivering a flurry of punches, most of which Raynor was able to block with wrists and forearms as he put his chin down and danced away.

"Come back here!" the red-haired boy demanded. "Come back and fight, you fekkin' dirt-pusher!"

That was when Raynor saw Harnack squint and realized that the sun was shining in his opponent's eyes. Raynor shifted his position slightly until he was sure Harnack was blinded by the glare, planted his feet, and threw a quick jab. The other teenager could see well enough to know something was coming his way, and raised his arms to defend against it. That opened his midriff to an attack, and Raynor was there to deliver a solid right punch to the gut. Three alternating blows, each powered by strong farm-boy shoulders, hammered Harnack's stomach like pile drivers.

The Harnack kid grunted as the air left his lungs, then he clutched his stomach, dropped to the ground, and vomited on the pavement. A cheer erupted as the locals celebrated a victory by one of their own, and a few of the adults stepped in to drag the bully away from the mob of youths that had closed in and was shouting slurs and threats.

Raynor started walking toward his truck—he just wanted to climb in and shut the door so nobody would notice that he was a little rattled from the fight—but Omer intercepted him. "Good fight, man," he said as he shook Raynor's hand. "That was killer."

Raynor muttered a series of expletives before spitting a wad of pink saliva onto the hot, dusty ground. Several of Jim's buddies jogged over to congratulate him, and after a round of cheerful high fives and slaps on the back, a smiling Raynor and his friends turned to watch the scene unfold.

One of the farmers climbed up into Harnack's truck and revved the engine, sending black smoke belching out of twin stacks, and drove the tanker onto the shoulder of the road. Then, with a burly man at each elbow, Harnack was escorted over to his rig and told to wait for the end of the line to arrive or head on home. He chose the second option.

As Harnack struggled up the drop step and into his truck, Raynor's friends howled with derisive laughter and shouted a few choice obscenities at him. The truck's air horn blared as the teenager hit the gas, up-shifted, and roared along the shoulder. Then, having spotted a gap, he cut between two trucks and swerved into oncoming traffic to yet another sounding of horns. Harnack steered into the right lane and headed north toward Bronsonville, waving a one-fingered salute out the window.

The line suddenly jerked ahead and everyone scrambled to get back to their trucks. Back in the cab, and having closed the gap in front of him, Raynor eyed himself in the mirror. That was when he realized that Harnack had scored a clean hit on his left eye, which was already turning blue and would soon be swollen shut. He swore. There wouldn't be any way to hide that from his mother, who was going to be less than pleased.

Raynor pulled into the station twenty minutes later, and was greeted with nods and smiles from his fellow truckers. It seemed as though he'd earned a fair amount of respect by standing up to the Harnack kid, and that felt pretty good.

He filled the tanker halfway, which was all his family could afford. As he started up the truck again, he hoped the fuel would be sufficient to get most, if not all of the crop in. That, at least, was better than nothing.

CHAPTER TWO

"Oh, sure, we've got bigger guns. Bigger guns and more of 'em. The problem, as I see it, is that we don't got enough hands to hold the fekkin' things. We need more soldiers, and we need them yesterday. What's the point in outgunning your enemy if your ordnances are collecting dust in the armory?"

Corporal Thaddeus Timson, Fort Brickwell, Shiloh
February 2488

THE PLANET SHILOH,
THE CONFEDERACY OF MAN

If it had been hot earlier that day, it was absolutely hellish by midafternoon. It was at least ninety degrees inside the CSX-410's open cab as Raynor drove the huge machine toward the south end of the field. There had been a time, starting back before Jim had been born, when the machine had been able to guide itself. But the robo-harvester's navigation system failed long before his family acquired the secondhand machine, which forced Jim to sit behind the wheel and manually steer the harvester as it cut a broad swath through the field of triticale-wheat.

Raynor neared the edge and turned the robo-harvester back in the other direction. Suddenly, his thoughts were interrupted by what looked like a dust devil off to the north. The windscreen was dirty so he stuck his head out of the cab in order to see more clearly, a feat made even more difficult because his left eye was swollen shut and hurt like hell. Then Jim realized that what he was looking at *wasn't* a dust devil, but a machine of some sort, coming his way. *What the hell . . . ?* Was it the neighbors? No, their crop was in, so there was no reason to roll their robo-harvester.

Raynor pulled his head back in, but kept an eye on the pillar of dust, as he guided the harvester toward the river. Then, once he was about halfway across the length of the field, he took a second look. What he saw surprised and worried him. The oncoming machine was a Confederate goliath.

Like every other kid on Shiloh, Jim had seen vids of the huge twelve-foot-tall walkers standing guard outside the Council headquarters on Tarsonis, marching through the streets in parades, and trudging through storms of lethal fire as their arm cannons dealt death to the Confederacy's enemies.

But Raynor had never seen a goliath marching

across the countryside before and felt a sudden stab of fear. Property taxes had been rising steeply for the last few years—and some farmers had been thrown off their land. Was that why the machine had been sent? To take possession of the farm? Maybe, but Jim couldn't see any sign of the ground troops that would normally accompany a walker. *What, then?*

He took the mic off its clip, and was about to alert his father to the goliath's presence, when Trace Raynor's voice came over the cab's speaker. "I can see it, Jim. . . . I'm on my way."

Raynor looked back over his right shoulder, saw the column of dust his father's beat-up truck was throwing up, and felt a sense of relief. Because even though he was good at schoolwork and could run every piece of equipment on the farm, there were a whole lot of things he didn't know how to do. And dealing with the government was one of them.

But he was curious, so as the brightly painted goliath splashed through the river and lurched up onto the field, Raynor brought the robo-harvester to a halt and switched the engine off to save fuel. He could hear the tinny sound of the Confederacy's anthem by then as the walker grew larger, and flags flew from dual antennas.

As his father arrived, the teenager took a swig of tepid water from the bottle on the floor before he exited the cab. The wheat crop was so sparse that his boots produced puffs of dust when his feet hit the ground. By that time the goliath had come to a halt, and stood not fifty feet away. As Jim entered the machine's elongated shadow, he was aware of the subtle vibration that the machine transmitted through the soles of his heavy work boots. There was something else, too, an acrid odor that he recognized as the smell of ozone, which hung heavy in the air.

The walker had a blocky cockpit where the pilot was seated, mounts for two sets of missile launchers, and articulated arms that were equipped with shovel-hands instead of the autocannons Jim had seen in the vids. But the armored body and sturdy legs were the way he remembered them.

With the exception of the machine's cockpit, which was painted dark blue, the rest of the goliath was red. A unit number was visible on both sides of the cockpit, and four dropship-shaped silhouettes had been painted onto the area just below the front canopy, along with that of a Hellhound—the Kel-Morian equivalent of the Confederacy's Avenger fighter craft. The mech was relatively clean except for a thin patina of dust, and the flags that had been flying so proudly a few minutes before hung motionless as if drained of spirit.

Trace Raynor's truck rattled as the engine shut down, the door opened, and he jumped out. He had a shock of gray hair, a neatly trimmed beard on a face so weathered it resembled a topographical map, and a body without an ounce of fat on it. His brown eyes were bright with anger as he came over to stand next to his son. "First the bastards raise our taxes so high we can barely pay them—and now they send a machine to trample our crops! They might as well shoot us and put us out of our misery."

Jim understood his father's resentment, but wondered about the wisdom of saying such things out loud, especially if the goliath was equipped with external audio pickups. But the thought was preempted as servos whined, and the canopy above what was painted to look like a snarling mouth opened to reveal the cockpit within. A uniformed marine rose to wave at them. "Good morning, folks!" his much-amplified voice said, booming through twin speakers. "My name is Farley . . . Gunnery Sergeant Farley. . . . I'll be down in a sec."

Farley gave a voice command. One of the goliath's massive shovel-hands rose up to meet him, he stepped onto it, and was gently lowered to the ground. The moment he stepped off, servos whined as the walker assumed a position akin to parade rest. "You must be Trace Raynor," the marine said, as he came forward to shake hands with the farmer. "And, unless I miss my guess, this is your son, Jim, proud member of the class of 2488. Good going, young man."

"Thanks." As Jim shook hands with the marine, he was impressed by Farley's high-wattage personality and the strength of his grip. There was something odd about the way he looked, though—the marine appeared to be too young for his middle-aged persona, and Jim noticed there was something strange about the way his jaw moved as he spoke. He had heard stories about how the Confederacy's doctors could "grow" new faces for people. So maybe the marine had suffered some terrible wounds and been given a more youthful look. There was no way to be certain, but Jim thought it was totally cool.

The marine's whites were barely wrinkled, which was no small trick, given how cramped the goliath's cockpit must have been. A double row of medals hung on the left side of his chest, a gleaming belt encircled his waist, and his shoes were mirror-bright. All of which made quite a contrast to Trace and Jim Raynor, both of whom looked slovenly by comparison.

Recruiters were a common sight on planets like Shiloh, although they had never made the rounds in a goliath before, which said something about the wars. It had been going on for several years by that time, and even though the Confederacy's spokespeople claimed that everything was going well, recruiting goals were increasing just as fast as taxes were. Which meant that when kids like Tom Omer and Jim Raynor graduated from upper school, they were targeted.

Realizing that he wasn't in immediate danger of being thrown off his land—not yet, anyway—Trace Raynor allowed himself to relax a bit. "Nice to meet you, Sergeant," he said. "Although I'd sure appreciate it if you could avoid trampling my wheat on your way out."

"Don't worry, sir," Farley replied understandingly. "I'll follow the river over to the road when I leave."

"Thank you," Trace Raynor said evenly.

"No problem," Farley said, as his eyes swiveled toward the teenager. "That's quite a shiner, son. How does the other guy look?"

Jim had been hoping that his shades would be sufficient to hide the black eye, but it seemed that Farley could see the margins of it. He forced a grin. "I'm pretty sure he looks better than I do."

Trace had taught his son to be modest, but he wasn't the type to let someone's honor be impugned. "There was a dustup in the fuel line. Some kid cut in line and Jim put him on the pavement," he said proudly.

Farley nodded. "Good for you, boy. It's important to stand up for yourself. So you're done with school. . . . Have you made any plans regarding what you're going to do next?"

"No," Jim answered honestly, staring into eyes that looked like two gun barrels. "Just work for my dad, I guess," he said with a shrug. The words came out with such a glum tone, he immediately felt guilty. He glanced up at his father and met his knowing gaze. Jim suspected that Trace knew he wasn't entirely happy with the future that awaited him.

Farley nodded agreeably. "That makes sense. . . . And I'm sure your parents appreciate it. Of course there are other ways to lend a hand. Take the current enlistment bonus for example. The government is paying a generous signing bonus to each person who joins up! That kind of lump sum would go a long way toward taking care of the bills."

A *generous* bonus? That got Jim's attention. A big chunk of money could fix everything for his parents, for the farm, maybe even his future. Was that why Tom had enlisted? After all, the Omers were even worse off than his folks.

He was about to ask the sergeant just how generous this lump sum would be, when his father frowned and gave an almost imperceptible shake of his head. *Keep your mouth shut.*

If Farley was aware of the interchange, he gave no sign of it as he turned to gesture at the goliath. "Then there's training to think about," he said. "You could learn to pilot a goliath, fly an Avenger, or drive a siege tank. Of course I'm a ground pounder myself—so I prefer the infantry. And that means wearing one of the new powered combat suits. There ain't nothin' like it, son. . . . Once you strap one of those bad boys on, you'll be ready to kick ass and scan names! Come on, step onto that shovel-hand, and I'll give you a peek at the cockpit."

It wasn't until Jim and the marine were off the ground and halfway up that he realized how skillfully his dad had been cut out of the conversation.

Now, some twelve feet off the ground, Jim Raynor was peering into the goliath's well-padded cockpit. "See that cradle?" Farley inquired as he pointed downward. "Once you strap in, all you have to do is move the way you want the machine to move. Input from the sensors feeds into the onboard computer, which passes instructions along to the machine, mimicking what you did. It takes some practice, of course, and it's more difficult when people are shooting at you, but so what? You can shoot back!

"This baby is retired now," Farley continued, "but the pilots who rode her scored plenty of verified kills. And I don't just mean infantry. We're talking mechs, tanks, vultures, and Hellhounds. . . . So this honey deserves some easy livin'."

As Jim leaned over the cockpit he saw a curved control panel, the worn cradle beyond, and could smell the combined odors of sweat, oil, and stale cigar smoke. All of which summoned up visions of what it would be like to strap in and stride across a cratered battlefield, as brave comrades marched on either side of him.

So cool . . . Jim thought. *But Mom and Dad would never let me go.* The teenager nodded politely, and let Farley do all the talking as the goliath placed them back on the ground. The visit came to an end shortly after that, and it wasn't long before Farley was back in his cockpit, marching his machine down into the river. He delivered his parting comment over the loudspeaker. "Remember the Marine Corps motto, son. . . . 'For family, friends, and the Confederacy.' People are counting on you."

Spray flew away from the goliath's heavy feet, and the walker headed off toward the road. That was when Trace Raynor summoned a wad of spit, aimed it at a rock, and uttered a one-word editorial: "Bastards."

Without another word the farmer entered his truck, fired it up, and took off. Seconds later he was on the dirt road that ran up toward the dome. The sun was high in the sky, there was work to do, and valuable time had been lost.

Jim watched the goliath until it vanished around the bend. He suddenly had a lot on his mind.

The sun was little more than a red smear on the western horizon by the time Jim Raynor parked the robo-harvester, walked across a dusty parking lot to the family's home, and made his way down the ramp. Like most of the homes on Shiloh, eighty percent of the house was underground, where it was relatively immune to both summer heat and snowy winters. The dome's top floor was protected by a semi-transparent eyelid-like membrane that could absorb sunlight during the day, send it off to be stored in the farm's power cells, and then open up at night. Which was when Jim liked to lie back in a lounge chair and stare up at the stars.

But that was for later. First it was time to take a sonic shower, throw on some clean clothes, and make his way into the kitchen where his mother was preparing dinner. Karol Raynor's ebony hair was streaked with gray, and wrinkles had started to appear around her green eyes, but she was still a beautiful woman. And smart too—she had been selected to attend the agricultural school in Smithson on a scholarship and was, as Trace liked to put it, "the brains of the family."

Karol kept up with all of the most recent developments in farming technology and constantly looked for ways to stretch the family's finances, including negotiating with creditors, a task Trace lacked the temperament for. She was a first-class cook, and thanks to her carefully sheltered vegetable garden, plus the fairly steady supply of meat provided by the local ranchers, the Raynors always had something to eat. Something Jim was especially good at. "Hi, Mom," the teenager said, as he entered the kitchen and paused to kiss his mother's cheek. "What's for dinner? I'm hungry."

Karol turned, opened her mouth to reply, and paused. "What happened to your eye?"

"Nothin' much," Jim replied evasively. "I got into a scuffle, that's all."

"A scuffle, huh?" Karol said cynically. "You know how I feel about fighting. We'll discuss it at dinner. And put some ice on that thing."

Once the family was seated around the kitchen table and everybody had been served, Jim had to tell his mother about the fight with the Harnack boy, and listen to a lecture about the importance of settling disputes with words rather than fists.

"Your mother's right, Jim," Trace put in. "Fighting's not the answer. But it's important to stand up for yourself, especially when it comes to bullies. The key is knowing when to get involved and when to walk away, because you never know what kind of mess you're getting into until you're up to your neck in it."

"I hear you, Dad," Jim said, "And I'll keep that in mind." He turned to Karol and manufactured a smile. "So, Mom, how was *your* day?"

Jim knew it was obvious that he was making a blatant attempt to change the subject, but felt relieved when his mother seemed pleased to end the discussion. She launched into what amounted to a local news report. Apparently, a new strain of drought-resistant triticale-wheat was about to become available, the Laughlins weren't getting a divorce after all, and the sonic clothes cleaner was acting up again.

Eventually the conversation came around to the recruiter and his goliath. Jim and Trace split the story between them. Once it was over, Karol shook her head. "Gosh, they're really getting aggressive, aren't they? They're saying everything's going fine out there, and the minute Jim's eligible to enlist they send a recruiter to our doorstep. What about your friends? Is anyone else getting targeted like that?"

"I don't know," Jim replied honestly. "But Tom Omer's shipping out right after graduation."

"I hope he knows what he's getting himself into," Trace said. "The military is not something to take lightly."

"No, he's really serious. And . . . I don't know, I've been thinking about it lately, too, what it would be like to join up. I mean, I've never been off planet, and the signing bonus might be enough to pay our taxes down. Who knows? Maybe you could fix up the farm, sell out, and move to Smithson. Then, when I get out of the Marine Corps, I could go to that university on Korhal like Mom wants me to."

His enthusiastic speech was greeted with utter silence. He didn't know what to expect; he'd been rehearsing it in his head ever since Farley's mention of the signing bonus, but that didn't make the notion any less shocking to his parents.

"No way," Trace finally put in. "The taxes are *our* problem, not yours. . . . Besides, the war with the Kel-Morians is none of our business. Let the people who care about it fight it—"

"Trace, you know the wars are our business, whether you like it or not," Karol interrupted. "But I agree with your father, Jim, there's no reason you should be saddled with our debts. Plus, I don't recall you mentioning the military before. That corporal must have left quite an impression."

"He's a *gunnery sergeant*, Mom," Jim said patiently, as he finished his stew. "And I *have* been thinking about it," he said. "Tom got me interested in the marines a long time ago, but . . ." Jim looked at his worried parents and felt a little guilty. Truth was, his mom was right: He had never actually entertained the thought of enlisting until that afternoon. When the recruiter said it could help his family, it was all he needed to hear; if he didn't help them, who would?

"Listen, I want to fight those scumbags, okay, because things are going to get worse before they get better, right, Dad? I mean, what if the Kel-Morians win? Then everybody would have to join an occupational guild . . . and do whatever the people in charge of the guilds say."

"It's a little more complicated than that," Karol said. "The people who lead the guilds are elected—but once in office they're just about impossible to get out. And the guilds *want* war, because if they can control all of the scarce resources they can control everything."

"That's one of the reasons we're paying higher taxes and dealing with shortages," Trace added. "They're hoarding strategic materials *and* trying to force us to accept their corrupt political system."

"Yeah, well, that's what I'm talking about," Jim replied earnestly. "If I were to join up, I could do something about the long fuel lines and food shortages. I could help a lot of people, including you guys."

Karol frowned. "This is kind of sudden, isn't it? I don't understand where all of this is coming from. You've never mentioned any of these feelings before."

"Your mother's right, Jim," Trace echoed. "I don't think you realize what you're up against here. That guy today, he's a recruiter! It's his job to make it seem adventurous and exciting, but war is war, no matter how you spin it. You have a fifteen-minute conversation with some propaganda spouter and suddenly you're ready to sign your life away."

"It's just not like you, Jim—to jump into something without thinking it through," Karol continued. "You can't blame us for being shocked—"

"I knew I *couldn't* leave before, that's why," Jim blurted, "not the way things are, so I never said anything! But now, with the bonus and all, there's a way to make things work!" He realized he was yelling, so he took a deep breath and continued calmly. "Plus, as much as I love the farm, it would be great to visit some other planets. Then, after a tour, I could come back and settle down."

As Jim said everything out loud for the first time, he started to feel truly excited at the prospect of joining the Marine Corps, and at the same time, frustrated by his parents' lack of support. It wasn't as if he hadn't seen it coming. He was their only child, after all, their little boy, and he'd never spent more than a weekend out of their sight.

An ominous silence once again filled the room. Jim looked back and forth at his parents. Karol was looking at her plate and shaking her head, turning the remnants of her stew over with her spoon. Trace was staring down at his folded hands, seemingly deep in thought. Not sure whether to excuse himself or wait for someone to speak, Jim passed the next few minutes by gingerly patting his swollen eye with a freeze-pak.

Eventually, Trace cleared his throat. "I'll say this. If Jim wants to get off planet and take a look around, this would be a good opportunity to do it." He exchanged glances with Karol before leaning back in his chair.

She doesn't look happy, Jim thought.

"You're going to have to give your mother

and me some time to think about this, okay, Jim?"

"Yeah, Dad," Jim replied, wondering whether he was doing the right thing, or if this was all a big mistake. He got up and cleared the table, then quietly left the room. His father, for the first time in Jim's memory, offered no words of guidance and Jim felt utterly alone.

The better part of three days passed with arguments back and forth, but on the third night there was a knock on Jim's bedroom door. He turned away from his computer. "Yeah?"

"Come on, your mom and I want to talk to you," Trace called out. He smiled warmly as Jim opened the door, and the two made their way down the hall.

As he sat back down at the table, Jim could sense that his mother had been crying. It was the worst feeling in the universe, and he suddenly wanted to take it all back. Every last bit of it. But then his father began to speak.

"Jim, your mother and I have never put pressure on you to follow in our footsteps, but up until now, you've had no say in the matter. We needed you here, so we just figured you'd stay, and that's unfair to you."

Karol, a sad smile on her face, reached over and clutched her son's hand in both of hers. Jim's heart was racing. Were they actually going to let him go? He looked back at his dad, whose expression had softened.

"If you want to enlist, son," Trace continued, "that's your choice. Because in this life, you are who you choose to be. And it doesn't surprise us one bit that our son wants to be a hero."

CHAPTER THREE

"Recent changes in the Confederate military hierarchy's structure have left several wings of the armed forces struggling to adapt. Charged with keeping lawlessness in check among the troops, the Internal Security Division has reported a lack of military police to deal with the growing recruit population. Analysts worry that these gaps in security may open vulnerable sections of the military to criminal abuse."

Max Speer, *Evening Report* for UNN
March 2488

THE PLANET RAYDIN III,
THE CONFEDERACY OF MAN

The sky was gray, huge thunderheads were building in the southwest, and it was a hot, humid day in the town of Prosser's Well. Tychus Findlay figured it would rain later, which was fine by him, since all of the dust made it hard to keep things clean. Like the company's weapons, for example.

There was a sudden roar, and windows rattled as a formation of Avengers passed overhead. Such events were so common, no one bothered to look up.

Lots of people were in town, still celebrating the fact that the Kel-Morian forces had been driven out of the area three days earlier, and were retreating toward the east. A good deal of the northern part of the settlement had been destroyed during the fighting, but the rest was relatively untouched, including the central business district.

There were dozens of variations, but all of the city's buildings had a boxy look because their components had been produced by the same on-site factory that had been dropped into position when the community was founded. A variety of domes, arched gateways, and walled courtyards had been added over the years and painted different colors. That gave Prosser's Well some additional character.

The town was laid out on a colonial grid so that it was easy for strangers to find their way around. A convenience that Tychus had reason to appreciate as he fell in behind a trio of half-drunk marines and followed them down the main drag toward the warehouse district at the other end of town.

The problem with being a noncommissioned officer in the Confederacy's Marine Corps was that it took so much time away from stealing things. There were exceptions, of course, his present errand being one of them. Because a civilian would never have been aware of the opportunity he had in mind. So maybe being a staff sergeant had its advantages after all.

Take the warehouse full of captured Kel-Morian weapons, armor, and other gear, for example. Only someone like him, who was positioned to monitor all of the communications that flowed past his CO, would be in a position to profit from the situation. The key was to act quickly, cut a deal with the supply sergeant in charge of the storage facility, and remove a large quantity of the captured gear *before* an official inventory could be carried out. Because, insofar as the Marine Corps mentality was concerned, items that aren't on a list don't exist! And if something doesn't exist, it can't be stolen.

The thought brought a grim smile to Tychus's square-jawed face as he ducked under a sign and paused to gaze at a window display filled with women's shoes. Or, more accurately, at the general area, because his peripheral vision was quite good, and if someone was following him, he wanted to know.

Not having spotted any MPs or suspicious civilians, Tychus turned a corner and followed an alley to the next street over. A hard left carried him into the warehouse district, and from there it was a three-minute walk to a low, metal-sided warehouse that would have been completely unremarkable had there not been sentries posted outside.

Tychus made his way over to the nearest guard. The fresh-faced youth immediately puffed out his chest to compensate for his significantly smaller stature. That reaction was not new to Tychus; at over six-and-a-half-feet tall, he was a giant compared to most, and his deliberate, hulking demeanor intimidated just about everyone he encountered. His brown hair was cropped into a flattop, and well-worn creases connected his chiseled features and set off a strong brow. Due to the relatively high concentration of methane gas in the planet's atmosphere, everyone on Raydin III had to wear nose plugs, a transparent air hose, and an auxiliary oxygen canister. The big noncom was no exception. In addition, he wore basic cammies and was armed with a pistol and a gauss rifle.

"Good afternoon, Sergeant."

"If you say so," Tychus growled. The sound of his voice was like a gravel crusher in low gear. "I'm looking for Gunnery Sergeant Sims. . . . Is he around?"

The private nodded earnestly. "He's inside, but I gotta see some ID first, Sarge."

Tychus grunted, waited for the sentry to pass a scanner in front of his eyes, and was already making his way toward the front door when the green indicator light came on. That was when the private spoke into his lapel mic, heard a one-word reply, and turned his back to the warehouse. For the first time in at least a minute, the private exhaled.

Having entered the dimly lit warehouse, Tychus spotted a distant light and made his way toward it. The air was cool and slightly musty. Piles of Kel-Morian cargo modules were stacked against the walls—while others stood like islands in the middle of the clean-swept floor. Now that Tychus was closer he could see the desk that sat directly below the light. A gunnery sergeant was seated behind the beat-up piece of furniture with his feet up. Had Tychus been an officer, this would have been a dangerous thing to do, so it was obvious that Sims was expecting his visitor and wasn't the least bit surprised when the other noncom came to a stop.

Sims had one pay grade on Tychus, but there are pay grades, and then there are *pay grades*. And, as every marine knows, the jump from staff sergeant to gunnery sergeant involves a lot of additional responsibility, authority, and respect. That, combined with the fact that Sims "owned" the warehouse, put him in the driver's seat.

The hair on Sims's head amounted to little more than brown stubble and, due to the way his ears stuck out, some of the men referred to him as "jughead." Never to his face however, which was dominated by coal chip eyes and an extra chin. Rather than use the plugs most people wore, Sims favored a minimal mask that covered his nose. It was held in place by an elastic band. Tychus nodded. "Gunny Sims? My name is Findlay. . . . You got a minute?"

Sims shrugged. "Sure, Sergeant. . . . Take a load off. What's on your mind?"

Tychus let the rifle slip off his shoulder, placed the weapon within easy reach, and sat down. The chair creaked and seemed to disappear beneath him. "We have a mutual friend," Tychus began cautiously. "Somebody who believes in the importance of free market capitalism."

"And who might that be?" Sims inquired levelly.

"The individual I'm referring to is Master Sergeant Calvin."

Sims nodded. "I know Calvin. . . . We were corporals together. He's a good man. What's he up to these days?"

"He's in charge of the 2nd Battalion's transportation company."

"Interesting," Sims said. "So, like I said earlier, what's on your mind?"

This was the point of no return. Because if Tychus told Sims what he had in mind, and the gunny turned him in, his next meal would be served in a military work camp up in the mountains. But if he *didn't* take that chance, no money could be made. So Tychus took the leap, as he'd done so many times before. "You've got a lot of stuff sitting around here, Gunny. . . . I'd like to take some of it off your hands."

Sims brought his feet down off the desk, pulled a drawer open, and stuck a hand inside. Tychus felt his stomach muscles tighten knowing that the other noncom could be reaching for a gun. But what Sims brought out was a box of cigars, which he flipped open. "Care for a smoke?"

Tychus produced a wolfish grin. "As a matter of fact I would, Gunny . . . thank you very much."

The next minute or so was spent cutting ends off and torching both cigars with the gold lighter that Tychus had stolen from a dead lieutenant. Finally, when both men were satisfied with the way their stogies were drawing, it was time to talk business. "Don't tell me," Sims said, "let me guess. Calvin is going to provide the transportation."

"That's the plan," Tychus confirmed. "With the Kel-Morians on the run, and our people in hot pursuit, the brass have been forced to push two convoys a day out of Port Haaby. But once they deliver, most of the trucks come back empty. And that's a waste of taxpayers' money, wouldn't you agree? Not to mention vespene gas."

Sims blew a column of smoke up toward the

lamp and chuckled. "So when do we get paid? And with what?"

"We get paid on delivery," Tychus answered. "We're talking silium crystals. They're small, lightweight, and you can sell them anywhere."

"I like it," Sims said approvingly, "or I will, assuming that the split makes sense."

Tychus knew that was coming, knew that the other man held the upper hand, and knew *he* knew. So he was negotiating from a position of weakness. "Each of us will take a third of the proceeds," Tychus said, "minus three percent each to pay the drivers and guards."

Sims shook his head. "Nice try, Sergeant. . . . Calvin deserves a third, given all he's bringing to the deal, and so do I. But what makes *you* so valuable? Your good looks?"

"My looks *are* an incredible asset," Tychus responded dryly, "but so are my connections. I'm the one who knows the customer and that's why I get thirty percent."

Sims was silent for a moment, as smoke from their cigars merged to join a common cloud. Finally, based on some personal calculus, he nodded. "Okay, Sergeant . . . you've got a deal. But it's important to move fast. A logistics team is scheduled to arrive in three days. They're going to count, label, and bar-code every item in this warehouse. So tell Calvin to get his ass in gear."

"I will," Tychus promised, as he got up to leave.

"Good," Sims said gruffly, and offered the box. "Grab a handful."

"Don't mind if I do," Tychus replied, as he settled the rifle sling over his shoulder. Then opening an enormous paw, he brought it down on the neatly ranked cigars, and made a fist. Once the hand was withdrawn, Sims realized that the box was nearly empty! He was about to object, but Tychus was a good six feet away by that time and headed for the door. A deal had been made.

CHAPTER FOUR

"I solemnly affirm my duty to support and defend the planets of the Terran Confederacy against all enemies, interstellar and domestic. I further affirm that I will bear true faith and allegiance to the same and that I will strive against any and all threats to the continued progress of mankind in this sector."

Confederate Soldiers' Oath

THE PLANET SHILOH,
THE CONFEDERACY OF MAN

Jim Raynor's swearing-in ceremony took place in the town of Centerville, where everyone knew the Raynors. So after Trace parked the truck, and the family made their way toward Main Street, all sorts of people came up to shake Jim's hand and exchange a few words with his parents. Trace's hand never left Jim's shoulder. Jim was beaming with pride.

About fifty people showed up to witness the

moment, a crowd that grew larger when a government-chartered bus pulled up in front of the colonial courthouse and sighed wearily as it came to a stop. Fifteen recruits got off. And even though most had joined earlier that morning, they swaggered around the town square as if they were combat veterans, much to the amusement of some *real* veterans who were sitting on a bench.

In spite of all the well-wishers, there was something a little bit sad about the dusty courtroom, the tired-looking bunting that had been draped across the front of Judge Guthrie's bench, and the limp flag that drooped from a pole. Guthrie did his best, though, administering the oath as if it had been handed down from on high, while pausing at regular intervals so Raynor, Tom Omer, and the other recruits could repeat the words after him.

Rather than the sense of excitement he thought he'd feel as he prepared to leave his home planet for the first time, Raynor felt a vague sense of foreboding instead, but put the emotion down to the fear associated with going off to marine boot camp. A hellish place by all accounts, where brutal drill instructors ruled, and recruits were routinely abused. But all for a good purpose, or so Gunnery Sergeant Farley had assured him, while processing his application because "boot camp produces marines! And we're the best of the best."

There were handshakes all around, and lots of

hugs, as Raynor worked his way out of the courtroom and onto the front steps. Then it was time to say one last good-bye to his parents. Much to Jim's embarrassment, his mother had packed a lunch for him, and tears were rolling down her cheeks as she kissed him. "Don't forget to write. . . . We're going to miss you so much."

Trace Raynor didn't say a word, but it was all there in his eyes and the strength of his grip. Jim's heart swelled with emotion, but he gritted his teeth and managed a weak smile. This is it, Jim thought, and a moment later was left to the mercies of a noncom named Corporal Timson who, if he had a first name, never chose to share it.

Timson was dressed in a reasonably clean uniform that was at least one size too small for him. Raynor noticed that there were four five-year pins on his left sleeve, which indicated that he'd been in the Corps for more than twenty years. So, either he'd been broken from a more lofty rank, or had been unable to rise above the rank of corporal. Neither of which spoke very well of his performance.

Whatever the case, Timson appeared worn out and eager to leave. "All right," he announced to those who had been sworn in earlier, "it's time to get back on the bus. We haven't got all day, you know."

Raynor gave a final wave to his parents and boarded the bus, carrying a small satchel and his lunch. There was a center aisle with seats on both sides, and a storage rack above.

Some of his fellow recruits were already aboard, shooting the breeze with each other or fiddling with their fones. The back of the bus appeared to be empty, so Raynor headed there and sat on the bench-style seat that ran from side to side. He looked around for Omer.

Moments later a boisterous group of young men entered the cabin and paused to give one of the girls some unwanted attention before shuffling toward the back. Their leader, a gangly red-haired youth, led the way. *Fekk!* Raynor's stomach dropped when he recognized Harnack, and one of his father's well-worn phrases came rushing back to him. *"Trouble is like a boomerang—the harder you throw it, the faster it'll come back at you."* Why did his old man *always* have to be right?

Whether he knew it or not, Harnack had become the butt of a lot of jokes around town the last couple weeks, thanks to Raynor and his iron fists. But now, as Raynor pretended to look casually out the window, he knew the bastard was looking for trouble, and could feel it coming straight for him. When he heard Harnack's boots stop short midway through the aisle, Raynor knew he'd been spotted.

Harnack pretended to sniff the air. "Damn! What's that smell?" Then, as if seeing Raynor for the first time, Harnack pointed at him. "Here's the problem. . . . Somebody took a dump in the back of the bus!"

Harnack's toadies erupted into laughter.

"What have we here?" Harnack demanded, as he snatched Raynor's lunch sack off the seat. "This yours?" Then, having dropped it on the floor, Harnack stomped it. "Oh, sorry . . . must'a slipped. Too bad there aren't any farmers around to protect you now."

Raynor knew he had to stand up for himself, and was halfway out of his seat when a florid Timson appeared. "What the hell are you jerk weeds doing back here?" the noncom demanded. "This ain't no fekkin' tea party. Sit down and shut up or I'll put a boot up your ass!"

The admonition left Raynor with no choice but to sit down, or complain about the other recruits, which was sure to make the situation even worse. Timson wasn't there to protect him—he just didn't want any trouble. *Where the hell is Omer*? Jim thought. And then he spotted him. Having just boarded the bus, Omer pretended not to notice the confrontation and immediately took a seat in the front row. *Well, so much for loyalty.*

Harnack straightened and nodded solemnly. "Sorry, we were working on seating arrangements, that's all. . . . We're good to go." Raynor was surprised by the bully's sudden deference.

Timson's beady brown eyes flicked from face to face. "Don't cause any trouble back here. . . .

You'll regret it if you do." And with that he turned back toward the front of the bus and proceeded to count heads as he made his way forward. Then, having matched the total to the number on his list, he gave the driver permission to proceed. Harnack flashed Raynor a wicked smile before taking a seat a few rows up.

The engine roared and the bus lurched into motion. Then, while the few remaining spectators looked on, the transport raised a cloud of dust as it followed the main street to the two-lane highway, which is where the journey to the next town began. There were two additional stops, each lasting an hour or so, which meant it was well after dark by the time the bus pulled into Burroughston.

But rather than the hotel that Raynor had been hoping for, the recruits were ordered to get out in front of the local upper school, where the custodian was waiting to lead them to the gymnasium. *They're going to make us* sleep *in this place?* he thought. It had high ceilings, simwood floors, and bleachers that were positioned along the south wall. The score on the electronic reader board was zero-zero. Raynor could have been back in Centerville.

"Welcome home," Corporal Timson said sarcastically. "You think *this* sucks? You ain't seen nothin' yet. This is a fekkin' paradise compared to your average barracks."

There was a scattering of mumbled replies,

which, judging from the expression on Timson's face, amounted to a personal insult. He stood with fists on hips. "What the hell was that?" he demanded rhetorically. "Eventually, should one or two of you be fortunate enough to get through basic, you will be entitled to call me Corporal. But until that unlikely day dawns, you will address every noncom and officer that you encounter as either sir or ma'am, depending on the type of plumbing they were issued. And you will do so in a voice that can be heard on Tarsonis. *Do you scan me, maggots?*"

Maggots? It was so melodramatic, Raynor had to battle a grin as he shouted "YES, SIR!" along with the other recruits. The response was still ragged, but a good deal louder, and phrased correctly.

"That's better," Timson allowed grudgingly. "Not perfect, but better. Draw your gear, pick a place to bed down, and report to me. We're eating field rats tonight, better known as barf boxes, and don't even think about trying to heat one of them up. If you burn this dump down it will be deducted from your pay. Do you scan me?"

This time the answer was nearly perfect. *"YES, SIR!"*

"All right, assholes," Timson growled. "Get your butts in gear."

It didn't take long for Raynor to get a mat, blankets, and towel. Then came the problem of where to put them. A good number of at least temporary friendships had been forged on the bus, but after being targeted by Harnack and his toadies, Raynor had been ostracized. Even Omer had deserted him. Not as part of a conspiracy, but because of a generally held desire to stay clear of the bully, as well as his pinheaded supporters.

So Raynor wound up throwing his mat down on the floor next to the north wall, a position that was a good fifteen feet from the nearest recruit, but would allow him to sleep with his back against something solid. Hopefully, assuming things went well, Harnack—whose name Raynor had discovered was Hank—would turn his attention elsewhere.

With that accomplished, Raynor went over to the line that led to Corporal Timson and three crates of A-rats—containers holding meals that could be eaten hot or cold—plus heat tabs they weren't supposed to use, an energy bar, and two contraceptives.

Two minutes later Harnack showed up, elbowed his way into the queue, and grinned menacingly. "Hey, sissy boy, mind if I cut in?" It was the fueling line situation all over again.

Raynor felt the anger begin to rise inside him, and was careful to channel it, as he snapped his head forward. It was a move that his father, who had been something of a brawler in his younger days, had taught him when he entered upper school—when his mom wasn't around, of course. *"Don't ever back down from a bully,"* Trace had said. *"Fight to win and end it as quickly as possible."* And the head butt worked extremely well as solid bone met the bridge of Harnack's nose, cartilage broke, and blood gushed onto the bully's chin.

Then, while Harnack was still trying to absorb what had happened, Raynor brought a knee up into his crotch. That was when Harnack produced a high-pitched keening sound, fell to his knees, and brought both hands in to guard his aching stones.

"Sure," Raynor said conversationally, "please feel free to cut in front of me anytime you want to."

Corporal Timson heard the disturbance, issued a long string of swearwords, and arrived on the scene thirty seconds later. He looked down at Harnack and up to Raynor. "Did you do this?"

Raynor was about to say yes when Harnack lurched to his feet and came to something resembling attention. This was when Raynor learned his first lesson about the military: the unspoken code that marines don't rat out other marines. "Sir, no sir," he lied. "I slipped and fell."

"Really?" Timson inquired cynically. "You fell on your balls?"

That got a laugh from everyone within ear range with the notable exception of Harnack's toadies, who shuffled their feet and glowered at Raynor.

"Yes, sir," Harnack said stiffly, his eyes straight ahead.

Timson shook his head wearily and sighed. "Okay, be more careful next time. Now hit the head, get yourself cleaned up, and report to me. I'll put a box of A-rats aside for you."

Harnack gave a stiff nod, said, "Yes, sir," and limped away. Once he was out of earshot, Timson looked Raynor up and down. "What's your name?"

"Raynor, sir. Jim Raynor."

"Well, recruit Raynor," Timson said in a voice pitched so low no one else could hear him. "I know Harnack has been up in your face . . . but what goes around nearly always comes around, which means you should keep a close eye on your six."

Raynor knew Timson was referring to the six o'clock position on a standard clock, which was to say, his ass. "Sir, yes sir."

"Plus," Timson added ominously, "if you do anything like that again you're going to piss me off. . . . And pissing me off is a very bad idea. Do you scan me?"

"Sir, yes sir."

"Good. Go get something to wipe up the blood with, get back in line, and don't screw up. I'll be watching you."

So Raynor went in search of a utility room and found one. Then, mop in hand, he went back to clean up Harnack's blood. And it was then that he noticed how things had changed. Recruits who hadn't been willing to speak with him before were openly friendly now—which meant he had people to sit with as the group explored their rations.

The fact that each of them had been issued *two* condoms came in for a good deal of humorous commentary, as did the political propaganda that was printed inside the lid of each barf box, urging "each member of the Confederacy's military forces to fight the Arbellan menace with all of his or her strength." The problem was, the Arbellan rebels had been defeated ten years earlier! The rations had apparently been sitting in a warehouse for a very long time.

Once the meal was over, Raynor returned to his mat, removed his fone from the travel satchel, and surfed the latest sports scores, followed by a news summary.

He readied his Dopp kit, and began what turned out to be a long surveillance of the men's bathroom. Raynor had taken Timson's—and his father's—advice seriously and knew there was a very good chance that a person like Harnack would come looking for revenge. And what better place to attack someone than in a restroom?

As he waited, Raynor brought up one of the digi-tomes he had uploaded for the trip. It came complete with a soundtrack that matched the story, continually morphing illustrations, and opportunities to pull up more information about the characters and their backgrounds. He watched out of the corner of his eye as Harnack and each one of his toadies had come and gone from the lavatory before he followed a group of three other recruits into the brightly lit space and took a quick sonic shower. Then, with a towel tied around his hips, he made his way over to one of the mirrors and went to work with his sonic toothbrush. That was when he heard the boy who had been singing in the shower stop suddenly.

Raynor turned, but not quickly enough, as a big bony fist hit him in the side of the head. He fell, and was still sprawled on the tiled floor when Harnack placed a size thirteen boot on his chest. Toadies formed a semicircle around him, and judging from the lack of other background sounds, the rest of the recruits had been ordered to vacate the room.

There was a black scab on the bridge of Harnack's broken nose, one eye was beginning to turn purple, and there was no sign of humor in the smile he produced. "Well, sissy boy, we meet again. You surprised me, I admit that—I didn't think you had the balls. But there's a big difference between head butting someone when they don't expect it and fighting like a man. So get up, sissy boy, and let's see how you do in a *real* fight."

Raynor considered mentioning the time he kicked Harnack's ass in the fueling line, but refrained. A foot belonging to a very angry person was pressing down on his chest, after all. It was not the time for brutal honesty.

Jim understood both the situation and the part he was about to play. Having been put down in the gym, and having lost face in front of his followers, Harnack had to whip him. Or at least seem to, although Jim realized the chances of a truly fair fight were pretty slim as he scrambled to his feet.

That didn't make any difference, of course, because what was, was, and all Raynor could do was accept the situation and make the best of it. Which was why he began the one-sided contest by taking a swing at the nearest toady. He felt his fist connect and had the satisfaction of seeing the youth go down.

That was a victory of sorts, but a short-lived one, as the other three rushed him. Raynor landed a punch on Harnack's cheek, but that was the extent of the damage he could do as a flurry of punches and kicks drove him to the floor.

Then, while blow after vicious blow landed, all Raynor could do was curl up into the fetal position and try to protect his head as the other recruits kicked him. "How do you like this *moron* now?" Harnack demanded from some place far away, as Raynor began to fall toward the bottom of a deep well.

Then the beating was over, the pain was gone, and Raynor was at peace.

CHAPTER FIVE

"This year's historic Reunion, an interplanetary summit of representatives from the original Old Families, will take place on Tarsonis, following a week of ceremony and celebration. More than a century has passed since the first supercarriers arrived in the Koprulu sector from Earth, and the descendants of those intrepid pioneers are slated to discuss a variety of topics regarding the economy and governance of terran space. Members of the Confederate government have already scheduled meetings with these representatives in order to incorporate their counsel into action more smoothly."

Max Speer, *Evening Report* for UNN
April 2488

THE PLANET TARSONIS,
THE CONFEDERACY OF MAN

The curtains made a hushed whisper as they rose far enough to let some sunlight in, the bed shivered ever so slightly, and the console that was built into the headboard of Ark Bennet's bed produced a soft chiming sound.

The teenager yawned, swung his feet over onto thick carpeting, and began the process of getting ready for a new day. He threw open the double doors that led to his private terrace. Tarsonis City was so vast that it stretched all the way to the horizon, where the details of it were lost in the early morning haze. The metroplex was both the capital of the Confederacy of Man and its largest city, which meant it was home to millions of people—very few of whom had the privilege of viewing it from the perspective of a sixty-three-room mansion every morning.

But as a member of an Old Family, such was Ark's birthright. And as his eyes swept across clusters of high-rise office towers, slab-like apartment complexes, and scabrous slums, he could *feel* the city's seething energy, the dark allure of its maze-like streets, and the siren call of pleasures he had heard about but never experienced. Because to be rich was to be the target of thieves, kidnappers, and paparazzi. So he rarely had the opportunity to venture out without a small army of heavily armed bodyguards who would report whatever he did to his parents. *So what good was wealth,* Ark asked himself, *if you're a prisoner to it?*

The city offered no answer other than the subdued roar of traffic as he closed the doors, turned back into the room, and crossed a broad expanse of carpet to his private bathroom. It was large enough to accommodate four. The walls were covered in exquisite marble, and at least a dozen fluffy towels were available for use, as Ark examined himself in a large, ornately framed mirror.

He was, according to his mother, "a very handsome young man," although Ark knew it wasn't true. His eyes were too far apart, his lips too thin, and his chin too narrow for that. Girls liked him nonetheless—or seemed to—but was that for real? Or the result of his family's wealth?

There had already been talk of an arranged marriage with the Falco family, which, though less prominent than his, owned one of the smaller shipping lines. It was a logical merger—interstellar shipping, building spaceships, and developing atmospheric craft-like military transports would provide strong horizontal integration. An arranged marriage would allow the Falcos to maintain a measure of independence. And if they were part of the larger family—so to speak—they would have a greater voice, which could make an important difference. But the prospect of marrying sixteen-year-old Hailey Falco had very little appeal for Ark.

He had finished upper school two weeks earlier—and the pressure was on to choose between two competing visions of who he would become. His father wanted him to learn the family business, his mother wanted him to become a scholar, and Ark was pretty sure that he wouldn't be any good at either one of those things.

The intercom buzzed as Ark ran a sonic razor over his face. The voice belonged to his father. "Ark, we're leaving in twenty minutes."

Ark sighed, said, "Yes, Father," and eyed himself in the mirror. A very young face stared back at him. *What should I do?* The other Ark was mute.

There were two ways that members of an Old Family could travel, and each had certain advantages. They could blast through traffic in a heavily armed convoy, or move covertly in vehicles that didn't look special but were. In this case Ark and his father were cocooned inside a groundcar that was tricked out with what dealers called "a city package." That included screened windows, a bulletproof skin, and solid run-flat tires. All of which was intended to ensure the Bennet family's privacy as well as their safety.

Unlike some of the Old Families, who clearly enjoyed "giving face" as the paparazzi referred to it, Ark's parents had gone to great lengths to keep both him and his sister under wraps. That was partly because they looked down on families who consistently played to the press as being crass, but it was a practical matter as well, because kidnappers frequently went after the most visible targets. And young people who were out on the town, traipsing from one nightclub to another, were easy to intercept. So Ark was used to playing his status down rather than up, and was constitutionally happy to do so.

Clearing a path for the nondescript car and its two passengers was what appeared to be a beat-up cab with a couple of armed guards inside. And bringing up the rear was a graffiti-covered delivery van, equipped with drop panels. Once the sides fell, two combat-suited ex-marines would be free to wade into traffic firing AGR-14 gauss rifles. Which should be more than sufficient firepower to defeat kidnappers or assassins.

But, for the moment, all three vehicles were waiting for a light to change. That was the problem with the low-key approach. The convoy was forced to blend in rather than blast through intersections with lights flashing and sirens bleeping.

The elder Bennet had a broad forehead, close-set eyes, and a prominent jaw. The businessman was dressed in a two-thousand-credit silk suit, which shimmered slightly as light from the moon roof hit it. Ark couldn't imagine wearing something like that; he preferred to dress the way most of his peers did, in a wire jacket that morphed from color to color depending on the nature of his surroundings, a Thump Band T-shirt, and the latest Street Feet shoes.

"So," Errol Bennet said dryly, as he eyed his son, "this will be your first conference—which is to say your first opportunity to see what awaits you."

Given the way his comment was framed, Errol Bennet clearly assumed that once everything was said and done, Ark would see things *his* way. The business—an empire really, that was built around interstellar shipping, but had holdings in related industries as well—was an endless source of fascination for Ark's older sister, Tara. She had been groomed for as long as he could remember to follow in their father's footsteps.

But the business held little interest for Ark, a fact that the youth had recently conveyed to his father in a particularly contentious family discussion. Errol had responded by sending Ark's mother and sister out of the room so he could have a man-to-man conversation with his "beloved son," as he put it. It seemed as though he'd uttered the phrase with a tinge of hostility, and Ark felt it like a kick in the gut. After Errol had effectively convinced the teenager that he had no other options—what with no natural talent and average intelligence, what could he possibly have to offer?—the deal was set: Ark would attend the meeting.

"Who will be there?" Ark asked as the light changed and the convoy continued.

"Representatives from the various families, as I told you before," his father replied. "We compete with each other, but we must cooperate as well, or risk tearing the system apart."

By "system," Ark knew his father meant the interlocking relationships between the Old Families, the government, and the public. All of which struck him as intensely boring. The prospect of going to meetings every day, of trying to figure out what each attendee's *true* motives were, building alliances, executing strategies, cutting costs, and boosting profits filled him with dread. Surely there was something *more* to life?

"I want you to pay very close attention today," Errol added. "I can't have you appearing ignorant in front of my associates because you can't be bothered to listen."

"Yes, Father."

The convoy had turned into the campus by then, having been forced to pause in front of a heavily fortified gate, prior to being allowed to proceed. The university was a private institution that owed its existence to the largess of families like the Bennets and was more than happy to provide the ruling oligarchy with a place to meet. Ten minutes later the vehicles were parked in an underground garage, where they would remain until the conference came to an end.

Ark accompanied his father upstairs, where the senior Bennet was quickly surrounded by well-wishers, oily enemies, and hopeful sycophants. He nodded to Ark, who smiled in return before going off to find his seat. It was as one would expect for a person of low status, high up and in the very back row.

The Hall of Reason was circular in shape,

which some wags claimed was a pun, foisted on the unsuspecting university by a cynical architect. Ark was impressed by the soaring domed ceiling and the unconventional manner in which the tiered seats were wrapped around the speaker's platform. Once the opening ceremonies were over, Ava Holt, the rather dowdy matriarch of Holt Enterprises, rose to introduce Ark's father.

The crowd rose to applaud Errol Bennet and continued to clap as he mounted the platform. The businessman gave Holt a hug and motioned for the audience to sit down. Bennet began his remarks by reiterating the need for harmony and what he called "an obligation to provide the Confederacy with support and guidance."

That's how the process was explained in all the textbook digi-tomes that Ark and millions of other students had been exposed to in school. The Old Families were expected to provide the democratically elected government with advice that it could accept or reject.

But, as the meeting continued, Ark was reminded that the reality of the situation was quite different. Especially when it came time for his father to address the Guild Wars. "The conflict with the Kel-Morian Combine has been very profitable by any measure," Errol Bennet intoned, as the platform under his feet slowly rotated.

"Those who manufacture uniforms, body armor, weapons, ammunition, vehicles, tanks, aircraft, naval vessels, communications systems, orbital defense platforms, and all of the other countless items supplied to our military forces have profited from the war. That includes every family represented in this room, although I'm sure every single one of us regrets the terrible cost borne by the Confederacy's brave soldiers, and by their families."

That was true, the families *had* profited handsomely, and Bennet's summary brought the representatives to their feet. The noise was thunderous, but as Ark clapped his hands, he wondered what the audience was applauding. The money they had made? Or the "brave soldiers" his father had referred to? Especially since none of his privileged friends were planning to join the military.

"But regrettable though it is, the conflict has had the effect of bringing our population together," Errol Bennet continued as the representatives took their seats. "And," he added, "to the extent that the UNN spends its time covering battles, it's not talking about *us*!"

That got a laugh, and it was supposed to, since all of those present had to contend with the press corps's eternal eagerness to run stories about the Old Families. A lot of it was society fluff focused on who was engaged to whom, coming out parties, and the like. But there were serious pieces, too, many of which were focused on allegations that certain officials were becoming rich by taking money from the Old Families in return for no-bid government contracts, favorable regulations, and a host of tax breaks. The stories were annoying, and potentially dangerous to the status quo, which everyone in the room had reason to protect.

Now Ark was beginning to understand why his mother hadn't wanted him to attend the meeting and why his father had insisted that he do so. Lisa Bennet wanted her son to pursue an academic career both as a way to "give something back," as she put it, and to insulate him from the family's financial dealings.

But his father wasn't having any of that. "We need both an heir *and* a spare," Errol Bennet had said. "After all, what if something were to happen to Tara?"

Which was fine, except that Ark didn't want to be a "spare."

Such were the young man's thoughts as Errol Bennet surrendered the platform to a guest speaker, who launched into what promised to be a very boring lecture on the need to raise colonial property taxes even higher so as to better recover the cost of military protection. Because on a per capita basis it was more expensive to defend a sparsely settled fringe world than a densely populated planet like Tarsonis. A perspective that was likely to find plenty of support from those in the chamber.

As the talk began, Ark got up from his seat and made his way downstairs. A quick check confirmed that his father's bodyguards were nowhere to be seen. That made sense, given all of the security in place around the university, and the fact that Errol Bennet could summon them within a matter of seconds if necessary.

So it was easy to slip out for a breath of fresh air. Getting back in would be a lot more difficult, of course, but Ark had plenty of ID, so there was no reason to be concerned. Having departed the carefully manicured campus, Ark felt his heart begin to beat faster, as he slipped into the city he viewed from afar each morning.

There were risks associated with what he was doing, Ark knew that, but the danger of walking the streets alone was far outweighed by the pleasure of doing so. Besides, Ark intended to limit himself to no more than an hour of stolen freedom before returning to the university.

Gradually, as the young man put some distance between himself and the campus, the upscale housing that bordered the university gave way to ten- and fifteen-story apartment buildings. They were part of a working-class neighborhood called Hacker's Flat. The name harkened back to an era when the area had been home to a number of farms.

Most of the street-level space was taken up by family-run bodegas that sold everything from deep-fried meat pies to high-end electronics. At least some of which were probably stolen. The sidewalks were cracked, the side passageways reeked of urine, and every accessible surface was covered with multiple layers of graffiti.

Lots of people were out and about, as was a small array of roving robots, each of which was equipped with a small holoprojector and enough artificial intelligence to match advertisements to the person it was pitching to. So it wasn't unusual to see an Advertising Artificial Intelligence that looked like a sonic clothes cleaner morph into a scantily clad young woman as it dashed across the street to present a different message to a businessman.

During the time it took Ark to walk a block he was approached by what appeared to be a five-foot-tall tube of underarm deodorant, a man who wanted him to "answer a few questions," and a nonprofit AAI looking for a donation. The machines were annoying, but he easily avoided them by circling around them and continuing on his way.

Ground transportation consisted of everything from powered speed skates to much-abused cabs and delivery trucks. They were often double-parked and subject to fines levied by an armada of traffic sensor feeds.

Ark estimated that he was less than a mile from the university at that point, but realized he had never ventured that far into the city without an armed escort before. So, just to make sure he had his bearings, Ark paused to bring up a street map on his fone. He took comfort from the icon that marked his position within the Hacker's Flat grid—and the knowledge that a couple of left- or right-hand turns would take him back to the university. After a quick look around to compare his surroundings to the image on his fone, Ark put the device back into his pocket.

It was a small thing. One that would have been completely unremarkable had it taken place within the context of a fashionable sky mall, but took on special meaning on the grimy streets of Tarsonis, where predators were eternally on the lookout for anything that might identify a possible victim. Such as a map.

Three locals took notice of the young man's moment of uncertainty, plus the fancy jacket he was wearing, but only one of them chose to follow up. Her name was Camy. She had long black hair, doelike eyes that looked even larger thanks to a generous application of makeup, and a pouty mouth. Camy's breasts were too large to be real, and were only barely contained by a leather vest that was cut in at her waist and decorated with silver ornaments. The girl's matching pants were so tight, they looked as if they had been sprayed onto her long, tapered legs. Ankle-high boots completed the outfit, and made a sharp rapping sound as Camy passed her prospective mark, and provided him an excellent opportunity to appreciate her shapely behind.

Having arrived at the next corner a good fifteen seconds ahead of the unsuspecting teenager, Camy examined a scrap of paper and frowned before shoving it back into her purse. As the young man arrived she turned and smiled. "Excuse me . . . I think I'm lost. Could you tell me how to get to the nearest bus station?"

"Yes," the mark said agreeably, "I think I can," and brought out his fone.

That would have been enough for a snatch-and-sprint artist, who would have been half a block away in a matter of seconds, soon to disappear into a maze of passageways. But Camy couldn't run in her high-heeled boots, and was after a bigger prize, although the mark's top-of-the-line fone might wind up in her purse as well. So as he brought the map up and began to scroll, Camy allowed her arm to touch his, and knew that her perfume was sure to reach his nostrils.

"Thank you so much!" Camy said gratefully, as the fone went back into her mark's pocket. "I was lucky to run into someone who knows the area so well."

"Not that well," the young man confessed modestly. "I'm a stranger here, too."

"Really?" Camy inquired, as her big brown eyes flirted with his. "Then I guess you wouldn't be able to recommend a restaurant. It's almost noon and I'm hungry."

Though no expert where young women were concerned, Ark knew an opening when he heard one, and was quick to respond. "I'm quite hungry myself. . . . There's got to be a restaurant around here. Perhaps you might give me the honor of buying you lunch."

The girl's face lit up. "That would be fun! How 'bout that place over there? It's close and wouldn't take either one of us very far out of our way."

That made sense to Ark, who felt a tremendous sense of accomplishment at having snagged such a pretty girl, and was careful to summon up his best manners as they crossed a busy arterial. He offered his elbow and she cheerfully latched on. The pub was called Jake's, and as Ark followed the girl past the wooden bar to a booth in the back, he noticed that a number of patrons turned to look. Of course that made sense, given how pretty she was.

Ark was thrilled when the girl invited him to sit down next to her rather than on the other side of the table. "My name's Laura," she said, "Laura Posy. And you are?"

"Ark," the teenager replied artlessly, unsure as to whether it would be dangerous to give his last name if she demanded it.

But if the lovely Laura was troubled by the breach of etiquette, there was no sign of it as she placed her left hand on his right thigh. "It's a pleasure to meet you, Ark," she said warmly. "Let's see what's on the menu."

By that time Ark was pretty sure that he was sitting next to a very attractive prostitute, which meant that if he played his cards correctly, he might be able to score the sort of experience he had heard other, more worldly boys brag about! And, as if to reinforce that notion, Laura gave his leg a gentle squeeze.

Ark's sandwich was surprisingly good. It consisted of a fresh roll, heaped high with sliced skalet meat, which was nearly invisible under a blanket of melted cheese. He didn't remember ordering a beer, but assumed that it came with the sandwich, and missed the moment when his companion passed a hand over it.

Ten minutes later, as Ark was finishing the sandwich and wondering how to broach the subject foremost on his mind, he began to feel a bit dizzy. Was the beer to blame? Yes, probably, although Ark was no stranger to alcohol.

He assumed the feeling would pass, especially if he left the beer alone and switched to water. But even as his mind processed the thoughts, the world around him seemed to slow. It became increasingly hard to focus and his head felt incredibly heavy. Then, it came to him: Laura was more than a hooker, Laura had slipped something into his beer, and Laura had plans for him!

There was just enough time to process a feeling of mixed embarrassment and shame before his forehead crashed onto the plate in front of him. Ark heard slow-motion laughter as two men came back to pick him up. He felt himself being carried for a short distance before being placed on a soft surface—maybe a cot. It swayed alarmingly, fell into a black pit, and took Ark along with it. His outing was over.

CHAPTER SIX

" 'Insubordination' is just a fancy word for 'washout recruit.' "

Lieutenant Marcus Quigby, Fort Howe, Turaxis II
May 2488

THE PLANET RAYDIN III,
THE CONFEDERACY OF MAN

A full day had passed since the meeting with Gunny Sims. Drops of blood-warm rain were falling, and Tychus could hear the muted rumble of thunder as he made his way over to the main street. Civilians and soldiers alike were moving faster as they sought shelter from the coming deluge.

Tychus would have done likewise had he been free to do so, but he was due back at Company HQ by 1600 hours local, where he and the other members of the Tactical Response Squad would sit around and shoot the shit until they were relieved at midnight. Which, based on a twenty-six-hour day, made for a long watch. There was plenty of comm gear at headquarters though—and all it would take was a quick call to Master Sergeant Calvin to set the illicit scheme in motion.

So rather than enter a bar for some well-deserved R&R, Tychus marched uphill to the north end of town. That was where his CO had set up shop in the same two-story office building where one of his Kel-Morian counterparts had been doing business just a few days earlier. The sentry posted outside the front door nodded, but didn't ask for ID, since nobody looked like Tychus except Tychus.

The noncom had to duck his head to clear the top of the doorway, which opened into an air lock, followed by the sparsely furnished office beyond. Supplementary oxygen was being pumped in through the air-conditioning system, which made it possible to remove his nose plugs and let them dangle on his chest.

The office was decorated with a well-executed drawing of the Kel-Morian outriders' famous death's head logo, plus dozens of scrawled signatures. Dead men for the most part—all buried in a mass grave outside of town. There were two desks up front, and Corporal Proctor was sitting at one of them. She looked up from her work as Tychus entered.

Proctor was pretty in an understated, no-

nonsense sort of way and completely uninterested in casual sex, which was the kind that Tychus specialized in. Her bangs were straight, her eyes were gray, and Tychus saw what might have been a warning in them. "The captain has been looking for you," she said, without inflection. "He's in his office."

Tychus's face was impassive, but alarm bells were going off in his head, because "Captain Jack," as his marines referred to him, was one of the few people in the Confederacy who scared him. Not physically, because the officer was no match for Tychus, but in other ways. Captain Jack Larimer was not only mean as hell, he had an inexplicable tendency to volunteer his unit for dangerous missions, and that was a threat to the most important person on Raydin III: Tychus Findlay.

So it was with a sense of trepidation that Tychus placed his rifle on a wall rack and approached the open door. He rapped three times and waited for the word "Enter!" before taking the requisite three paces forward. A lot of officers would have forgone such formalities under the circumstances, but not Captain Jack. "Staff Sergeant Tychus Findlay reporting as ordered, sir!"

Captain Jack was about thirty years old and loved to run. There were some people who said he could run the ass off a wheel. And because of that he was not only lean but very sure of himself. In fact, self-confidence seemed to ooze out of every pore of the officer's whipcord-thin body as he lounged behind his desk and took pleasure in the fact that a man like Tychus had to follow his orders. The smile arrived slowly. "At ease, Sergeant. Have a seat."

Tychus accepted the invitation, settled his weight onto a metal chair, and waited to find out what kind of shit detail his CO had in store for him. It didn't take long.

"I'm going to take the Tac Squad out on a mission tonight," Captain Jack announced, "and you'll be second in command."

Tychus nodded woodenly. "Yes, sir. What's the objective?"

"We're going after a civilian collaborator," the officer replied. "A man who took money to provide the enemy with information about his neighbors."

"Sounds like a picnic, sir," Tychus commented. "Why wait? Let's pick him up now."

"I said he was a civilian," Captain Jack replied. "What I *didn't* say is that he lives about fifteen miles north of here, in a fortified house, on top of a hill. There have been periods of civil unrest on Raydin III—and his home was built to take some punishment. So a bit of circumspection is in order. We're going to dress like Kel-Morians and arrive in a Kel-Morian transport, which was captured along with the town. It was in need of some repairs, but our people put the ship right and it's ready to lift."

"So if we arrive at night, the collaborator will believe we're there to pick him up," Tychus mused, "and allow us to land unopposed."

"Something like that," Jack agreed vaguely. "Round up your men, get some food in them, and order the duty driver to take you down to the warehouse where the stuff we captured from the Kel-Morians is stored. Do you know Gunnery Sergeant Sims?"

Tychus felt his heart beat just a little bit faster. "We've met . . . yes."

"Good. He'll help you get the team set up with all the proper gear. Meet me at the landing strip at 2000 hours. And don't be late, Findlay. . . . You know how that pisses me off."

Tychus knew it was time to leave, and stood. He was halfway out the door when Captain Jack stopped him. "One more thing, Sergeant. . . . Bring a rocket launcher. We might need it."

After spending a couple of hours getting ready, Tychus and his squad drove onto the airstrip at precisely 1930, thereby ensuring that they would have plenty of time to run one last check on the team prior to liftoff. Lightning flashed in the eastern sky as the big truck came to a halt and the marines bailed out.

All the necessary arrangements had been made by Corporal Proctor, so none of the Confederate soldiers opened fire on what appeared to be a squad of Kel-Morian outriders splashing across what had been a city park, to the row of aircraft parked beyond.

Kel-Morian battle dress was a good deal less formal than the color-coded gear issued by the Confederacy. In fact, in many cases the protective gear that each soldier wore consisted of CMC armor plating patched together with pseudo-leather padding. The uniforms were covered with guild symbols and insignias that marked their specialty, a tradition that started all the way back with Moria's original mining guilds. The rippers were known to be the best-equipped soldiers in the Combine, but even they had a preference for Confed armor when they could get their hands on it; a fresh coat of black paint easily erased its origins—and the blood the soldier surely would have spilled in procuring it.

The Kel-Morians knew where the improvised airstrip was, of course, but there was no reason to make the war easy for them, so, with the exception of handheld lamps and the spill of light that came from inside the Kel-Morian dropship, the entire area was blacked out. However, out beyond the area that was under the direct control of the military, some of the local citizens were making no effort to comply with the blackout, and the marines lacked sufficient personnel to chase them down.

"All right," Tychus said as his team assembled

next to the ship. "Pair off and check each other's gear. Wasser, you're with me."

Corporal Wasser, better known to the rest of the squad as "the troll," was short but extremely powerful. So strong, in fact, that it was necessary for Tychus to actually exert himself to beat Wasser at arm wrestling.

But Wasser's *real* claim to fame was his relationship with Captain Jack, which some likened to the bond between a man and his dog. Tychus knew that if Wasser was present, Captain Jack wouldn't be far away, and that proved to be the case as the squad members completed their checks and trooped into the cargo bay. Captain Jack, now *Overseer* Jack, according to the Kel-Morian insignias on his clothing, was chatting with the pilot. Once the squad was aboard and properly strapped in, he came back to sit with them.

"Lock and load," the officer said, as the engines ran up and the Kel-Morian dropship wobbled into the air. "We'll be over the target in about five minutes."

The trip was so short there wouldn't have been any reason to use a transport if it hadn't been for the deception involved. But Tychus was glad of it, because the faster they could complete the mission and return, the sooner he could check on Operation Early Retirement. Calvin was supposed to send two trucks in at 0300 and Tychus wanted to be present.

Both of the ship's side doors had been removed to make way for an automatic weapon on one side and a rotary rocket launcher on the other, both of which were manned by helmeted crewmen. The slipstream blew cold air and rain in through the doors, but Tychus was glad of the openings nonetheless, because they allowed him to catch an occasional glimpse of the countryside whenever a bolt of lightning crackled across the sky.

As the ship flew north he saw clusters of lights and knew he was looking at homes that should have been blacked out. And that raised an interesting question. . . . Since he could see them—did that mean *they* could see the ship? And would they recognize it as a Kel-Morian aircraft if they did?

The fact that the dropship was flying low, only a couple of hundred feet off of the ground, seemed to suggest that it *would* be identifiable during a lightning flash. Tychus felt something cold trickle into his bloodstream. Did Captain Jack *want* people to spot the Kel-Morian aircraft? And if so, why?

There was no way to know as the ship banked and circled to port. That revealed a brightly lit house. *The* house, or so Tychus assumed.

Captain Jack was communicating with the pilot via his helmet comm, and while Tychus couldn't hear what was said, he saw the officer's lips move.

Tychus wondered why he had been cut out of the conversation. Normally, as Captain Jack's number two, Tychus would have been privy to all the interactions on the command channel. So was this an anomaly? Or was the officer hiding something? There was no way to know as the transport lost even more altitude and the circle tightened.

Tychus, who was seated opposite the opening on the port side, caught a glimpse of a large house, outbuildings, and a landing pad with civilians running every which way. Then he saw the strings of lights and realized that a party was under way. He opened his mouth to speak, but was cut off as spikes began to rattle against the fuselage. "That's what we've been waiting for," Captain Jack said grimly, his voice flooding all of their helmets. "Let the bastards have it."

The rocket launcher was on the starboard side of the dropship and therefore pointed upward. But the gauss cannon was operational and it sent streams of red tracers down to explore the estate below. Men, women, and children were tossed about like rag dolls as the supersonic spikes found them. Empty casings flew through the air, bounced off the deck, and rolled away.

But the battle wasn't one-sided. The door gunner's head jerked as a spike smashed through his visor, scrambled his brains, and blew a gout of goo out through the back of his helmet. As he fell a marine stepped in to take his place.

Tychus was out of his seat by then and hurried to confront Captain Jack. "I suggest that you tell the pilot to land this thing now, sir! The transport makes an easy target."

"Soon," the officer agreed grimly, as a shoulder-launched rocket exploded against the hull. "Let's make sure everyone in the area sees the markings on the ship first."

Now Tychus understood the *real* reason for using the Kel-Morian dropship and the disguises. The Confederate civilians weren't collaborators, they were something else, dissidents perhaps. People the government planned to eliminate. And having seen the ship's markings, witnesses would report the attack as a Kel-Morian raid! Thereby reinforcing all of the Confederacy's propaganda about enemy atrocities.

And the plan would probably work unless Captain Jack got them all killed, which appeared to be increasingly likely as more enemy fire hit the hull, and holed it. A marine screamed as a piece of shrapnel took his leg off just below the knee and a corpsman rushed to his side. "Put it down, sir! Put it down *now*," Tychus insisted as he stared into Captain Jack's stony eyes.

"You're a coward, Findlay," the officer replied tersely as a bullet came in through the open door, hit metal and ricocheted past his head. "And I'll have you up on charges the minute we return to base."

Enraged, Tychus lifted his weapon and smashed Captain Jack in the side of the head. The officer was wearing a helmet, but the rifle butt hit so hard it broke through the protective shell, and delivered a blow to the company commander's skull. The ship dropped ten feet, then recovered as the pilot fed more power to the retros. Tychus stumbled back.

Captain Jack's unconscious body was still falling to the floor as Wasser uttered a roar of outrage. He jumped onto Tychus's back and called for reinforcements. Tychus managed to drop the marine who came straight at him, but when two more tackled his legs, he went down. Wasser wrapped two hands around Tychus's throat and cut off his air supply. Tychus felt the ship vibrate as the pilot maxed the retros, wondered how he could have been so stupid, and fell into a black hole.

CHAPTER SEVEN

"Of the thousands of new soldiers recruited into the Confederate armed services over the past few months, there have been several dozen complaints filed with the Bureau of Personnel regarding illegal drafting. The bureau claims that these allegations of unsanctioned conscription are unfounded and based on 'the typical panic and unrest found in civilian populations during wartime.' Out of respect to our audience, UNN has chosen to drop this investigation until tensions dissipate to peacetime levels."

Max Speer, *Evening Report* for UNN
May 2488

THE PLANET TARSONIS,
THE CONFEDERACY OF MAN

The unconscious boy lay on the cot with his eyes closed and his arms hanging down to the floor as Camy rifled through his pockets and two men looked on. The wallet was right where she expected it to be, inside the still morphing jacket in a self-sealing pocket.

The con artist kept her back to the onlookers as she opened the leather folder and went straight for the cash. *Bills . . . nice.* Camy knew right then that she'd snagged a good one. It was rare to find bills these days—especially among the low-life scabs she usually came across in Hacker's Flat.

Having stuffed the cash into her bra, she took an inventory of the rest. And that was when she saw the name "Ark Bennet" on a holocard, and frowned. Could it be? Could the naïve, slack-jawed youth lying on the cot really be the scion of the famous Bennet family? After shuffling through the rest of the boy's wallet, she concluded that he was. Not because she'd seen him on the vids, but because of the name. She'd never met anyone named "Ark" before—much less an "Ark Bennet."

Camy's first reaction was greed. How much would the Bennet family be willing to pay to get their boy back? A hundred thousand? A *million*? The notion of a ransom was tempting. Very tempting. But it was scary, too . . . because the Bennet family was extremely powerful, and the moment they reported their son missing the Tarsonis Police Force would scour the city looking for the boy. The thought of that, and what they might do to her, made Camy's heart pound.

There was another party who would be willing

to buy Ark Bennet, however. He wouldn't pay as much as the Bennets would, but the transaction would be a lot safer, and would put a layer of protection between Camy and the police.

"So, pay up," one of the men demanded. "We've got some serious drinking to do."

"Don't worry," Camy replied. "I will. I'll pay ten each, plus whatever you can get for that jacket, which will be ten times more. It could be traceable though, so take it at least six blocks away, and sell it quick. That goes for the rest of his stuff, too. I want one of you to strip him down—while the other goes for some street clothes. The faster we do this the better. So *move*!"

The grubby, smoke-filled room was located over the onetime garage that had long served as Harley Ross's command post, and there was a strong possibility that he was the most unkempt recruiting sergeant stationed on Tarsonis. Something the marine was proud of, because while other noncoms were spending their time in upper schools, strutting about and telling lies about how wonderful the Marine Corps was, he was out sifting through working-class neighborhoods where only two out of ten teenagers finished school and work was hard to find. And his numbers were better than anybody else's. Which explained why Captain Fredricks left him alone.

So that's where the recruiter was, playing cards with three of his cronies, when his fone began to rattle on the table just as Dicer upped the ante. A sure sign that he had a winning hand. So rather than throw good money after bad, Ross looked at the incoming number and flipped the device open. "Hey, sweet cakes, what you got for me?"

The other men watched cynically as Ross nodded, said, "I'll be right over," and broke the connection. "Don't tell me," Dicer said. "Let me guess. I raise the ante and you have to leave."

Ross smiled apologetically. "Sorry about that, but duty calls! There's a war on, you know. . . . Somebody has to keep the Kel-Morians at bay, or they'll land on Tarsonis and go after your wife."

"She'd probably welcome a squad of KM rippers after all the years living with Dicer," one of the other men observed, and Dicer glowered by way of a response.

"How 'bout it?" Ross inquired, as he cashed out. "Anyone want to make fifty credits? I could use some muscle."

"Count me in," a man named Vic responded. "I could use some scratch."

Ten minutes later Ross and Vic were in the unmarked van and on their way. Traffic was bad as usual, so it took a full twenty minutes to reach the Hacker's Flat neighborhood and pull up to the loading dock behind the pub. Camy was there waiting as the two men got out of the van. She was clearly annoyed. "What the hell took you so long?" she demanded. "The stupid sonofabitch is starting to come to."

"That's no way to talk about a young man who is about to join the Confederacy's armed forces," Ross replied sternly, as he mounted a short flight of concrete stairs. "Show some respect."

Camy produced a snort of derision, pivoted toward the door, and led the men into the back room. A young man was laid out on the cot, but was trying to sit up and form words that refused to come. Both the fancy jacket and shoes had been replaced by used clothing purchased at a bodega a few doors down. "Good work!" Ross said, as he stood over Camy's latest find. "He's in good shape. Where'd you get him?"

Camy shrugged. "I think he's a college student. . . . He wandered off the campus and was strolling along the street when I spotted him."

Ross eyed her. "You think he's a college student? Or you *know* he is? Let's see his wallet. There's bound to be some ID in there."

"He didn't have a wallet," Camy responded vaguely. "Maybe he forgot it or something."

Ross shook his head in disgust. "So you cleaned out his wallet. . . . What else did you get?"

Camy stood her ground. "What difference does it make? It isn't like you need his real name or something. A girl has to make a living. Which reminds me . . . Fork it over."

Ross, who was wearing a rumpled suit, removed two separately packaged ounces of crab from his coat pocket and handed them over. Crab was the nickname for a powerful narcotic substance that was both a depressant and an intoxicant. "You ought to cut back, Camy. . . . That stuff is bad for you."

"And you ought to kiss my ass, *Ross,*" Camy snapped back, as the packets disappeared into her purse.

"I'd be happy to handle that responsibility for him," Vic interjected, and leered at her.

"You wish," Camy responded darkly. "Now quit screwing around and get the meat out of here. There hasn't been any sign of a search so far, but there's bound to be one, and I'd like to be somewhere else when the heat arrives."

"Roger that," Ross replied. "Vic, you grab him under the armpits, and I'll take his legs. Camy, if you would be so kind as to go out and open the back door, I would be eternally grateful."

Having struggled mightily, Ark managed to sit up at that point, and voiced his objections. "Gibo tell orby im pop."

The man named Ross swore, let go of Ark's ankles, and adjusted the ring on his right hand.

Once the Marine Corps emblem was rotated inward, he slapped the booster against the boy's neck to fire a powerful sedative in through the pores of his skin. Ark jerked convulsively, saw the brute's face roll out of focus, and felt himself float away.

ABOARD THE CONFEDERATE TROOPSHIP *GLADIATOR*

Consciousness returned slowly. Ark heard noises, occasional snatches of conversation, and the persistent rumble of something. Engines? Air-conditioning? There was no way to be sure. Then someone pried open his left lid and aimed a penlight into his eye. The woman had a pleasant middle-aged face and was wearing medical scrubs. "This one is coming around," she announced. "Let's get him off the table and into the holding area."

Two men, also in medical scrubs, came to assist, and they were anything but gentle as they pulled Ark up into a sitting position. "Where am I?" Ark inquired blearily, as he eyed the medical equipment around him. "You're on a system runner, headed for the troopship *Gladiator*," the woman replied cheerfully. "I hope you enjoyed your going away party . . . 'cause you're going to pay with one helluva hangover."

Ark wanted to tell her that there hadn't been

any going away party, but the men had him on his feet by then and were walking him out of the sick bay. There were a number of twists and turns, but Ark's head hurt, and he couldn't keep track of them. A hatch irised open two minutes later, and he was pushed into a compartment half-filled with ratty-looking young people, all of whom regarded him with empty-eyed stares. As the men let go, Ark felt dizzy and quickly sank to the deck.

Nobody said anything as the hatch closed, but a girl at the other end of the compartment was sobbing softly, and a boy was humming a pop tune. The youngster stopped when a muscular youth slapped the back of his head and said, "Shut the hell up."

So an uneasy silence settled over the group and remained in force until the ship entered the *Gladiator*'s docking bay and put down. Then, once the cavernous space was repressurized, Ark and the rest of the recruits were led off the smaller ship to stand on the blast-scarred deck.

That was when three sharply dressed marines appeared and went about the job of pushing and prodding the recruits into three perfectly spaced ranks. Once the task had been accomplished a staff sergeant appeared. He had dark skin, and even though he was no more than five-and-a-half-feet tall, his personality filled the bay.

"My name is Wright . . . *sir* to you. You are now aboard the troopship *Gladiator*, which is about to break orbit, and take you to Turaxis II. Once there you will be transformed into warriors. And not just *any* warriors, but the *best* warriors in the whole friggin' galaxy, even if it kills you . . . which would be fine with me. Now we're going to hold roll call. When I call your name you will say 'present.' Allen."

"Present!"

"Alvarez."

"Present!"

And so it went until Wright called for "Kydd" and nobody answered.

The noncom touched a button on his remote terminal console, eyed the picture that was displayed there, and scanned the ranks until he spotted Ark. Then, having pushed his way between two street thugs, Wright brought his face to within inches of Ark's. "Are you trying to mess with me, recruit Kydd?"

Ark was surprised. *Kydd? Who the heck is Kydd?* Clearly there had been a mix-up of some kind. He shook his head. "No sir, my name is Bennet . . . Ark Bennet. If you'll contact my father, Errol Bennet, he'll give you a reward."

"Yeah, sure," Wright responded. "And I'm the finance minister—but I work as a sergeant to supplement my income. Now, I have your name down as Ryk Kydd, so that's who you're going to be until you file the necessary forms, collect affidavits proving that you're really someone else, and find some civvy in the Bureau of Personnel to cut you loose. Is that clear?"

Ark found it difficult to answer with Wright only inches away. Especially since he had bad breath. "Yes, sir. When can I file the forms you spoke of?"

There was very little humor in Wright's long, slow smile. "You can file them after you graduate from boot camp. So work hard, sweetheart, because people who don't make it through basic training the first time start all over again. And that ain't no fun!

"Now, having wasted my time, drop down and give me thirty push-ups. Oh, and one more thing. Welcome to the Marine Corps."

CHAPTER EIGHT

"It's a good idea to take your time making friends: I usually give it six rounds. Whether they're bullets, beers, or bouts depends on the day."

Lance Corporal Jim Raynor, 321st Colonial Rangers Battalion, in an interview on Turaxis II
July 2488

ABOARD THE TROOPSHIP *HYDRUS*,
EN ROUTE TO TURAXIS II

The *Hydrus* was more than fifty years old, but she was *big*, in keeping with her original purpose, which was to transport settlers to colony worlds like the one Raynor had been born on. But those days were over, and the ship had long since been purchased into military service, and was currently being used to support the Confederacy's war effort. Which was why Raynor and more than two thousand other "boots" were camped out in the vessel's cavernous hold.

And "camped out" was the operative term, since there weren't cabins for anyone other than the crew and the two hundred or so uniformed personnel traveling to Turaxis II for a variety of reasons. So, with the exception of a section of deck that the noncoms in charge referred to as the "parade ground," Hold Two was a no-man's-land of individual encampments, each of which served as home for up to fifteen recruits.

The arrangement led to occasional turf wars, which the noncoms sought to squelch. But in spite of their beady-eyed vigilance, and the stunner-armed patrols tasked with keeping things under control, the "zoo," as many of the inhabitants referred to it, was a dangerous place to live.

All of which had come as a surprise to Jim Raynor, who, based on everything he'd seen and heard on the news, believed that the military was highly organized, perfectly integrated, and fully supplied. And that was why taxes were so high, or so everyone had been told, to make sure the military had everything it needed. Except that they *didn't* have everything they needed. Including adequate transportation.

That became even more apparent as Raynor drew his daily rations, and was carrying them toward his squat, when a Klaxon began to beep. An official announcement followed: *"This is Lieutenant Freeson. Due to a security breach, unauthorized personnel have gained access to Hold Two. Military police are en route. Those individuals assigned to Hold Two are to avoid contact with the intruders, take up positions with their backs to the port and starboard bulkheads, and await further instructions. I repeat, this is Lieutenant Freeson . . ."*

Raynor might have listened to the message all over again, but he was distracted as a mob of people rushed his way. One of them bumped Raynor's arm and sent the boxes of rations spinning away. Raynor was clambering to retrieve them—it was either that or go hungry—when a scuffle broke out nearby. "That's right, freak," he heard a familiar voice bark, "it's time to go back into your cage."

Raynor straightened, peering through the crowd to get a glimpse of the melee. His suspicion was confirmed. The voice belonged to Hank Harnack. Most of Raynor's injuries had healed since the beating he received in the lavatory, but the skin around his eyes was still purple, and hurt whenever he touched it.

Corporal Timson had followed up on the incident, of course, but having heard Harnack refuse to rat him out, Raynor had been careful to do likewise. Something the noncom clearly approved of. Timson had been careful to keep the two combatants away from each other after that, and once the original draft was combined with others from different parts of the planet, the recruits had been separated. Up until now, that is.

After breaking out of the forward hold, several hundred violent criminals were on the loose—the hold had been abuzz with a rumor that the *Hydrus* was carrying prisoners on their way to some sort of military work camp or reformatory. Now, most of the captives were trying to lose themselves in the larger crowd, or steal personal items from the squats, but half a dozen of them were circling Harnack like a pack of wild dogs.

Tom Omer materialized at Raynor's side. "Uh-oh," he said ominously. "It looks like Harnack is about to get his. Couldn't happen to a nicer guy."

Raynor couldn't help but smile, his gaze fixed on Harnack, who was now offering the thugs a supercilious smirk while kissing each bicep and striking a weight lifter's pose. "Yeah, he's a sweetheart all right."

Omer snorted as the constantly shuffling circle tightened around Harnack. "Wonder what he did to crack them off," he mused aloud. "It could have been anything. These guys are animals."

That wasn't far from the truth. The prisoners were allegedly offered the chance to join the Marine Corps after a brief stint at the reformatory, as an alternative to doing hard time in prison. But old ways die hard, and with nothing else to do, the criminals had broken out of the area assigned to them. He pitied any poor social workers or counselors who would be assigned to help these guys become upstanding citizens—they sure had their work cut out for them.

Now, like it or not, Raynor was faced with a choice. It would be incredibly satisfying to see Harnack receive some of his own medicine. But he knew exactly what his father would say if he were there: "Remember, son . . . the *true* measure of a man is whether other people can count on him when it makes a difference."

"Here," Raynor said, as he handed his rations off to Omer. "Take care of those, will you? I'd appreciate it."

"Don't do it," Omer advised ominously. "You'll be sorry."

Distant shouts were heard, followed by three shrill blasts from a whistle and the thunder of feet on steel.

"Yeah," Raynor agreed, as he removed his jacket and placed it on top of the rations. "I probably will."

Some of the recruits had placed their backs against the bulkheads by then, but others were caught up in the moment and eager for entertainment. They began to chant, "Blood! Blood! Blood!" as Raynor navigated his way between a scattering of encampments and into the open area beyond. The circle was tighter by then, so much so that Harnack was starting to fend off blows, as more whistles blew in the distance.

One of the onlookers had a sprained ankle,

and was leaning on a crutch, which Raynor jerked out from under her as he strode past. The girl swore as she went down, made a grab for the recruit on her right, and both of them fell in a tangle of arms and legs.

"Shit. Sorry, miss," Raynor uttered hastily as he continued on.

A pang of fear dropped into Raynor's gut as he entered the fray with the improvised weapon. By now a con had wrangled Harnack into a headlock. The crutch made a whirring sound as it slashed through the air, caught the con behind the knees, and brought him down.

Having been freed from one attacker, Harnack launched a spin kick at another. As he completed the move and sent the con reeling backward, he looked at Raynor and grinned. "Okay . . . You *aren't* a sissy. But you're stupid as hell!"

There was no time for a response, as Raynor took a glancing blow to the side of the head, and brought the crutch around by way of a response. It struck one of the attackers in the mouth, broke some of his teeth, and put him on his ass.

The whistles were louder by then, as a phalanx of noncoms began to work their way across the deck, stunning anyone who failed to obey orders. But it was slow going because they had to pause frequently in order to take escaped cons into custody.

So as Raynor rammed the crutch into a con's

gut, he knew it would be at least three or four minutes before help arrived. And a lot of things could happen in that time.

Raynor swore as somebody took hold of the crutch and jerked it away from him. Then a fist hit him in the right kidney. The pain was intense, and he was starting to fall, when a badly bloodied Harnack grabbed him by the belt. "Stay on your feet!" he shouted. "They'll stomp you if you don't."

Having been stomped by Harnack's friends in the lavatory, Raynor understood the wisdom of the other youth's advice. So he battled to stay vertical, as the two of them fought back-to-back, and bets were placed all around. Then, as Raynor landed a roundhouse punch on a hate-filled face, the noncoms arrived.

The uniformed marines were swinging their stunners at anything that moved by that time, which was why Harnack pulled Raynor down. "Go limp!" he commanded. "They're gonna stun you!"

Raynor obeyed, but some of the cons fought back, which earned them a high-voltage clubbing and a presumption of guilt. Once the criminals had been cuffed and led away, Harnack scrambled to his feet. "You're one crazy sonofabitch," he said admiringly, as he reached down to give Raynor a hand.

"Thanks," Raynor replied. "I think."

That was when Omer arrived with a leather

bag full of coins. There was a jingling sound as he shook it. "Look at all the money I won betting on you guys! We'll split it three ways."

When Harnack grinned, a bloody film covered his teeth. "Great. . . . It was worth it then."

Raynor put a hand on his kidney. It hurt like hell. "I'm not so sure about that. . . . What triggered the fight anyway?"

"It was their fault," Harnack said defensively. "I called one of them a freak and he threw a punch. That's when I decked his ass."

Raynor sighed and rolled his eyes. "I should have known."

Omer chuckled.

"I'm hungry," Harnack announced suddenly, as he snatched the bag of coins from Omer. "I hear somebody smuggled some *real* food on board and they've got a brew-up goin' back in the corner. Come on . . . lunch is on me."

Omer made a grab for the bag, but Harnack had already spun around and started to leave. A few seconds later, he stopped abruptly and looked back. "You losers comin'?"

"This should be good," Raynor mumbled cynically, as he threw an arm across Omer's shoulders. "Assuming we survive the trip to boot camp, we should be able to survive anything the KMs throw at us."

* * *

Four intervals and several warp jumps later, the *Hydrus* entered orbit some three planetary diameters off of Turaxis II. Under normal conditions the ship would have cut it closer, say one diameter out, but with Kel-Morian raiders on the prowl it was necessary for the old transport and ships like her to form a convoy before entering orbit.

Though originally built for peaceful purposes, the enemy ships had been armed and armored using materials and skills furnished by the Morian Mining Guild. The KMs didn't have a fleet as such, so members of the Kelanis Shipping Guild were filling that role, and had proven themselves to be quite formidable despite a lack of military training.

The KMs were unpredictable for one thing, which made it that much more difficult to defend against their constant attacks, as the admiral in charge of organizing the Confederate ships sought to order, cajole, and sometimes shame the merchant captains into placing their vessels where they were supposed to.

Meanwhile down in the *Hydrus*'s hold, there was very little for the recruits to do except worry, because the ship was secured for battle, and in the absence of acceleration couches they had to lie under drift nets for hours at a time.

Raynor, who was flat on his back next to Harnack, understood the need. Because, should the vessel come under attack and the argrav generators fail, everything, including unsecured recruits, would suddenly become weightless and drift all about. So to protect them, as well as the ship herself, it was necessary to immobilize the boots.

Each of them handled the situation differently. Omer was frightened, his body tense and perfectly still, and his face drained of color. Raynor was concerned, knowing that the *Hydrus* would have to depend on other ships for her defense, but figured the swabbies knew what they were doing. There was no way to know how Harnack felt, because he was asleep, and snoring loudly.

"Will you shake him or something?" Omer asked.

"Be careful what you ask for," Raynor responded. "He's so peaceful at the moment."

"It sounds like his nostrils are too small for that melon head of his."

"Or maybe he's been punched in the face one too many times. That's my guess."

"Why are we hanging out with him again?" Omer asked.

"I don't know. Entertainment? Pity?"

"I can hear you . . ." Harnack mumbled, smacked his lips, and launched directly back into his snoring. Raynor and Omer cracked up.

"I guess we should try to sleep, too," Raynor said. He took a deep breath, closed his eyes, and wondered what his parents were up to.

So as the hours passed, Raynor took catnaps and tried to read, without much success. Alarms sounded at one point, followed by an announcement that the convoy was under attack, but the captain gave the all clear ten minutes later. Then a thin, watery likeness of his face appeared on every functioning monitor. The hair he still had was wrapped around the sides of his head. He had bushy brows, serious eyes, and a softly rounded jaw. The uniform he wore looked as though it had been slept in.

"We lost the Cyrus*,"* he said soberly, *"but the attacking ship was destroyed by our escorts within a matter of minutes. We expect to enter orbit approximately one hour from now. Confederate forces control all of the best slots at the moment. But since the strategic situation remains fluid, and the Kel-Morians own roughly half of the planet's surface, the disembarkation process will take place on the double.*

"For that reason recruits will be asked to form up into groups of fifteen, and when it's your turn to board a dropship, you will proceed with the utmost dispatch. Any recruit who fails to comply with orders, or otherwise impedes progress, will be stunned.

"Two squadrons of Avengers will be waiting to escort our dropships to the surface," the captain continued, *"but it's likely that the enemy will respond with fighters of their own. So you may have a front row seat in a real dogfight.*

"Once on the ground you will be ordered to deass the dropships on the double so that they can clear the area and make another trip. I'm told it's nighttime where

you're headed, about fifty-five degrees, and raining. Good luck, and don't forget to shoot at least one of the bastards for me."

A click was heard as the captain disappeared and was immediately replaced by one of the standard images that the recruits had seen at least a hundred times before on their journey. It showed a clearly dispirited young man slouched on a set of stairs that led up to a tenement. The caption read: "The Marine Corps . . . you owe it to yourself."

Harnack pushed the net up away from his face and yawned. "What the hell was that all about? Doesn't the old geezer realize that some of us are trying to sleep?"

"We're about an hour out," Raynor replied. "The dancing girls have been notified of your arrival, free beer is available in the mess hall, and you were promoted to general."

"Sounds good," Harnack replied agreeably, as he began to extricate himself from the net. "Save my place. The general needs to pee."

CHAPTER NINE

"Combat escalated today between Confederate forces and the Kel-Morian Combine. Two new regiments of the Terran Confederacy saw their first action in the battles that cut across the plains of Turaxis II, and casualties were heavy. When asked about today's losses, Lieutenant Colonel Vanderspool of the 3rd regiment was quoted as saying, 'Although tragic, these numbers are not unusual for regiments made up of newly recruited battalions. What your figures fail to take into account is that today saw the creation of veterans. I will take ten experienced soldiers over a hundred greenhorns any day of the week.' Vanderspool refused to respond to further questions concerning today's loss of life, and our cameras were soon escorted off the base."

Max Speer, *Evening Report* for UNN
July 2488

ABOARD THE TROOPSHIP *HYDRUS* TO TURAXIS II

It was more than two hours before the *Hydrus* dropped into orbit, and the first group of recruits was ordered to leave the hold. But because Raynor and Harnack were slated for the *third* flight of dropships, they had to endure another hour-long delay before it was their turn to go.

Once the fifteen-person group was lined up with standard issue kit bags in hand, a harried sergeant took the time required to check each name off a list before shouting final instructions. "You will follow me, keep your mouths shut, and do exactly as you are told!"

So saying, the noncom turned her back on the group and took off at a jog. Raynor welcomed the chance to stretch his legs. He was keenly aware of everything around him as he followed Harnack through a maze of corridors and down a level to the point where a hatch labeled LAUNCH BAY blocked further progress.

There was a three-minute delay before it irised open and ozone-laced air flooded the lock. Then they were on the move again as the sergeant led them out into a large compartment that was temporarily sealed off from the vacuum beyond.

Rows of dropships were waiting; judging from appearances, some of them had seen a lot of action. And given all of the different insignias on display, Raynor got the impression that the squadron had been assembled from at least half a dozen units.

Did that imply that a lot of individual commands were under strength? Raynor thought it might. The group pounded across the blast-scarred deck to a much-patched ship. A hand-painted image of a scantily clad, dark-haired vixen could be seen near the bow, immediately over the name: DADDY'S GIRL.

The forward section of the hull was convex, so as to provide some lift while operating in an atmosphere. Two extremely powerful engines were mounted where the fuselage narrowed slightly before splitting into twin booms that extended back to support vertical tail fins.

But there was no time to gawk as the noncom led her charges to the vessel and stopped next to an open belly hatch. Her right arm windmilled as she urged them inside. "Move! Move! Move!"

Once inside, the pilot was waiting to herd the passengers into the built-in seats that lined both sides of the ship. They were ordered to clip their bags to the ringbolts located between their boots, strap in, ". . . and prepare for liftoff."

Raynor tried to think of a way to "prepare" and came up empty. That left him free to look around. Four large crates were strapped to the deck. One was clearly full of medical supplies, given all the red crosses that had been stamped on it, and another bore a label that read: SHOTGUNS, TORRENT (20).

As Raynor continued to scan his surroundings he saw that there were a lot of black-and-yellow decals on the bulkheads, all warning against a host of sins he had no plans to commit. A handwritten note from one of the previous passengers was visible directly across from him. It read: SO WHAT'S YOUR RECRUITER DOING RIGHT NOW?

Raynor knew the answer—or thought he did. Gunnery Sergeant Farley was probably drinking beer, sweet-talking a country girl, and looking forward to a steak dinner. *The bastard.*

The ramp made a prolonged whining sound as it was retracted, the airframe started to vibrate as the engines spooled up, and a barely audible Klaxon began to bleep outside. That was the signal for everyone *not* dressed in space armor to evacuate the flight deck. Exactly three minutes later, the outer doors opened, air was expelled into space, and the first pair of dropships rode it out.

Then it was their turn, and Raynor felt the bottom drop out of his stomach as *Daddy's Girl* left the relative safety of the launch bay for the dangers that waited beyond. There weren't any windows or viewscreens to look at, so they couldn't see Turaxis II and the blacked-out landmass below. But all of them were aware of free fall, as their weightless bodies attempted to float up off their seats, and a loose stylus cartwheeled through the air.

The dropship began to shake violently as it entered the planet's upper atmosphere. Raynor felt his teeth start to chatter, opened his mouth, and saw others do likewise as everything around them rattled loudly. That was when the pilot spoke over the intercom. His voice was even and controlled. *"Sorry about the vibration—but it will disappear soon.*

"That's the good news. . . . The bad *news is that Kel-Morians want to kill us! So a shitload of Hellhounds are on their way up to try to ruin our day. Fortunately our fighter jockeys will be waiting to greet them—and I'm the best dropship pilot in the Confederacy. See you on the ground."*

There was a click as the announcement came to an end. Harnack grinned approvingly. "He's full of shit—but I like his style!"

Then *Daddy's Girl* shuddered as something hit her. And, without warning, she flipped over onto her back, corkscrewing toward the planet below. "We took a hit!" Omer shouted, his eyes wide with fear. "We're going to die!"

"Shut up, Omer," Raynor snapped, although the same possibility had crossed his mind. The other recruit looked resentful—but did as he was told.

At that point smoke began to fill the cabin and the dropship came out of its spin. It was still going down at a sharp angle, however, and Raynor wasn't surprised when the announcement was made. *"We're going in,"* the same voice they had heard before said matter-of-factly. *"Brace for impact."*

Oh, hell. Raynor didn't know what that meant, even so, he reflexively laced his hands behind his head and pulled his elbows in tight. The ship's glide path flattened out, and the bottom of the fuselage hit something hard and bounced off. Raynor's chin hit his chest and came back up again. That was followed by a very short flight, *another* impact, and a series of successive jerks as *Daddy's Girl* skittered across Turaxis II's surface before slamming into an outcropping of rock. Raynor was thrown to the left, as were all the others on the starboard side of the ship, but the three-point harnesses held them in place. As the cabin lights went off, emergency lighting came on, and an alarm began to beep plaintively.

There was a moment of stunned silence as the passengers caught up with the fact that they were still alive. That realization was followed by the crackle of flames and a series of loud moans from a recruit named Santhay. Raynor waited for someone to tell him what to do. The recruits were panicking as they checked on one another, and Omer's voice wailed above the din, "What should we do? Somebody in charge, please tell us what to do!" *Silence.*

Suddenly the odor of smoke invaded Raynor's nostrils. *Oh, no.* Desperate to find help, he whipped his head toward the cockpit and felt a jolt of pain in his neck. Wincing, he fumbled with his harness. *The pilot's gotta be dead or injured, and there's a god-*

damn fire. The emergency lights flickered and Santhay began to make dreadful keening noises. *I gotta do something.*

Decision made, Raynor finally released his harness and stood. "Omer . . . the belly hatch is blocked. Open the side exits and count heads as people bail out.

"Harnack . . . check the cockpit. If the pilot is alive, pull him out of there!

"Chang . . . open those cargo modules. Some weapons might come in handy. I'll go aft and see how many people are injured."

Then Raynor made his way in. People were using emergency fire extinguishers by then, but the air was still thick with smoke and he was coughing. What he found at the back end of the ship wasn't pretty. It looked as though the entire tail section had been shot off, holing the belly and leaving the ship rudderless. Maybe the pilot *was* the best. The fact that most of the passengers were still alive was either a testament to his skill, or nothing less than a miracle.

There had been two casualties however, which included the decapitated pilot, whom Harnack was dragging from the cockpit. His torso was drenched in blood, but the needle-gun was safe in its holster, so Raynor bent over to retrieve it. His stomach felt queasy, but he managed to ignore that as he stuck the pistol into the waistband of his pants.

"Come on!" Harnack yelled. "This thing could blow!"

With help from another recruit, Raynor carried Santhay forward and out through an emergency exit on the port side. Rain was falling, with the exception of a spill of light from inside the ship, it was pitch black. Harnack was waiting on the ground. "When the swabbies decided to call these things dropships, they weren't kidding!"

"Come on, let's put some distance between ourselves and the ship," Raynor said.

Two of the recruits gently hoisted an unconscious Santhay onto their shoulders, and the group slogged through puddles of dank mud into the darkness. Seconds later, a muffled thump was heard behind them as the fire found the dropship's fuel supply, and the entire vessel exploded into flames. A series of popping noises resounded as ammo cooked off inside the hull, followed by a couple of muted blasts, and a sharp bang as an overheated air tank blew, firing chunks of shrapnel in every direction.

Fortunately they were a safe distance from the ship by then. Raynor raised his voice so they could hear him over the roar of the flames. "Let's find some shelter. Then we'll hole up and wait for help."

"Who died and put you in charge?" one of the recruits demanded.

"The pilot did," Raynor replied grimly. "But if you have a better plan, let's hear it."

After a few seconds of silence, Raynor nodded. "All right then. Do any of you have medical training? No? Well, Santhay needs some sort of stretcher, and then we need to clear the area. That fire is like a beacon. It could bring a shitload of KMs down on us."

It took a good fifteen minutes to improvise a sling-style stretcher for Santhay, distribute half a dozen shotguns, and move out. An emergency lantern Raynor had salvaged from the ship sent a blob of white light skipping up ahead as he led them down into a gully, through a swiftly flowing stream, and up onto the opposite bank. He knew there was a chance he was leading them into enemy hands, and if that was the case, the lantern would surely expose them—but he had no other choice. The area was pitch-black.

The group was on flat ground at that point, which, judging from the piece of rusting equipment they passed, had been farmland prior to the wars. What they needed was cover and a place to hide until the sun rose, when they could better determine where they were. So when the circle of light slid across the side of what might have been a barn, Raynor had reason to hope. *Now we just have to find the cellar,* he thought, relieved.

But the emotion was short-lived as someone shouted a warning, bright lights stabbed down from the sky, and the unrestrained roar of engines was heard as two ships swept in from the west.

Harnack brought his shotgun up and pointed it at the nearest source of light. Raynor pushed it down again. "Don't tempt the bastards, Hank . . . we're outgunned."

Harnack lowered the weapon as retros stabbed the ground, and both ships came in for nearly simultaneous landings. But who was aboard them? Because the nearest ship was backlit, Raynor couldn't see the vessel's markings. A cold wind sent shivers through his rain-soaked body. He was scared.

But there wasn't much the recruits could do except stand there and stare as the ship put down, the belly hatch opened, and light spilled onto the ground as a ramp deployed. Once that process was complete, a backlit soldier in a bulky combat suit jumped to the ground and stopped fifteen feet in front of them. Bright lights projecting from the front of his armor made it impossible to see. The much-amplified voice was male. "My name's Master Sergeant Hanson. . . . Who's in command here?"

There was a moment of silence. Finally, when the rest of the recruits looked at him, Raynor took a pace forward. "I guess I am, sir . . . recruit Jim Raynor."

A servo whined as Hanson's helmeted head swiveled incrementally and gravel crunched under his boots as his weight shifted. The voice was incredulous. "*Recruit* Raynor?"

"Sir, yes sir," Raynor replied. "The pilot was killed when our dropship crashed. We didn't know where we were, so I figured we should find a place to hole up."

Hanson was silent for a moment. "Understood. All personnel will place their weapons on the ground and board the ship. Wounded first."

Raynor felt an emptiness at the pit of his stomach. "No offense, sir, but which side are you on?"

"I collect my pay from the Confederacy," Hanson replied. "Welcome to Turaxis II, son. . . . If you like to fight, you came to the right place."

CHAPTER TEN

"Why do they call it 'boot camp'? Because if they called it 'beat your ass camp,' nobody would go."

Staff Sergeant Tychus Findlay, 321st Colonial Rangers Battalion, in an interview on Turaxis II July 2488

THE PLANET TURAXIS II

The flight from the crash site to the base called Turaxis Prime took about half an hour. And having just survived a Kel-Morian attack, Raynor knew how vulnerable the ship was as it skimmed the gently undulating terrain below. If they were lucky, the eyes in the sky would lose the aircraft in amongst the ground clutter.

Meanwhile, there had been almost total silence since recruit Santhay had stopped breathing, and the corpsman had been unable to resuscitate him. Now Santhay's body was covered with a blanket, and made for a sobering sight as it lay strapped to the center of the deck. *That could've been me,* Raynor thought. *What did I get myself into?*

Even Harnack was subdued as forward motion stopped, and the pilot announced their arrival and brought the dropship's engines up into the vertical position. The ship rocked gently as a side wind hit the port side and the transport dropped through the opening below. Once the aircraft was in the hangar, and two outward-bound Avengers were clear, a pair of thick blast doors rumbled closed.

Moments after the ship's skids touched down, two privates entered the transport and loaded Santhay's body aboard a stretcher. Raynor could tell they had done the same thing many times before. They were gone a few moments later.

At that point Master Sergeant Hanson ordered the boots to deass the ship, and as Raynor followed Harnack down the ramp, he got his first glimpse of Turaxis Prime. The underground hangar deck was *huge.* Large enough to house hundreds of dropships, Avengers, and lesser aircraft, which were parked in orderly rows.

A few of the ships were so pristine they might have been new, but most showed signs of wear. Power wrenches chattered, fusion cutters hissed, and lifters hummed as crews of hardworking technicians in space construction vehicles worked to make repairs.

As a corporal ordered Raynor and his companions to follow her, a steady flow of incomprehensible announcements was coming in over loudspeakers mounted high above, a jitney loaded with dispirited looking pilots whirred past, and servos whined as a clutch of SCVs bustled along in the opposite direction. The overall impression was one of organized chaos, and Raynor felt as though he were finally seeing the *real* Marine Corps, rather than the glamorized version marketed to the public. The two couldn't have been more different.

A couple minutes later the newly arrived recruits made their way onto an elevator large enough to accommodate a siege tank. The corporal, who was half Harnack's size, felt no compunction about pushing, shoving, and even *kicking* the recruits in order to form a column of twos with the shortest members at the front and the tallest in the back. The purpose of the exercise was to limit the formation's maximum speed to that of the slowest recruits while simultaneously creating a military appearance.

The cacophony of noise coming from A Deck faded quickly as the platform descended. And it wasn't until the elevator coasted to a stop four levels below that the boots were marched out onto what they would soon come to know as the grinder. It was a vast parade ground on which they would perform endless calisthenics, learn how to march, and listen to boring speeches. The first of which was about to begin.

But before they could listen they had to reach the assembly area and do so in a military manner. That meant marching in step. "You will lead with your *left* foot," the corporal announced, as the column lurched forward. "No, stupid," she said. "Your other left! My God . . . what did they send us? A draft of idiots?

"Now, try again . . . your left, your left, your left, right, left. That's right. . . . Now you're getting the hang of it. Bring that left heel down *hard*!"

And so it went as the recruits completed the trip to the assembly area with only occasional missteps and outbursts of frustration from the corporal. Other boots, some of whom Raynor recognized as having been aboard the *Hydrus*, were already present. They had been fortunate enough to land safely, after which they had been formed into training companies and fed, prior to being marched onto the grinder.

They were standing at parade rest with feet spread and hands behind their backs. Most were smart enough to keep their eyes forward, but one of the recruits couldn't resist the temptation to eyeball the incoming troops, and was soon pumping out push-ups for his impertinence.

So Raynor was careful to keep his eyes on the platform directly in front of the assemblage as a neatly uniformed officer mounted a short flight of stairs and made his way to the podium. It was made out of real wood and the Marine Corps insignia was prominently displayed on the front of it. That was when a sergeant shouted, "Atten-hut!" The result was uneven to say the least and would have earned all of them a lap around the grinder had the circumstances been different.

The officer clearly prided himself on his appearance. His cap was correctly positioned on his head, his mustache was perfectly trimmed, and his pink cheeks were freshly shaven as his eyes darted from face to face. His nod was short and precise, like a bird pecking at a scattering of seed. "Good morning. . . . As you were."

There was a prolonged shuffling sound as the recruits went back to parade rest and the noncoms frowned disapprovingly.

"My name is Major Macaby," the officer began, "and I am in charge of basic training on Turaxis II. It's somewhat unusual to have a training facility this close to a combat zone, but these are unusual times, and we marines are adaptable. In fact, I think it's safe to say that there are certain advantages to be derived from the situation, as will become clear once you enter the final stages of boot camp.

"The purpose of your training is to prepare you to fight the Kel-Morians. And for good reason. Many of you come from planets where fuel rationing and food rationing are everyday realities. That's because the Kel-Morians are trying to take control of all the natural resources they can in a blatant attempt to replace the Confederacy's duly elected government with their own corrupt guild-dominated political system. Which, were the effort to succeed, would result in virtual slavery for us . . . since none of our families and friends would be allowed to join one of the largely hereditary guilds. So there's every reason to fight, and to fight hard, lest our way of life be stolen from us."

Macaby paused at that point and allowed his eyes to roam the faces before him as if to make sure that they understood the full import of what had been said. Then, seemingly satisfied with the expressions he'd seen, the major consulted a scrap of paper. "With that in mind you will be interested to know that the exigencies of war require us to shorten your training cycle to nine weeks from the standard twelve weeks."

A solitary clapping sound was heard, followed by a noncom's stern order, "Take that man's name!"

Macaby smiled indulgently. "Yes, I rather expected that announcement would meet with your approval! However, that being said, steps will be taken to ensure that the intensity of the basic training experience will be increased so that you will be fully prepared for combat when you join a line unit.

"So pay attention to your instructors, be ready for anything, and give it all you have. The life you save could be your own. That will be all."

A sergeant shouted, "Atten-hut!" and as Macaby left the stage, Raynor considered the implications of what had been said. Boot camp had been shortened. Did that mean the wars were going poorly? What else *could* it mean?

It was a sobering thought as the latecomers were integrated into the existing training companies. Both Raynor and Harnack were placed in D Company, which consisted of three platoons, with three squads to a platoon, for a total of seventy-two men and women. That was light by combat standards, since each squad was supposed to include three four-person fire teams, but there weren't enough recruits for that.

And somehow, by a process invisible to Raynor, he was named as a temporary "recruit sergeant," and placed in charge of the 1st squad, 2nd platoon. A dubious honor since he instantly became responsible for seven peoplc in addition to himself. One of them was Harnack, who smiled wickedly and offered Raynor a one-fingered salute.

As the newly re-formed companies were marched down a ramp to the dormitory-style living quarters below, Raynor was nervous. All the noncoms seemed so angry—and now Raynor was sure to be singled out because of his new position.

Each platoon had its own long rectangular room, and once racks were assigned, the recruits were given permission to "fall out, grab a shower, and get some sleep." All seven hours of it, before they would be expected to get up and double-time to chow. Later, after haircuts, they were scheduled to receive personal gear, uniforms, and weapons.

But all of that was six-plus hours away, after a sonic shower and some much-needed rest. So Raynor stripped down to his skivvies and was about to head for the communal showers when three heavily armored Kel-Morian rippers emerged from a solid wall, swiveled toward the unsuspecting recruits, and opened fire.

Raynor saw the assault rifles sparkle, and felt a tingling sensation as half a dozen electric impulses accelerated through his chest, followed by a cry of consternation as they hit a person behind him. The enemy soldiers weren't real, of course, but Raynor's heart was pounding nevertheless, and there was nothing fake about the fear he felt.

That was when the spectral rippers exploded into a thousand motes of light and another phantom appeared. Though nearly transparent, he looked like a recruiting poster come to life, and there was something about his synthesized voice that reminded Raynor of Farley. *"My name is Gunnery Sergeant Travis,"* the hologram announced, *"and I have been ordered to assist with your training. An attack like the one you just experienced took place three months ago when a Kel-Morian special operations team managed to infiltrate a base on Dylar IV. Seven marines died that night, three were wounded, and one of them is still on life support. So remember, the enemy can strike anywhere, and at any time. You are never safe."* And with that Travis disappeared.

Ryk Kydd was in love with his Bosun FN92 sniper rifle. Or, more accurately, in love with the way he felt when he fired it. Because hitting targets that other people couldn't made him feel strong and competent. The weapon had a skeletal stock, a telescopic sight, and an extremely long barrel. And that was critical. Because the more time the bullet spent inside the metal tube, the more likely it was to hit the target. And during the last few weeks, that had become very important to him.

So as Kydd elbowed his way up onto a rise, it was with the intention of qualifying as a Marine Corps sniper while still in boot camp. Something only two people had achieved before him.

At that point Kydd had completed two earlier "crawls," and having scored simulated kills in both situations, it was time for one final test of his marksmanship on a specially designed indoor range. Kydd was wearing a helmet, light body armor, a standard combat harness, and protective earplugs.

"Okay," Sergeant Peters said in his ear. "Here's the scenario. . . . A very important general is going to appear in the enemy encampment about a thousand yards in front of and below your position. A number of other people may be present, but the general is the only one who will be wearing a beret and smoking a pipe. The mission is simple. Identify your target and kill him with one shot. Good luck, son. . . . I know you can do it."

Kydd heard a click, followed by the soft whisper of an artificial wind as a computer-generated panorama blossomed around him. The sky was pewter gray, the surrounding slopes were green, and the camouflaged trucks and hab-units had a mottled appearance. A sensor array could be seen rotating above one of the vehicles, two sentries stood guard, and a wisp of vapor was issuing out of the exhaust stack on the generator truck. Other than that, there wasn't much to see.

Kydd was grateful for that, because if the target had been visible right off the top, before he had time to prepare, he would have been faced with a difficult decision. Take a poorly prepared shot, knowing that it might be the only opportunity, or wait and hope the target would reappear.

While the beret-wearing general was nowhere to be seen, one of the sentries would serve as a good stand-in, and there was plenty to do. The first step was to chamber a round and make sure the safety was on.

Then it was time to use the rifle's built-in range finder to see how far away the target was. Kydd eyed the information available on the heads-up display (HUD) projected onto the inside surface of his visor and saw that the sentry was 996 yards away. It was a long shot but well within the Bosun's reach.

With that information in hand, it was time to check for data related to the temperature, humidity, altitude, and barometric pressure. All of which would have an effect on how the .50 caliber slug was going to fly through the air.

Having absorbed the information and processed it, the computer built into Kydd's helmet produced a drop chart complete with a recommended windage and elevation. And as the conditions around him continued to change, Kydd knew the document would update itself on a continuous basis.

He was about to move to the next step, and actually set the windage and elevation, when a tent flap opened and a rectangle of light appeared. It flickered as a succession of soldiers stepped outside. Kydd could see them talking to one another.

That was when a very real combat car arrived and stopped about twenty feet away from the tent. Wait a minute . . . was the general about to get out of the vehicle? No, the car was a distraction and Kydd forced himself to ignore it. *Beret,* he thought to himself, *I have to find the man with the beret.*

But as the telescopic sight swung left to right, Kydd realized that *none* of the men in front of him was wearing a beret. Maybe the general was still inside the tent. Maybe . . .

Then Kydd saw a sudden spark of light, panned to the left, and saw that one of the soldiers was lighting a pipe! Was that enough? Should he kill the man even though he wasn't wearing a beret? The instructors were throwing the problem at him on purpose. Kydd knew that, but it didn't make the decision any easier. And the longer he dithered the less time he would have to make the shot.

As if to punish Kydd for his indecision, it began to rain. And the water that fell from the sprinklers located high above was not only real but very distracting. The man with the pipe looked up, said something to the man standing next to him, and made his way over to the combat car. Kydd swore under his breath. The general was going to get in the car and leave! Having made up his mind, Kydd hurried to set both the windage and elevation as the officer stepped up into the open car and took the seat next to the driver.

At that point there was even less light, the rain was obscuring Kydd's vision, and the part of the target's body still exposed was the general's head. It was little more than a dark smudge in the quickly gathering gloom. And making the situation even worse was the fact that the combat car was about to pull away.

Kydd's thumb seemed to move of its own accord as the safety came off. It was necessary to nudge the barrel a fraction of an inch to the left in order to compensate for the steadily increasing wind that was blowing left to right. Then Kydd entered a strange alternate reality in which time seemed to slow. So that even as the car began to pull away, Kydd had enough time to compensate and squeeze the trigger.

He heard the rifle bark and felt the recoil as the projectile sped away. Then Kydd saw the target's head explode and heard Sergeant Peters whoop with joy, "You did it, Kydd! You took forever, and you let the easiest shot go, but you nailed the bastard! Congratulations!"

It wasn't his father's voice, or his mother's for that matter, but that was okay. Finally, after eighteen years, Kydd knew what he'd been born to do. And it felt good.

The windowless office was many levels underground. An effort had been made to personalize it with laser-inscribed plaques, framed awards, and other mementos. Private Ryk Kydd was standing at attention, staring at the wall.

Meanwhile, Major Lionel Macaby continued to review the recruit's P-1 file, which was displayed on the screen in front of him. The youngster hadn't been in the Corps long enough to pile up a lot of fitness reports, training endorsements, and other bureaucratic nonsense, so there wasn't much substance.

But one entry in particular caught the major's attention. It stated that after only eight weeks of boot camp, Kydd was the best shot in the entire training battalion and had already earned the much coveted sniper's badge. An honor most aspirants achieved only after attending a special school. But, according to the boy's drill instructor, a seasoned veteran named Peters, "Private Kydd has a sharp eye, outstanding eye-hand coordination, and the X factor. After racking up some field experience, he should be considered for advanced sniper training."

Macaby knew what Peters meant. The so-called X factor was marine shorthand for a talent that only one out of a thousand good marksmen had—the ability to seemingly slow the passage of time as they took their shots. An absolutely devastating talent that was very much in demand throughout the Marine Corps. Experts had been hired to study the phenomena, in hopes of finding a way to duplicate it, but none had been successful so far. Although one psychologist believed that Kydd could have "psionic capabilities." Whatever that meant.

The other entries of interest were all related to the same thing: repeated claims that Kydd had been drugged, abducted, and sworn into the Marine Corps under a false name. Furthermore, according to affidavits submitted by Kydd since his arrival on Turaxis II, his *real* name was Ark Bennet. Which, if true, would make him a member of a very prominent family.

Of course Kydd, like so many others, was probably just trying to get out of the Marine Corps. But what if the claim was true? And what if Kydd, a.k.a. Bennet, really was who he claimed to be? There were only a few vidsnaps of Ark Bennet in the public domain, and the ones he'd seen were of what looked like a much younger boy, with a more rounded face. There was some degree of physical resemblance, however, and Macaby was a realist. So he knew that while most of the young men and women in basic were volunteers of one kind or another, a small number, say one or two percent, were forced to join by unethical recruiters intent on hitting their increasingly high quotas. Which was okay with him so long as the practice didn't get out of hand.

But if some damned fool had been lazy or reckless enough to press-gang the VIP's fair-haired son, then there would be hell to pay once the truth came out! And the repercussions would start at the top and flow downhill. So what to do?

Fortunately the answer was right there in front of him. Thanks to the accelerated training schedule, Kydd was about to graduate from boot camp. That meant he would join a line unit within a week or two. All Macaby had to do was buck the problem up the line and keep his head down, knowing it would take the chain of command weeks to respond. Because later, when the shit hit the fan, Kydd's *new* commanding officer would have to deal with the cleanup! The plan was clean, smart, and in the finest tradition of the Marine Corps.

Macaby cleared his throat portentously. "Congratulations on qualifying as a sniper, son. That's a very impressive accomplishment. As for the claims regarding the manner in which you were recruited, I want you to know that I take them very seriously. That's why I plan to forward your package to the Bureau of Personnel—along with a request for a division-level review. In the meantime you have an excellent record. Don't mess it up. Do you have any questions?"

Macaby saw a look of satisfaction flicker across Kydd's face and disappear. "Sir, no sir."

Macaby nodded. "Dismissed."

Kydd's uniform was smooth, creased, and spotlessly clean as he completed a textbook-perfect about-face and marched out of the office.

It would be a real shame, Macaby thought to himself, *to lose such a promising recruit.*

CHAPTER ELEVEN

"Although losses have been substantial in the most recent skirmishes with the Kel-Morian Combine, Confederate sources report that troop morale is at an all-time high. Analysts credit this to increased military discipline throughout the unified terran forces, including new changes that have been described as 'strict, thorough, and rigorous.' "

Max Speer, *Evening Report* for UNN
August 2488

MILITARY CORRECTIONAL FACILITY-R-156,
ON THE PLANET RAYDIN III

The day began as it always did with the harsh sound of the Klaxon that signaled when to get up, when to eat, and when to do everything else of any importance. That was followed by the sound of Sergeant Bellamy's belligerent voice as he entered Barracks #3. "Hit the floor! This ain't no flickin' resort. That includes you, *Sergeant*

Findlay . . ." he mocked. "Get your ass in gear."

Yeah, rub it in, you waste of life. The day you actually see combat is the day you can shit on my parade.

Bellamy made it a point to broadcast daily that Tychus wasn't a sergeant anymore. He'd been demoted to private the day he had appeared at the summary court-martial, and been sentenced to three months' hard labor.

Tychus's feet were sticking out over the end of the steel-frame bed, and he was in the process of pulling them in when the swagger stick struck. The blow hurt. Tychus swore and Bellamy grinned. "How 'bout it? Have you had enough? Is today the day? You can take me. . . . So have at it."

Bellamy was a small man, commonly referred to as "the runt" behind his back, and eternally on the lookout for opportunities to impose his will on the larger prisoners, Tychus being his favorite target. He was dressed in a parade ground–perfect uniform, his nose plugs were dangling on the front of his chest, and his right hand rested on the swagger stick that was clenched under his arm.

Back during the Roman Empire on Old Earth, swagger sticks had been functional implements that were used to direct military maneuvers or to administer physical punishments, but they had long since become symbolic in nature. Some officers and noncoms continued to carry them, especially those who were insecure, and Bellamy fit the pattern. His was a handmade affair carved out of highly polished wood with silver caps at both ends. Bellamy stuck his jaw out as if inviting Tychus to take a swing at it. An offense that could double the prisoner's sentence.

Tychus was on his feet by that time. He knew that Bellamy's comments were intended to provoke a violent reaction so he would receive an even harsher sentence. But more than that, Bellamy was trying to intimidate the other prisoners by demonstrating his mastery of a much larger man. "Thanks for the invite," Tychus rumbled, "but I think I'll pass." *You rat-faced sonofabitch.*

Bellamy grinned. "Life sucks, doesn't it, Findlay? You're damned if you do—and damned if you don't. But one thing's for sure . . . if you aren't dressed and present for muster in ten minutes, you'll be hauling the cart today . . . and all by yourself."

Tychus sighed. It was all part of the game. A game Tychus himself had found great pleasure in playing—on the other side of the field, of course. He knew the key was to stay cool, and never react. *I'd like to see you haul that cart, you twitchy little rodent,* Tychus thought, but didn't bat an eye as Bellamy studied him, frowning.

While Bellamy had been messing with him, the other prisoners had been busy hitting the sonic showers. Now it was impossible for him to shave, shower, and be ready for inspection in ten minutes. So he took the only course open to him.

"That sounds good, Sergeant . . . I could use a good workout."

None of the prisoners who were in earshot were foolish enough to laugh, but there were plenty of grins, as they hurried to get ready.

Tychus was two minutes late when he left the barracks, accepted a nose-hose and an air bottle from a private and put the rig on. Bellamy was waiting, and wasted little time announcing that because of his late arrival, Tychus would have to haul the cart all by himself. But since most of the prisoners already knew about thc punishment, the gasps of astonishment the noncom had been hoping for weren't forthcoming.

Once the roll had been called and the inspection was over, the prisoners were marched across what had originally been a parking lot before the Confederacy had acquired the rock quarry from its owners for use as Military Correctional Facility-R-156. There were twenty-three prisoners representing the marines, rangers, and the fleet.

The low, one-story kitchen and attached mess hall had originally been built for use by the quarry's employees, who presumably enjoyed better food than the crap the prisoners ate every day. On that particular morning the entrée was generally referred to as SS. That stood for "squib special," which consisted of dried meat drenched in a watery gravy, served on a piece of soggy toast.

It was disgusting, but given the lack of other

options, plus the heavy labor that was expected of them, the prisoners had no choice but to choke the salty mess down and chase it with massive quantities of water. And that, according to a medic who had been sent to R-156 for going AWOL, was a deliberate strategy to prevent hyperthermia.

A lot of fuel was required to power his big body, so Tychus ate his share and accepted donations from others. He had just gobbled his last bite when the Klaxon sounded and it was time to follow the other prisoners outside, where Bellamy ordered them to form a column of twos and led them up a switchbacking road.

The noncom was jogging, so the prisoners were forced to do likewise, and to Bellamy's credit he was in good shape. So much so that he ran backward part of the way, swagger stick clamped under his arm, yelling cadence as he did so.

Five minutes later they arrived on a level area where two of the trucks used to haul rocks down to the flatlands were parked. The quarry was located at the end of a narrow canyon with steep slopes on three sides. The process of mining the rock was primitive, to say the least—Tychus figured the added danger was part of the punishment. Explosives were used to separate tons of rock from the mountain above. Then *more* explosives were used to make the big pieces smaller before they were loaded into the cart, which was emptied into one of the waiting trucks.

But before the grueling process could begin, it was first necessary to fall in for another head count. And while that was taking place, Tychus knew the rest of the prisoners were looking at the rusty metal box that was sitting in front of them—and thinking about the man locked inside. When Sergeant Bellamy opened the box, would Sam Lassiter be alive or dead?

Lassiter had been sentenced to serve five days in the cargo container for spitting in Bellamy's face. Of course Bellamy had "boxed" prisoners for less serious infractions. And being boxed for more than a day or two was usually a death sentence. Especially given the cold nights and the fact that Bellamy provided the subjects of his wrath with only ninety-five percent of the supplemental oxygen they needed to stay alive. But Lassiter had already been locked away for three days, and some of the prisoners thought he might even make it to four. Tychus wondered when it would be his turn; Bellamy had threatened him on plenty of occasions, and it was only a matter of time before he followed through.

The steel container was eight feet high, four feet wide, and eight feet long. It was furnished with a single blanket, a pail to crap in, and a plastic jug full of water. Food was delivered twice a day via a narrow slot. As Bellamy unlocked the door, Tychus knew what the noncom *wanted* to see, which was a body lying on the floor. Because if

Lassiter died inside the box, it would prove that prisoners couldn't beat the system *or* Bellamy, assuming there was a difference.

Rusty metal squealed in protest as Bellamy stood to one side and pulled the door open. That was when the prisoners saw Lassiter. He was not only alive, but crouched over a pail, with his pants down around his ankles. "What's wrong with you perverts?" he croaked. "Give a guy some privacy."

All fear of Bellamy was momentarily forgotten as the prisoners broke into laughter and the noncom slammed the door and locked it. Then, having turned his back to the box, Bellamy glared at the now silent prisoners. "Okay, girls, the fun is over. There's a pile of rocks waiting for you—"

That was when Lassiter shoved his hand out through the food slot, got a grip on Bellamy's belt, and jerked the sergeant up against the door. The prisoner stabbed the noncom through the slot with his breakfast fork. He was still at it, plunging the tines in again and again, as Bellamy *yelped*, and the guards broke the sergeant free.

"You'll pay for this!" Bellamy raged, as a corporal kneeled down beside him, cut his shirt away, and slapped a plastiscab over the bloody puncture wounds.

Judging from the amount of blood, Tychus figured it would take more than a bandage to close up Bellamy's wounds. He smiled and silently thanked Lassiter for brightening his day.

"I wonder where they're taking him," Tychus inquired of no one in particular.

"I hear they have a special place for guys like Lassiter," the man standing next to Tychus said. "A place where they can get inside your head and screw around with it."

"I don't know what they're gonna find in there," Tychus replied unsympathetically. "But they got their work cut out for 'em."

The prisoners watched calmly as armed guards wrestled Lassiter to the ground. He was yelling unintelligibly, growling, and snapping his teeth as they shackled his wrists. Once he was restrained, they took him by the elbows and led him down the road.

Lassiter jerked his arms away and proceeded to walk under his own power. He had a thatch of unruly hair, many days' worth of stubble on his face, and wore the filthy remnants of a uniform. But in spite of all that, there was something regal about his bearing. *You are a truly magnificent sonofabitch,* Tychus thought.

Next came Bellamy, who limped along with the help of a guard until a groundcar swung by to pick him up. Tychus lifted his face toward the bright sky, closed his eyes, and smiled. He was sure that Bellamy's absence would take him off the hook where the cart was concerned.

"Fall out and take a short bio break before proceeding up the slope," Corporal Carter ordered.

"Findlay, prepare to haul the cart." *Damn.* The peon had his orders and was determined to enforce them.

That was when Tychus spotted Bellamy's precious swagger stick lying on the ground in front of the steel box. It was covered with a thick layer of dust, so no one had noticed it.

Tychus knelt next to the stick and pretended to tie his bootlace as he scooped it up. One end went up his pant leg, the other into the top of his boot. Then, having secured his prize, it was time to head uphill.

With the single exception of Tychus the prisoners were herded past the wooden ramp upon which the cart sat, and up to the big pile of broken rocks that awaited them. Tychus was ordered to tow the cart up the incline so the others could load it.

The air was beginning to warm up a bit by then, so Tychus stripped down to the waist before making his way over to the dented cart. Coffinlike, it sat on parallel tracks and weighed three or four hundred pounds. Normally two or even three prisoners were assigned to haul the container up the five-percent grade, so Tychus knew it wouldn't be easy.

But faced with a choice to either ask for help or fail a test of strength, he was determined to succeed. So, taking hold of the thick rope used to pull the cart uphill, he passed it over one massive shoulder and leaned forward. With nothing else to do for the moment, guards and prisoners alike stopped to watch.

Tychus's shoulders were nearly forty inches across, and as he put his head down and began to pull, the onlookers could see cordlike muscles ripple as metal squealed and the cart's wheels began to turn. Steps had been cut into the rocky slope, and rather than think about the amount of weight he was pulling, Tychus focused on the placement of his feet instead. One foot, and then the other, each taking him closer to his goal. Finally, to the accompaniment of light applause, he made it to the top, where a lever-operated metal plate came up to block the cart's rear wheels.

Not even Corporal Carter questioned Tychus's right to take a break as chunks of granite were loaded into the metal box, the first truck was backed into place, and the brake lever was thrown. The track rattled noisily as the load sped downhill, slammed into a pair of stops, and tilted forward. The rocks made a hollow booming sound as they landed in the truck. Then, with that accomplished, it was time to repeat the whole process again. And so it went as Tychus and the cart made four additional trips up the slope before the Klaxon sounded and it was time for a box lunch that consisted of soggy sandwiches, a cup of fruit, and an energy bar that most of the prisoners saved for later.

Unfortunately, Bellamy arrived along with the

meal. He was seemingly none the worse for wear in the wake of Lassiter's attack, and immediately began to prowl the area, looking for things to complain about.

But as Tychus chewed and watched Bellamy's movements, he thought he saw a pattern. The runt wasn't just wandering around—he was looking for his stick! Because if he announced that the implement was missing, and one of the prisoners came across it, Bellamy knew it would be destroyed. Especially given how many people had been hit with it. Tychus could feel the sore spot where the damned thing had been rubbing his leg and couldn't resist a grin. Here at least was something to enjoy.

Exactly thirty minutes after the lunch break had begun, it was over. Then it was back to work, with Bellamy in charge this time, constantly shouting insults at Tychus.

For his part Tychus was starting to tire. What had been difficult earlier was nearly impossible now. His feet felt as though they were made of lead, time seemed to slow, and it became more difficult to breathe even though he was still receiving supplemental oxygen through the nose-hose. "What's the matter, *Sergeant*?" Bellamy scoffed, from two feet away. "Is the workout you wanted too much for you? How 'bout I give the job to someone else? All you have to do is ask."

Tychus couldn't reply—there wasn't enough

extra energy for that—so he kept on going as Bellamy walked along next to him. Finally he heard a clank as the metal plate came up to block the wheels, and Tychus knew that particular journey was over.

Tychus felt slightly dizzy, not to mention thirsty, but knew it was important to focus. Would Bellamy see the bait? And if he did, would it be possible to engineer the rest of the plan? The answer came quickly.

"Hey, Sarge," Carter called out. "Look down there . . . between the tracks and about halfway up the slope. . . . Is that your swagger stick?"

Tychus followed the pointing finger and was satisfied with what he saw. Having been surreptitiously washed off during the lunch break, the swagger stick was easy to see and Bellamy immediately set off to retrieve it. Tychus waited for the noncom to take half a dozen steps, saw him step between the tracks, and shouted, "No!" But the noise of the machinery operating nearby drowned him out, as he lunged forward, appearing concerned for Bellamy's safety. A carefully targeted hip bumped into the prisoner in charge of the brake lever. He fell against the handle, there was a clang as the plate fell, and the cart began to roll.

Bellamy was bending over the swagger stick by then. He looked up in response to the ominous rattling from above. That was when he threw up his hands as if to stop the steel box, realized his mistake, and turned to jump clear. But there wasn't enough time. His throaty scream was cut short by a meaty thump, as metal met flesh and Bellamy was sucked under the cart and split into three chunks of bloody meat.

Everyone was in shock, including Corporal Carter, who feared that he might be blamed for the accident. Rather than go after Tychus, who had been heard shouting a warning, the noncom chose to blame the hapless brake operator for throwing the brake handle. He was sentenced to five days in the box but lasted only two. It was, as Tychus put it, "a damned shame."

CHAPTER TWELVE

"Once my eye is locked tight on my quarry, the whole world just goes quiet. Almost peaceful. It's just me, my target, and my heartbeat softly measuring out the last seconds of that poor sucker's life. When the job is done and I can put the rifle away . . . well, that's when I like to make the world get noisy again!"

Private Ryk Kydd, 321st Colonial Rangers Battalion, in an interview on Turaxis II
July 2488

THE PLANET TURAXIS II

A one-hundred-yard-deep free-fire zone surrounded Turaxis Prime and was intended as a last line of defense should the base be attacked by Kel-Morian ground forces. The strip of raw, vegetation-free dirt was mined, regularly swept with a variety of scans, and surrounded by weapons emplacements.

Having weathered nine long weeks of training

without a pass, and with graduation ceremonies scheduled for the next day, more than a thousand recruits were streaming toward Gate Alpha. It was the closest gate to the town of Braddock.

Even though the town's civilian community might complain, the truth was that they looked forward to the river of money that was about to flow through town, even if there was some collateral damage as a result.

As Ryk Kydd passed through Gate Alpha and followed a jubilant group of his peers toward the delights that waited beyond, he felt the same sense of excitement that he had during his last day on Tarsonis. In this case it was because, hijacked or not, he was about to become a real honest-to-God marine! And that meant doing what marines do when they go on liberty, which is raise hell.

Not alone, because there was no fun in that, but with his buddies Raynor and Harnack. They weren't the sort of people Kydd had been exposed to on Tarsonis or been allowed to associate with. The bond between the three of them had been forged during the third week of training, when they wound up on the same shit detail, and Kydd had figured out a way to reprogram a maintenance robot to do the job for them.

As a child he loved taking the Bennet family's bots apart and putting them back together again—usually with half a dozen parts left over. But practice made perfect, and he was correct: a maintenance robot *could* be taught to peel potatoes.

So Raynor and Harnack were waiting when Kydd cleared the free-fire zone and arrived in front of a bar so famous that its name was tattooed on thousands of arms, legs, and other body parts throughout the Confederacy. Because tradition required each boot to hoist his or her first pre-graduation beer somewhere inside the sprawling maze of rooms that the owners called Bloody Mary's before continuing down Shayanne Street to enjoy the pleasures beyond. All three of the recruits wore maroon kepis, gray waist-length jackets with maroon trim, and matching trousers with knife-edge creases. Their shoes were mirror-bright and relatively unworn—they had always been reserved for inspections and little else.

Kydd exchanged clumsy shoulder bumps with Raynor and Harnack, who both chuckled with amusement at Kydd's continued struggle to adopt their basic social customs. For weeks, they had been tutoring him in everything from using slang words, to making a bed, to using a sonic mop, and he'd already made a great deal of progress. They were proud.

In fact, all three teenagers had changed significantly since starting boot camp. They were lean, strong, and in Kydd's case, a good deal more confident. The miniature sniper's rifle that he wore on his left breast pocket was a source of pride to both him *and* his buddies. "So, how did it go?" Raynor asked. "Did Macaby believe you?"

"He said he was going to bump my case up to division," Kydd answered. "So I ought to hear back in a week or two."

"Make that a month or two," Harnack put in cynically. "Still, that's good news, buddy, because the minute the ol' man springs you, we're gonna have one helluva party! And *you* can buy."

Kydd knew it wouldn't go down like that, and so did Raynor, but both were used to allowing Harnack to be Harnack. "Well done," Raynor said, as they turned toward Bloody Mary's. "Now for that beer and some decent grub! I'm tired of the crap they serve in the mess hall."

"Roger that," Harnack agreed. "Form a single column, follow me, and don't take prisoners." With that, he turned on his heel and strutted through the crowd, waving his arms and hollering, "Make way for His Eminence, the Emperor of Tarsonis. . . ."

An hour and a half later the threesome left Bloody Mary's thirty credits poorer, having consumed two beers each, plus enormous steaks and huge servings of the fried potatoes that the bar was justifiably famous for.

It would have been completely dark by then on many planets. But thanks to Turaxis's three small moons, all of which reflected light onto the surface on clear nights such as this one, nights were no more than six hours long and were preceded by a long, moody twilight.

Music pounded as they walked down the street, and even though melodies changed from bar to bar, the backbeat seemed to remain the same as a man grinned at them from a doorway. Chemicals that had been injected under his skin made it glow bright blue. "We have girls, men . . . *all* nude, *all* hot, and *all* yours!"

"Thirsty, boys?" a tired-looking woman with long, luminescent hair droned from atop a rickety stool. "Every third drink is free—and we got the best band this side of Turaxis."

"I'm the guy you've been looking for," a binked-out drug dealer said, as he sidled up to Raynor. "Crab, snoke, turk . . . I have it all."

"Some turk might amp things up a bit," Harnack suggested, stopping abruptly in his tracks.

Raynor turned around and brushed the dealer off. "Not today, man." He nudged Harnack to keep moving. "Don't worry, Hank—you're amped enough. Hey, let's find the Black Hole. . . . I hear the floor show is great."

The other two were ready for just about anything at that point, and happy to follow Raynor as he took a left off Shayanne and led them past a group of bored MPs to the cluster of dives beyond. That was when they saw a spectral image form directly in front of them and Harnack groaned. Multiple versions of Gunnery Sergeant Travis had been dogging them day and night for weeks by that time and had apparently followed them into town, where a network of carefully placed holoprojectors were being used to push Travis at them again.

"So you're on liberty, having a good time," Travis said. *"That's when a Kel-Morian agent spots you. They only gave him one grenade, but that was enough to kill three of our boys in the Dylarian Shipyards. The war ain't over just because you dumbasses got a pass! One grenade could kill you all."*

"Come on," Harnack said disgustedly. The image shivered as he walked through it. "Travis is full of shit. He makes that stuff up."

Raynor didn't think so, but kept that opinion to himself, as the insistent *thump, thump, thump* of loud music drew them toward a large section of pipe that extended from a two-story building out onto the sidewalk. It was painted black, in keeping with the nightclub's name, and guarded by two brawny bouncers. They eyed the trio skeptically, but allowed them to pass, as a spiral lighting scheme led the recruits inside.

"What a dump!" Harnack shouted over the pounding music, grabbing Raynor and Kydd by the shoulders as he followed them into the Black Hole. Raynor couldn't help but agree—the place was loud, dark, and reeked of stale beer and sweat.

But all was forgiven when the stage at the bottom of the spiraled room came into view.

"Whoa," Kydd uttered. The three recruits stared down at the platform, upon which a young woman with pink hair was dancing seductively. The largely male crowd roared with approval as her top came off and sailed through the air.

Harnack gleefully shoved the guys forward. "First round's on me!"

That was when a scantily clad waitress wearing too much eye makeup appeared and led the threesome down one level to a recently vacated table. As they walked, Raynor noticed that most of the patrons were fellow recruits, along with a scattering of regular marines and noncoms.

The latter sat at their own cluster of tables, surrounded for the most part by empty seats. It appeared none of the boots wanted to party next to them.

"What'll it be?" the waitress chirped as the guys sat down.

"Three shots of Scotty's No. 8 plus beer chasers," Harnack answered authoritatively as he patted her rump. If the waitress felt the contact she gave no sign of it and sashayed away.

"What is Scotty's No. 8?" Kydd asked. His father was very particular about the liquor he kept in the house—this one apparently didn't make the cut.

"Scotty Bolger's Old No. 8 is the good stuff," Harnack said. "Trust me . . . you'll like it."

"Uh-oh," Raynor said ominously. "Look over there . . ." he indicated with a subtle nod of his head. "See the marines sitting at that table? Two of them were in the gang we fought on the *Hydrus*."

"Well, I'll be damned," Harnack responded. "I do believe you're right! Maybe this would be a good time to finish kicking their asses."

"You gotta be kidding me," Raynor replied incredulously. "The way I remember it they were kicking *our* asses when the noncoms got there."

"Look at that!" Kydd exclaimed. "One of them waved."

Raynor snorted, shaking his head. "Kydd, you didn't see what went on up there. Don't make jokes . . . these guys are criminals."

"Holy crap, the twerp isn't lying!" Harnack declared, his eyes widening. "Those bastards *are* waving at us!"

Raynor peered across the room at the grinning ex-cons. "What the . . . ? " He smiled and skeptically lifted his hand into a high sign. "You've got to hand it to the drill instructors . . . they did one helluva job with those guys—" Raynor suddenly realized Harnack had left his seat and looked up to find his friend casually strolling toward the marines, cracking his knuckles.

"Hank! Damn it!" Raynor called out as he leaped from his chair. He turned toward Kydd. "I'm gonna kill him."

"I'll wait for the drinks," Kydd said.

"Good. Order another round. We need to sedate this sonofabitch before he gets himself in trouble." Raynor turned and headed straight for Harnack.

"Hel-lo, ladies!" Harnack hollered as he approached the marines.

"Good evening," one of them responded with a smile, nodding politely. The others followed suit.

"It seems you fellas don't remember me too well. Let me refresh your memory," Harnack said tauntingly as he leaned forward, fists on the table. "I'm the guy who drop-kicked your sorry asses and left you cryin' for your mommas!"

Raynor jumped in, throwing his arm around Harnack. "Gentlemen, please pardon my friend here. He's had a few too many, and we're just gonna get on our way—"

"Nonsense," one marine interrupted. "We're all brothers here, fighting for a common cause. Whatever may have happened between us in the past . . . consider it long forgotten. Please . . ." He motioned to two empty seats. "Care to join us?"

"Hell no," Harnack snarled.

With one hand, Raynor pinched a pressure point on the back of Harnack's neck—a move he'd picked up in combat training—and steered him away from the table. "Again, sorry for the interruption," he offered over his shoulder.

"Get off me!" Harnack shrugged his way out of

Raynor's grip. "Those guys are damn freaks. What the fekk happened to them?"

"I don't know, Hank," Raynor said as he guided Harnack back to his seat. "The reformatory must be really top-notch, or maybe they got their asses kicked into submission by some hard-core DI or something." Even as he said it, Raynor couldn't shake the feeling that something weird was going on. Those marines were just *too* nice.

The waitress set down their drinks, and Raynor nodded his appreciation. "Anyway," he continued, "I'm glad they were so understanding, because otherwise you'd have just gotten yourself into a shitstorm of trouble, Hank, and I ain't in the mood to bail you out again. Consider yourself lucky."

Hank offered Raynor a one-fingered salute by way of a response.

"Ugh!" Raynor cried after taking a sip of his drink. "This tastes like crap! Why do you drink this stuff?"

"Eh, you get used to it," Harnack responded.

Just then the dancer kicked her panties out into the crowd, and five marines fought to take possession of them. A beefy corporal won the contest and jumped up onto a table to wave the trophy over his head. The crowd roared with laughter, inspiring the noncom to pull them onto his head like a hat.

"I'm gonna go see if I can buy those panties off him," Harnack said excitedly, leaping out of his seat and jogging over to the corporal. Laughing, Raynor and Kydd shook their heads in disbelief, and the two watched with quiet amusement as Harnack offered money, got denied, and strode back to his seat wearing a mischievous smile.

"No luck?" Kydd asked.

"Nope. Looks like I'm gonna have to find my own pair of panties. What color are yours, Kydd?" he asked, winking. Kydd playfully shoved Harnack on the shoulder and all three guys cracked up.

As the dancer waved and the stage sank out of sight, two trapeze artists dropped from above and began a series of death-defying stunts. The fact that they were naked made the performance all the more interesting, and the whole crowd was mesmerized—even Harnack. In the meantime the second round of drinks arrived and went down smoothly—followed by another round twenty minutes later.

The Black Hole was full to overflowing by then, and even though Raynor was feeling a little light-headed, he did notice that the composition of the crowd had changed. There were more crewmen in the bar by then—all dressed in space-black uniforms and all apparently off the same ship.

The usual jibes could be heard as the eternal rivalry between the fleet and the grunts continued to play itself out, but things went well until a drunken swabbie spilled a drink on a belligerent recruit, and all hell broke loose.

Harnack uttered a whoop of joy as fists flew and the fight began to spread. Raynor noticed that the ex-cons were still sitting at their table as more people got up to take part in the mayhem.

In the meantime someone attacked Kydd as he was returning from the restroom, and Harnack jumped immediately to his friend's defense. That brought *more* swabbies their way and Raynor suddenly found himself at the center of a brawl.

It wasn't the first such fight to take place in the Black Hole, which was why all of the tables and chairs were bolted to the floor. That kept the furniture from being used as weapons, thereby limiting both the severity of injuries suffered and the amount of damage done to the bar.

The proprietors didn't *want* to host a fight, however, so it wasn't long before distant whistles were heard and the MPs arrived. Raynor, who was trading blows with a burly petty officer at that point, threw a right cross. As it connected with the swabbie's jaw, the shock of the blow traveled all the way up Raynor's arm. When he saw the noncom's eyes roll back in his head, he knew that particular battle was won.

As the MPs began rushing the crowd, Raynor knew that he and his friends needed to escape or be arrested. He took advantage of his momentary victory to shout, "Harnack! Kydd! Follow me."

And just as they had for the last nine weeks, the other two obeyed willingly. Unfortunately, some of the combatants were blocking the path to the kitchen. So when a bleeding marine stumbled into Raynor's path, he pushed the man into a swabbie, who swore as both tumbled to the ground.

Raynor led the charge, stepping over the grappling foes—and inadvertently slammed the swinging kitchen door into a stunned waitress as they burst through. Mortified, Raynor glanced down to see that the front of her minidress had been plastered with chocolate cake on one side and what looked like framberry pie on the other.

He opened his mouth to apologize, and was greeted by a bone-crunching closed-fist punch to the nose. He stumbled back into Harnack and Kydd as the cursing woman continued her assault by scooping a gob of chocolate off her apron and smashing it into his face.

"Ow, damn it! Knock it off . . . we're just tryin' to get outta here!" Raynor pleaded, slurring from drink, wincing in pain, and mumbling through the heavy smear of sticky chocolate and blood that now coated his nostrils and mouth.

Two white-clad cooks appeared behind the waitress. One of them lifted her by the armpits as she thrashed about. "Let go of me! What are you doing?"

"Don't worry, April, we got this," the cook said as he put her down. April stomped off, furiously wiping her dress.

"Hey, chef man," Harnack said, as he battled a hiccup, "let us get the hell outta here and no one gets hurt. Otherwise, I'm gonna break your fekkin' bones, one by one. . . ."

The cook made use of a meat cleaver to point toward the back of the kitchen. "Get out. And don't you idiots ever come back here. I specialize in *butchering meat*. Get me?" He waved the cleaver and the other chefs snickered behind him.

"Okay, let's go!" Raynor yelled as he scrambled up and dashed toward the back. He snatched a rag off the counter and quickly ran it over his face before tossing it haphazardly on the floor.

Raynor saw Kydd hesitate as he edged nervously past the cooks, who stood watching with their thick arms folded. "Come on!"

The three recruits bolted out the back door, aware that the MPs were no doubt making their way through the brawling crowd and would be there to arrest them at any moment. They exited into the rear parking lot.

They split up, searching for a means of escape, but found nothing until Raynor spotted an olive drab vulture hover-cycle idling next to a marine combat car—it probably belonged to one of the MPs who was called to the scene. *How the hell am I going to drive this damn thing?* Raynor wondered, his head swirling with doubt. But he knew he had no other choice. "Okay! Here's our ride, men . . . hurry, climb on the back."

Harnack chuckled as he approached, getting his first clear look at Raynor's face since the chocolate incident. "Jimmy, my brother, you are *shit-faced*! Literally, you have *shit* on your *face*!"

Kydd howled with laughter.

Raynor self-consciously wiped the last of the chocolate off his face with his sleeve and then straightened. "Okay, seriously. We gotta go *now*." The vulture rocked slightly as Raynor swung a leg over the seat and eyeballed the controls. With its long streamlined nose, a seat large enough for an armored soldier to sit on, and two powerful engines, the vulture was equipped with standard handlebars, plus some simple instrumentation. What could go wrong?

Thanks to the fact that Raynor wasn't wearing armor, there was enough room for Harnack to swing in behind him, but that left Kydd with nowhere to sit. "Think you can stand behind Hank?" Raynor asked, eyeing the rear of the machine over his shoulder. "Yeah . . . just put your feet on the floor and lean backward. Looks like the engine compartment will support you."

Kydd clearly didn't want to be left behind, so as Raynor revved the engines experimentally, he straddled the seat. It was a tight fit, and the additional weight caused the vulture to sink alarmingly. But there was no time to consider the mechanics of the situation as someone yelled, "Halt!" and a whistle blew.

Raynor twisted the left handle, felt the bike jerk, and saw the letter "D" appear on the control panel in front of him. Then, as a couple of MPs pounded across the parking lot, Raynor opened the throttle. That was a mistake because with two engines, and no wheel-generated friction to slow the vulture down, the machine was *fast*. Kydd was nearly thrown back over the engine compartment as the bike took off, Harnack howled with delight, and Raynor experienced a moment of panic as the nose hit the side of a parked car and glanced off.

Having backed the throttle off, and cranked the handlebars over, Raynor managed to guide the vulture out of the lot and onto the street beyond. Sparks flew as the badly overloaded bike bottomed out, rose an inch or two, and accelerated away.

Perhaps Raynor would have been able to drive the vulture down a quiet side street and abandon it there if it hadn't been for the combat car that gave chase. Though not as fast as the vulture, the four-seat vehicle was better driven, and therefore able to keep up.

Raynor glanced into a rearview mirror, saw the flashing lights, and turned onto a main street. The sun had set, but thanks to the planet's moons and a clear sky, there was still enough light to see by as Raynor wove in and out between other vehicles. The bottom of the vulture scraped the pavement each time it tilted more than two or three degrees to the left or right and sent sparks arcing away.

"They're gaining on us!" Harnack warned, as he shouted into Raynor's right ear. "Go faster!"

So Raynor twisted the throttle and felt the machine accelerate. Signs flashed by, one of them said something about "Police," but Raynor missed the rest of the message as he blew through the intersection, saw the T-shaped warning sign, and knew he should turn right or left. But he was going too fast.

A curb rushed at him, and there was a horrible grating sound as the vulture lurched up and over the obstruction before landing on a perfectly manicured lawn. The grass led up a gentle slope to a low-lying sign that read POLICE STATION, which shattered into a dozen pieces as the vulture plowed through it.

Kydd was thrown clear, Harnack was wedged between Raynor and the engine compartment, and the hover-cycle's onboard computer shut everything down as the vulture skidded to a stop only steps from the building's front door.

Raynor struggled to his feet and turned to assist Harnack as Kydd tottered across the lawn to retrieve his kepi, which had landed several yards away.

"I'm driving next time," Kydd said calmly as he brushed off his uniform. "And *you* can fekkin' stand up."

It wasn't much of a joke, but the other two thought it was hilarious, and fell down laughing.

All three were arrested four minutes later.

CHAPTER THIRTEEN

"Confederate troops provided critical support to nuclear fortifications on Char today during heavy fighting, helping to drive Kel-Morian forces into retreat. Colonel Trelmont of the 2nd regiment congratulated the soldiers in a news conference later this evening, saying, 'If it weren't for loyal Confederate citizens bolstering our ranks, men and women picking up arms to defend our unified accord, we would have lost a planet today.' "

Max Speer, *Evening Report* for UNN
August 2488

THE PLANET TURAXIS II

After a night spent in the city's spacious drunk tank, Raynor awoke to the sound of someone banging on a garbage can, while shouting, "The party's over! Time to go home." He had a throbbing headache, and groaned miserably as he sat up and put both feet on the floor. The bunk bed shook as Kydd jumped down from above. There was a thump when his shoes hit the floor. "Good morning, Jim!" he said cheerfully. "You look like hell."

Raynor was about to say, "And so do you," when he realized it wasn't true. Kydd's uniform was wrinkled and a little dirty, but he was otherwise ready for inspection, all the way down to a pair of glossy shoes.

Raynor frowned. Even that hurt. "How come you look so good?"

"Because I got up, took a sonic shower, and used one of the free shaving kits the jailers hand out," Kydd replied brightly. "We're going to be marines today, you know. . . . We have to look sharp."

"You're not a marine," Raynor complained bitterly. "You're a friggin' freak. Where's Hank?"

"Right here," Harnack said while yawning, as orders were shouted and the other prisoners began to file out. His kepi was missing, his shirt was ripped, and there were grass stains on his pants. His eyelids were heavy with sleep, but he still managed a smile as he staggered along. "Did we have a good time? I can't remember."

"We had a *great* time!" Kydd reported. "Come on . . . the MPs are going to march us back to base."

"They're going to *what*?" Raynor inquired, but Kydd was already three feet away by that time and headed for the door. So all the others could do was follow as the military personnel were ushered into a parking lot where a squad of MPs was waiting to receive them. Most wore knowing grins rather than the angry expressions Raynor expected to see. "Why is everyone being so nice?" Raynor wondered aloud.

"Fall in!" one of the noncoms ordered gruffly. "Make two formations of six ranks each with the tallest idiots in the back. Marines over here—swabbies over there."

"I think they've done this before," Harnack observed as the three of them fell in.

More orders were given and the first two ranks of swabbies were magically transformed into a column of twos. Once the fleet personnel were in motion, the marines followed.

"I have to take a piss," Raynor muttered.

"Aim for Kydd," Harnack responded, loud enough for the sniper to hear. "He's on my nerves today."

Kydd glanced back and grinned. "You're a mean sonofabitch, you know that?"

"Oh, come on. You've seen Raynor shoot—you know he can't aim worth shit."

"Oh, wow. You are *so* going down." Raynor stealthily planted a foot in Harnack's path. After a quick stumble, Harnack regained his footing and the three recruits hid their smirks as the MPs led them out onto the street.

They might have been subjected to a long humiliating shuffle through the center of town, had it not been for a sergeant wearing a beer-stained uniform and sporting a black eye. He began to call cadence, the marines fell into step, and the swabbies did likewise. Heads came up, shoulders went back, and the age-old command of "Your left, right, left," echoed between the surrounding buildings as the troops marched through town.

Suddenly Raynor felt better. It was a bright, sunny morning, he could see distant contrails clawing the sky, and he was glad to be where he was—even if his head hurt each time he brought his left heel down hard. Somebody began to sing a marching ditty. More voices joined in, and the trip back to base was transformed from a retreat to a triumphant parade. The town of Braddock had been sacked and conquered.

Once Raynor, Harnack, Kydd, and the rest of their company were back on base, they were ordered to report to their quarters, where Gunnery Sergeant Red Murphy was waiting for them. The drill instructor had lost one arm, one leg, and one eye in battle, and having opted for electro-mechanical prostheses rather than the lab-grown limbs that most people preferred, he was more cyborg than man. And his replacement parts whirred and clicked whenever he moved.

But even though the replacement parts might not have been as pretty as their flesh-and-blood counterparts, they were very functional and granted Murphy a level of grim credibility he would not have had otherwise. Like most DIs, he was a pretty good actor, but his threats rang hollow, since the boots knew they were going to graduate at 1500 hours.

By that time it was clear that Macaby and the citizens of Braddock had been well aware of what would happen when the Marine Corps turned hundreds of recruits loose on the town. But appearances were important to discipline, so Murphy pretended to chew them out and the recruits pretended to listen.

Finally, when the speech was over, the noncom sent them off to "take showers, get some chow, and prepare for inspection at 1400 hours."

Neither Raynor nor Harnack felt like eating, but Kydd did, much to their disgust. But what Raynor *did* want to do was call home. He had no idea what time it was for them on Shiloh, but figured his parents would be glad to hear from him regardless, especially on such an important day. It was going to cost several weeks' pay to use the interplanetary fone, he knew that, but figured the sound of their voices would be worth it.

But before he could place the call, it was first necessary to wait through a fifteen-minute line before gaining access to one of the two dozen public comm units that were available for the boots to use. Finally, having been routed through an intricate series of signal boosters and relays, Raynor heard a series of beeps as the fone rang. Then, on the sixth ring, he heard his father's voice. A vid-feed would have cost twice as much, so he had to settle for just audio. "I don't know who this is," Trace said, "but you'd better have one helluva good reason for calling at two in the morning."

"It's me, Dad," Raynor said. "I just wanted to let you know that I'll be a marine two hours from now. We're about to graduate from boot camp."

Raynor grinned as his father said, "Wake up, hon, it's Jim!" Then, clearly awake by that time, Trace Raynor said, "Damn, it's good to hear your voice, son. . . . I wish we could be there to see the ceremony."

"They're going to give each one of us a vid-snap," Jim replied. "I'll send it along as soon as I get it. How are things going?"

"Fine," Trace answered, "just fine. Hold on a sec. . . . Here's your mother."

Jim knew all of his father's inflections, and the hesitancy in the older man's voice made him wonder if things were going well, or if Trace Raynor was hiding something. So after his mother asked about his health, and where he was likely to be sent after boot camp, Jim put the same question to her. "So, Mom, Dad says everything is fine . . . but that's what he would say even if the robo-harvester blew up. I'm counting on you to tell me the truth."

"Well," Karol Raynor said, "there's a new regulation. Every farmer has to buy a business license. And they cost two thousand credits each. So that was something of a blow . . . but here's the good news. Thanks to your signing bonus we were able to pay it! So in that sense everything is fine."

What his mother hadn't said was that the cost of the license had consumed two-thirds of the bonus, which meant they wouldn't be able to pay their taxes as planned. Suddenly Jim wondered if joining the Marine Corps had been such a good idea after all. But it wouldn't do to say that, so he told his mother that he was happy to hear it, and was careful to change the subject.

"You should see Tom now . . . he lost about ten pounds, he can do a hundred push-ups, and he claims to be good-looking. He says 'Hi,' by the way, and wants you to know that the cookies you sent me were really good. And he should know, 'cause he ate six of them."

Karol laughed. "You tell Tom that another package is on the way!" Then, after some heartfelt good-byes, it was time for Raynor to surrender the fone to the next person in line. It was nice to know his parents were okay, but the conversation still left Raynor with an uneasy feeling in the pit of his stomach.

* * *

Once the recruits had showered and shaved, it was time to put on the antiquated CMC-200 series armor that they'd been training in for weeks. Each suit had logged thousands of hours of use before being repurposed for use in boot camp, and smelled funky inside.

Only about twenty percent of the hardskins were fully combat-ready at any given time, but they *looked* good, thanks to the countless hours that each recruit was required to spend washing, polishing, and applying touch-up paint to them. And the attention to detail didn't end there. Each gauss rifle had been cleaned, lubricated, and inspected to make sure that not so much as a tiny fleck of dirt or rust could be found on it.

Then, having checked one another for flaws, the recruits filtered out onto the grinder for the final inspection that would precede the trooping of the colors. During the ceremony each company would carry a flag that belonged to a serving battalion. This would honor the line units that many of the newly graduated marines would soon be part of.

Could the people on the reviewing stand actually see a ding from hundreds of feet away? Murphy claimed that they could, but Raynor knew that was absurd, not that it made any difference.

So they stood inspection, Murphy pronounced himself happy with the results, and was visibly proud as the flag for the 2nd Battalion, 3rd Marines was given to the company's four-person color guard for safekeeping. Kydd, who had been chosen to march on the right side of the battalion's flag with a gauss rifle on his shoulder, was beaming with pride.

There was a fifteen-minute wait for all of the units to get into position, followed by a barely heard order from the training command's sergeant major, and a swift flurry of drumbeats as the troops went into motion. The band played *To the Eternal Glory of the Confederacy* followed by a sequence of stirring marches as each company completed a full circuit of the grinder before coming to a much-practiced stop in front of the reviewing stand.

As luck would have it, Kydd's company was toward the center of the large formation and the four-person color guard was directly in front of the stand. So when Macaby rose to introduce the battalion's guest of honor, Kydd could not only hear, but *see* the Honorable Cornelius Brubaker, who was one of his father's best friends!

As Brubaker began to speak, Kydd was tempted to break ranks and run forward, thereby rescuing himself from the Marine Corps. He couldn't bring himself to do it, however, because even though the strategy would almost certainly be successful, it would ruin the graduation ceremony for his friends. Plus, given Macaby's promise to buck his case up to division level, Kydd figured there was no need to make a scene. Once the people at the top took action, justice would be done. In the meantime, it felt wonderful to be truly *good* at something, and to be included in an organization on account of his personal accomplishments, rather than the name he had been born with.

So Kydd stood at parade rest, eyes front, as Brubaker thanked the newly graduated marines for their dedication and sacrifice. And that was when Kydd remembered that the rifle on his shoulder had been manufactured by a subsidiary of Brubaker Holdings—which meant that both the businessman and his family had profited handsomely from the wars. Just as Bennet Industries had. In fact, the more people and equipment that were destroyed, the better it would be for the Old Families! No wonder Brubaker had been willing to speak.

Once Brubaker's comments were over, and he returned to his seat, Macaby stepped up to the podium again. "It is my pleasure, and my lasting honor, to welcome you to the Confederacy's Marine Corps," the officer began. "As you know, once marines complete basic training they are normally sent on to Advanced Infantry Training, or AIT. However, due to the somewhat unusual situation here on Turaxis II, we have an opportunity to provide you with *actual* combat experience, rather than further training scenarios."

At that point the battalion's sergeant major

shouted, "Hip, hip . . ." and the marines shouted, *"Hooray!"*

Macaby smiled knowingly, as if to suggest that he could scan minds. "I know all of you want to get out there and fight the Kel-Morians as soon as possible! But it wouldn't be a good idea to drop you directly into a combat situation without some additional seasoning—so you will spend your first few weeks well back of the front lines. Then, when your commanding officers decide that you're ready, they'll move you up. All in all it will be a good way to support our line units while providing you with the extra training you need.

"Once you return to quarters you will receive your orders, load-out schedules, and an additional issue of field gear. Your armor will be issued to you when you arrive at your receiving command. Again, congratulations, and good luck."

At that point the sergeant major shouted, *"Atten-hut!"* and a *crash-thump* was heard as the training battalion obeyed.

Then, after three beats came the order, *"Dismissed!"* and a cheer went up as Raynor, Harnack, and all the rest removed their helmets.

During the celebration none of them noticed the semi-transparent figure that had materialized on a steel walkway high above their heads, or heard what the apparition had to say: *"Some of you will lead—and others will follow. Those who lead must spend lives wisely—and those who follow must give themselves gladly. For you share a common bond, and when you die, it will be for each other."* Then, like the spirit he was, Gunnery Sergeant Travis disappeared.

BORO AIRBASE, ON THE PLANET TURAXIS II

The trip from the airstrip adjacent to Turaxis Prime to Boro Airbase covered more than seven thousand miles, all aboard a maxed-out four-engined Bennet Industries heavy transport aircraft. The huge transport had been designed to haul anything from troops to tanks—which meant scant attention had been paid to the creature comforts. So the three hundred–plus troops packed into rows of removable seats could do little more than shoot the breeze, make use of whatever was stashed on their newly returned fones, and take uneasy naps as the large vehicle droned toward its destination.

Raynor and Kydd, both of whom enjoyed reading and listening to music, took the trip in stride, but it was more difficult for Harnack, who slept some but spent a lot of time fidgeting and bothering those seated around him.

Raynor, who was listening to the latest music file that Kydd had sent him, frowned and pulled one of his earbuds loose. "This stuff is kind of slow, Ryk . . . and what the hell is a fugue?"

"It's an imitative polyphonic composition, in which a theme or themes are stated successively in all of the voices of the contrapuntal structure," Kydd replied matter-of-factly. "Keep listening—it will grow on you."

Raynor nodded, put the earbud back in, and surreptitiously switched to a tune called "The Mar Sara Shuffle" by Harvey and the Heartbreakers.

When the transport entered Turaxis II's eastern hemisphere, four Avengers took up stations around it, because the aircraft was a juicy target for the KM fighters. So once the landing gear finally thumped to the ground, and the transport taxied to what looked like a new terminal building, the marines were glad to deass the plane and collect their gear from the jumble of bags that came out of the cargo compartments. "Damn, it feels good to get off that piece of crap," Harnack exclaimed, as the three of them lined up to retrieve their bulky B-2 bags.

"Since my family built that 'piece of crap,' as you call it," Kydd replied cheerfully, "I'll pass your complaint along to Father the moment he shows up."

"Which will be in about a hundred years," Harnack replied skeptically. "Face it, rich boy, you're in for the duration."

"And *you're* in the way," Raynor put in, as the marines in front of them got their bags and left. "Get your butt in gear."

Then, having been sorted into numbered contingents, the heavily burdened newbies were herded through a guarded gate and into what had once been a hangar. Awaiting them were rows of open crates and a long line of tables. There was barely a pause as Raynor's retinas were scanned, he was told to advance, and a corporal shoved an E-9 rifle across the table at him. Kydd produced a whoop of joy as he was issued a Bosun FN92, and Harnack took delivery on an SR-8 shotgun. Rifle slings, cleaning kits, and ammo were distributed as they progressed down the line and past a grim-faced sergeant whose sole responsibility was to say, "Do not load your weapons until instructed to do so."

There was more, *much* more, as the newly arrived marines were given instructions on everything from how to find the mess hall to what sort of gear to take with them in the morning. A half hour later they were dismissed, and as Raynor left Assembly Area Alpha, he noticed that something was different. Rather than being *marched* to dinner, they were free to find their own way. Not a huge change, perhaps, but an indication that they weren't boots anymore, and that felt good.

After being rousted out at 0500 hours, the marines were fed, ordered to pack up their gear, and hustled onto three military trucks. A fourth was loaded with B-2 bags that they weren't going to see again until they arrived at Fort Howe. Wherever *that* was. In the meantime Raynor figured it was going to be a long, tiresome day as the trucks pulled out onto a four-lane road. There they became part of a metal flood that was headed southeast, where most of the fighting was.

The temperature began to climb as the sun arced higher into the sky, so the marines raised the waterproof fabric that protected the cargo area and let muggy air flow through the back. They sat facing one another, with their backs to the road, but Raynor tried to see what he could.

Everything looked pretty normal at first as the long convoy wound its way through scenic farmland, across rural bridges, and through little towns. But eventually, after a stop to eat their rations in a dusty turnout, the bucolic setting began to change.

Raynor saw the first signs of the wars on the equipment that was beyond repair. SCVs were making field repairs, but there had been no way to salvage the flame-scorched tanks and chunks of unidentifiable wreckage that he watched roll by. It was a sobering sight.

Then the convoy began to pass through small cities that had clearly been attacked from the air, past burned-out buses that had been pushed off the road, and fields that had been transformed into civilian shantytowns. Those were the hardest to look at, as hollow-eyed adults stood and stared, and skinny children ran along beside the trucks, holding their hands up. Raynor tossed every bit of food he had over the side, and others did likewise, but he knew that a few cans of fruit and some energy bars weren't going to make much difference.

"There hasn't been any fighting back home yet," Raynor said to Kydd, as they left the latest encampment behind. "But if the war spreads to Shiloh, my mom and dad could wind up like that."

Kydd nodded, but looked away, clearly thinking about *his* parents. They, like most members of the Old Families, were safe on well-protected Confederate core worlds like Tarsonis.

"I can't believe it's this bad," Raynor said.

"Me, neither."

"It just seems so hopeless. What can we possibly do to help these people?"

"I don't know. I guess just do what we're told, and hopefully it'll make a difference."

"This isn't what I thought it was gonna be like," Raynor said.

"Tell me about it."

They sat in silence for a while as the depressing scenery rolled by. After a while Raynor turned around and found Harnack quietly throwing dice with a hollow-faced marine named Max Zander. Raynor was glad to see that his boisterous friend had found something to do besides piss everyone off—even if he was destined to lose most of his money.

Still, all of the people he'd known in boot camp were starting to change, and that included

Hank. He was still hair-trigger, and a bit unpredictable when off duty, but squared away the rest of the time. In fact, it was very rare for a noncom to find fault with either his uniform or his weapon.

That night was spent in a military rest area, which consisted of underground dormitories that had been scooped out of the ground and covered over with a thick layer of soil. The water tanks, septic system, and supply depots required to sustain the facility were buried as well. In fact, the only items visible on the surface were the command center, the comsat station adjoining it, and an engineering bay. It wasn't fancy, but comfortable enough, all things considered.

Raynor caught an hour of guard duty that night, which sucked because his watch was a "splitter," meaning that he had to get up in the middle of the night and then go back to bed again. But at least the watch was uneventful. He was able to get back to sleep without any difficulty, and felt reasonably rested when he got up in the morning. Then it was time to clean up, eat some rations, and reboard the trucks.

The sun was little more than a yellow bruise in a gray sky. The air was warm and humid, hinting that it might rain later in the day, and Raynor could feel his undershirt stick to his back as he followed Harnack up onto the truck. The vehicle had been left running, and for no good reason insofar as Raynor could see, especially given the fuel shortage back home. That pissed him off, but he lacked enough rank to do anything about it.

Having been cleared for departure, the trucks rolled onto the busy highway for what promised to be another boring day. One of the marines had a beat-up media box loaded with a selection of Rilian techno riffs, which he proceeded to play full blast, so that the vocals and the backbeat merged with natural sound to create what amounted to a sound track for the trip.

At some point it began to rain, but not that hard, so the marines elected to leave the side panels up even though that meant getting sprayed by vehicles headed in the opposite direction. The convoy entered a verdant valley, where mounds of burned-out rubble marked what had once been profitable moss farms.

Were the farmers still alive? And living in refugee camps? Or had they been killed? There was no way to know, and Raynor was thinking about his parents, when the first Kel-Morian Hellhound dropped through the overcast and opened fire. A truck exploded, another ran into the fireball, and somebody began to scream.

CHAPTER FOURTEEN

"UNN's four-part documentary series The Price of War *has been pulled from the air by military censors. Called 'derogatory, dishonest, and unpatriotic' by the True Flag Forum, the series attempted to show a clear perspective on the lives lost during the Kel-Morian engagement. Preston Shale, president of UNN, will hold a press conference this afternoon."*

Max Speer, *Evening Report* for UNN
September 2488

THE PLANET TURAXIS II

There were three enemy aircraft in all. They skimmed along no more than a hundred and fifty feet off of the highway, firing as they came. Nose cannons spewed beams of coherent radiation at the tubby transports even as rockets leaped off their wing racks and wove in for the kill. Some struck their intended targets and some missed. The resulting explosions sent columns of debris soaring into the air.

By a stroke of good luck, truck two, which Raynor and his buddies were riding in, was spared during the first pass and he found himself on his feet yelling, "Get out! Run like hell! Take cover!"

The Hellhounds pulled up, flew a lazy circle around the far side of the valley, and turned north again. Raynor and the rest of the marines were crouched in a neighboring field at that point, weapons raised, firing madly. "Lead them!" Raynor shouted, as he remembered the lessons learned in boot camp, but knew the likelihood of bringing one of the flyers down was next to nothing.

A succession of explosions marched up the highway as the KM pilots strafed the motionless convoy for a second time and a storm of small arms fire converged on them from both sides of the road. Raynor heard shouts of joy as the second Hellhound in line staggered, produced a thin trail of black smoke, and was forced to break away. The marines hadn't brought the craft down, but they had inflicted enough damage to send it limping toward home, with the other Hellhounds providing cover.

The entire battle consumed just minutes, but destroyed two trucks and damaged a third. The fourth vehicle, the one loaded with gear, was untouched. Surprisingly, given the extent of the destruction, casualties were limited to one KIA and two WIAs.

Because the marines were replacements, and hadn't yet been integrated into regular companies at Fort Howe, they didn't have their own command structure with them. The sole surviving driver, Corporal Hawkes, took charge and got on the horn to the nearest source of potential help, which was an outpost designated as Firebase Zulu. His face was expressionless as he listened to a series of profanity-laced orders. Then when the download was over, he nodded. "Roger that, sir . . . I'll get things going. Over."

Hawkes's first task was to choose three temporary squad leaders, which he proceeded to do based on what he'd seen from the newbies so far. That was how Raynor wound up in charge of the second squad, which included Harnack, Kydd, and Zander. Hawkes eyed Raynor. "Can you drive a truck?"

"Yes, Corporal, I can drive just about anything," Raynor answered honestly.

"As long as it isn't a vulture," Harnack said sotto voce from a few feet away.

"Good," the corporal replied. "Use truck four to push one and two off the highway before traffic starts to back up. As for number three, I'm not sure if it's operational or not. Do we have anyone who knows their way around engines in this group?"

"I could take a look at it," Zander offered modestly, and the noncom was quick to take him up on the offer.

"Great! You do that. . . . If you can't get it going, tell Raynor. He'll push it out of the way. As for everyone else," Hawkes said as he looked around, "you have ten minutes to round up your B-2 bags if they still exist and get ready for a nice little stroll. Because even if we get truck three running again, there won't be enough transport for everyone."

With his squad in tow Raynor made his way past the still-smoking wreckage of trucks one and two, saw Zander peel off to examine three, and made a beeline for the last vehicle, which was battered but still running. "Hey, Hank!" he yelled, as he swung up into the cab. "It looks like traffic is starting to back up. Take the rest of the squad down the line and tell the vehicles behind us to take ten. And don't let anyone below the rank of general push past. I need room to maneuver."

Harnack looked back, saw a traffic jam that included both military and civilian vehicles and waved an acknowledgment.

It took half an hour to clear the road, get truck three up and running again, and load twenty marines into the back. Those who were on foot were ordered to report to Firebase Zulu as soon as they could. It was going to be a slog—and those fortunate enough to ride waved cheerfully as their trucks pulled away.

Altogether thirty-eight men and women were left behind, with nineteen marines to a squad, and

Raynor in charge of the entire detachment. The latter being a last-minute decision by Hawkes that came as a surprise to Raynor but to no one else.

Those who still had B-2 bags had put them aboard the trucks, so all the marines had to carry was their weapons, a full load of ammo, plus first aid kits, canteens, and one box of rations each. With only ten miles to cover, and a solid surface to walk on, Raynor figured the group should be able to reach Firebase Zulu in a few hours.

Raynor sent two scouts forward. He came next, followed by squads one and two, with Private Phelan bringing up the rear. Once across the highway, the column headed south, facing oncoming traffic so they could jump into the drainage ditch if one of the vehicles came too close.

The clouds were starting to burn off, the air was warm, and the Snakeback mountain range could be seen off to the southeast. From what he'd heard, Raynor knew it marked the western edge of the disputed zone, which meant the enemy wasn't far away. *I hope I'm not leading these people into a bloodbath,* he thought.

He had a comm, albeit not a very powerful one, which generally produced little more than snatches of guarded conversation, bursts of static, or the yowls that occurred when one side or the other sought to jam communications. So if there *was* danger ahead, he had no way to confirm it. Raynor worked hard to conceal his anxiety.

Eventually, after crossing a wooden bridge, Raynor called a halt. It was well past noon, he figured they were at least halfway to their destination, and the riverbank would make a good place to eat and rest. There were the usual complaints when he insisted on sentries, especially from Harnack, who was dispatched to keep an eye on their western flank.

Having opened his box of rations, and stashed various components in his pockets to snack on later, Raynor ate his cold entrée while he walked around. That was something he'd seen Red Murphy do back in boot camp. It was a way not only to make himself available to the troops, but to see who had their boots off in order to deal with blisters, and warn groups of marines that "one grenade would kill them all."

A few minutes later Raynor found himself next to the highway where one of the sentries was posted. Outside of the intermittent rumblings to the south, it was so quiet that he could talk to the other private without raising his voice. It took a minute for the significance of that to sink in. The reason there wasn't any noise was that all of the traffic had stopped! In fact, when questioned, the sentry reported that it had been at least fifteen minutes since a vehicle had crossed the bridge.

Raynor felt a cold fist grab his stomach. The fact that there wasn't any traffic meant that the highway had been cut off! Probably to the south, where the sounds of battle could be heard. Meanwhile, back behind the column somewhere, the MPs were probably blocking southbound traffic to prevent it from running into Kel-Morian forces farther on down the road. But how far? Beyond Firebase Zulu? Or north of it? With all these unknowns, Raynor feared he might lead the column into a meat grinder.

He could order them to stay put, of course, or turn back, and no one would blame him given the fact that he wasn't a real noncom. But he could practically hear his father saying, "Doin' nothin' ain't an option, son. . . . It's *always* better to be wrong instead of worthless." And that piece of advice was very much in tune with his own instinct, which was to follow the orders he'd been given and reach Firebase Zulu.

Raynor felt a renewed sense of urgency, and immediately cut the break short. They were going to have to double-time it down the road. All of them were in good shape, so the run was easy at first as they jogged down the empty highway, ready to take cover at a moment's notice. And there was a scary moment when the sound of engines was heard and two dropships passed over, clearly headed for the battle that was taking place to the south.

As Raynor ran, the comm unit signal cleared and gradually he was able to hear a series of terse but understandable conversations between someone called Zulu-Six and a variety of other people. Was Zulu-Six Firebase Zulu's commanding officer? Yes, that made sense, and from what Raynor could make out, things weren't going well. In fact, assuming he understood the situation correctly, two gangs of Kel-Morians had split off from a larger force and were threatening to overrun the outpost.

Raynor thought about Corporal Hawkes and the marines who had been fortunate enough to ride in a truck, and wondered what they were doing at the moment. Fighting their first battle, probably—assuming they were still alive. War had been entirely theoretical up until that point—situations and tactics that had been described to him at boot camp—but suddenly it was very real.

Raynor didn't have a map, but didn't need one at that point, because as the column rounded a curve and passed between high banks, they could see the firebase atop a low-lying hill. A half-dozen armored personnel carriers were positioned along the bottom edge of the slope, and the weapons mounted on each vehicle were firing up at the bunkers that fronted Firebase Zulu.

While of a similar size, each vehicle was different, having been pieced together from whatever the KM armorers could lay their hands on at the moment. So some were equipped with reactive armor salvaged from Confederate personnel carriers, while others were protected by sheets of metal that had been welded to their flanks and angled to deflect bullets. They were positioned to protect a siege tank, which was firing uphill and blowing huge chunks out of the revetments above.

Lower down, the dome-shaped bunkers intended to prevent infantry from charging up the slope were on fire, and two SCVs could be seen trying to extinguish the flames. But others were intact and putting out a heavy volume of fire. They would be critical if the men and women of Firebase Zulu were going to hold on.

Meanwhile, troops wearing a wild assortment of refurbished CMC armor were battling their way up the hill as fire lashed back and forth. One of the KM soldiers was equipped with a sculpted helmet he had picked up somewhere, armor plates that were bound together with a variety of leather straps, and a bandolier of ammo pouches.

Raynor couldn't help but admire the man's bravery as he paused to wave his comrades forward, only to disappear in a flash of light as a shoulder-launched rocket hit him from behind. The resulting *BOOM* was nearly lost in the chatter of assault weapons, the steady beat of a gauss cannon, and the dull thump of mortar rounds as they cut unlucky soldiers down. Each death left a red blotch on the face of the hillside.

"Get off the highway!" Raynor shouted, and waved his troops into the orchard off to the right. Some of the gnarled fruit trees had been shattered by artillery fire during a previous battle, but enough remained to provide cover, and Raynor went person to person until all of the marines were organized into four-man fire teams. Except for Kydd, Harnack, and Zander, that is, who were sent forward to find a path. *Was that the right thing to do?* Raynor thought so, because it was consistent with what he'd been taught. *"Run, think, and shoot."* That's what Gunnery Sergeant Red Murphy always said. But thinking was the hardest part. What if he was wrong?

Raynor waited for a break in the comm traffic to announce himself. All transmissions on both sides were automatically scrambled and descrambled. Raynor didn't have a call sign, so he made one up. "Zulu-Two-Three to Zulu-Six. Over."

There was a long pause, followed by a burst of static, and a suspicious voice. "Zulu-*who?* Over."

"Corporal Hawkes can vouch for me," Raynor replied. "In the meantime this is to let you know that we are half a mile north of the firebase and closing with the KM armor. We will attempt to put some of those personnel carriers out of action. That should bring at least a few of their troops back downhill. So be careful who you shoot at. Over."

This time the response was quick and precise. "This is Zulu-Six. I scan you, Two-Three . . . and I like the way you think. Execute. Over."

Harnack, Kydd, and Zander had returned by

then and were ready with a report. "We found a path," Harnack announced. "It leads down the gully in front of us, up along that stone wall, and in behind those outbuildings. The personnel carriers are a stone's throw beyond that point."

"Okay," Raynor agreed. "You'll lead us up there. Meanwhile, I want Kydd and Zander to head for what's left of the farmhouse and set up shop there. Ryk, see how many of the KMs climbing the hillside you can bring down, and don't worry about your six. Max will take care of that. Right, Max?"

Zander's eyes were very bright. He nodded. "Count on it."

"All right," Raynor said. "Get going."

The farmhouse was off to the right, where it sat inside what had been a rectangle of trees before some of them were destroyed during an earlier battle. The structure itself had taken a hit, and been partially burned. But half of the second story was still intact—and Kydd knew that was where Raynor wanted him to go. Because from up there his long-barreled rifle would be able to reach all the way up the hillside, to the point where the Kel-Morian guerillas had already destroyed two bunkers plus the SCVs sent out to repair them.

So time was of the essence as he ran, hunched over, behind the stone wall that ran east to west across the farm, and scrambled up the slope behind the house. He was about to pass through the back door when Zander grabbed hold of his combat harness and jerked him back.

Then, holding one finger up to his lips, the shorter man went in through the back door, E-9 rifle at the ready. Five seconds passed, followed by two shots, which brought Kydd on the run. The kitchen was empty, but as the sniper entered the hallway beyond, he heard a low whistle, and looked up a staircase to see Zander motioning from above.

Kydd made his way up the stairs to where a Kel-Morian soldier lay dead in the middle of a debris-littered hallway. A comm unit rested inches from his fingertips. "He was an observer," Zander said evenly. "Pick your spot. I'll be down below making sure that no one sneaks up on you."

"Take the comm," Kydd suggested. "And listen in. Maybe you'll hear if they're sending people this way."

Zander nodded, scooped the comm up off the floor, and disappeared down the stairs.

Secure in the knowledge that Zander would cover him, Kydd entered a bedroom and made his way over to a shattered window. Something bit into his knee as he placed it on the floor. A bit of broken glass, most likely, but the cut could be dealt with later.

The sill was high enough to provide a good

rest for the long-barreled rifle, and having already chambered a .50 caliber round, all he had to do was put his eye to the scope and tilt the weapon upward. It was a moment Kydd had given a good deal of thought to in boot camp—because killing a real human being was no small thing. But when he saw the desperation of the scene before him, his doubts faded away.

A group of Kel-Morians had closed in on the last defensive bunker and one was using a flame-thrower to cook the people inside. And those people were Kydd's people—even if he hadn't met them before. And the fact that he couldn't see the KMs' faces made it that much easier for the sniper to consult the data displayed on his HUD and make some final adjustments before shifting gears.

The crosshairs settled over the target. Time seemed to slow as Kydd's right index finger began to squeeze the trigger, then there was the moment of release as the rifle butt kicked his shoulder, and the weapon released a bang so loud it made his ears ring. That was when the heavy slug plowed through the air, Kydd realized he had forgotten to put his earplugs in, and his right hand worked the bolt as if it was operating without input from his brain.

Then the bullet was there, striking the Kel-Morian guerilla behind the left knee, where his armor was weakest. It wasn't a lethal shot, nor was it intended to be. Kydd's FN92 ammo was designed to pierce armor, but the sniper didn't want to take unnecessary chances. His mission was to bring the enemy soldiers down and bring them down fast. The slug smashed through armor, destroyed the Kel-Morian's knee joint, and bounced off the rounded cap designed to protect him from frontal shots.

As the soldier fell, his self-sealing suit was already injecting painkillers into his bloodstream and applying a tourniquet to his lower leg. So by the time he rolled down the slope to the bottom of the hill he was out of action for good.

But Kydd wasn't thinking about the first Kel-Morian anymore. He was focused on the *third*, and lost in the aim-fire-reload sequence of what he was not only doing, but doing *well*. Better than he'd done in school, better than he'd done working for his father part-time, and better than he had ever hoped to do. And it felt good, *very* good, as the fourth target fell and he forced himself to pause.

"Save the last round long enough to look around," Sergeant Peters had told him. "Because some bastard could be closing in on *you*. Then, if it's safe to do so, take your final shot before loading the next magazine."

Kydd scanned, came up empty, and fired. The target wasn't wearing armor this time and his head blossomed into a bloody mist. Kydd barely noticed. A killer had been born.

* * *

It had taken the better part of fifteen long minutes for Raynor and Harnack to get all the other marines into position in and around the farm's outbuildings. Such a thing would have been impossible had the Kel-Morian overseer placed some soldiers north of his armored personnel carriers. But, having met only minimal resistance as he swept into the area at the base of the hill, and eager to take Firebase Zulu quickly, the overseer had apparently chosen to send *all* his troops against the objective.

Now, as Raynor prepared to lead his fellow marines into battle, he suddenly felt short of breath, his heart racing. He was frightened—not for his own safety, but because of his lack of experience and the possibility that he might screw up. So it took an act of will to emerge from hiding, wave his troops forward, and shout: "Follow me!"

Two fire teams remained behind to provide covering fire. The rest of the marines charged across the intervening space, firing as they ran. All of the Kel-Morian turret gunners were shooting uphill. That left their lightly armored backs exposed, and two died almost immediately as slugs ripped into them from behind.

Then the marines were on three of the vehicles, shooting down into the compartments below, but they lacked enough manpower to tackle the rest. The Kel-Morians turned all of their weapons on the captured personnel carriers, and Raynor saw three of the marines closest to the enemy swept away by a hail of spikes. His heart sank. Was Omer one of them?

Enraged, Raynor climbed up onto the nearest carrier and jerked a dead gunner up out of her firing position. Projectiles pinged, spanged, and rattled as they peppered the metal around him. Having dropped into the blood-splashed turret, Raynor placed both boots on the shiny pedals below. There was a satisfying whine as the double-barreled weapon swung around and came to bear on the enemy. The KMs saw the threat, and Raynor felt his anger turn into fear as the vehicle took hit after hit.

That was when Raynor thumbed both triggers and sent parallel streams of spikes toward the carriers that were still under KM control. The overlapping explosions merged to produce a continuous roar of sound as the devastating rounds ate their way through layers of neosteel armor to seek out the ammo bins within.

Raynor's entire body was shaking in reaction to the adrenaline pumping through it. He was shouting words he couldn't understand and wondering if the moment would ever end. Then came an earthshaking *CRUMP!* as a pillar of fire propelled the top of the enemy vehicle fifteen feet into the air, where it appeared to hang momentarily before crashing down.

Raynor sensed movement to his right, swiveled his weapons in that direction, and was preparing to open fire on a new target when a much-amplified voice was heard. "This is Zulu-Six. . . . Hold your fire! The battle is over."

It took a moment to process the officer's words, but once he did, Raynor pushed himself up and out of the turret. He looked around at the scene. The few remaining Kel-Morian soldiers were being disarmed and taken into Confed custody.

Raynor took a deep breath as he looked down at his hands. They were smeared with blood. He wiped them on his pants but the red stuff wouldn't come off.

Then, as Raynor surveyed the scene around him, he was overwhelmed with guilt. Both the area around the vehicles and the hillside above it were strewn with dead bodies. An empty feeling flooded the pit of his stomach, and Raynor was forced to reswallow a portion of his lunch. He took a quick look around, fearful that someone had spotted his weakness, and was glad to see that his friends were busy with other things as he jumped to the ground and ran to the point where he thought he'd seen Omer go down.

The ground around Omer was covered with blood. Plastiscab battle dressings covered one side of his chest, and the lower part of the soldier's left arm was missing. One of the firebase's medics was working on him, and Raynor could tell that the painkillers had kicked in, because Omer smiled dreamily as he looked up. "One battle . . . that's all I was good for. Now they're probably gonna send me home."

"Maybe not . . . I'm sure they can patch you right up." Raynor smiled. "Your parents will be proud," Raynor said, as he knelt next to his friend. "*Real* proud."

Omer frowned. "I was scared, Jim. . . . Were you scared?"

"I was very scared. I think I crapped my pants."

Omer managed a laugh. "I'll tell your parents about everything."

"Tell them about boot camp," Raynor responded. "But not about this."

"No," Omer replied soberly. "I won't tell them about this."

As Omer was carried away, Raynor heard the whine of servos and the thump of heavy feet. He turned to face a suit of battle-scarred armor. There was a soft hiss as the visor opened and a man peered at Raynor. He had blue eyes, and deep creases bracketed both sides of his mouth. "I'm Captain Senko—otherwise known as Zulu-Six. Are you Zulu-Two-Three by any chance?"

Raynor nodded.

"I thought so. . . . You and your team did a good job. A *real* good job."

"Thank you, sir. . . . I'll pass that along." The officer turned to leave. "Sir?" Raynor broke in. "How many people did we lose? Or is it too early to say?"

Senko placed an enormous hand on Raynor's shoulder. It felt heavy. "The same as always, son . . . we lost too damned many."

And that, Raynor discovered over the next few hours, was absolutely true.

CHAPTER FIFTEEN

"Any member of the armed services caught removing military assets from a government installation without sanction will be tried as an enemy agent and subject to the death penalty."

From section 14:76.2 of the *Confederate Uniform Code of Military Justice*

FORT HOWE, ON THE PLANET TURAXIS II

More than a week had passed since Tychus had been released from Military Correctional Facility-R-156 and ordered back to duty. It had been a tough three months, but that was behind him now as a dropship named *Fat Girl* skimmed over what had been the city of Whitford, and Tychus took the opportunity to eyeball the ruins through an open side door. The slipstream blasted his face and forced him to retreat. But not before he caught a glimpse of devastated buildings, cratered streets, and burned-out vehicles all laid out on a tidy grid.

Whitford had been overrun by what the press liked to refer to as "the breakout." Although Tychus thought it was more like a *break-in*, since the Kel-Morians had been able to fight their way through Hobber's Gap and lay waste to an area between Burr's Crossing to the south and an outpost called Firebase Zulu up north.

But what they *hadn't* been able to do was overrun Fort Howe. That was the home of the 3rd Battalion, 4th Marines, also known as "the Thundering Third." The battalion had not only pushed the KMs out of Whitford and back toward the mountains, it was currently following the enemy home.

In the meantime Tychus was about to join the 3rd Battalion's holding company at Fort Howe, where, with any luck at all, he would be able to return to work on Operation Early Retirement. A much-neglected aspect of the war effort that Tychus hoped to refocus his attention on.

The transport began to slow a few minutes later, circled the base below, and lowered itself onto the main landing pad of a starport. The dropship carried eleven other passengers, replacements mostly, who would soon become members of the Thundering Third. They were already pulling their belongings together as the skids touched down and a green light appeared.

When the ramp was extended, Tychus followed a couple officers and some noncoms onto the pad. Once there, he was struck by the fact that, except for one other ship, the area in front of the starport structure was empty! A sure sign that most of the battalion was elsewhere.

All of his original gear had been lost during the transfer from Prosser's Well to MCF-R-156. So all Tychus had to carry was his duffel bag containing some extra underwear and a Dopp kit. Tychus entered the starport to get directions to the admin building and went back outside to wait for an open-sided jitney.

The five-minute ride served to confirm his initial impression: Fort Howe had been stripped of troops in order to battle the Kel-Morians off to the east. A barracks building had been lifted off the ground and was in the process of being repositioned, and the occasional squad could be seen double-timing from one location to the next. But the facility had an empty feel.

He entered the admin building and discovered that half the people who had been on the dropship with him were already there—and lined up in front of a single sergeant who was doggedly working to help them. So a good forty-five minutes passed before it was Tychus's turn to belly up to the counter and surrender the chip containing his personnel file and his orders.

The clerk assigned Tychus to holding company Echo, scheduled him for a medical exam, and a follow-up appointment with Fort Howe's "morale" officer. Meaning a shrink who among other things was charged with keeping track of marines fresh out of a military correctional facility.

Having completed those arrangements and assigned Tychus to the barracks where Echo Company was quartered, the sergeant looked up at Tychus with strangely soulless eyes. Was it because the guy was a stylus-pushing rear-echelon functionary? Or was it something else? Whatever it was came across as kind of spooky. "That should take care of it, Private. . . . Check the monitor in your quarters for chow times."

"How 'bout some gear?" Tychus demanded. "I lost everything I had at my last duty station. All I have is a change of underwear."

That problem lay outside the realm of the expected, so the sergeant frowned disapprovingly and tapped a series of keys. Then, having found the necessary entry on the screen in front of him, the frown disappeared. "Here we are," the clerk said apologetically. "You *are* authorized to receive a full issue. I missed that, for which I sincerely apologize."

Tychus's eyebrows rose. An *apology*? From a clerk? And a sergeant at that? That was downright weird. "Take this over to Supply Depot 7," the clerk said, as he passed a chip across the counter. "Give it to the person on duty. They will take care of you."

* * *

After exiting the admin building and catching another jitney ride, Tychus got off across from a low, one-story, metal-clad supply depot with a big white SUPPLY DEPOT 7 painted on the front. Heat shimmered as it rose from the concrete, a dropship roared as it passed overhead, and a file of sweat-soaked marines jogged past. They were singing, "One, two, three, four—I love the Marine Corps."

Tychus knew it was a lie as he made his way toward the supply depot. The homely structure was protected by a defensive blast wall. Not far away, to either side of the structure, two missile turrets sat poised to defend the base against enemy aircraft.

In order to reach the front door, Tychus had to walk a zigzag course between prefab obstacles. It was five degrees cooler inside the building, and Tychus was reminded of Gunnery Sergeant Sims and the supply depot full of Kel-Morian supplies back on Raydin III. Had Sims and Calvin been able to sell off some of the war booty before the logistics team arrived? No, he thought, not without a customer!

That thought made Tychus feel better as he crossed a spacious waiting area to the counter that separated him from long rows of storage racks beyond. Two-person teams could be seen in the back, pulling items off of shelves and scanning them.

A lance corporal was positioned under a sign

that read NEW ISSUE, and nodded as Tychus approached. "Morning . . . what can I do for you?"

"All my gear was lost in transit from one duty station to another," Tychus explained. "They told me to report here to receive a new issue. Here's my A-chip."

The lance corporal looked young and had probably been in the marines for a year or so, given his rank. He passed the chip by a scanner, eyed the results, and nodded agreeably. "Yup, you're authorized for a new issue, all right . . . but we're in the middle of an inventory at the moment. Come back at 1400 hours and we'll fix you up."

Tychus frowned, put both fists on the counter, and leaned forward. "I have a better idea. . . . Why don't *you,* or one of your supply weenies, draw my gear right now? Because I don't feel like coming back at 1400 hours—or any other time for that matter! *Do you scan me?"*

"Oh, I scan you all right," Lance Corporal Jim Raynor replied calmly. "Only trouble is that you have me confused with someone who gives a crap. *Private."*

Tychus was momentarily stunned as the other man mirrored his posture, eyes narrowed, looking straight at him. When confronted with his overwhelming size, most people took two involuntary steps backward. But this marine hadn't flinched, and showed no signs of backing off. Having put himself on a limb, Tychus had no choice but to reach both hands across the counter and grab a generous handful of the other man's shirt. He gave it a twist for emphasis. Tychus scowled as the marine's eyes drifted toward his tattooed knuckles. "That's right, boy. P-A-I-N, something you're about to become very familiar with," Tychus growled. "Now, maybe I wasn't clear. . . . *Get my stuff, and bring it here, or I will rip your fekkin' head off and piss in the hole!"*

That was when Tychus felt something hard jab the back of his skull, heard the familiar *click-clack* sound, and knew someone was holding a shotgun to his head. "That's one possibility," a third voice drawled, "or I could blow *your* head off and check to see if there's anything inside. My guess is no."

Tychus was still holding a fistful of shirt as the lance corporal smiled slowly. "I would listen to Private Harnack if I were you," the marine said reasonably. "He shot three Kel-Morians last week—so he might be suffering from post-traumatic stress disorder. Of course, it's hard to tell where Hank's concerned."

Tychus was furious, but, determined not to let his emotions show, he released his grip. Then, having snatched the A-chip back, he turned to go. The red-haired marine, with his supercilious smile still firmly in place, stood well out of reach. A rectangle of bright sunlight beckoned—and Tychus made for it. A skirmish had been lost—but the battle was far from over.

THE RAFFIN BROTHERS MINE
NEAR FORT HOWE ON THE PLANET TURAXIS II

The Kel-Morian rippers had been living deep underground for six days. The main chamber was lit with emergency lanterns, and strings of lights crisscrossed the area above. Power was supplied by a generator that had been liberated from the Confeds and brought down into the mine.

Dozens of matte black powered combat suits lined the walls. Soldiers sat in small groups talking, gambling, or fine-tuning various pieces of equipment. They wore every scrap of clothing they had, because despite the meager heat emanating from a few jury-rigged heaters, it was cold in the mine.

Foreman Oleg Benson didn't know very much about the mine, and didn't need to know anything more than the fact that it had been abandoned at some point, and was deep enough to hide in. He sat off by himself, as befitted a Kel-Morian foreman, sucking on an unlit pipe and wondering how much longer he and his men would be required to wait. One day? Two? Certainly no more than that, because he and his troops were running short of food.

But if his superior's plan was successful, Benson and his rippers would play a pivotal role in one of the most daring raids of the war. Because the mine was only a few miles east of Fort Howe, which, having been stripped of troops, was ripe for the plucking. And in more ways than one.

Because once Benson and his grunts overran the base and secured a landing zone for an airborne assault team flown in from the east, there would be ample opportunity to loot the base. An activity Overseer Scaggs not only approved of, but insisted upon!

It was Scaggs who had the clarity to see an opportunity for victory and sent the rippers into hiding even as the marines from Fort Howe pushed Kel-Morian forces toward the east. A move that could convert a loss into a victory if successful. A group of guerillas began to sing and Benson smiled.

FORT HOWE, ON THE PLANET TURAXIS II

After grudgingly returning to collect his new gear from the supply depot at 1400 hours, Tychus was about to go to chow, when a cute, ginger-haired corporal on a motorized cart arrived in front of the barracks. "Is Private Findlay here?" she asked sweetly as she hopped out.

Tychus ran his eyes up and down the corporal's petite, curvy frame. "Who's asking?"

"So it *is* you, then." She looked up at him. "You're much bigger in person than in your picture," she offered innocently.

Tychus smiled—a genuine smile that reflected

the bevy of impure thoughts that were running through his mind at that particular moment. "Yes, I'm Findlay," he acknowledged. "Did I do something wrong?"

"Beats me," she shrugged as she motioned to the cart. "Hop in! Lieutenant Colonel Vanderspool wants to speak with you."

Tychus swore under his breath as he walked around to the passenger side. Had he been assigned to a shit detail of some sort? Yes, probably. He was both surprised and worried. Lieutenant Colonel Vanderspool was in charge of both the 3rd Battalion and the base. So if he wanted to talk with a lowly private, then it was probably because of an infraction. But what? There hadn't been enough time to steal anything.

Still, Tychus had no choice but to get in the cart and allow himself to be transported to the command center. Suddenly Tychus was painfully aware of the fact that his uniform was wrinkled and his boots were in desperate need of some polish.

But there was nothing Tychus could do about those deficiencies as he followed the sexy little corporal inside, stepped onto the lift platform, and walked into the well-furnished waiting area outside the base commander's office on the observation deck. Tychus caught a glimpse of Vanderspool through his open door, as he sat on the corner of his desk chatting with an officer.

Tychus got the impression of a man whose handsome features had begun to blur as a result of age and too much good food. Vanderspool was, according to what the corporal had said, just in from the field. But if that was the case, Tychus couldn't see any signs of hardship as he examined the officer's starched uniform and immaculate boots. A hands-off type then, somebody who preferred to sit around and shoot the breeze with staff officers, rather than spend time on the front lines.

The visitor laughed at something Vanderspool said, got up out of the guest chair, and exited the office. That was when the corporal stuck her head in and said something Tychus couldn't hear, before motioning for him to enter.

Tychus took three steps into the office, came to attention, and announced himself. "Private Tychus Findlay, reporting as ordered, *sir*!"

Now that Tychus was closer he could see that Vanderspool had hard eyes, a tracery of broken veins that wandered over the bridge of his nose, and a thin-lipped mouth. "At ease," Vanderspool said approvingly. "Sorry about the short notice, but I've been commuting between the fort and Hobber's Gap, where we're about to push the KMs back into the disputed zone. Please, have a seat."

The tone had been congenial so far, so Tychus felt somewhat relieved as he sat down, but still on guard. Because he'd been summoned for a reason, and odds were he wasn't going to like it.

Vanderspool had circled the big desk by that time. The executive-style chair sighed as he lowered his weight onto it. "You have an interesting record," Vanderspool commented, as he plucked an old-fashioned letter opener off the desktop and began to toy with it. "You worked your way up to staff sergeant, struck an officer, and were sent to a correctional facility on Raydin III."

The officer paused at that point, but Tychus knew better than to speak. Some officers like to run their mouths, and Vanderspool was clearly one of them. But where was the one-sided conversation headed?

"It's only fair to remind you that you are on what amounts to parole," Vanderspool continued sternly. "One word from me and you'll be back in a correctional facility." His voice darkened. "And if you think hard labor was bad, you can only imagine what else we're capable of. If you mess with me, boy, you might just end up a prisoner in your own body. Scan me?"

Tychus had no idea what Vanderspool was referring to and didn't want to find out. And technically, he *wasn't* on parole, but it didn't seem up for discussion. Besides, he wanted to get the hell out of there, so Tychus gave the answer that every officer likes to hear. "Yes, sir."

"But," Vanderspool said, brightening. "I believe in second chances. Which is why I'm going to give you *this*."

Vanderspool slid a patch across the table. Tychus couldn't hide his surprise when he saw three inverted chevrons. "That's right," Vanderspool said. "You're a sergeant again. Not a staff sergeant like before—you'll have to earn that rocker, but a *buck* sergeant. Congratulations!"

Tychus was not only shocked, but exceedingly pleased, because sergeants have more opportunities to steal things than privates do. "Thank you, sir . . . thank you very much."

"You're welcome," Vanderspool replied indulgently. "The battalion suffered a lot of casualties during the last week—and I'll find a slot for you in one of my line companies."

"Thank you, sir," Tychus said. "In the meantime, could I ask a favor?"

"Well, that depends," Vanderspool answered. "I'm afraid a pass is out of the question at the moment."

"No, sir, it isn't anything like that," Tychus assured him sanctimoniously. "If I can make a difference during the next few weeks, then I'd like to do so."

THE RAFFIN BROTHERS MINE NEAR FORT HOWE ON THE PLANET TURAXIS II

Having received the necessary order, the Kel-Morian rippers were armed and ready to attack. There were dozens of them, all standing in a rough semicircle and wearing the flat black armor for which they were famous. The last-minute briefing by Foreman Oleg Benson wasn't absolutely necessary, but was appreciated, since they were a close-knit group and fought for each other as much as for the Kel-Morian Combine.

There was very little chance that the Confeds would pick up a comm unit signal originating from underground, but rather than run that minimal risk, Benson ordered his troops to listen with visors open. "All right, men," he said, as his voice echoed off the walls of the mine. "This is the moment we've been waiting for! The eve of what will be one of our most celebrated victories.

"Think about it. . . . We are only miles from Fort Howe, the base has been stripped of personnel to fight our regulars up in the mountains, and those who remain don't know we're coming! Who could ask for more?"

The reply was the time-honored cry of *"HEGERON!"* which paid homage to the famous battle on a Kel-Morian mining world named Feronis. According to legend, a gang of armored rippers had taken on an entire battalion of motorized infantry on the plain of Hegeron and defeated them. The extent of the victory had probably been exaggerated over the years, but it was still a point of pride.

"That's right," Benson agreed. "Tonight is the night to remember not only the battle of Hegeron, but the evil that dwells in the high-rise towers of

Tarsonis, where members of the Old Families grow rich off those who slave in their factories. Like Kel-Morian soldiers everywhere, the rippers will never forget that workers have a right to a fair wage, to basic social services, and to free elections!" And by that, he meant wealth, possessions, and power. What else was worth fighting for?

The cry of *"HEGERON!"* was much louder this time, and a fitting moment for Benson to close his visor, which was a signal for the others to do likewise.

Then, walking single file, the warriors made their way up to the surface, where near total darkness was waiting to cloak them. They split into smaller teams at that point, turned toward the west, and began to jog. Smaller predators, those to whom the night normally belonged, scattered in every direction. Death was on the loose and it was time to hide.

CHAPTER SIXTEEN

"UNN broadcasting offices were closed earlier today as Confederate officials moved in to confiscate 'seditious and slanderous materials' in the station's library. This action follows the unauthorized airing of actual war footage by unknown individuals within UNN. Confederate investigators are currently searching for any leads to the whereabouts of these traitors."

Max Speer, *Evening Report* for UNN
September 2488

FORT HOWE, ON THE PLANET TURAXIS II

One of the planet's moons was still arcing toward the western horizon, the lights were turned down, and Raynor was lying on his rack listening to some very retro tunes that Kydd had passed along to him when the door to the dormitory-style barracks room slammed open, and a basso voice said, "Hit the floor! It's time for all of you ladies to dance!"

Raynor dropped his fone and sat up just in time to see Tychus Findlay stroll down the center aisle sporting a brand-new set of sergeant's chevrons. *Oh no,* Raynor thought, *How the hell did I step in this pile of shit?*

"That's right," Tychus announced cheerfully, casting a wicked smile directly at Raynor. "Your worst fekkin' nightmare just arrived! You thought basic sucked? Just wait till *I'm* done with you. Now get dressed."

"I don't believe it," Harnack said. "Who would be crazy enough to make *you* a sergeant?"

"I'm glad you asked," Tychus replied, as he made his way over to where Harnack was standing. Large though he was, Harnack found himself looking *up* as a huge fist got a grip on the front of his shirt and hoisted him up off the ground.

Tychus was smoking a stogie, and as their faces came level with each other, Harnack could feel the heat from the glowing red ember on the tip of his nose. Tychus exhaled and Harnack coughed. "You're the asshole with the shotgun," Tychus observed, as Harnack's feet dangled uselessly in the air.

"And you're one crazy sonofabitch," Harnack responded insolently.

Tychus might have bounced Harnack off the wall at that point, but Raynor was there to intervene. "You made your point, Sergeant. Hank, shut the hell up! Or do you *want* to wind up in the infirmary?"

Harnack's answer was forever lost as a Klaxon sounded and the loudspeaker over their heads came to sudden life. "This is Lieutenant Colonel Vanderspool. . . . The base is under attack! I repeat, the base is under attack! All duty personnel will report to their pre-assigned rally points. All off-duty personnel will report for duty. Again, this is Lieutenant Colonel Vanderspool. . . ."

Tychus put Harnack down and squinted at Raynor. "Which rally point is Echo Company supposed to report to?"

Raynor shrugged. "I don't know. We're in a holding company waiting to be slotted into a line unit. We've been reporting to a supply sergeant on a temporary basis and pulling shit details for days. We didn't have any noncoms until now. I was the acting squad leader."

Tychus eyed Raynor and frowned. "How long have you been a lance corporal?"

"About a week," Harnack chimed in. "Ever since we kicked a starload of Kel-Morian ass at Firebase Zulu!"

"Well, at least you bunnies have seen some action," Tychus allowed grudgingly. "Get your weapons, gear up, and grab all the ammo you can carry. At least some of the Kel-Morians will be wearing armor—but we don't have time to suit up. Put on your chest protectors, and remember ladies, the zipper goes in front."

The orders set off a mad scramble as Raynor,

Harnack, Kydd, Zander, and a marine named Connor Ward rushed to get ready. The building shook from a series of explosions as Tychus slipped into his body armor. The cigar was still clenched in his teeth and some ash cascaded down over his chest protector as he fastened the straps.

"The noise you heard was a set of demolitions charges going off," Tychus predicted. "So it's safe to assume that the bastards are on base by now."

"Good," rumbled the husky, dark-skinned Ward as he settled a pack loaded with extra rockets onto his broad back. "I want to kill as many Kel-Morians as possible! It's payback time."

"I'm gonna light those bastards up!" Harnack proclaimed enthusiastically, as he came forward to stand next to Ward. He was wearing protective goggles plus a two-tank backpack. He held the flamethrower's tube-shaped igniter across his torso the way a mother might cradle her baby.

Like Ward's rocket launcher, the flamethrower was a squad weapon that would normally be assigned to someone with the proper training. But given the circumstances, and with no one to tell him no, Harnack had appropriated the weapon for himself and was clearly eager to try it out.

"So where are we going?" Zander inquired pragmatically, as he pointed the stubby barrel of his grenade launcher at the ceiling. "I say we defend the officers' club," he quipped dryly. "That's where the important stuff is."

"I think we should head for the armory," Raynor put in, as the insistent *pop, pop, pop* of small arms fire was heard in the distance. "That's what the Kel-Morians will try to destroy first."

Tychus realized that Raynor was correct, and, not having a plan of his own, was quick to agree. "General Raynor has the right idea. Let's go, girls, on the double!"

The six-man squad slipped out of the barracks just in time to see one of the fort's elevated turrets fire a salvo of missiles at an unseen target and then explode as two Kel-Morian Hellhounds roared overhead. The light generated by the explosion strobed the surrounding buildings and left after-images floating in front of Raynor's eyes as he followed Tychus down onto the half-lit street.

Someone—it wasn't clear who—was firing flares up into the darkening sky. They went off with a distinctive pop, and threw a ghastly green glow across everything below, as tiny retros lowered them to the ground.

A firefight was under way up ahead, and as the squad drew closer, Raynor saw that a group of lightly armed marines had taken cover behind a plascrete blast barrier as a trio of Kel-Morian rippers marched toward them. The flat black armor was hard to see, or would have been without the light from the flares, which threw long, hard shadows toward the embattled marines. Projectiles sparkled as they hit the enemy armor, and two grenades exploded harmlessly in front of the enemy grunts. They were rocked back on their heels, but recovered and kept on coming.

"Ward!" Raynor snapped as the group continued to advance on the barrier. "Can you reach them?"

"I can and I will," the marine rumbled, stepping between a couple of marines and raising the launcher. "Watch out for my back blast."

There was a loud whoosh, followed by a roar, as the armor-piercing round raced up the street. It scored a direct hit on the Kel-Morian who was at the center of the three-man formation. The result was a loud boom followed by a reedy cheer, as pieces of the ripper flew in every direction.

But as Ward worked to reload his single shot launcher, the enemy grunts were closing with the marines, firing as they came. Raynor saw two men fall as Harnack readied his weapon.

"Eat this!" Harnack proclaimed as he pointed the igniter over the barrier and pulled the trigger. A gout of fire shot up the street, wrapped a ripper in a fiery embrace, and set him to dancing inside a cocoon of orange-red flames.

Zander dropped a series of grenades into the conflagration, and the resulting explosion sent the Kel-Morian's helmet and head shooting straight up, trailing fire as they went. Then there was a flash of light as the suit came apart—and shrapnel flew in every direction.

That was spectacular stuff, but not as amazing as what occurred next, when Tychus jumped the barrier and charged the remaining grunt with his weapon blazing! As the two of them collided, Tychus bowled the ripper over and landed on the Kel-Morian's chest. It shouldn't have been possible, but Tychus was not only bigger than most men, but amped on adrenaline as well. He brought his rifle butt down on the other soldier's visor, swore when it didn't shatter, and hit it again and again.

The Kel-Morian was trying to buck Tychus off, but the marine was already in the process of bringing the rifle butt down for a sixth time. As solid metal smashed into the face beyond the visor—a sliver of bone was forced up into Foreman Oleg Benson's brain.

Raynor, who had been rushing to help, skidded to a halt. "Damn! Remind me not to piss you off!"

"Too late for that," Tychus responded, as he got up off the corpse. "But at least you and your girlfriends know how to fight. . . . That's more than I expected. Come on! Let's head for the armory!"

Without helmets or comm units, the squad had no way to communicate with the command structure as they ran up the street. Not that it made much difference, because while there were pockets of organized resistance, chaos ruled.

Nowhere was that more evident than in the vicinity of the armory, as the squad crossed a parking lot littered with a dozen dead marines and began to close in on a brightly lit loading bay. One truck was already halfway down the street and another was in the process of pulling away. That left two more in the final stages of loading. A guard hut offered momentary cover for the group. Kydd was the last one in. He broke out a window, placed his weapon on the sill, and began to scan.

"Damn it!" Raynor exclaimed, as two rippers opened fire from the shadows. "What's going on here?"

"They're stealing stuff, that's what's going on," Tychus replied knowingly, as spikes buried themselves in the plascrete and the noncom jerked Raynor back out of the line of fire. "Which is real interesting because you'd expect the KMs to blow the place up!"

Raynor's mind was racing. "That's right! How long since the first announcement? Fifteen minutes max? They must've been loading at least some of those trucks *before* the attack began!"

"Well, I'll be damned," Tychus replied in mock amazement, "you aren't as stupid as you look! So General, let's kill those fekkin' rippers and find out where those trucks are going."

It was a good idea, but before the squad could act on it, all of Fort Howe's surviving turrets began to fire missiles up into the inky black sky as three

Kel-Morian transports loaded with troops came in for a landing. As some of the missiles struck their targets, orange-red blossoms appeared and Kel-Morian transports died. There was a prolonged clatter as debris fell all around.

"There's act two," Tychus observed, as an explosion lit his upturned face. "An airborne assault intended to take and hold the base."

"Why steal arms if you plan to capture them?" Raynor demanded.

"For the money," Tychus growled. "Some rotten bastard *knew* the KMs were coming—and knew he could blame the loss on them once the battle was over. Come on. . . . We have work to do."

The other four members of the squad had engaged the grunts by then, and as the two men rounded the east side of the guard hut, heavy fire was sleeting back and forth. Then Tychus saw one of the enemy soldiers jerk as if slapped in the face. The Kel-Morian fell over backward as a *second* .50 caliber slug smashed through his protective visor, which was made of cheap, low-grade plasteel. "That's some nice shooting," Tychus observed loudly as he fired a short burst. "Who's the kid with the long gun, anyway?"

"That depends on who you ask," Raynor replied, as one of Ward's rockets struck the second grunt and blew the man in half. "But the kid answers to 'Kydd.' "

"We're taking fire from the south!" Harnack shouted, as he began to back toward the loading dock. A long tongue of fire swept the area where the dead marines lay—cremating both them and half a dozen Kel-Morian troops.

Then, as Harnack continued to pan the igniter back and forth, he accidentally swept it across the back end of a fuel truck. Ward shouted, "Watch out!" but it was too late, as the tanker exploded. There was a throaty *BOOM* as a chunk of flying metal cut two enemy soldiers in half, a column of flames shot straight up into the air, and a wave of fiery fuel flowed out to lap around Kel-Morian ankles.

To conserve on weight, the KMs weren't wearing hardskins, and they began to scream as they ran in circles. Zander put them out of their misery with a series of well-placed grenades as Harnack stared in wonder. "Did *I* do that? Holy crap, I'm in love."

Meanwhile, as Kydd and Ward turned to help their buddies defend against the new threat, Tychus was pulling a door open and jerking the driver out of a truck. He was a civilian, and a terrified one at that, which offered support to the theory that somebody was not only stealing weapons but colluding with the enemy to do so!

Raynor had taken possession of the other truck by then even as the firefight grew more intense. So he slid behind the controls and sounded the air horn, in hopes that the rest of the squad would take notice. They did, and Kydd and Zander rushed to board Raynor's vehicle, while Harnack and Ward piled into the one that Tychus was driving.

Then, as spikes shattered the windscreen and perforated the front hood, Raynor pulled away. He had a sick feeling that they weren't going to make it. But then, suddenly, all the firing stopped. It seemed choreographed, as if someone *wanted* the trucks to escape. Someone who didn't know they had been taken over.

Raynor thought it best to find a safe place to park it before rejoining the battle, but Tychus clearly had other ideas as he passed on the left, and his voice sounded over the truck's radio. "This is Echo-Six to base command. . . . The enemy looted the armory and my squad and I are giving chase. Over."

That was a partial truth at best, but Raynor never got a chance to complain, as a second voice was heard. "This is Hotel-One to Echo-Six. . . . Break it off. . . . I repeat, break it off and report to rally point seven. That's an order. Over."

Then came Tychus's reply. "You're breaking up, Hotel-One. Repeat, breaking up. Will try again in five. Over."

At that point Raynor realized that he and his fellow squad members had been hijacked by their new sergeant and were being drawn into a dangerous combination of criminal activity and dereliction of duty. That went against everything he had been taught to believe in, and that made him feel guilty, not to mention scared.

On the other hand, there was no question about what he had seen with his own eyes. Confederate marines had been loading the trucks *before* the attack started. So it appeared as though at least some of the good guys weren't all that good. And how could they get away with something like that unless somebody higher up was in on it? Truth was, it was hard to tell what was right and wrong anymore.

Suddenly Raynor could hear his father's voice ringing in his ears. *"We keep working and they keep taking. . . . It just ain't right."*

And it wasn't right. So, Raynor decided, *if I can take something back, and pass it to my family,* at least something good will come of this. The battle faded behind them as the trucks passed through a shattered gate. Fifteen minutes later the two-vehicle convoy entered the already devastated suburbs of Whitford. The night was black, the headlights were white, and the highway was gray.

CHAPTER SEVENTEEN

"I used to light fires as a kid. A lot of fires. My folks were always giving me grief about it. They just didn't understand. It wasn't pyromania: it was a career move."

Private Hank Harnack, 321st Colonial Rangers Battalion, in an interview on Turaxis II
July 2488

FORT HOWE, ON THE PLANET TURAXIS II

Two days had passed since the Kel-Morian rippers had launched their surprise attack on Fort Howe, and as a jitney carried Tychus toward the command center, there was plenty of activity to be seen. Dozens of SCVs were hard at work repairing half-slagged defenses, filling craters, and clearing away debris. Civilian crews had been brought in to help, but there was still plenty left to accomplish.

The jitney Tychus was riding in was forced to detour around the burned-out wreckage of a Kel-Morian aircraft before continuing on its way.

The battle had been far from one-sided, however. More than a hundred of Fort Howe's marines were wounded or killed, and it was very likely that the base would have been overrun had it not been for some very good luck. The rippers' commanding officer was killed early on in the battle, a squadron of Avengers arrived quickly enough to destroy three Kel-Morian transports, and half a squad of enemy soldiers was wiped out when a marine ran over them with a truck.

Meanwhile, miles to the east, the Thundering Third had broken through the Snakeback Mountains and pushed a contingent of Kel-Morian regulars back into the disputed zone. A victory for which Vanderspool was given credit despite the fact that Fort Howe had nearly been lost. It was a glaring miscarriage of justice that Raynor was still struggling to accept—and Tychus regarded with his usual cynicism. Vanderspool was a player, and a successful one, so what else was new? If it hadn't been Vanderspool it would have been some other officer.

The question is, Tychus thought, *why does the sonofabitch want to talk to me? He doesn't know that we took the truck, not for sure anyway, because he would have sent the MPs after us if he did.*

The jitney arrived in front of the command center, and Tychus jumped off as a couple of other people got on. He was dressed for the occasion this time, in crisp cammies and glossy boots. Rather than lug a rifle around, Tychus was armed with a pistol in a shoulder holster.

In the wake of the surprise attack two marines were posted outside the building. They demanded that Tychus submit to an identity scan, and like the clerk Tychus had dealt with on the day he arrived, the guards were *too* polite. *Where are these people coming from?* the noncom wondered. There was something strange about them.

Tychus went upstairs and entered the waiting room outside of Vanderspool's office. The same red-haired corporal he had met before was on duty and instructed him to sit down. It was a longer wait this time because Vanderspool was being interviewed by a UNN reporter, so rather than let the opportunity go to waste, Tychus spent the next five minutes mentally undressing the corporal one item of clothing at a time. She was down to a pair of panties and her combat boots by the time the journalist left the office. "You can go in now," she said brightly, and smiled.

Tychus thanked her, made his way over to the door, and knocked. Then, having heard the word "Come!" he took three paces forward and announced himself. "Sergeant Findlay reporting as ordered, sir!"

Vanderspool looked up from his calendar as a pressed and polished Tychus Findlay entered the room. *I'll be damned,* he thought, *the guy looks like he just stepped out of a recruiting poster.*

Vanderspool had mixed feelings about his newly appointed sergeant. During the Kel-Morians' sneak attack—the magnitude of which came as an unpleasant surprise to Vanderspool, who was expecting a simple raid—Findlay had led his squad to the armory with plans to defend it. Upon seeing that the facility was being looted, he and his men had not only given chase, but had actually recovered one of the trucks. Having it returned to Confederate hands didn't help Vanderspool or his Kel-Morian partner financially, of course, but it did make him look like a hero. And for that, he was rewarded handsomely, with the honor of being named full colonel, a title he'd schemed long and hard to attain.

The missing truck was still nowhere to be found, however, which was very costly for both parties. At an emergency meeting the next day, his KM partner, Aaron Pax, was furious, accusing Vanderspool of double-crossing him by stealing the truck for himself. Vanderspool convinced him otherwise, promised he'd get to the bottom of it, and countered with his own questions about the attack. Why had things gone down the way they had, with so many extra men and firepower? All their other schemes had worked like clockwork, but this one was a total disaster. His partner claimed ignorance, but the colonel was not so sure.

But after interrogating the two captured drivers from the armory, Vanderspool had the name of a Kel-Morian superior, and was able to piece together why the small operation had turned into a full-scale assault. It was a classic case of greed gone wrong: The superior had discovered the scheme and piggybacked onto the mission, sending out his own troops and hiring civilian drivers to steal the trucks. But it was poorly planned, and, thankfully, turned out to be a failure for the interloper; as the trucks left in a convoy, they were intercepted by their rightful captors and reclaimed, which at least made Vanderspool feel a little better—he'd hate to think that the scheming pig had made off with any loot. Even so, Vanderspool was hell-bent on revenge, and he would get it. He always did.

For now, though, he needed to find the missing truck; it was the most valuable of them all by a huge margin—it was filled with components for weapons and armor upgrades, which were worth nearly eight million credits all by themselves—and Vanderspool was determined to find it. So where was it? Findlay was a convicted criminal, after all. . . . Not for theft, but the guy was depraved enough to attack his commanding officer. Something wasn't right with him. Did *he* know where the truck was?

And what about the other members of Findlay's squad? Were they a bunch of degenerates that finally found their rightful leader? Or was the entire group pure as the driven snow? There was no way to know—but he would do his best to find out. "At ease," Vanderspool said, and forced a smile. "It's good to see you again, Findlay. . . . Please, have a seat."

"Thank you, sir." Tychus sat down. He felt uncharacteristically nervous. What was Vanderspool's angle? What was he after?

"It took guts to chase those looters and recover that truck," Vanderspool said, "and I'm proud of you."

The truth was that Tychus had been hell-bent on stealing *both* vehicles and hiding them in the ruins of neighboring Whitford. Raynor had talked him out of it. Because, as the younger man put it, *"if you bring one of the trucks back, they'll believe your story. And if you don't it will look like the entire squad went AWOL in the middle of a battle. Which strategy sounds better to* you?"

Tychus had been resistant to Raynor's smart-assed input at first, but was glad he had listened now, as Vanderspool's dark eyes bored into him. Maybe Jim Raynor would prove to be of some value, after all. "Thank you, sir."

"So," Vanderspool continued, "thanks to your outstanding performance, it's my pleasure to inform you that you and your men are going to be part of a new mixed-force unit that I will have the honor to lead.

"The 321st Colonial Rangers Battalion is going to be an elite outfit—but the team you'll be part of will be even more remarkable. We're calling it the Special Tactics and Missions platoon, or STM. It will receive the very latest armor and related technology. Sound good?"

It sounded *bad*. Very bad, because anytime the Marine Corps said that something was "special," it wasn't. And membership in elite units always meant more work, more inspections, and more attention from above. All of which would be detrimental to Operation Early Retirement. "Yes, sir," Tychus lied. "I can hardly wait to get started."

"That's the spirit!" Vanderspool replied cheerfully. "You'll be pleased to know that we're bringing in a young fire-breather to lead the STM platoon. His name is Lieutenant Quigby, and you'll have an opportunity to meet him shortly."

By that time Tychus had taken note of a change to Vanderspool's uniform. So he took the opportunity to suck up, in hopes that doing so would help put whatever doubts the officer might have had to rest. "I look forward to working with Lieutenant Quigby, sir . . . and congratulations on your promotion."

Tychus could sense the wheels turning as Vanderspool smiled. "Thank you, Sergeant. Good luck with your new assignment. I plan to keep an eye on you."

Did the last comment constitute a threat? Yes, Tychus thought that it did, but forced a smile anyway. "Thank you, sir. I'll do my best." And with that he got up to leave.

Vanderspool watched the other man go. Maybe he was wrong. Maybe Sergeant Findlay was exactly what he appeared to be. A big, simple-minded brute that would continue to be a useful tool until such time as the Kel Morians killed him. And maybe the men who reported to him were choir boys. But maybes could be dangerous, especially with so much at stake, so an insurance policy was in order. And, unless Vanderspool missed his guess, there was bound to be one just waiting to be used.

Three days after the official creation of the 321st Colonial Rangers Battalion, Lieutenant Marcus Quigby mustered his platoon on a field adjacent to Fort Howe's firing range and took the opportunity to introduce himself. The platoon consisted of three squads—none of which were up to full strength.

That didn't stop Quigby from strutting back and forth in front of his tiny command as if it were a full regiment, a brand-new swagger stick under his arm, as his other hand jabbed the air. Quigby loved to give long, boring speeches, insisted on following every regulation to the letter, and micromanaged everything his subordinates did. None of which endeared the officer to his troops.

But thanks to his talent for engineering—and the fact that his father was a general—Quigby had been given a slot in what might become a very visible organization. Just the thing to jump-start his career if everything went well. None of which mattered to Raynor, who found it difficult to take the young officer seriously. "What an asshole," he said out of the corner of his mouth, which caused Zander to grin.

Quigby's tirade had clearly reached a climax as he jabbed a finger toward the sky. "So," he said portentously, "with all that in mind, the time has come for a *new* generation of hardskins. I'm talking about armor with advanced capabilities that will enable this platoon to clear obstacles during conventional attacks, carry out missions behind enemy lines, and reinforce units temporarily cut off from a larger force. Behold the future!"

Somebody's timing was off, so Quigby was left standing there, his finger pointing at the clear blue sky for a good four seconds before a muted roar was heard. That was when Raynor and the rest of the troops saw something leap into the air a thousand feet down-range and come their way.

The bright red hardskin arrived a few seconds later, turned a full circle as if to display the jet pack that kept it aloft, and lowered itself to the ground. The big boots produced twin puffs of dust as they hit, and the power pack made a high-pitched whining noise as it spooled down.

It was an impressive demonstration and Quigby was clearly proud of it. His beady eyes, framed by disproportionately bushy eyebrows, darted from one face to the next. "Not bad, eh?" he demanded in a high, squeaky voice. "This is a demonstration model, which was modified to meet Technician Feek's needs. But it's similar to what each member of the platoon will receive after you qualify on standard CMC-225s. Fortunately for us, Sergeant Findlay is an expert where the 225s are concerned—and will be able to bring the rest of you up to speed. Isn't that right, Sergeant?"

The whole thing was news to Tychus, who came to attention. "Sir! Yes, sir."

"I thought as much," Quigby said to no one in particular. "Once we move on to the CMC-230-XEs and -XFs, it will be time for Mister Feek to take over the training effort."

"Hello," the man in the hardskin said, his voice booming through external speakers. "My name is Hiram Feek. I'm looking forward to providing you with instruction on how to operate a Procyon Industries 230-series hardskin, otherwise known as

Thunderstrike armor. The unit I'm wearing today is a CMC-230-XF, sometimes referred to as a fire-bat, due to its unique capabilities."

That was when a whirring sound was heard as the CMC-230's helmet was removed and the suit cycled open to reveal the man inside. Harnack let out an audible gasp. Feek was only about four feet tall and stood on special risers. He had a shaved head and a generously proportioned mustache that bobbed up and down as he addressed the men.

"As is the case with any new weapons system, the 230-series suits will require some fine-tuning before thay are put into service. So please keep me informed regarding any operational issues that you run into over the next few weeks. Your feed-back will help Procyon Industries to perfect this new generation of hardskins."

And with that the suit cycled closed and the helmet clicked on. Feek raised an arm, pointed it over their heads, and shot a gout of flame into the air.

"That's beautiful!" Harnack said reverently. "Can I have one?"

"Yes," Lieutenant Quigby answered indul-gently, "you can."

Fleet Petty Officer Third Class Lisa Cassidy had been confined to Fort Howe's brig for two days.

Not all that long a period of time for most brig rats, but Cassidy was addicted to a drug called crab, a powerfully intoxicating depressant. And two intervals was a long time to go without a hit. So she was grumpy, twitchy, and a bit paranoid as a series of clangs were heard outside of her cell and two female MPs came to collect her.

Enlisted people had a tendency to stick together, so when a corporal opened the door to Cassidy's cell, there was something akin to sympathy in her eyes. "Time to come out, Cassidy. You got a visitor."

Cassidy frowned. "If it's the chaplain, or the morale officer, tell them to go flick themselves. Or each other."

The MPs laughed. "No, it ain't either one of them," the corporal responded. "Colonel Vanderspool wants to talk to you."

"What'd you do, girl?" the other MP inquired. "Get up in some general's face?"

"Not that I remember," Cassidy replied, as she stood. "Are you going to shackle me?"

"Sorry," the corporal replied apologetically. "Them's the rules."

Cassidy held her wrists out, felt cold metal tighten around them, and heard the usual click. With that formality out of the way she was ordered to precede the MPs down a gleaming corridor to a checkpoint, and from there through a maze of hallways to a room labeled VISITOR 2.

Once the shackles were removed, she was ordered to enter. The room was empty except for two chairs and a table, all of which were bolted to the floor. So she sat on the table and looked around. It didn't take long to spot the spy eye mounted up in a corner. She gave the camera a one-fingered salute, felt a wave of nausea, and knew her stomach was already empty. The cramps would start soon and she wondered if she'd be able to get through the meeting first.

Vanderspool, who was watching a monitor in a surveillance room, smiled grimly as the young woman flipped him off. "So this is the one?"

Captain Marvin Ling was in charge of both the brig and base security. He'd been wounded while trying to defend the main gate and still had a bandage wrapped around his head. Ling's eyes shifted from the monitor to Vanderspool. "Yes, sir. She fits the description. Petty Officer Cassidy is intelligent, good at what she does, and addicted to crab. And, according to an evaluation performed six months ago, she may be addicted to the adrenaline rush associated with combat as well."

Ling's hand went up to touch the bandage that was wrapped around his head. "She was in the thick of it the other night, gave aid to at least a dozen swabbies, and shot a Kel-Morian Air Wolf in the face."

Vanderspool eyed the woman on the monitor. She was clutching herself as a series of tremors ran through her body. "And then?"

Ling shrugged. "And then she went to her stash, got binked, and passed out. Some of my people found Cassidy unconscious in a lavatory and brought her in. According to her personnel file this is the third time she's been in the brig for a drug-related offense, and that makes her a prime candidate for a work camp."

"Or maybe she can find redemption in some other way," Vanderspool replied as he got up to leave. "I'll find out. And Captain Ling . . ."

"Sir?"

"Have someone turn off the camera and audio pickup in that room. The matter that Petty Officer Cassidy and I are about to discuss is classified."

Ling nodded. The motion made his head hurt. "Yes, sir."

An MP escorted Vanderspool down a corridor, through a checkpoint, and from there to the door labeled VISITOR 2.

Having unlocked the door, the MP pulled it open, allowed Vanderspool to pass through, and returned to the hall. There was an audible click as the door closed. Cassidy stood and was about to come to attention when Vanderspool waved the courtesy off. "There's no need for that, Petty Officer Cassidy. I'm Colonel Vanderspool. Please have a seat."

Now that he could see Cassidy more clearly, Vanderspool realized that the medic was quite pretty. Something that could be advantageous, given what he had in mind for her. Cassidy had short, brown hair worn in a shaggy cut that might have made her appear boyish except for the fact she had a very feminine face. The look in her large, luminous eyes was worldly and vulnerable at the same time. A combination that exerted a definite pull on Vanderspool and would probably appeal to other men as well. Like those in Findlay's squad. There was no way to be certain, but the odds were pretty good. "So, my dear," Vanderspool said, adopting an avuncular tone. "I hear you are a crab addict."

Doc had been in the Colonial Fleet long enough to know that something unusual was taking place. Colonels didn't come to visit lowly medics unless there was a reason. Vanderspool wanted something from her, but what? Sex? Yes, she could tell he was attracted to her, but figured there was something else in play, too—something he wanted and she had the power to give. And, being an expert at getting what she wanted, Doc knew how to play it. *If* she could fight off the withdrawal symptoms long enough to take advantage of the opportunity. "Yes, sir."

Vanderspool nodded. "Good. I'm glad you

chose to admit it. Had you said anything else I would have left you to your fate. You'll be happy to know that I'm not here to lecture you about the evils of crab or to threaten you with punishment. Word is, crab has become increasingly hard to find these days. So I'm here to offer you a continued opportunity to ply your skills as a medic, and access to a reasonable amount of crab, in return for regular reports on a certain group of soldiers. Soldiers who may or may not be engaged in illegal activities. Would you be interested in such a role?"

Something shifted deep inside Cassidy's brooding eyes. "And if I say no?"

"Then you'll be sent to a work camp. Not as a punishment for saying 'No,' but because that's where you were headed before this conversation took place."

"Then my answer is yes."

"Excellent," Vanderspool replied. "You won't be sorry."

CHAPTER EIGHTEEN

"Three members of the UNN reporting staff were apprehended by Confederate officials today under charges of sedition related to last week's unauthorized airing of war footage. UNN president Preston Shale released a statement condemning the reporters for acting against the interests of the Universal News Network and Confederate citizens across the sector. He also thanked the new staff member responsible for blowing the whistle, a journalist named Handy Anderson. We'll be interviewing Anderson tonight for his insights into the case as well as the road that led him from the battlefield to the news desk."

Max Speer, *Evening Report* for UNN
October 2488

THE CITY OF WHITFORD, NEAR FORT HOWE,
ON THE PLANET TURAXIS II

As the last moon dropped below the horizon, and day finally faded to night, stars appeared in the sky. Occasional rectangles of buttery light could be seen here and there, but most of what had once been the city of Whitford was soon engulfed by the steadily encroaching darkness and everything that went with it.

By some miracle the city's two-story bell tower was still standing and provided an excellent vantage point from which to survey the mostly deserted ruins below. There were still some inhabitants, of course, citizens who had chosen to live in the rubble rather than follow one of the highways out into the countryside to lead a miserable life in one of the teeming refugee camps.

Such individuals were cautious, however, and had to be, since all manner of predators prowled the city's remains. Thanks to the night vision capability built into his helmet, Raynor could see occasional rectangles of brighter green that marked internally heated structures, all of which had to be fortified.

There were individual blobs of light, too, some standing sentry duty on rooftops, while others hurried through the ruins trying to complete some errand or other before complete darkness lay claim to the land. The occasional *pop, pop, pop* of small arms fire could be heard as people shot feral dogs, fought off intruders, or settled scores. Whitford was a dangerous place to live—and a dangerous place to do business. "Who did you say our customer is?" Raynor asked.

Tychus spoke around the cigar that was clenched between his teeth as he continued to examine the city via his own visor. "Why clutter up that busy little head of yours with unnecessary information? Suffice it to say that he's a friend of a friend."

"Glad to hear it," Raynor said lightly. "I was afraid he might be a criminal or something."

The whole question of what to do with the loot had been discussed over beers the night before. Tychus had claimed to have a buyer lined up and was willing to pay each member of the team a fee if they would help deliver the goods.

Most of the team was enthusiastic about the idea, Raynor being the exception, since the whole truck-stealing episode had continued to weigh on his conscience. *"Absolutely not. I don't want anything to do with it,"* Raynor had said.

As the guys discussed it further, Raynor became irritated at the notion that Tychus would get to keep most of the money. *"Why wouldn't everybody share equally?"* Raynor demanded.

"I'm the one with the contacts—so I should get a bigger share," Tychus responded, eyeing the faces around him.

"That's a crock," Raynor replied heatedly. *"There wouldn't be any loot without the team!"*

Tychus seemed to consider it for a moment, then leaned back, as a lazy smile appeared on his face. *"You have me there, Jim . . . equal shares it is."*

"That's right!" Raynor said.

And it was only then, as Tychus took a swig of beer, his smile spreading across his face, that Raynor realized he had been conned. The guy was smooth, *very* smooth.

"Come on," Tychus said, pulling Raynor out of his thoughts. "It's time to go down and collect our money. The kid will keep an eye on our neighbors. Ain't that right, Kydd?"

Like the rest of the squad, Kydd was supposed to be thirty miles to the west, getting drunk in the town of Orley, where an officially sanctioned R&R facility had been established for that purpose. And with any luck at all they would be there later that evening, once the deal was done. Strangely, given his former station in life, the prospect of providing security for an illegal transaction didn't bother him in the least. Perhaps that had something to do with the way he had been recruited into the Marine Corps—and the fact that he was doing something he was good at for a change. Kydd looked up from the Bosun FN92 sniper rifle and nodded. "No worries, Sarge. I have you covered."

Raynor, who thought there was plenty to worry about, followed Tychus down a circular staircase to the chapel below. All of the windows were blacked out, and thanks to a liberated battery, lights hung here and there. The nave was barely large enough to hold the truck, which had been backed into it. An absolute necessity to prevent the vehicle from being spotted from the air.

Heavily draped double doors opened onto a courtyard and a shattered gate beyond. A luminescent Harnack was visible to the left, and Zander to the right. Both were standing adjacent to box-shaped structures that resembled tombs.

Raynor hoped the deal would go down smoothly. He wanted to score some money for his parents, but hoped he wouldn't have to kill anyone to get it. Since they were dealing with criminals, he knew violence was a possibility, so he was prepared for the worst. Of course now, having taken part in the theft of the trucks, he was a criminal himself. A shocking notion that he was still trying to assimilate.

Raynor's thoughts were interrupted by a burp of static and the sound of Kydd's voice in his ear. *"I have two vehicles approaching from the northeast,"* the sniper said. *"Both are about the right size and shape. Over."*

"Roger that," Raynor said, knowing the rest of the team had heard as well. "You know what to do. Over."

There was a double *click* by way of a response.

"Okay, everybody," Tychus said, "it's showtime!"

A few moments later two green blobs appeared at the gates and disgorged smaller green blobs, which entered the open courtyard. There was a pause while the various players eyed each other suspiciously, followed by another pause as the buyer's chief of security circled the area. Then, satisfied that the courtyard was reasonably safe, he spoke into a lip mic.

That was when the buyer entered the courtyard and paused to look around. Because of the night-vision technology Raynor was using, the details were hard to discern, but he had the impression of a portly middle-aged man wearing night goggles and a white suit. "What a shame," the man said sadly. "My daughter was married here. That was a very special day. What about you, citizen Smith?" the buyer said, as he looked from Raynor to Tychus. "Do you have children?"

"Probably," Tychus admitted. "But who can keep track? Did you bring the crystals?"

"Of course," the buyer said airily. "You know my reputation. So let's take a look at the components . . . the very latest in jammers if I'm not mistaken."

Raynor knew that Kydd was keeping watch, but he couldn't help but look around nervously. He still couldn't believe he had let Tychus rope him in—again. *This will be the last time,* he told himself.

"Follow me," Tychus replied, and led the man inside. If the buyer was shocked to discover that stolen electronics were being stored inside a chapel, he gave no sign of it as two of his employees jumped up onto the truck and began to inventory the cargo. All the crates had already been opened, in order to speed the process along, but it was still necessary to inspect the boxes on the bottom. So a good twenty minutes passed before the entire process was completed.

Finally, having received a positive report from his chief of security, the buyer declared himself satisfied. "It appears that everything is in order. . . . Here's your payment."

With that, the pear shaped blob waved one of his bodyguards forward. The functionary was carrying a metal case, which he presented to Tychus. The noncom opened it, inspected the crystals stored within, and passed a small, multi-spectrum analyzer over them. Then, having scanned the readout, he nodded approvingly. "They look good. . . . It's been nice doing business with you. Will you need help getting the truck out of here?"

"No, that won't be necessary," the buyer assured him. "Farewell, my friend . . . and stay safe. These are dangerous times."

With that the buyer returned to his vehicle while one of his men started the truck, and drove it out through the double doors and into the courtyard beyond. Dust kicked up as it passed through the gate.

Once the buyer was gone and peace had settled over the scene, Connor Ward slid the top of a tomb out of the way and stood up. His rocket launcher was loaded and ready at his side. "Damn . . . That's the last time I spend time in a tomb—until the last time I spend time in one!"

The comment might have been sufficient to elicit a chuckle from the others except that Kydd preempted the moment. *"Uh oh, here comes company, Sarge! I have about fifteen heat signatures. They're on foot and closing from the south. Over."*

Raynor swore bitterly. He'd been hoping for a clean exit.

"They were waiting until the buyer left, the bastards," Tychus observed, as the first muffled shot was heard. "They saw our customer arrive, figured some sort of deal was in progress, and now they plan to steal the proceeds."

Raynor knew that these people were prepared to kill his friends to get what they wanted, and he wasn't about to let that happen. "All right, Ryk . . . you know what to do. Thin them down. Over."

A shot rang out. "Hank . . . Max . . . get the combat car and drive it into the courtyard. Once you're in position we'll pull Kydd down out of the bell tower."

Both men nodded and vanished into the night. The combat car was hidden inside what had once been a store located two blocks away.

"Come on," Tychus said. "Kydd won't be able to get 'em all. Let's go out back and say 'howdy.'"

Tychus, Raynor, and Ward slipped out the back of the church as Kydd fired again. *"I missed that one,"* the sniper said flatly. *"Be careful! I think they plan to rush you. Over."*

Kydd's prophecy came true as a small army of

green blobs broke cover and were forced to weave their way between headstones as they sprinted forward. In the wake of the attack on Fort Howe, and the theft of the trucks, the team had been quick to bond. Now, faced with another common enemy, it was as though they had been fighting for years.

"I have them," Ward rumbled, and fired a rocket. The range was so short the missile barely had time to arm itself before striking the first attacker and exploding.

Raynor's visor automatically dampened the sudden flash of light, thereby preserving his vision. Once the explosion was over, only three blobs were visible, all running away. "Let 'em go, Ryk," Raynor said, "and come on down. We have what we came for. Let's get out of here."

Kydd, whose finger had already been in the process of tightening around the two-stage trigger, let go. Then, as the targets disappeared into ruins out beyond the graveyard, a question occurred to him. The hijackers, if that's what they were, had been running away. So why was he about to fire on them? Was it a game now? Made easy because blobs aren't people? The answer was painfully obvious. The problem was that he didn't feel all that guilty about it.

Kydd got up, made his way downstairs, and followed Raynor through the much-abused double doors. His buddies were waiting, the engine roared, and cool air wrapped him in a chilly embrace. The chapel, still radiating warmth collected during daylight hours, continued to glow.

FORT HOWE, ON THE PLANET TURAXIS II

Tychus liked Lisa Cassidy from the moment he first saw her. It was during the morning muster, and she was already present when the rest of the platoon arrived, standing at parade rest behind Lieutenant Quigby, who always made a point out of being there first. The medic was pretty, for one thing, and judging from the way she filled out her uniform, she was shapely as well. Qualities that Tychus was always on thc lookout for.

But in addition to Cassidy's obvious physical appeal, there was her attitude, which the entire platoon got a preview of when Quigby launched into one of his rants. This particular lecture was focused on the horrors of venereal disease, the negative impact that sexual relationships could have on unit cohesion, and the need for abstinence on the part of the entire platoon. That was when Doc came to attention and delivered a one-fingered salute to the officer's back, before returning to parade rest.

It was all that Raynor, Harnack, and the rest of them could do to keep from breaking out into laughter as Quigby finished his sermon and turned to introduce the medic. "Petty Officer Cassidy will monitor each one of you for symptoms," the officer said sternly, "and report them to me. I should add that she's part of an experiment to see if medics should be added to the table of organization for standard infantry units, and we're lucky to have her."

Not too surprisingly, Cassidy—upon whom Tychus had bestowed the nickname "Doc"—was invited to join Tychus, Raynor, and the rest of them as they left Fort Howe that evening. By the time they returned to base, Tychus had a possessive arm draped across the medic's shoulders, and, judging from her expression, she was happy with the arrangement. A fact that was something of a disappointment to Harnack, who would otherwise have taken a run at her. The whole thing was smoothly done, and when Doc made her first report to Vanderspool, he smiled.

More than two weeks had passed since the sale in Whitford. Long, hard weeks for everyone, including Lieutenant Quigby, Hiram Feek, and, to a lesser extent, Tychus, all of whom served as instructors. But once the steadily growing platoon mastered the CMC-225s, and graduated to the new CMC-230 series suits, Tychus went from instructor to student overnight. Because the Thunderstrike armor required a whole new set of skills—as crash after painful crash proved. It took both experience and good judgment to decide exactly how much power to apply during liftoff, maintain what Feek called "a heads-up posture" during transit, and to land without "making an ungodly mess" as Quigby referred to "non-compliant landings."

And Quigby was a stickler. Everyone suffered under his arrogant tutelage, but no one more than Doc Cassidy. The reason for that wasn't entirely clear, but probably had something to do with her lack of respect for him, which she signaled in subtle and not so subtle ways. Like forgetting to salute, call him "sir," or comply with regulations that she considered to be stupid.

As a result Quigby rode her constantly, always looking for fault, and always finding it. That made Doc angry, which led to the incident in which he was forced to take a full course of inoculations all over again because his medical records had been "lost."

It had gotten so bad that Quigby tried to have Cassidy transferred out, only to have the request turned down by the company commander, who claimed that Colonel Vanderspool was "monitoring the situation." Whatever that meant.

But now, as the officer sucked a mouthful of water through the tube in his helmet and swallowed it, he had every reason to feel proud as he made his way down the line of fully armored soldiers that comprised the mixed-forced battalion known as the 321st Colonial Rangers.

Sergeant Findlay and the first squad stood ramrod straight, their blue armor gleaming in the morning sun. Quigby had come to rely on the huge noncom, who, in spite of his criminal record, was clearly more trustworthy than the rest.

Lance Corporal Raynor was next in line, but a bit too smart for his own good and therefore presumptuous. It would be a long time before he was promoted.

Quigby was slightly disappointed to see that Doc Cassidy's hardskin looked good. Her armor was different from all the rest; it had red crosses on both shoulders and the word MEDIC emblazoned across her chest. Would that save her from a Kel-Morian rocket? No, probably not, but it was worth a try.

Suddenly Quigby felt slightly dizzy. Was it the Vilnorian curry he'd consumed the night before? Yes, probably. His mouth felt dry, so he drank some water, and was grateful when the vertigo disappeared.

Private Harnack's red firebat suit was noticeably different from the blue armor the others wore, and not just because of the color. The tanks built into the hardskin gave it a bulky profile, which the enemy would soon learn to fear.

And then there was Private Ward, whose suit was equipped with two rocket launchers, one mounted on each shoulder. Both were capable of firing four fire-and-forget missiles. Just the thing for battling armored Kel-Morians, which Ward was clearly eager to do.

And so it went as Quigby eyed Zander and the rest of squad one before turning his attention to squad two. That was when the dizziness returned. He staggered and nearly lost his balance. Sergeant Stetman, who was in charge of the second squad, was there to steady him. "Are you okay, sir? Should I have Doc take a look?"

"I'm fine," Quigby insisted impatiently, as he shook the noncom off. If there was a worse possibility than submitting himself to Cassidy's not-so-tender ministrations, the officer couldn't imagine what it was.

Besides, Colonel Vanderspool was in the process of reviewing the new battalion on the parade ground nearby. In fact, Quigby could hear the sound of martial music, the occasional clash of cymbals, and knew his father was among the VIPs seated near the carefully arranged buffet. And opportunities to impress *General* Quigby didn't come along every day.

So Quigby fought off the vertigo and accompanying nausea long enough to complete a perfunctory inspection, checked the readout in the upper right-hand corner of his HUD, and saw that it was time to prepare for what was intended to be a very spectacular jump. The idea was to leap *over* the audience as the last of the battalion's conventional troops marched past, and land facing the VIPs in perfect formation! It was the sort of thing that was bound to leave a lasting impression.

There was a problem, however, a very urgent problem, which Quigby was powerless to solve. Suddenly he needed to go to the bathroom! And unlike some combat suits that were equipped to recycle waste, the prototype was not. Sergeant Findlay could lead the troops, of course, but that would mean missing a rare opportunity to impress his father, so Quigby chose to gamble instead.

Thanks to the fact that the ceremonial jump had been practiced at least fifty times, the orders came naturally, as Quigby instructed the platoon to stand by, and watched the last few seconds tick away. Then, as he said, "Jump!" the entire platoon took to the air.

There wasn't much to do on the way up, as thirty-six sets of armor soared over the line of trees that bordered the parade ground and quickly reached apogee. At that point it was necessary to cut power for a second and fire steering jets as gravity pulled the hardskins down. The problem was that Quigby had lost control of his bowels by then, along with the CMC-230-XE itself.

The result was an amazing and almost perfectly synchronized *THUMP* as thirty-five sets of boots hit the ground at once, each gleaming soldier standing at attention. All except for Quigby, that is, who landed on his back in the middle of

JIM RAYNOR OUR MOST FAMOUS PATRON
321ST COLONIAL RANGERS BATTALION, HEAVEN'S DEVILS

RAYNOR'S RAIDERS
FIGHT FOR FREEDOM
JOIN THE BATTLE AGAINST THE DOMINION TODAY

the buffet table, thereby destroying it and showering all of the VIPs with flying food!

People began to scream.

That was bad enough, but the moment was made immeasurably worse when the suit's onboard computer decided that Quigby was in need of immediate medical attention and blew itself open so that medical personnel could access his body. That left a mostly naked Quigby lying spread-eagled on top of the wreckage with a dazed expression on his face, and semi-liquid feces all over his light-colored pants. General Quigby was not amused. Nor was Colonel Vanderspool.

Without opening his visor, Tychus communicated with his squad over the comm. "Doc? What the hell happened? What's wrong with Quigby? Over."

There was a long moment of silence—followed by Cassidy's voice. *"It's really hard to say, Sarge, but if I had to guess, I'd say it was something in the water. Over."*

That was followed by an explosion of laughter, the sound of an approaching siren, and an order from the battalion's furious executive officer. The review was over.

CHAPTER NINETEEN

"No question about it; I'm gonna be strong and tough and smart, and I'm gonna help all the farmers here get free from them bankers. Stick by your people: that's what Pa says."

Tom Omer, in an excerpt from a 5th grade report entitled "When I Grow Up"
June 2478

FORT HOWE, ON THE PLANET TURAXIS II

The sun was low in the sky, shadows lay long on the ground, and the air was starting to cool as Lisa Cassidy prepared to leave the base. Although the nearby city of Whitford lay in ruins, and the Honky Tonk District that adjoined Fort Howe had suffered some collateral damage during the recent attack, the HTD—as the troops referred to it—was not only resilient but still open twenty-five hours a day. And as Doc slipped out through the west gate, the two-block-deep strip of tawdry bars, strip joints, and flophouses took her in.

The HTD was her *real* home in many respects, since none of the bartenders, thieves, or hookers who lived there thought less of Cassidy because she was a crab addict. On the contrary, they understood her in a way that her military buddies couldn't. And that granted Doc a sort of sleazy legitimacy her fellow rangers couldn't hope for and weren't seeking.

Still, Cassidy liked the other members of her squad well enough, even if they were absurdly easy to manipulate. Something that made her feel slightly guilty but a bit smug, too. Because, at the end of the day, it was each person's responsibility to look out for themselves.

And in her case that meant feeding Colonel Vanderspool a steady stream of information in return for relative freedom and a steady supply of crab. And that was a delicate task. Because if she said too much, her squad mates might find out, and if she said too little, Vanderspool would send her to a work camp.

"Hey, hottie, you need some company?" a soldier inquired hopefully, as Doc made her way past the sidewalk table where he and his buddies were seated.

"I'll let you know if I get that desperate," the medic said as she cleared the bar and took a right. She could hear the soldiers laughing as she followed a narrow passageway back between two buildings. It reeked of urine, was littered with empties, and decorated with graffiti.

The walkway emptied into a rather pleasant courtyard that fronted a restaurant called The Gourmand. The establishment was way too expensive for enlisted people, which was one of the reasons Vanderspool chose to eat there. That and the fact that his mistress had an apartment on the second floor.

So Cassidy weaved between linen-covered tables to the restaurant's south wall, climbed a set of stairs to the second floor, and followed a wraparound balcony to the front of the building, just as she had on prior occasions. Vanderspool was sitting on a wicker chair near a pair of glass doors. They were open to the apartment beyond, and the faint strains of classical music could be heard from within.

Like his guest, the officer was dressed in civvies. His outfit consisted of a yellow silk shirt, nicely tailored brown slacks, and a pair of basket weave slipons. He held a glass of red wine in his right hand and there was a bottle at his elbow. He nodded formally. "There you are, my dear . . . right on time. Punctuality is a military virtue, isn't it? And it has to be since lives are often at stake. Please sit down. Would you care for a glass of wine?"

"No, sir. Thank you," Cassidy replied politely, as she took a seat.

Vanderspool winked knowingly. "It can't compare to ten milligrams of crab, I suppose. . . . Although it's a helluva lot cheaper!"

Doc forced a smile. "Yes, sir."

"So," Vanderspool said reflectively, as he took a sip of wine. "What can you tell me about the unbelievable fiasco that took place the day before yesterday?"

Cassidy knew the officer was referring to the review—and the manner in which Lieutenant Quigby had been publicly humiliated. "Tell you, sir?" she inquired innocently. "I'm not sure what you mean."

"Don't be coy," Vanderspool said sternly. "You aren't very good at it—and it pisses me off. We had the water from Quigby's suit analyzed. It was laced with a couple of powerful drugs, plus a fast-acting laxative. The lieutenant thinks *you* were out to get him—but I'm betting on Findlay or one of his men."

Doc's first instinct was to blame Tychus, since that was the path of least resistance, but on second thought she realized how stupid such a course might be. Because if the colonel had one spy, he could have *two,* and the whole squad knew she was responsible. So she looked Vanderspool in the eye and told the truth. "Lieutenant Quigby is correct, sir . . . *I* was responsible."

Vanderspool was so surprised by the admission that he sloshed wine onto the tablecloth as he set the glass down. *"You?"* he demanded. "But why?"

"Two reasons," Cassidy answered calmly. "First, I really detest the little bastard. And, no offense, sir, but some officers behave like assholes just for the fun of it.

"Second, these guys have a very tight relationship. I'm in, but jerking Quigby around solidified my position. Now they really trust me. Wouldn't you say that's important, sir?"

A full five seconds of silence passed. During that time the medic saw a number of expressions come and go on Vanderspool's face, including anger, calculation, and a grudging smile. "I have to give you credit," the officer said. "You are a scheming bitch. No offense intended," he added sarcastically.

Doc felt a sense of relief. "Thank you, sir. No offense taken."

"So, how is it going?"

"It's going well, sir. Once I leave here I'll join the rest of the squad at Three Fingered Jack's down the street. That's where they like to hang out."

Vanderspool nodded. "Good. Now, one last thing before you go . . . I don't give a damn about Lieutenant Quigby, but I *do* care about his father, the *general,* and your scheme made all three of us look bad. I don't like that. I don't like that at all. So here's a piece of advice: *Don't ever do something like that again."*

Doc heard a floorboard creak and began to turn but it was too late. Two flat-eyed soldiers, both in civilian attire, stood directly behind her. One jerked the medic out of her chair and put a full nelson on her as the other came around and positioned himself in front of her. "Give her three shots," Vanderspool said grimly. "But leave her face alone."

Cassidy was tough, or believed that she was, but after three successive blows to the stomach she fell to her knees and threw up. Some of the vomit oozed down between the floorboards and fell on the table below.

Doc heard a woman's voice from somewhere inside the apartment. "Javier? I'm tired of waiting."

Vanderspool rose. His voice was hard. "Take her out to the street. That's where trash belongs."

Cassidy held up a hand to stall the marines off, made use of the bottom part of the tablecloth to wipe her mouth, and struggled to her feet. Then, having executed a near perfect about-face, she left.

When Cassidy arrived at Three Fingered Jack's she was surprised to see that her normally high-spirited squad mates were sitting around slumped in their chairs. And if his hang-dog expression was any guide, Raynor was the most upset of all.

Feek was standing on the bench next to Raynor, apparently offering words of comfort. "What's going on?" Doc inquired, as she took a seat next to Harnack.

"This guy Tom Omer . . . one of Jim's good friends from home," Harnack said soberly. "We all shipped out together from Shiloh. Well, Tom got tore up pretty bad during the fight at Firebase Zulu. He lost one of his lungs and one of his arms. Anyway, we just got the news that Tom died. The wounds were too much for him."

Harnack looked toward Raynor and back. Cassidy saw that the others were listening, too. "Jim was leading our squad the day Tom was hit so he feels like it was *his* fault. But that's bullshit. I was there and it was bad luck. Nothing more."

"That's true," Kydd chimed in. "There wasn't anything Jim could have done."

"They're right," Doc said, as she looked at Raynor. "I've seen a lot of people die in this war, and most of the time there isn't any rhyme or reason to it."

Raynor looked up from the tabletop. There was a haunted look in his eyes. "His parents are going to be devastated, and it's all my fault. What if I'd stayed home? What if I was there right now? Maybe Tom would be alive."

"Yeah," Zander put in, "and maybe the rest of us would be dead. Because if you hadn't been there, somebody else would have been in charge and who knows how *they* would have handled the situation."

"Exactly," Kydd agreed, as Tychus arrived with a fresh bottle of Scotty Bolger's. "All I know is that you did a lot better job than *I* could have. Tom would say the same."

"This is for Tom Omer," Tychus rumbled, as he refilled Raynor's glass. "I didn't know him, but you say he was a good soldier, and that's good enough for me. Because *you're* the real deal, so Omer's the real deal, and that's all we need to know. Now, pick up that glass, and let's drink a toast . . . to Tom Omer, who went to war, and did the best he could. We won't forget him."

It was the longest speech, maybe the *only* speech, Raynor had ever heard Tychus give. And unlike so much of what the older man normally had to say, there hadn't been a trace of sarcasm, condescension, or irony. The words couldn't make the pain go away, nothing could accomplish that, but they were the source of some much-needed comfort. It was a side of Tychus Raynor hadn't seen before and one that he welcomed.

"Hear, hear," Feek said, as he raised a glass. "Here's to Tom Omer."

The words echoed around the table, and as Cassidy raised her glass, she felt like what she was: a fake.

* * *

The sun had barely broken company with the eastern horizon as the old truck came to a screeching stop next to the heavily guarded gate, and Hiram Feek jumped to the ground. It was a long drop for someone of his stature, but he was used to that, and he absorbed the shock with bent knees.

Then, having waved good-bye to the elderly driver, Feek hurried across the street to the west gate, where his retinas were scanned and the machine whirred as it ate his Priority One Civilian Pass and spit it back out again.

Seconds later the technician was inside Fort Howe, where he made straight for the barracks in which the first squad, STM platoon, 321st Colonial Rangers Battalion was quartered. Though not a member of the outfit himself, Feek felt a natural bond with the men and women who were slated to wear his creations. And the squad had adopted Feek as one of their own. Like them, he had left his family behind in order to fight—in his own way—for the cause. But right now, he had even more important matters to attend to.

Having arrived in front of the building, Feek pulled the door open, pounded up a flight of stairs, and went looking for Raynor. Because even though Tychus was bigger and had more stripes on his arms, Raynor was generally the man with a plan. And given the kind of trouble Zander and Ward had gotten themselves into, it was going to take one helluva plan to get them out.

* * *

Raynor was dreaming a good dream when someone shook his shoulder. He opened his eyes, saw Feek, and closed them again. "Go away. . . . We have two days off and I plan to spend both of them in bed."

"You can't," Feek insisted. "Zander and Ward are in trouble. You need to get them out."

Raynor swore, sat up, and swung his feet over onto the cold floor. It was early, and the entire platoon had the weekend off, so just about everyone was still in bed. Except for Zander and Ward, that is. Their racks were empty and neat enough to pass an inspection. Raynor yawned. "Where are they? In the brig?"

"No," Feek replied urgently. "They're almost twenty miles northwest of here, unless the bandits took them somewhere else, and I wouldn't know—"

"Wait—*bandits*?" Raynor demanded incredulously, suddenly alert. "What the hell are you talking about?"

"It all started a couple of weeks ago," Feek explained patiently. "Suddenly Zander had lots of money. I asked him where it came from, but he wouldn't say."

Raynor knew the source but saw no reason to explain. He trusted Feek, but the fewer people who knew about the theft the better. "So?" he asked. "Where do the bandits come in?"

"Zander bought a lot of food with the money and hired a truck," Feek responded.

Raynor groaned and held up a hand. "Don't tell me. . . . Let me guess. He loaded the food onto the truck and headed for some refugee camp or other."

"That's right," Feek agreed. "Ward and I agreed to go with him and provide security in return for a couple of beers. But somewhere along the line word of the shipment must have leaked out—because we were only about halfway there when we ran into a Confederate checkpoint—"

"—except it wasn't a Confederate checkpoint," Raynor finished for him. "It was a roadblock put in place by the bandits."

"Right again," Feek conceded. "So they took all of the food, plus Zander and Ward. I managed to slip away." He indicated his small stature. "I had to hitchhike back—but I came as quickly as I could."

Raynor felt as though he'd been punched in the stomach. "Thanks, Hiram." He rubbed his eyes and held his hand there for a few seconds, deep in thought. Finally he lifted his head. "Okay, roust Harnack, Kydd, and Doc. But don't bother the rest of the platoon. Understood?"

Feek nodded. "What about Tychus?"

"I'll take care of Tychus."

"How?" Feek asked. "I mean, no offense, Jim," he added, "but Tychus isn't known for random acts of philanthropy."

"These people are bandits, right? So they have loot," Raynor responded. "That'll get his attention. Plus, don't underestimate Tychus. He may look hard—but he has a heart of gold."

When Feek smiled, his mustache went up and sideways at the same time. "And a liver of gold, lungs of gold, and kidneys of gold," he responded.

Raynor forced a chuckle. "Yeah, something like that. . . ." He patted Feek on the shoulder approvingly. "We're going to need a vehicle."

Feek nodded. He had the truck that was used to ferry the Thunderstrike armor around and run errands. "I'll supply that."

"Good," Raynor said. "It's nice to know that we won't have to steal one."

The better part of an hour was required to get everyone up and off base where Feek was waiting to pick them up. The civilian was driving, Doc was riding shotgun, and Tychus, Raynor, Harnack, and Kydd were sitting in the back of the truck, sorting through the weapons that Feek had hidden there prior to leaving base. They had absolutely no idea where their friends were being held. But Raynor had a plan.

The single cargo light was on, but most of the illumination was coming in through the open roof vent. "This is farm country for the most part," Raynor said, shifting position so Harnack, Kydd, and Tychus could see him, "and I know something about farming. This area might *look* empty, like nobody's around, but believe me, there are eyes everywhere. So the locals know where the bandits are, and are either afraid of reprisals, or related to them! So they aren't going to talk. Not to the authorities, anyway. But if we can find the right person and make it worth their while, we might get a lead."

"Or we could take someone aside, kick his ass, and choke the location out of him," Harnack suggested hopefully.

"We'll use that as the backup plan," Raynor replied agreeably. "I told Feek to stop in a little town called Finner's Crossing. Odds are they have a pub there—that seems like a good place to start."

"*And* have a beer," Tychus put in. The truth was that he figured both Zander and Ward were dead. But he wasn't about to say that to Raynor, especially in light of Omer's recent death. Plus, it was to his benefit to hold the squad together. "A few brews and this trip will actually seem worthwhile."

"Ignore Sergeant Sunshine," Raynor advised as he shifted his gaze from Harnack to Kydd. "Kidnappings have been common around here ever since the wars started and the economy tanked. Some people will make money any way they can. Odds are the bandits are hoping that someone will come along and pay a price for our friends."

"Our *idiots* is more like it," Tychus said sourly. "You give them more money than any private has a right to and what do they do with it? They buy food and then give it away! Now that's stupid."

"Getting kidnapped *sucks*," Kydd mused aloud. "Look where it got *me*: I got drugged by some hooker and now I'm stuck with you jerk weeds for God knows how long."

A palpable silence filled the truck as everyone turned to look at the blank-faced sniper. Several seconds passed before Kydd erupted into boisterous laughter, and the rest of the crew followed suit.

Tychus shook his head in wonderment. "Look at Kydd, talkin' like he's one of us grunts and not some frou frou Old Family prick. The military's done you good, boy."

The small door that provided access to the cargo compartment from the cab was open, so Doc had been able to listen in. And she knew that if her squad mates had large sums of money there had to be a reason. That was the sort of information Vanderspool would want to know about.

It was too early in the day for a dose of crab, especially if some sort of fight was in the offing, but the stimpack was legal, and would help tide her over. The device made a gentle hissing sound as she pressed it against the back of her neck.

NEAR THE TOWN OF FINNER'S CROSSING, ON THE PLANET TURAXIS II

Finner's Crossing was five miles short of the spot where the food shipment had been hijacked. Rather than roll into the center of town where the vehicle would almost certainly attract attention, Raynor told Feek to park on the outskirts of the community next to a fueling station.

Then, after a good deal of argument from Harnack, it was agreed that Raynor and Tychus would walk into town while the rest stayed back to guard the truck. "We'll bring you something to eat," Raynor promised. "And remember, two of you should be awake at all times. That includes you, Hank."

That request provoked more complaints, and Raynor was in the process of explaining why his instructions were necessary when Tychus cut the conversation short by slamming the door and walking away.

The main road led the men past simple, wood frame houses that were equipped with solar-collecting roof tiles and satellite dishes. The dishes weren't operational, of course, not since the battles in space had begun, but might become functional again someday.

"Here's what we're fighting for," Raynor observed. "Neighborhoods like this one."

Tychus directed a sidelong glance his way.

"You're kidding, right? We're not fighting for the people who live in these houses, we're fighting for the people who run the government, and believe me, there's a big difference."

They passed a few isolated stores and came across what was obviously the town's main street. It was a sad-looking affair that consisted of one- and two-story commercial buildings, many of which were in desperate need of paint. "No, these people *are* the problem," Tychus continued, "because they choose to believe all the lies, and allow themselves to be victimized."

Raynor frowned. "Maybe some of them are like that—but plenty aren't. Take my parents. They know the government isn't perfect, but what's the alternative? The Kel-Morians? I don't think so."

"Nor do I," Tychus replied, peering left, then right, down the street. "Which is why I want to put a shitload of money aside, find a comfortable hole, and crawl inside. Which way?"

"I'm guessing left," Raynor replied.

"Left it is," Tychus replied, and turned in that direction.

They walked half a block before Tychus broke the silence. "What a dump."

Raynor, who still felt homesick from time to time, frowned. "Spoken like someone from a big city," he said neutrally.

"No," Tychus replied. "Spoken like someone from a crummy little nowhere dump. A place where truckers stopped to take a leak, where the smartest person in town was the waitress in Pappy's Café, and each day felt like it was a year long."

As they approached Hurley's Bar, Raynor realized that these were the only details Tychus had ever shared about his past. They'd gotten closer, but Raynor felt as though he knew nothing about Tychus. He wondered if he'd ever really know him, or whether it even mattered.

The tavern was housed in a low one-story building with plenty of empty parking places out front. Once inside, Raynor found himself in an atmosphere so familiar he might have been back home. A bar backed by what was clearly a kitchen occupied one corner of the large space. A row of sturdy posts supported the low, smoke-stained ceiling, and four-person booths lined the outer walls. A man who might have been a truck driver was seated at one of the mismatched tables at the center of the room, the bartender was drying glasses, and an elderly dog came out to greet them.

Raynor paused to give the animal a pat on the head before following Tychus over to the bar. The man standing behind it had a shaved head, bushy eyebrows, and the fist-flattened nose of an amateur prizefighter. Pictures of him could be seen here and there on the walls. Most were of him standing in some ring or other, bloodied fists raised in victory. Hurley perhaps? Yes, Raynor thought so.

The proprietor ran an eye over Tychus as if sizing him up before nodding politely. "Good afternoon, gents. What'll it be?"

"A couple of beers," Tychus responded.

"Coming up," the bartender replied, as he removed two mugs from the shelf over his head. "Would you like anything else? Something to eat, maybe?"

"Yes, we would," Raynor replied genially. "We'll take a look at your menu in a minute. . . . But first maybe you can help us out with some information. Some friends of ours were passing through the area recently, and they haven't come back. We'd like to find them. Any idea of who we might talk to? Or where we could look?"

Raynor saw the man's eyes cloud over as some suds ran down the side of the second mug. "Sorry to hear about your friends, mister. . . . But these are troubled times. People shouldn't travel at night. That'll be five credits."

"I didn't say they were traveling at night," Raynor said evenly, as he slipped some coins into the other man's hand. "But they were. We aren't asking you to name names. We're just looking for some information, that's all. Keep the change."

Hurley opened his hand to see two large coins. "Why don't you gents have a seat at one of the tables?" the proprietor suggested. "I'll bring a menu."

"How expensive was my beer?" Tychus asked as they went to sit down.

"Fifty credits," Raynor replied.

"That makes a hundred altogether," Tychus observed. "These beers had better be good. *Sucker.*"

Raynor and Tychus ordered enough food to feed themselves, Doc, Kydd, Harnack, and Feek. Then, with take-out bags in hand, they left. It wasn't until they were back in the truck, passing out thick sandwiches, that Raynor found the hand-drawn map. He grinned and gave it to Tychus. "Don't spill anything on my hundred-credit map. . . . How's your lunch?"

CHAPTER TWENTY

"Confederate sources today announced an exciting new plan that would allow UNN reporters onto actual military bases to observe the course of the war. This should silence many of the critics who have dubbed the Kel-Morian engagement 'the Quiet War' due to the Confederacy's hand in limiting media exposure. As one of the journalists selected for this opportunity, I'm very excited to get into the action and document the bravery of our soldiers. My security monitoring detail has assured me that it will be as unobtrusive as possible."

Max Speer, *Evening Report* for UNN
November 2488

The hand-dug pit was located in the middle of the barn, where it wouldn't be spotted from the air, and was sheltered from both sun and rain. Silas Trask, the man who made decisions for the gang, called it "the tank." As in "storage tank," because that was where he kept the women he doled out to his men, and captives that someone might be willing to pay for.

Half a dozen people occupied the miserable hole at the moment. That included the soldiers, who had been held for nearly two days, an elderly couple, and two terrified teenage girls—both of whom were slated to serve as entertainment the next time the bandits decided to party.

All of them stood in six inches of muddy groundwater and stared upward as a bright light appeared over their heads. "Hey, you two scumbags," a male voice called out, "you're up."

There was a splash as a ladder came sliding down to hit the bottom of the tank. Zander went up first, closely followed by Ward, as the other captives watched from below. It was hard to know what to hope for. The tank was horrible—but so were the men above. And once summoned there was no way to know what would happen to them next. Some people were returned to the tank and some were never seen again. Were they free, having been ransomed? Or were they dead? Zander prayed under his breath.

Heavily armed bandits were waiting. One of them pushed Zander toward the tractor-size door. The soldier could see that it was evening. "Get moving," the man said, and pushed again.

As he stumbled forward, Zander's eyes darted from side to side, searching for anything that might help. He was shorter than his captors, but he was strong, and all he needed was some sort of weapon. A shovel, a pitchfork, anything would do. But nothing of the sort was within reach as the two men were pushed, shoved, and kicked into the barnyard beyond. Two of the planet's moons were still up and arcing across the velvety blue sky.

The soldiers were marched across an open area to a modest farmhouse that was lit from within. That was something of a surprise to Zander, since he would have expected the bandits to black it out, but maybe they wanted the place to look normal.

Three wooden steps led up to the front door. It was already open and gave access to a brightly lit but mostly empty interior. Part of the ceiling had been damaged by a leaky roof, which explained why the bandits were living in the vehicle shed instead.

Trask, a dark-haired man with flashing white teeth and a taste for gaudy, clearly stolen jewelry, stood waiting for them. He scowled as the captives entered the room. "Look at that! Muddy footprints on my clean floor. . . . Have you no manners?"

Zander rolled his eyes and glanced over at Ward, who was quietly looking at his feet. Zander turned back toward Trask just in time to receive a swift knee to the groin. He doubled over, groaning, but was pulled back to a standing position by the thugs. "No, I guess you don't," Trask said patronizingly. "Please, gentlemen, have a seat."

Trask indicated two chairs that were positioned in the middle of the brightly lit living room, which, thanks to the shattered windows, was open to the outside. Zander didn't want to comply, not if Trask wanted him to, but was forced to step forward when a gun barrel jabbed him from behind. Ward was equally recalcitrant, but submitted with less of a struggle because he could see the odds were stacked against them. He was far from cowed, however, as was apparent from both his facial expression, and the set of his shoulders.

The chairs were positioned directly in front of the windows and securely fastened to the floor. Trask came around to stand directly in front of the two men as they were tied in place. "You want to hear something funny?" he inquired cheerfully. "Two men came looking for you! It appears your stupidity is contagious. They paid one hundred credits for a map that will lead them here. That means they have money. *My* money. Or it will be soon." And with that Trask chuckled contentedly as he and his men left the house.

"The bastard is using us for bait," Ward rumbled. "When the guys move in on the house they'll run into an ambush."

"Yeah," Zander said thoughtfully. "That's the plan anyway, but our buddies aren't stupid."

"Jim isn't," Ward agreed soberly, "but what about Tychus and Hank? They'll just come barreling in here without a second thought."

"Or a first." Both men let out a chuckle, which faded into contemplative silence.

"I'm sorry I got you into this mess," Zander said regretfully.

Ward shrugged. "It don't make much difference, Max. I'm not afraid to die."

"I just . . . I feel terrible is all. This was my idea and I screwed up. If we would've made it, we could've helped so many people, but . . . I shouldn't have brought you into this."

"Max, I'm ready anytime. Those Kel-Morian bastards killed my entire family—and I've been waitin' to get up there with my wife and kids. Only thing is, I was plannin' on taking a lot more of those sons of bitches with me. A *lot* more." He paused. "It's bad enough to see a soldier cut down by flying shrapnel. But when it's your daughter, and she bleeds out in your arms, you can't forget. That's what I see when I close my eyes, Max. . . . I see Dara looking up at me with those big brown eyes. 'Am I going to be okay, Daddy?' That's what she asked me, and I said, 'yes.' So that's why I want to live for a while longer. So I can kill as many of those murderers as I can."

"It ain't over till it's over," Zander replied, in an attempt to cheer the other man up. "So it's the Kel-Morians who oughtta be worried!"

The two men were silent for several minutes as they struggled with their bonds, trying to loosen them without success. Because of the thick cloud cover, evening had faded into complete darkness, and from under the bright lights of the living room, nothing could be seen outside. Which only added to the feeling of being on display.

"You know," Ward said, finally interrupting the sustained silence. "It was my fault. . . ."

"How so?"

"It was about six months ago, back on Tyrador VIII," Ward replied. "My wife said we should head out into the country, get away from the refinery. But I said, 'No, the KMs'll never come here.' That's what I said. And then they came! I'm the one who should have died. You understand, Max? *I'm* the one."

"Connor, I'm so sorry. It was bad luck, that's all. But hey, we all make mistakes. I know I have. All you can do is—"

Suddenly, a loud crash was heard, and Hiram Feek fell through the roof.

Moments before Feek fell through the roof, Raynor was lying next to a freshly deceased sentry about a hundred yards away, calculating his next move. Though not as powerful as the .50 caliber weapon Kydd normally carried, the lighter weapon Feek had provided from a surprisingly large stash of so-called test weapons was just as effective, and equipped with a silencer.

Within seconds, Kydd neutralized enough

sentries to allow Raynor to close in on the farmhouse and catch a glimpse of the way his friends had been positioned in the brightly lit living room. Once he figured out what the bandits expected him and his friends to do, he called Feek in for his jump.

And it was a thing of beauty! From liftoff to landing the textbook-perfect arc brought Feek and his armor crashing down through the farmhouse's roof and an upstairs bedroom to land only a few feet from the hostages.

The problem was, his right boot went through a couple of floorboards, leaving Feek in an awkward position. Wood splintered as Feek jerked his foot out, and the rifle made a clattering noise as he shot the lights out. The hostages were safe.

Then, just before the *real* battle began, there was a brief opportunity for Ward to speak. "Nice of you to drop in, Feek—what the hell took you so long?"

Tychus liked a good fight, especially when there was the prospect of profit and he knew the battle would go his way. As he and Harnack readied their weapons, there was a sudden crash, and the bandits, who had lost control of the hostages, came rushing out of various buildings, firing their weapons wildly.

The two marines weren't wearing armor, and

didn't need to, as the green blobs appeared on their HUDs and both men opened fire with carefully controlled bursts. Their assault weapons chattered, and blobs stumbled and fell, as Doc slipped into the barn. An M-1 bag was slung over her shoulder, and the pistol she always carried into battle was in her hand.

Cassidy paused in a shadow. That was when Trask turned away from the slaughter taking place out front and cut diagonally across the floor toward the side door. He was holding a needle-gun, and gold jewelry winked as he passed under a dangling glow strip.

Doc brought the pistol up in the approved two-handed grip, took careful aim, and shot Trask in the head. He staggered, tripped, and fell headfirst into the pit.

She heard girlish screams, followed by a sudden commotion down in the hole, and spotted a ladder. Then, having lowered it into place, she was there to help the hollow-eyed prisoners escape from the tank.

"You're an angel," the older woman said gratefully, as Doc gave her a hand.

Cassidy smiled. "I'm a lot of things, ma'am," she said grimly, "but an angel isn't one of them."

Once all the shooting was over, and the squad had complete control of the farm, they came together in the open space in front of the barn. "Damn," Harnack said as he looked around. "Are we good, or what?"

"Good for nothing," Zander said, straight-faced. "It would have been nice if you had arrived a bit earlier."

"And it would be nice if *you* would spend your money on booze and hookers," Tychus put in as he emerged from the barn. "And not necessarily in that order." Having stripped Trask of his jewelry, he was trying to force a garish-looking ring onto the little finger of his left hand.

"Which raises an important topic," Kydd interjected. "It seems to me that the people who got rescued should buy the beer."

"Count on it," Ward said with a smile. "The first round is on Zander."

"Good," Tychus said, "because I happen to know of a bar that would benefit from our business."

Raynor groaned. "Not Hurley's . . ."

Tychus grinned wolfishly. "Of course Hurley's! We need a refund on those overpriced sandwiches."

"Gimme some!" Harnack said, as he raised his hand.

The high fives generated a series of slapping sounds.

Doc was the last person to join in the celebration.

FORT HOWE, ON THE PLANET TURAXIS II

Four days had passed since the raid on the farmhouse, the squad was back at Fort Howe, and Doc was pissed. She and the rest of the squad had been training hard, and were in the middle of a hard-earned break when a message arrived ordering her to report to the command center. That was definitely not in keeping with the reporting process that she and Vanderspool had agreed on.

So having been told to report to Vanderspool's office, Cassidy blew through the waiting room and entered in a huff. The door slammed behind her as she stomped across the room. Vanderspool, who had been busy stuffing printouts into a briefcase, looked up in surprise as a very angry medic came forward to lean on his desk. "What the hell are you trying to do?" she demanded. "Get me killed? If Tychus figures out I've been ratting him out he'll squash me like a bug—"

Vanderspool was a desk jockey, but hadn't always been one, and Doc was surprised by the speed with which his right hand shot out to grab a fistful of shirt. A fancy clock, two vidsnaps, and a brass shell casing filled with writing implements went flying as he dragged her across the surface of the desk until her nose was only inches from his. *"You will address me as 'sir' . . . and as for having you killed, that could happen today! Do you scan me, bitch?"*

Doc saw the anger in his dark eyes and knew

she'd gone too far. That was one of the problems associated with using crab. Any time she had too much or too little of the drug, it affected her judgment. "Yes, sir. Sorry, sir."

Vanderspool pushed her away. "That's better. . . . I don't have time to play meet-the-drug-whore in the HTD today. . . . General Thane wants me to fly to Boro Airbase for a strategy session. But before I go I want a report on Sergeant Findlay and his group of misfits.

"Civilian authorities claim that a man matching his description entered a pub called Hurley's the day before yesterday, challenged the owner to a fistfight, and nearly killed him. Plus, if what they say is true, other soldiers were present as well . . . one of whom was described as being a female with short hair and a pretty face. Sound familiar?"

Cassidy stood with her head bowed, looking down at the mess on the floor. She began by saying, "Yes, sir," in a subdued voice, and went on to tell the story as she knew it, starting with being awoken by Feek.

Vanderspool listened intently as Doc described the trip to Finner's Crossing, what she had overheard regarding large quantities of money, the map, the attack on the farm, the manner in which the hostages had been freed, and the subsequent delivery of Zander's food shipment to a refugee camp nearby. Vanderspool's blood was boiling. All his suspicions were confirmed—the whole lot of them were worthless, pitiful crooks. His temples throbbed and his jaw tightened as Cassidy continued her narrative.

"Then, on the way back to base, Tychus, I mean Findlay, insisted that we stop at Hurley's Bar, because Hurley was the one who gave Raynor the map and ratted us out." She shrugged. "You know how Findlay is. Hurley was good with his hands—but not good enough. In fact, if it weren't for Lance Corporal Raynor pulling Findlay off him, the bastard might be dead."

"But they say you gave him first aid," Vanderspool said.

"That's what I do," Cassidy said offhandedly.

"That's *one* of the things you do," Vanderspool countered tightly. "You are dismissed."

Doc looked up. Her surprise was obvious. "Dismissed?"

"Yes," Vanderspool responded. "What did you expect? A medal?"

"You aren't going to throw us all in the stockade?"

"No," Vanderspool replied. "I told you I'm on my way to a meeting. Now get the hell out of my office!"

Doc came to attention, did an about-face, and left.

Vanderspool slammed his hands down on his

desk. So he'd been right all along. . . . Findlay and his cronies *had* stolen the truck, sold its contents to the highest bidder, and split the money. *His* money.

Vanderspool stalked into his lavatory and clutched the sides of the sink. Leaning in toward the mirror, his jaw clenched, the colonel peered intently at his reflection. *Those goddamn thieving bastards,* he thought. *I'm going to kill those sons of bitches. I knew it!* Furious, he smashed his fist into the mirror. It shattered into a thousand pieces, shards of glass clattered as they fell, and Vanderspool looked at his knuckles. His skin was ragged.

The colonel's mind was flashing with rage, but he needed to focus. He wanted to kill them, brutally, mercilessly—or worse, turn their brains to mush so he could see their smiling, worshipful faces as they were forced to do his bidding.

But that would have to wait. As infuriating as it was, he needed them—the STM platoon were the only soldiers who had undergone the weeks of training required to use the new hardskins, and there was no one else who could execute the strategic plan he was about to present at the conference. It would be his shining moment, and one that could not be tarnished—by anyone, not even them.

With a dropship waiting for him, Vanderspool left for the airstrip. The corporal, who had no idea what was going on, was left to clean up the mess on the floor.

CHAPTER TWENTY-ONE

"These rumors are based on the worst kind of propaganda, something our enemy is intimately familiar with. All the prisoners of war being held in our internment facilities receive three nutritious meals each day, are given excellent medical care, and are treated with respect."

From a statement released on behalf of the
Kel-Morian Combine
November 2488

FORT HOWE, ON THE PLANET TURAXIS II

The sky was gunmetal gray, it was unseasonably cold, and the troops were wearing water-slicked ponchos as they crossed the rain-lashed grinder. Puddles had formed in the low spots and produced tiny geysers each time a droplet of water fell into them.

The first thing that members of the STM platoon noticed as Tychus Findlay led them into the base theater was the fact that a squad of heavily armed MPs was patrolling the perimeter of the building. Harnack, who was walking next to Raynor, produced a low whistle. "What's with all the security?"

Raynor shrugged. "Beats me . . . maybe they know the briefing'll be so boring they'll need guards to keep us in there."

"Or maybe something important is in the wind," Harnack theorized. "I'd like to fry me some more Kel-Morians."

"It's a good plan," Raynor said dryly, "so long as they don't fry *you*."

Harnack might have replied, but the two men were inside the lobby by then, and being herded into the auditorium beyond. It was large enough to hold hundreds of people, so every member of the thirty-five-person platoon got a seat in the first row.

It took a few minutes to get everyone settled in, but once they were, Colonel Vanderspool appeared from the wings and marched to the center of the stage. Then, looking down at Tychus, he said, "Sergeant, is everyone accounted for?"

The officer was wearing a lip mic and his voice boomed over the theater's sound system.

Had Tychus known that Doc's effort to humiliate Lieutenant Quigby would cause the officer to be transferred, thereby leaving *him* in charge of the platoon, he would have put a stop to the harassment. Because the last thing Tychus wanted was to be in charge of anything other than a large bank account. But Quigby was gone and there was a shortage of line officers, which meant he'd have to fill the slot until a replacement came in. So all he could do was look up at Vanderspool and say, "Yes, sir. All present, sir."

"Excellent," Vanderspool responded as a carefully crafted smile appeared on his handsome face. "I have some very good news for the STM platoon. After weeks of training, you have a mission! And not just *any* mission. This is the sort of outing we had in mind when those CMC-230 suits were issued to you.

"In fact, if this effort goes the way we hope it will, our goal is to use you and your new hardskins to help capture the Kel-Morian strategic resources repository in the city of Polk's Pride. It's a critical objective—one that we are certain will decide the outcome of the war on Turaxis II." His smile broadened even more as he swept his gaze across the line of soldiers. "How would you like to be the Confederacy's most celebrated war heroes?"

The reaction from the soldiers was glum in spite of Vanderspool's enthusiastic pitch, and a few whispers were exchanged. "Ah, yes," Vanderspool continued cheerfully. "Some of you may know that we have attempted to cross the Paddick River and attack the repository before. Unfortunately, we failed. But trust me—we *will* try again, and we *will* succeed. You have my word.

"But, before we get started with Polk's Pride, let's take a look at the immediate objective." As the lights went down and a holo appeared on the stage, Vanderspool moved to one side.

"The image you're looking at was captured by an orbiting battle cruiser," Vanderspool explained. "The pictures they took were computer enhanced and combined to create the map you see on the screen."

As Raynor studied the image, he saw what he took to be three hills, each crowned with a fortification. Between them, and surrounded by what appeared to be a plascrete barrier, was what looked like a military camp. Six long, narrow buildings could be seen side by side. Two more were set off from the others, and a command center with a comsat station was located next to several supply depots and a water tower. Access roads wound here and there, dotted with blister-shaped bunkers that bracketed all of the main entry points.

"What you're looking at is a prisoner of war camp," Vanderspool informed them gravely. "It's called Kel-Morian Internment Camp-36, or KIC-36, and more than four hundred of our brave soldiers and pilots are being held there. And not just held, but *tortured,* and in some cases murdered. But there's no need for me to describe what goes on inside the camp, because we are about to have the privilege of hearing about it firsthand from one of the few people to successfully escape, a young pilot who proves that anything is possible." He stepped back and clapped for several seconds before extending a hand toward the approaching figure, a sympathetic smile on his face. The battalion offered a polite round of applause.

Aided by a cane and accompanied by a medic, a frail-looking figure shambled out to join Vanderspool. She looked like a skeleton over which parchmentlike skin had been stretched. "This is Captain Clair Hobarth," Vanderspool said soberly. "Her dropship was shot down; she was captured and taken to KIC-36, where she was held for three months before she managed to escape. The two prisoners who tried to flee with her weren't so lucky. I was opposed to her coming, but she insisted, because she regards the men and women she left behind as brothers and sisters. Captain Hobarth?"

Hobarth's voice was hoarse, but thanks to the mic she was wearing, her words could be heard. "Good morning . . . thank you all for what you have already accomplished—and *will* accomplish on behalf of the prisoners of KIC-36." She drew a slow, deep breath. "I'm not here to tell you a sob story about the months I spent there. I'm here to tell you how to attack the camp, kill the animals who run it, and rescue our people."

Somebody started to clap, more fervently this time, and Raynor joined in. Here, after the attack on Fort Howe and the looting of the armory, was what he'd been waiting for: something he could believe in. "Thank you," Hobarth said humbly, as she produced a laser pointer, and a red dot began to roam the 3-D image. Each item it passed grew larger and began to rotate, so that the audience could view it from various angles.

"By now you've noticed these hills," she said. "They're all about the same height and topped with missile turrets, defensive guns, and pop-up turrets. And, because there are three of them, anyone who tries to attack the camp will enter a cross fire.

"That's bad," Hobarth croaked, "but making the situation even worse is the fact that some of these weapons could be depressed to fire on the camp itself. And believe me, the camp's overseer, the man we called 'Brucker the Butcher,' wouldn't hesitate to do so."

Hobarth paused at that point as if to let the information sink in before continuing the briefing. "So, if you're going to rescue our people, you've got to neutralize the hilltop fortifications first. . . . And that's where your special capabilities come into play."

Hobarth paused at that point, as if to summon

more energy, before continuing on. "Here's how it's going to work," she continued. "Dropships will fly you over the site. You'll jump, land on all three hills at the same time, and destroy the weapons installations there. At that point you will make your way downhill, engage the guards, and take control."

Raynor watched the red dot draw a line around the camp. "Having blown holes in the charged shock wall, you'll evacuate the POWs to the landing pad located *here*." As the red dot came into contact with it, the 3-D image grew larger and began to rotate. "By that time other members of your battalion will have landed to provide you with support and a succession of dropships will arrive to evac the POWs. A squadron of Avengers will be on hand to keep the Kel-Morian Hellhounds off your backs. Oh, and one more thing. . . ." she added, with all the volume she could muster. "When you get back—the beer is on me!"

That announcement produced a very enthusiastic cheer, and Vanderspool smiled indulgently as he returned to center stage. "Thank you, Captain Hobarth. . . . That was an excellent presentation. And I hope you know what you're getting yourself into—because the men and women of the 321st are very thirsty!"

The audience chuckled appreciatively as Hobarth raised a skeletal hand, smiled weakly, and plodded offstage.

"Okay," Vanderspool said soberly, "that's the overview. Obviously it will be necessary to solve a lot of tactical problems before you'll be ready to carry out a mission of this complexity. And that's what we'll be working on over the next couple of weeks. In the meantime, remember this: Security is of the utmost importance. Surprise is a key element of the plan that Captain Hobarth described to you, and there are Kel-Morian sympathizers in the area. So don't discuss the mission when you're off duty. Not even with each other. Do you scan me?"

"Sir, yes, sir!"

"Good. Training will commence at 1400 hours. Acting platoon leader Findlay will be in charge. Dismissed."

Raynor looked left, saw his friend scowl, and grinned. Tychus might not be much of a strategist, but he was a natural leader, and the perfect person to lead the raid on KIC-36. Even if he was going to bitch about the responsibility twenty-five hours a day! The next couple of weeks would be interesting.

Tychus stood up and eyed the faces around him. "So what are you people waiting for? An engraved invitation? Get your butts in gear. . . . We have work to do." Preparations had begun.

Camp Crash, as it soon came to be known, was located about ten miles southwest of Fort Howe. It consisted of two hills, with an old gravel pit centered between them, and a couple of ramshackle buildings off to one side. And, because the STM platoon had been given its own dropship to train with, they could travel to and from Camp Crash in a matter of minutes.

As training day three dawned, and the platoon prepared to board the *Sweetie Pie,* Tychus gave them his version of a pep talk. "You people are pathetic," he began. "The plan is to jump out of the dropship and land on your feet, not your heads! Control is the key. . . . So quit screwing around."

They had heard it all before. Control *was* the key. But how to accomplish it? Piloting the Thunderstrike armor during carefully monitored training exercises was one thing, but controlling it under combat conditions was something else, and only a third of the platoon's thirty-five soldiers were any good at it.

Unfortunately Raynor wasn't one of them, and as he boarded the *Sweetie Pie* it felt as though ball bearings were rolling around in the pit of his stomach. He was among those who had crashed the day before, which forced Feek to stay up all night repairing Raynor's CMC-230-XE.

The truth was that "flying" one of the hardskins took as much skill as piloting an Avenger. So how many 230-XEs could the Confederacy realistically put into service? Not very damned many, not in Raynor's opinion anyway, because it would be too expensive and time consuming.

The dropship took off and began to climb. Raynor was nervous, but Tychus was there to comfort him. "Try not to embarrass me again," the noncom said, as he stopped in front of Raynor. "You looked ridiculous yesterday. If you're determined to kill yourself," he growled, "the least you could do is wait for the actual mission, and dive headfirst into a missile turret! Then I could put you in for a medal. Your parents would like that." He produced a cheerless, fake smile, and was gone half a second later. Having spread his own special brand of joy, Tychus moved on to speak with the next team member.

A few minutes later the ship reached 8,000 feet, turned toward the southwest, and began the first run of what promised to be a long day. Both of the side doors and the specially rigged floor hatch were open, so the dropship's slipstream was buffeting the soldier who was acting as jump master. Protected as he was by the CMC-230-XE, Raynor barely noticed the breeze as he lined up behind a private named Pauley. She was one of the "naturals," a person with a natural affinity for Thunderstrike armor, and showed no signs of hesitation as she fell through the hatch and disappeared.

Raynor, who had been careful to skip breakfast, felt slightly nauseous as he took the final step into nothingness. He wanted to piss, his heart was thumping in his ears, and he was short of breath. He couldn't see the target as the CMC-230 plunged toward the surface below. Not directly, because the only way to look down would be to bend at the waist, a move that would send him spinning out of control. But he could see the gravel pit via tiny cameras built into his boots.

His target was Hill Bravo, which was a quarter mile to the right, meaning it would be necessary to steer himself in that direction. A scary prospect, since things were going well so far, and any action he took could result in disaster.

But Raynor had no choice. Not if he was to land on target. An AGR-14 gauss rifle was clamped to his chest. That left him free to deploy his arms as well as the computer-controlled vanes that were built into them. Having done so, Raynor shifted his weight. The result was a satisfying turn to the right, followed by a tight spiral, which he was forced to correct.

Then, just when Raynor was beginning to feel that he had the hang of the process, an unexpected burst of wind sent him tumbling out of control! His boots flipped up where his head should have been, an alarm sounded inside his helmet, and everything except the suit's readouts became a blur. Raynor was a bullet now, speeding toward the planet's surface, where a very symmetrical crater was about to appear.

Had the jet pack fired yet? No, and a good

thing, too, because that would propel him toward the ground at an even higher rate of speed. Raynor knew he would have to use his arms and body to correct his orientation relative to the ground or end up buried in it. The key was to act slowly and deliberately, even though every fiber of his body wanted to hurry, knowing that the ground was coming up at 160 miles per hour.

So Raynor straightened his body, deployed his arms the way he'd been taught to, and felt his head flip up. The gravel pit reappeared on his HUD. Tychus, who had seemingly been born knowing how to use the new suits, witnessed the move via one of the tracking cameras on the dropship. His voice filled Raynor's helmet. *"This ain't no game, jerk weed! Save the tricks for someone who cares. Over."*

Raynor grinned as the jet pack fired, the CMC-230-XE began to slow, and Hill Bravo grew larger below him. Tychus thought he was screwing around! Doing tricks when he was supposed to concentrate on training. "Sorry about that, Sierra-Six. . . . I got carried away. Over."

In spite of Raynor's reasonably successful jump, not everyone fared so well, and by the time the *Sweetie Pie* returned to Fort Howe, Doc had not only been forced to treat various broken bones but deal with a couple of fatalities as well. Feek took the deaths especially hard. After all, he was responsible for the way the CMCs were designed.

Plus the hardskins would have to be replaced from Feek's quickly dwindling supply of spares, while other suits were going to require major repairs, and almost all of them had at least minor problems.

So when the dropship put down, and UNN reporter Max Speer went out to meet it, Tychus was already in a pissy mood. "Look over here!" Speer said, as he pointed at a hovering cam bot. "That's right. . . . Give me that 'I'm gonna kick some ass' look."

Only it was more than a look. Speer saw something *huge* fill his field of vision as he was hauled off his feet. Tychus threw the other man over an armored shoulder, and Speer was subjected to a jarring ride as the platoon leader carried him toward the command center located nearby. The camera followed them.

Sentries stared in openmouthed amazement as Tychus brushed past them, ducked under the top of the doorway, and pounded up the stairs to the point where he was forced to duck again. Then he was in the waiting room on his way to the office beyond.

A lieutenant was sitting in Vanderspool's guest chair, and she uttered a surprised shriek as an armored giant barged into the room and dumped what she assumed to be a dead body on the base commander's desk. "I brought you a spy, sir," Tychus rumbled, as Speer rolled onto his feet. "Look!" Tychus said as he plucked the cam bot out of the air. "The bastard has been taking pictures of us!"

Vanderspool scowled as he came to his feet and turned to the lieutenant. "Would you excuse us? Thank you."

Once the lieutenant was gone Vanderspool spoke again as he walked around his desk to stand beside Speer. "Have you lost your mind? This is Max Speer. . . . He's a reporter for UNN—and he's been cleared to accompany you. Max is going to show the citizens of the Confederacy what a fantastic job our soldiers are doing—isn't that right, Max?" he said, giving the reporter a friendly pat on the back.

Speer smiled broadly, and said, "At your service, Colonel."

Tychus looked at Speer and back again before releasing the cam bot. It pulled back in order to get a wide shot.

"No way, sir. . . . There isn't enough time to teach him how to jump. Besides, we're going to have enough to do without tracking any civilians."

Vanderspool raised a hand. "Don't worry, Sergeant. Speer will arrive with the second wave on one of the dropships. Now, if you would be so good as to return to your duties, I have work to do."

Speer had fully recovered from being thrown

onto the desk—he had more important things to worry about. "Hold that position for a sec," Speer said as the cam bot took up a position directly in front of Vanderspool. The officer flashed a bright smile. Neither one of them turned to look as Tychus left the office.

After their first full week of training, Raynor offered to take Tychus into the HTD for a beer, knowing full well that the other man wasn't likely to decline a free drink. The truth was, the two had forged a solid friendship, and Raynor had become Tychus's unofficial second in command, even if a couple of sergeants outranked him. That didn't mean Tychus would agree to the proposal Raynor had in mind, however—especially since the idea ran counter to one of his most cherished sayings: "Never volunteer for anything."

When the time came to meet Tychus, Raynor saw that Doc was clinging to one of the big man's arms. Raynor shouldn't have been surprised, because the two of them had been groping one another for weeks by then, even though certain members of the platoon disapproved. Tychus and Doc were in the same chain of command after all, which raised the possibility of favoritism if nothing else, but no one had the balls to complain about it.

So the three of them ventured into the comfortable sleaziness of the HTD, where everyone seemed to know Doc, and, minutes later, they were shown to their favorite table at Three Fingered Jack's.

Knowing Tychus the way he did, Raynor waited until his friend had consumed several glasses of Scotty Bolger's before making his case. "I've got an idea," Raynor said, having checked to make sure that no one was close enough to hear. "Something that will help our mission succeed."

"Yeah?" Tychus responded. "What's that? You plan to shoot Max Speer in the head?"

Raynor laughed. Speer had proven to be as annoying as they'd all expected—and forever underfoot. "That would be incredibly gratifying, but no," Raynor replied. He straightened. "My concern is this. . . . You saw Captain Hobarth. How many of the POWs are just like her—injured, weak, *slow*?"

Doc, who was busy giving Tychus a shoulder massage, appeared to be oblivious to the conversation. From the dreamy look in her eyes, Raynor could tell she was high. But so were most of the other people in the bar—difference being that they preferred alcohol to crab. And, so long as Doc was sober while on duty, Raynor figured what she did the rest of the time was up to her.

"So, here's the problem," he continued. "The flaw in Vanderspool's plan is that once we blow the shock wall, the POWs *won't* come pouring out. Partly because they won't be expecting us—

and partly because at least some of them will be in bad shape. And loading them will take a long time. Maybe *too* long. The Hellhounds will be on us by then. How long can the Avengers hold them off?"

"This all makes sense," Tychus allowed, "but I'll be damned if I know what we can do about it. Of course you do, or *think* you do, which is why you're buying the booze."

"As it happens I *do* have something in mind," Raynor agreed lightly. "And it goes like this: I want to drop into the area one day early. I'll enter the POW camp, mingle with the prisoners, and help them get organized. Then, when the platoon falls out of the sky, they'll be ready to go."

There was a moment of silence as Tychus emptied his glass, followed by a solid thunk as he put it down. Then, having wiped off his lips with the back of one hand, he belched. "That," Tychus proclaimed, "is one of the worst ideas I have ever heard! Have you been shooting some of Doc's crab?"

Raynor glanced at Doc, whose attention was still somewhere far, far away. "What's wrong with it?" he demanded defensively.

"I'm glad you asked," Tychus replied. "First, if anything goes wrong with your jump, the entire mission could be compromised. Second, how the hell would you enter the camp, supposing you're lucky enough to survive the landing? And third, what if you succeed, and Colonel Vanderscum scrubs the mission?"

"Yeah," Doc put in vacantly. "That would suck."

"It certainly would," Raynor conceded. "But given the fact that Speer is still on the job, I'm pretty sure our little outing is good to go.

"And as far as how I'm going to land and get inside the camp, I got that idea when our scouts captured a KM Hellhound pilot yesterday. He was shot down over the disputed zone—they're holding him on the base.

"All *you* have to do is get the colonel to put a lid on the news that we have him. Then with help from the intel people, I'll put on a Kel-Morian flight suit, stroll up to one of the gates at KIC-36 and show them some very official-looking ID. Once they let me in, I'll ask them for a ride back to my base. But, since it's more than two hundred miles away, it'll take them at least a day to arrange for transportation. Meanwhile, I'll find a way to make contact with the POWs and warn them."

Tychus looked Raynor in the eye. "Tell me something, Jim," he asked skeptically, "because this all sounds completely crazy. What's in it for *you*?"

Raynor was silent for a moment. "You might think this is bullshit. . . . But this mission is something I actually believe in. Something pure and clean, no underlying motives, no greed—these are our people, and they need our help. I want to bring them out. Maybe it sounds stupid, but this is what I had in mind when I joined up."

Tychus eyed him cynically. "Vanderspool wants to make general. What's so pure and clean about that?"

Raynor shrugged. "It doesn't matter so long as the prisoners escape."

"Okay," Tychus said reluctantly. "I'll tackle it first thing in the morning. In the meantime, go grab some more drinks. All this talking is making me thirsty."

CHAPTER TWENTY-TWO

"As the Kel-Morian engagement marches toward its fourth year, we have received several reports of heightened criminal activity in the civilian sector. Although some analysts blame this new wave of lawlessness on the dynamics of a wartime economy, the consensus among Confederate pundits is that this criminality represents the exposure of certain portions of the citizenry. One analyst, who asked to remain anonymous, said, 'It is our belief that patriotism shows its true colors in times of hardship.' "

Max Speer, *Special Evening Report from the Front Line* for UNN
November 2488

FORT HOWE, ON THE PLANET TURAXIS II

The sun was still rising, the air was crisp, and Tychus was in a good mood. Much to Tychus's amazement, Colonel Vanderspool liked Raynor's proposal. That made sense in a way, because the battalion commander wanted the mission to succeed, but Tychus was so cynical about officers in general—and Vanderspool in particular—that the green light was a surprise.

So Tychus was on his way from the command center to the building where the KM pilot was being held, when he saw someone he had never expected to see again: Sam Lassiter.

Somewhere along the line the soldier had undergone a near miraculous transformation. Rather than the rebellious, unkempt figure that Tychus had last seen being escorted out of the rock quarry by armored guards, *this* Lassiter had short hair, was clean-shaven, and wore a uniform so perfect it looked like something straight out of a recruiting video. The soldier cut across Tychus's path but paused when his name was called. "Hey, Private Lassiter," Tychus said. "The last time I saw you was at MCF-R-156. I'm surprised they let you out after what you did to Bellamy."

Lassiter's eyes were blank. "MCF what? Bellamy? I don't understand. You must have me mixed up with someone else."

"I don't think so," Tychus replied, as he eyed the private's name tag. "You don't remember the quarry, the box . . . attacking Sergeant Bellamy?"

Lassiter was clearly aghast. "Attack a sergeant?" he said disbelievingly. "You must be joking. I would never do something like that. Now, if you'll excuse me, I'm due at the command center in five minutes and I don't want to be late." And with that he walked away.

Tychus turned to watch him go. Besides the fact that the guy was completely delusional, there was something weird about Lassiter's demeanor . . . something that reminded him of the overly courteous admin clerk, the bright-eyed sentries assigned to keep Vanderspool safe, and something the colonel had said: *". . . if you think hard labor was bad, you can only imagine what else we're capable of. You might just end up a prisoner in your own body."* What did that mean, anyway? Had the Confederacy come up with a new program? A way to take a wild man like Lassiter and turn him into a human robot? There was no way to be sure, but as Tychus continued on his way, he had one more thing to worry about.

There were only three people aboard the dropship. The pilot, Feek, who was acting as jump master, and Lance Corporal Jim Raynor. Tychus had offered to come along and shove his friend into the abyss, but Raynor had declined.

Five extremely busy days had passed since his meeting with Tychus, and now, with Colonel Vanderspool's blessing, Raynor was about to drop into Kel-Morian-held territory alone. It was a stupid, stupid thing to do, and he knew that now. But maybe, just maybe, the mission was a way to atone for stealing the trucks. And it was something he knew his parents would be proud of.

One thing was for sure—there would be no turning back, since the blacked-out transport was already over enemy territory. Raynor had taken the utmost care to learn everything he could about the Kel-Morian prisoner he would be impersonating. Fortunately, they were about the same height and had similar builds. Raynor had watched intelligence officers interrogate the pilot via a closed circuit feed, and had been given access to his personal property as well, which included the contents of his fone. So Raynor knew all sorts of things about Ras Hagar, including his wife's name, how many children he had, and what kind of music he liked. Would it be enough? No, not if the Kel-Morians scanned his retinas, but there was little chance of that. From what the captured pilot said, they were so short on tech supplies, scanners were nearly impossible to find. All he had to do was play his role right, and there wouldn't be any doubt as to who he was.

Raynor was trying to focus on remembering his alter ego's story, but his mind was swirling with worry. The dropship was flying in from the west as a half-dozen Avengers were conducting a raid a few miles to the south as a diversion. Would the KMs notice the additional blip on their screens? Yes, they would, but Raynor and the crew were taking a gamble that the dropship would come off their list of threats as soon as it turned back.

Feek came back to see him. The technician's visor was open so Raynor could see his expression. What was it anyway? Admiration? Pity? Or some combination of the two? He would never know. "We're five minutes out," Feek said. "It's time to get in position and start your final check."

"Thanks," Raynor said. He was already standing up. Having shuffled forward to the point where the rectangular-shaped black abyss awaited him, it was time to run a last check on the suit. *Here's your chance*, an inner voice said. *If there's something wrong with your suit you can't jump. Nobody would question that.*

But another voice could be heard as well. And it belonged to his father. *"A lie is like an infection, son. . . . It burrows deep inside and makes you sick."*

Besides, there were the POWs to think about, and the memory of the way Hobarth looked was enough to strengthen Raynor's resolve. So Raynor ran one last check, saw all of the indicators come up green, and gave a thumbs-up to Feek. He nodded, the pilot said, "Good luck" over the intercom, and it was time to close his visor as the final countdown began. He could see it on his HUD and hear it in his ears. "Five, four, three, two, one."

Knowing how important timing was going to be, Raynor started moving on three, was halfway through the hatch on two, and in free fall as the countdown hit "one." Everything was pitch-black. There were no visual cues to go by other than the displays on his HUD. But practice made perfect, and Raynor was pleased to discover that his body knew what to do. As the altimeter in the upper left hand corner of his vision continued to unwind, he was head over feet and stable.

When the jet pack came on, it felt as though he were being propelled *upward,* but only for a moment, as the CMC-230-XE began to slow, and surface winds threatened to tip him over. But Raynor knew how to compensate, and did so, as the thrust continued to increase and a ghostly green landscape began to populate his HUD.

However, there wasn't any time to admire the view as the ground rushed up, Raynor flexed his knees, and the hardskin did likewise. Then came the impact as his boots hit, the jet pack shut itself off, and he was down. Ironically, it was the best landing he had ever executed, day *or* night, and there wasn't anyone around to appreciate his accomplishment.

Well, there wasn't *supposed* to be anyone, but the possibility of bad luck was always a factor, and Raynor took a quick look around to ensure that he hadn't come down right on top of a KM patrol. But there was no sign of anything other than a glowing green animal that eyed him for a moment before scurrying away.

Satisfied that he was safe, for the moment at

least, it was time to look for a suitable hiding place. After casting about for a bit, Raynor came across a depression and went about the clumsy process of lying down in it. Which, given the jet pack on his back, was more like leaning on something rather than lying flat.

Then it was time to exit his armor. Raynor chinned a control, opened a latch, and was rewarded with a hissing sound as the hardskin opened and pressures were equalized. Raynor pushed the top half aside, kicked his way free of the control interfaces, and struggled to his feet. With only a Kel-Morian flight suit to protect him, the night air was cold.

But there was work to do, beginning with the need to arm a self-destruct system that would destroy both the CMC-230-XE and everything within a twenty-foot radius were someone to tamper with it. With that out of the way, it was time to cover the hardskin with a thin sheet of protective camo cloth and a layer of loose rocks to keep the rig from being discovered. That took Raynor more than an hour and left him feeling as tired as Hellhound pilot Ras Hagar would be after seven days of making his way out of the zone.

And the fact that he hadn't showered or shaved for that same period of time would support his story. *If* he got to tell it. But first he had a five-mile hike to complete. That was the bad news. The good news was that there was a seldom-used mining road he could follow that would take him to a point within half a mile of the POW camp. Plus he had a compass and a pair of KM-manufactured night-vision goggles with a built-in compass to help him find his way.

Raynor ate an energy bar, took a moment to wash it down with a swallow of water, and set off. Now, as the second phase of his mission began, the night was his armor.

FORT HOWE, ON THE PLANET TURAXIS II

Cassidy needed a fix, but she was out of crab, and had been for two grueling days. There was a shortage of the stuff in the HTD due to the war and police crackdowns. That was the bad news. The good news was that she was going to score a week's worth of the drug in the next hour or so! All she had to do was fight back the withdrawal symptoms, make her way through the HTD to Colonel Vanderspool's hidden hideaway, and rat her friends out. *But hey,* Cassidy thought, as she turned, tense and shaky, into the narrow passageway. *What are friends for? To give you a helping hand, right? Well, I sure as hell need a helping hand right now.*

Vanderspool was waiting for her on the balcony above The Gourmand restaurant. He was wearing civilian clothes, and looked reasonably happy, which meant his mistress was on duty and performing well. But the most important thing was the small metal container on the table in front of him. That was full of crab, *her* crab, and she could smell it. Or was that a hallucination? It was difficult to tell.

"Hello, my dear," Vanderspool said warmly. "You look ravishing as usual. . . . Please have a seat."

So Cassidy sat down, and with a minimum amount of prompting from Vanderspool, delivered her report as she fumbled with her hands to keep them from quivering. There wasn't much to say, truth be told, since the squad had been too busy training for the raid on KIC-36 to get into trouble, but there were always a few minor infractions she could report on—such as the booze Harnack kept in his locker.

Vanderspool listened patiently, but didn't seem to be all that interested, and neglected to ask any follow-up questions whatsoever. "So," he said, once Cassidy's report trailed away. "Is that it?"

Cassidy struggled to keep her unfocused eyes up and off the metal container. "Yes, sir . . . that's it."

"Okay," Vanderspool said agreeably. "Well done! Now listen carefully. . . . There's something I need you to do for me. Something important."

As soon as Doc realized she'd have to wait longer to get her fix, a jolt of pain shot through her nervous system, and her body twitched involuntarily. Her skin moistened and suddenly she felt very cold. As Vanderspool spoke, leaning in close, every puff of his breath sent sickening shivers down her spine. He was enjoying this.

It took him more than ten minutes to give Doc her orders, which she concentrated hard to take in—and because each minute felt like an hour, the meeting seemed to last forever. As she listened to Vanderspool's orders, she realized her role was changing from snitch to something far more sinister. Cassidy would have agreed to anything at that point just to get her fix, not that Vanderspool gave her much choice.

Finally, just as she began to fear that she was going to lose control of her crab-starved body, the meeting came to an end. By now, Doc's jaw was clenched so tight, her vision blurred each time her pulse throbbed in her head.

Three minutes later, in the shadow cast by the dumpster behind the restaurant, Doc was transformed. Suddenly she felt whole again, life was worth living, and the pain was behind her. As she exhaled what felt like her first breath of life, her dry eyes burned with a sudden swell of tears.

KEL-MORIAN INTERNMENT CAMP-36,
ON THE PLANET TURAXIS II

The headquarters building was located inside the plascrete barrier, and was home to both the internment camp's offices and the overseer's living quarters. And with plenty of slave labor to call upon, the previously modest space had been expanded to include a dining room, sitting room, and private deck. And that's where Overseer Hanz Brucker was, sitting on a comfortable chair and smoking a cigar as he looked out onto his private kingdom.

His was an extremely important job. Or that's what he thought anyway—and most people would have agreed. Overseer Brucker was responsible for a large contingent of troops that included rippers, armor, and artillery.

Plus, he was in charge of KIC-36, an internment camp that was packed with more than three hundred extremely dangerous enemy combatants. All of whom should have been put to death. But killing Confederate POWs would inevitably result in reprisals against Kel-Morian prisoners, so it was necessary to keep them alive. But just *barely* alive, since there was no point in coddling people who had taken the lives of Kel-Morian fighters, and would do so again if given the chance.

Brucker's thoughts were interrupted as a door opened behind him and Taskmaster Lumley made use of a discreet cough to announce his presence. "I'm sorry to disturb you, sir. . . . But dinner is ready."

It was welcome news since Brucker was a man of strong appetites. The cigar butt's red ember looked like a shooting star as it arced toward the prisoners' quarters and fell short of the edge of the deck. Lumley scurried over and stomped it out with his boot. Brucker's chair made a scraping noise as he hoisted himself up and out of it. "Thank you, Lumley. . . . What am I having?"

Lumley had a cadaverous countenance and the manner of an undertaker. "Roasted near-pig, sir, with the skin on."

"Excellent," Brucker replied eagerly. "And what wine can I expect?"

"A rather dry white, sir," Lumley replied, as the overseer shuffled toward the door.

"Not a red?"

"No, sir. Not this time."

"Well, you know best," Brucker allowed, as he paused to negotiate the threshold. The sitting room was nicely furnished, considering the circumstances, the emphasis being on oversized chairs and subdued lighting.

At that point the melodic sound of a string quartet could be heard originating from the adjoining dining room. As Brucker entered he was pleased to see that the table was covered with white linen, the silver gleamed under the glow of a gracefully shaped candelabra, and the gaunt-faced musicians were seated in their usual corner. They hated playing for him, of course, but that was part of the pleasure, as was consuming an enormous meal while they were forced to watch.

The POWs' faces were blank, but Brucker

could feel the weight of their stares as he shuffled to the head of the table. Lumley was there to hold the chair for him, lay an extra-large napkin across his midriff, and bring the first dish of what would be a seven-course meal.

The quartet consisted of two violins, a viola, and a cello. The group wasn't quite as good as it had been a few weeks earlier, before the viola player had been gunned down as he tried to climb the fence, but life is full of setbacks. And it was Brucker's hope that the newest addition would improve with practice.

And so the meal went, from appetizer to main course, and from Haydn to the Kel-Morian composer Odon. Then, as Lumley came in with dessert, he brought news as well. "I have a message for you, sir. . . . The shift boss sent word that one of our flyers presented himself at the north gate. A Hellhound pilot, I believe. He was shot down over the disputed zone and hiked back to our lines."

"Excellent!" Brucker said enthusiastically. "Please send for him. . . . And tell the cook. The poor devil will be hungry by now."

After jumping out of a dropship while wearing experimental combat armor and hiking five miles cross-country, Raynor should have been tired. But after talking his way into the Kel-Morian POW camp, he was so high on adrenaline he felt as if he could run for twenty miles straight. He felt as though he could see better, hear better, and even taste better. So far, Raynor's disguise was working.

Having been escorted from the north gate to the command center where he'd been given a place to sit down, he was sipping a glass of water when a door slammed and a Kel-Morian entered the office. The man's stooped shoulders made him appear shorter than he actually was, and given the way his head tilted forward, it appeared as if there was something wrong with his neck. "Airman Hagar?" the man inquired, as he regarded Raynor from under bushy brows. "I'm Taskmaster Lumley. Overseer Brucker would be honored if you would join him in the dining room."

Dining room? Raynor was surprised to hear that the POW camp had one. But he forced a smile as he stood. "Of course!" he said agreeably. "Although I fear I am far from presentable."

"The overseer understands," Lumley said with the surety of the family retainer that he was. "Please follow me."

Raynor thanked the man who had seen to his needs thus far—and followed Lumley through a door and into the private quarters beyond. He was immediately struck by the quality of the furnishings, the dim lighting, and the music that grew steadily louder the farther they went.

But even with something of a lead-in, Raynor wasn't prepared for the scene that greeted him as

Lumley led him into the dining room. The huge, fat man who rose to greet him, the richly set table, and the animated skeletons who occupied one of the corners were like elements in a bad dream. Raynor had practiced coming to attention Kel-Morian style, and was just about to do so, when his host turned to extend a pudgy hand. "There you are, my boy!" Brucker said heartily. "I'm Overseer Brucker. . . . Welcome to Internment Camp-36."

Brucker's grip was soft and slightly damp, and he held on for one second too long for Raynor's comfort. He was glad when the contact was broken. "Thank you, sir. . . . I'm very glad to be here, as you can imagine. Three Avengers jumped me over the zone. I nailed one of the bastards, but the others put me down."

"Three to one," Brucker said disapprovingly, as his already florid face grew even darker. "That's the kind of scum we're dealing with! Still, you showed them! Well done, lad. . . . Well done."

Brucker was shorter than Raynor by a good three inches. A few strands of brown hair had been combed over an otherwise bald pate, and little beads of perspiration could be seen on his heavily creased forehead.

But while Brucker wasn't a handsome man, Raynor sensed that he was a dangerous one . . . something that was evident in the other man's stony eyes. They glittered with intelligence as they darted here and there, and Raynor felt himself start to sweat. "Thank you, sir. I'm afraid my boss will be far less understanding, however!"

Brucker laughed, just as he was supposed to, and gestured to a new place setting. "Please . . . you must be hungry. I have already eaten, so I hope you won't mind dining alone while I go out to make the evening rounds. Lumley will see to your needs."

Raynor felt a tremendous sense of relief. He'd been dreading the prospect of a prolonged conversation with the man. "That's very thoughtful of you, sir," Raynor replied, as he sat down.

"You're welcome," Brucker said, as he shuffled toward the door. "I'll see you in the morning."

Moments later the overseer was gone—and Raynor turned toward the POWs. They looked back at him with carefully blanked faces as their bows sawed, music flowed, and time seemed to slow. Raynor was faced with an important choice. Would he have a chance to pass the word the following day? Or was this the best opportunity he would get?

Knowing that Lumley might arrive with food at any moment, Raynor glanced at the doorway and confirmed that it was empty. Then, having made his decision, he turned toward the quartet and spoke in a hushed voice. "Listen carefully. . . . I have a message from Captain Hobarth. . . ." He glanced again at the doorway, then continued, articulating every syllable to make his message absolutely clear. "Tomorrow night, at 2300 hours, be ready."

Eyes widened at the mention of Hobarth's name, and one of the men had just opened his mouth as if to speak when Brucker reentered the room. He was faster on his feet this time, and three armed guards followed him in. Raynor thought about reaching for the pistol tucked under his left arm—but knew that doing so would be suicidal. "Place your hands on top of your head," Brucker growled, as a taskmaster hurried forward to snatch the handgun out of its holster.

"There," Brucker said, once Raynor had been disarmed. "That's better. . . . It looks as though the enemy sent a spy to Internment Camp-36! Perhaps next time they will do their homework. Let me tell you something about the fraternity of Hellhound pilots, my Confederate friend. . . . Do you see *this*?" Brucker demanded as he held up his right hand. The "HH" outline on his palm was vague, but a permanent groove seemed to have formed after years of wear. "Each pilot has two side-by-side steel Hs implanted into the palm of his hand once he qualifies. As a result you can *feel* the raised area when you shake hands with them. I guess your *handlers* must have missed that. It's a shame you're going to die before you get the chance to tell them."

Raynor offered no response, nor was one expected.

Brucker turned to the taskmaster. "Take him to the wet room. I'll be there shortly."

The guards hauled Raynor out of the room, and Brucker was about to follow when he remembered the POWs. He paused to look back. "You played well tonight . . . not perfectly, but well. You have my permission to clean up the scraps." And with that he left.

The POWs stood, looked at one another, and shuffled toward the head of the table. One by one they spit on Brucker's dessert plate before passing through the door on their way back to the bleak buildings where they spent each night. Would the spy tell Brucker what he had told them? Yes, that was the way of things at KIC-36, and the dark-haired stranger would be grateful when death came for him.

CHAPTER TWENTY-THREE

"They say that clothes make the man. My suits make the man into a fekkin' monster."

Hiram Feek, designer of the CMC-230-XE and civilian member of the 321st Colonial Rangers Battalion, in an interview on Turaxis II November 2488

KEL-MORIAN INTERNMENT CAMP-36,
ON THE PLANET TURAXIS II

Judging from the look of things, the torture chamber doubled as a morgue. Or was it the other way around? Not that it mattered. A scattering of instruments lay on a stand, indicator lights marked pieces of electronic equipment, and the air was chilly.

Raynor was naked except for a pair of trunks, and the framework that supported him was slanted away from the floor and positioned over a drain. Bright lights burned his eyes, but when

Raynor managed to penetrate the glare, he could see a hazy figure that he knew to be Overseer Brucker. The officer's thronelike chair was positioned on a raised platform that gave him a better view of the proceedings. "So," Brucker said, "how are you feeling?"

Raynor thought the torture had been going on for at least half an hour by then, although he had no way to keep track of time. The Kel-Morians hadn't brought out the hot irons. Not yet anyway. Brucker's so-called "truth monitor," a man named Dr. Moller, preferred to use needles. And thanks to his medical training, he knew exactly where to insert them to inflict the maximum amount of pain.

So Raynor's throat was sore from screaming, his body was soaked with sweat, and as he tilted his head down he could see clusters of needles protruding from various parts of his body. All of them hurt like hell. "I could use an aspirin," he croaked.

"You'll be glad to hear that Dr. Moller can relieve pain as well as inflict it," Brucker replied. "But, before we move to that stage, let's review what we have so far. . . . You were sent to gather information about my base. Correct?"

"Yes," Raynor replied hoarsely.

"And," Brucker continued, "you claim that Confederate forces are scheduled to attack us at some point during the next two weeks."

Raynor knew that the leads attached to his body were connected to some sort of lie detector. So the key was to tell the truth as frequently as he could without divulging the most critical fact. *Find spider holes and hide,* he kept repeating in his head, fearful that the pain would make him momentarily lose his lucidity. An attack was coming all right—but in hours rather than weeks. If he could hold that piece of information back he could protect his friends and prevent a massacre. "Yes, they're going to attack you," Raynor agreed.

Raynor blinked the sweat out of his eyes and saw Brucker's hazy form turn toward a barely visible Moller. The doctor answered the unspoken question with an elaborate shrug. His voice was flat and emotionless. "It appears that he's telling the truth, or some version of it. One thing seems clear, though. . . . The attack isn't imminent. Not if they're still in the process of gathering intelligence."

"All right," Brucker said agreeably, "let's switch topics for a moment. Tell me about the neural resocialization program. I want to know who runs it, how it works, and what results have been obtained."

Raynor's mouth was dry. He tried to summon some saliva but couldn't. " 'Resocialization'? I have no idea what you're talking about."

Moller stepped in at that point, pushed one of the needles in deep, and flicked another with his forefinger. Raynor screamed, and screamed again, as Moller shoved a third needle in under one of his toenails.

"Now," Brucker said, as the screaming died away. "Let's try that again. Perhaps you call the program something else. . . . But based on information obtained by our intel, criminals and other troublemakers are being taken to special centers, where experimental treatments are used to erase their antisocial tendencies. What a sick group of people you are. Kel-Morians would never do anything so cruel. We hear you have quite a few of these brainwashed dullards serving in your armed forces. Now, provide me with all of the relevant details, or suffer some more."

There was so much pain that Raynor found it difficult to think. "I can't tell you," Raynor croaked. "I don't know."

"He *doesn't* know," Moller agreed. "Or so it appears."

"I don't believe it," Brucker responded cynically. "Who knows? Maybe *this* one has been brainwashed. Try again."

Moller obeyed, and Raynor experienced a jolt of pain so powerful that if felt as if his skull might crack open. So, when the tidal wave of darkness arrived he was grateful for it, and allowed himself to be carried away.

* * *

Raynor had died and gone to hell. That's what he assumed anyway, given his inability to see, and the pain that racked his body. There was light, he knew that, because he could see it through his lids, and feel the heat of it. So he attempted to open his eyes—but it felt as if they were glued shut. The obvious solution was to reach up and rub them. When he tried to do so he discovered that his hands were bound behind him.

So Raynor tried again, *willing* his eyes to open, and this time his efforts met with success. His left eye popped open, followed by his right, but the light was so bright that he was forced to close them again.

Raynor's eyelids fluttered, his pupils made the necessary adjustment, and his vision was restored. Now he realized that the bright orb was the sun! It had risen over the hill Vanderspool had designated as "Charlie" during mission training and was spearing him with its rays.

That was the moment when Raynor discovered it was possible to be alive and in hell at the same time. Because as he struggled to summon some saliva in his bone-dry mouth it became apparent that he was dangling from a rope. A fact made even more obvious when a breeze caused his body to spin. His harness creaked in protest. *Oh, God.*

It wasn't long before Raynor realized that he wasn't alone. A prisoner named Cole Hickson, a twenty-year-old soldier who had been captured during a skirmish in the zone, was suspended, unconscious and badly beaten, off to Raynor's left. They had shared a cell, and just before Raynor was taken out to be interrogated, Hickson had offered some sage advice. *"Try to hide, if you can. Find spider holes in your mind, and crawl into them."*

That advice had carried Raynor through the worst parts of the torture. He had been trained at boot camp to withstand interrogation techniques, but he knew a person could easily forget those skills in the presence of physical pain. He hoped Hickson would survive, but more than that, he hoped the mission to save the POWs would be a success, so that if he himself died, it would be for *something*.

But that seemed unlikely as Raynor looked past Hickson and saw the bird-pecked remains of a third man. He was little more than a tattered skeleton. They were hanging from spokes attached to a central column. It squeaked as the wind attempted to turn it. Then, as the breeze grew stronger and the spokes began to rotate in earnest, shadows flickered across the camp below.

It didn't take a genius to figure out that the display was intended to instill fear in the prisoners. Raynor could see a line of POWs shuffling along below, and noticed that none of them were looking up. They had no desire to be reminded of where they were or what could happen to them. And for good reason.

As the sun continued to crawl across the sky Raynor drifted in and out of consciousness from time to time. Eventually a number of such interludes blended together to become one endless nightmare. Something important was supposed to happen once darkness fell, but for the life of him, Raynor couldn't remember what.

FORT HOWE, ON THE PLANET TURAXIS II

A force of unseen Avengers was flying cover as the dropships waited to be loaded. The *Sweetie Pie's* engines were idling, the ramp was down, and the STM platoon was beginning to board. Other dropships, those that would fly in empty to pick up the POWs, were on standby, and would remain so until all the troops were in the air and on their way.

It had been a mistake to let Raynor go. That was something Tychus had come to realize as he watched the soldiers enter the ship. Because while he had plenty of leadership experience, Tychus had never been in command of a unit larger than a squad before. Had Raynor been present, he would have been the logical person to lead the first squad. *And* handle the sort of pissy personnel issues that Tychus wasn't very good at.

He was also concerned about Raynor. What if the ruse hadn't been successful? All he knew was that Raynor had landed outside the zone without incident, but what happened after that was still unknown.

Making the situation worse was the fact that the platoon was supposed to land on three different objectives. A plan that required him to delegate authority to his squad leaders, which went against all his instincts and put him on edge.

In Raynor's absence, Tychus had been forced to choose between Harnack, Zander, or Ward to lead the first squad. Various arguments could be made for each one. But given that Harnack was too impulsive, and Ward was arguably suicidal, the logical choice was Zander.

Tychus's thoughts were interrupted as a suit of armor lurched out of the surrounding gloom. "Excuse me, Sergeant," Speer said, "would you unload your troops please? I have a wide shot already, but I'd like to shoot something tight as they come up the ramp, so I can change it up later on."

A moment of ominous silence passed as Tychus sought to control his temper and failed. "Are you stupid?" he demanded angrily. "Or crazy? *No,* you fekkin' asshole, I won't unload the troops! Now get outta my face."

Speer had been on the receiving end of the sergeant's wrath before and had a very thick skin. "Okay," he replied cheerfully. "How 'bout a quick sound bite then?"

Tychus opened his mouth to release a blast of profanity that would take the finish off Speer's armor, but the reporter was already backing away. "Just kidding, Sarge . . . just kidding," the civilian said as he turned away from the ramp.

Tychus was still mumbling under his breath as he boarded the *Sweetie Pie.* Due to the jet packs on their suits, none of the soldiers could sit, but they could lock their joints and relax inside their hardskins during the trip.

Then it was time to give the kind of rousing speech officers like Quigby specialized in. "Okay," Tychus said. "Remember the plan, watch your six, and don't shoot Jimmy or any of the POWs. You got any questions? No? I'll see you on the ground."

The dropships were in the air five minutes later, running with the lights off as they turned toward the east. That was when the first part of the hour-long flight began. At that point each soldier was a prisoner to his or her hopes and fears as the dropship's engines whined and the vessel bored a hole through the darkness.

All except for Harnack that is, who had convinced Feek to equip his armor with some unauthorized memory and a closed circuit playback capability. So while his comrades wrestled with their personal demons, Hank was watching a personalized video mix on his HUD and bobbing his head in rhythm to the music.

Tychus found out about the vid mix the same day he discovered Doc had been crab-free for twelve hours, that Ward had tiny pictures of his wife and children affixed along the upper edge of his visor, and that Zander was carrying ten grenades over his authorized load out. Weight a larger man wouldn't have been able to get away with. What Tychus *didn't* know was how many of his platoon would be coming back or why part of him cared.

After what seemed like an eternity the pilot's deliberately neutral voice came over the comm channel in Tychus's helmet. "We're ten minutes from the drop zone . . . repeat, ten out. Give the KMs my best. Over."

Rather than remain aboard the *Sweetie Pie* and supervise the jump, Tychus had granted himself the privilege of being the first person to drop, and therefore the first to land. Because if something went wrong, he figured it would go wrong right away, and he wanted to be there to deal with it.

After the long wait Tychus was conscious of the tension he always felt just prior to combat, but a sense of anticipation as well, since it would feel good to *do* something for a change. He was eager to find out if Raynor had succeeded in infiltrating the camp, and if he'd been able to warn the POWs. Tychus felt pretty good about the odds; knowing Jim, the poor bastards had been briefed, re-briefed, and alphabetized!

The thought brought a smile to Tychus's face

as the dropship entered a tight turn, the deck tilted under his boots, and the final seconds ticked away. "Three! Two! One!" The jump master brought her hand down and Tychus dropped into the abyss. The sun was busy shining on the other side of the planet, but two moons were up and casting a ghostly glow over the landscape below.

It was pitch-black due to a high overcast, or would have been, without the technology that was available to him. Tychus was gratified to see both his night-vision display *and* a computer-generated terrain map appear on his HUD. He was slated to land on Hill Bravo. The movements were so automatic by that time that the glowing target seemed to shift toward him rather than the other way around. The altimeter unwound, the jet pack fired, and Tychus took hold of the weapon that was clipped to his chest.

His boots hit seconds later, as a green Kel-Morian turned toward the unexpected threat, and shook spastically as half a dozen spikes hit his chest. "Hello," Tychus said to no one in particular. "That was for Captain Hobarth. No need to get up . . . I'll let your boss know I'm here."

KEL-MORIAN INTERNMENT CAMP-36,
ON THE PLANET TURAXIS II

The gently spinning world was black with occasional blips of light. Raynor was lost, and had been for hours by then. He was aware of a sense of expectation, however, although it wasn't until he saw flashes of light on the surrounding hilltops and heard a series of resonant booms that he remembered why. The platoon was landing!

The next fifteen minutes were a mix of excitement and fear as Raynor heard gunfire, saw tracers pass within feet of him, and wondered if one of his squad mates was going to shoot him. Then he heard confused shouting and felt a series of jerks as he was lowered to the ground. Tychus was waiting in the glow created by four suit lights as members of the first squad gathered around. Was that concern on his face? "Enough hanging around," the platoon leader said as he cut Raynor free. "It's time for you to go to work."

Raynor nearly choked as Doc gave him a sip of water. "It's nice to see you, too," Raynor said, once he had recovered.

"Boy, Raynor, you're looking pretty sexy in those trunks," Ward chided.

"I don't want to look," Zander put in. "I'll never get the image out of my head."

"What the fekk *is* this?" Tychus demanded, as he eyed the people around him. "A tea party? We have POWs to load. Get to work."

As the others left, Tychus put a huge arm around Raynor's shoulders and helped him walk. "You done good," Tychus said gruffly. "Thanks to you the POWs are ready to go."

Raynor stopped short and looked back at Hickson, who was being carried away on a stretcher. He was awake now, and even managed a wave.

Raynor gave him a nod, took a shallow, excruciating breath, and allowed himself to be led away. Just then three Hellhounds broke through the screen of Avengers circling above and blew one of the incoming dropships out of the sky. Huge chunks of flaming debris cartwheeled down and cut one of the buildings in two. That triggered a fire, which lit up the night. *"Cap-One to Sierra-Six,"* a voice said, as a second dropship went down. *"I'm sorry to say that we have ten bandits at angels five. Your buses are turning back. They'll try again later. Over."*

"Roger that, Cap-One," Tychus said, and swore once the connection was broken.

"The dropships aren't coming, are they?" Raynor inquired.

"No," Tychus replied, as a Hellhound cut across the valley, guns spraying red death at the ground below. "They were forced to turn back."

"I had a good view from up there," Raynor said, as he jerked a thumb back over his shoulder. "The KMs have quite a few trucks on the base and some other vehicles, too. Let's load 'em up and haul ass."

Tychus frowned doubtfully. "To where?"

"The disputed zone," Raynor replied. "It sucks, but it's better than this."

A series of rockets slammed into the camp as if

to emphasize Raynor's point. It was clear that the KMs planned to kill the POWs rather than allow them to escape. "Roger that," Tychus said calmly. "We'll give it a try. And find some clothes. You look like shit."

Max Speer had been aboard the single dropship that managed to touch down safely. He smiled broadly and continued to record as the soldiers departed.

The Avengers had regrouped by that time and took off after the Hellhounds. One of the enemy fighters took a hit from a missile, roared over the camp, and slammed into the hill designated as "Charlie." The fighter was carrying a full load of ordnance plus lots of fuel. The resulting explosion shook the ground and a red-orange fireball floated up into the sky as members of the STM platoon rushed to collect the POWs.

And that was when they discovered that, having been tipped off by Raynor, the prisoners had organized themselves into small groups and were ready to board the dropships. The weakest POWs had been spread across all of the groups so that the stronger ones could assist them, and all the "platoons" were gathered near the Kel-Morian landing pads waiting for ships that weren't coming. It was a bittersweet sight for Raynor, who was determined to finish what he started.

High on the stimpack Doc had given him, Raynor insisted on taking charge. He could see the drug's appeal for the first time; it seemed to erase his pain, at least for a little while. The mental anguish he'd just suffered would take more than a drug to ease—but there was no time to think about that now.

Raynor knew where the camp's factory was, and led a posse that consisted of Zander, Doc, and a couple of STM troopers to the low-slung structure. And just in time, too . . . because as he and his companions jogged up the road Raynor saw headlights and knew some of the KMs were going to make a run for it. "Stop them!" he shouted. "But don't destroy the vehicles."

There was a sharp exchange of gunfire as the groups clashed. Some of the KMs—those who'd been on guard duty when the attack began—were wearing armor. The rest were wearing vest-style chest protectors. As the defenders charged, Ward fired a salvo of rockets at them even as Harnack opened up with his flamethrower. There were three overlapping explosions, so only two of the armored KMs staggered out of the raging inferno, and they were on fire. The STM troopers triggered their gauss rifles and the enemy soldiers fell.

As Raynor stepped under a harsh light and bent to retrieve a Kel-Morian assault rifle, he heard a powerful engine start. Zander shouted, "Watch out!" and Raynor found himself pinned in the glare of two headlights as tires screeched and a huge saber command car barreled straight at him!

Raynor threw himself to the right, felt a searing pain as the loose gravel ripped some skin off, and fired a short burst. The fact that a bullet whipped through the driver's side window and blew Taskmaster Lumley's brains out was a matter of luck rather than marksmanship.

But the effect was the same as the vehicle swerved, skidded, and came to a halt. By the time Raynor got up and rounded the back of the vehicle, Overseer Brucker was out of the car and waddling away.

"There! Behind the car!" Doc shouted.

"Stop, or I'll shoot!" Raynor yelled as he scrambled toward Brucker, positioning himself within range, but the Kel-Morian officer kept going. Then, before Raynor could pull the trigger, Zander fired a single shot. Brucker stumbled and fell.

Doc had chosen to shuck her armor because it was difficult to treat patients with the hardskin on. By the time Raynor reached them she was already kneeling next to Brucker with her medical pack opened at her side. A red stain could be seen on the officer's right thigh and he was gritting his teeth in pain. "It looks like the bullet missed bone," Doc said matter-of-factly. "He'll be fine."

"That's Overseer Brucker," Raynor said, "the guy the POWs call 'the Butcher.' They'll be thrilled to hear that he's going to recover."

"I need to slip a plastiscab bandage in under the exit wound. Do me a favor, reach under his knee and lift it up."

"I should have shot you," Brucker said bitterly, as Raynor lifted the officer's leg.

"Yeah, life is filled with missed opportunities," Raynor observed.

"Thanks," Doc said. "You can put it down now. And Jim . . ."

"Yeah?"

"Once you find some clothes, track me down. I'll give you some more happy juice and put antibacterial dressings on the worst of those needle holes."

"Okay," Raynor agreed as he eyed a trooper. "You'll guard him?"

"Sure," the other soldier agreed. "No problem."

As Raynor left, Doc applied a plastiscab bandage to Brucker's entry wound and taped it in place. Then, having removed a disposable syringe from her bag, she withdrew ten cc's of clear liquid from a small bottle. "What's that?" Brucker inquired.

"It's a painkiller," Doc replied, as she examined the inside surface of Brucker's arm. The light was poor, and the patient was obese, so it took a moment to find a vein. But once Doc had it the needle went in smoothly.

That was when she leaned in close. Her voice

was little more than a whisper. "Colonel Vanderspool asked me to give you this message. . . . If you thought you could get your grubby little hands on his trucks, you thought wrong. Attacking Fort Howe was a serious mistake, and the last one you're ever going to make."

Brucker's eyes opened wide and he tried to jerk his arm away as he realized what was going to happen. But it was too late by then. The poison was already in his bloodstream. He jerked convulsively, tried to say something, and died.

"Damn it!" Doc said regretfully, as she got to her feet. "The fat bastard had a heart attack! Oh well, you can't win 'em all. Drag him off the road, Max. . . . The last thing we need is a speed bump."

CHAPTER TWENTY-FOUR

"This week's program lineup showcases the heroism, valor, and strength of all our fighting men and women. Tune in to Courage for the Confederacy *at 2100, followed by the acclaimed documentary series* Honored Few *at 2200, only on UNN, your home for up-to-the-minute information, analysis, and commentary on the war."*

Max Speer, *Special Evening Report from the Front Line* for UNN
December 2488

KEL-MORIAN INTERNMENT CAMP-36,
ON THE PLANET TURAXIS II

Having captured the factory, the next challenge was to assemble a convoy and load it. Once Zander completed a quick inventory of what was available, Tychus learned that he had six trucks, two buses, two tracked, armored personnel carriers (APCs), and a saber command car at his disposal.

So he put the saber at the head of the column, followed by an APC, the trucks, the buses, and the second armored personnel carrier.

Three members of the STM platoon had been killed in crash landings, and two had been taken out subsequent to touchdown. That left Tychus with thirty-one of his own people, plus a dozen rangers who had been lucky enough to survive a dropship crash. That gave him a force of forty-three soldiers to protect some three hundred POWs, roughly ten percent of whom might be healthy enough to fight, and were busy arming themselves just in case.

Could the convoy break through into the zone? He hoped so. The only alternative was to stay at KIC-36 and wait to see who would arrive first. A contingent of Kel-Morian troops? Or some Confederate dropships? Given the fact that they were well inside Kel-Morian-held territory, it would have been silly to put his money on the dropships.

There was a sudden roar as gravel flew in every direction and a dusty vulture hover-cycle came to a stop. Not only was Jim Raynor at the controls, he was wearing goggles he'd acquired with the vehicle, a collection of garments scrounged from the factory's locker room, and a pistol he had taken off a dead pit boss. There was a big grin on his face as he revved the engines. "Look what I found!"

Kydd had been forced to jettison his armor

and initiate its self-destruct device when its control system crashed. He looked small standing next to Tychus. "Don't let him do it, Sarge. . . . The last time he drove one of those things we wound up in jail."

But it was too late as an overmedicated Jim Raynor waved and took off down the road. His voice could be heard over the comm in the saber. *"I'll scout ahead,"* Raynor said, *"and let you know what to look out for."*

Tychus swore as he saw an Avenger chasing a Hellhound across the valley, gave orders for everyone except Ward to shuck their armor, and did so himself. It was too bad, since the hardskins would have given his people an edge in a head-on fight, but they were too large for the already crowded vehicles and wouldn't be able to keep up no matter how fast they walked or jogged. But there's an exception to every rule, and since Ward had the capacity to launch eight independently targeted rockets, he was ordered to ride in truck one.

Having freed himself from his suit, Tychus entered the saber, snatched a mic off its clip, and gave the necessary orders. "Keep the vehicle ahead of you in sight, but stay three truck lengths back, and kill your headlights. The comms can be monitored by the enemy. . . . So don't use them except in an emergency. Over."

Zander gunned the engine and put the saber

in motion. They had a long way to go, and the clock was ticking.

THE DISPUTED ZONE,
ON THE PLANET TURAXIS II

As part of Overseer Brucker's regiment, it was the Kel-Morian Snakehead Komando's mission to keep a close eye on the northern sector of the zone, send in regular intelligence reports, and interdict any Confederate patrols that happened along.

The unit was camped in and around a scattering of house-sized rocks, with a clear free-fire zone all around, and good visibility for the sentries perched atop of the biggest boulders. So Foreman Kar Ottmar felt reasonably secure inside his boxy command vehicle as he typed another letter into his hand comp. He couldn't send it of course, not until the Komando returned to base, but doing so every night was part of a long, frequently interrupted conversation with his wife, Hana.

He could imagine her getting the electronic letters ten or fifteen at a time, and the flicker of firelight on her pretty face as she read them aloud to the children. He never spoke of the fighting in hopes that his family would never face the horrors of war. So he was telling them a story about the dusty brown lizard that had taken up residence in one of his hats, and what the reptile liked to eat, when a comm technician rapped on the half-open door. "Sorry to bother you, sir, but Assistant Overseer Danick is on the horn. He sounds pretty upset. It seems the Confeds attacked KIC-36 and laid waste to it."

Ottmar swore silently as he hit "save" and left the lizard story half-told. The comsat truck was parked about fifty feet away and protected by light-dispersing camouflage netting. A minute later he was inside the vehicle and sitting on a fold-down seat. A bare-breasted pinup named Viki smiled down on him from her spot just above the comsat terminal as he pulled a headset down over his head and adjusted the lip mic. "This is Snake-Six. Over."

"The bastards dropped out of the sky!" Danick proclaimed, as if such a thing wasn't fair. *"They weren't wearing parachutes, they were using some kind of flying armor, which enabled them to land with pinpoint accuracy. We're still in the process of sorting everything out, but it's clear that Overseer Brucker and about forty of his guards are dead, with ten WIAs, and major damage to the base.*

"That's not the worst of it, though," Danick continued hotly. *"The Confeds freed the POWs and they're headed your way! I want you to stop them, Kar. . . . More than that, I want you to kill every one of the bastards and leave their worthless carcasses to rot in the sun! Do I make myself clear? Over."*

Ottmar could visualize the lick of hair that

would be hanging down across the other man's forehead, the bulging intensity of his eyes, and his slightly purplish lips. "Yes, sir. Very clear. Over."

"Put your comm tech back on the line," the assistant overseer instructed. *"We'll feed you everything we have on the column's position and direction of travel."*

"Yes, sir," Ottmar replied, and surrendered the headset to the comm tech.

As the officer stepped down from the truck, he wasn't surprised to find Taskmaster Kurst waiting for him. Somehow Kurst always knew when something was about to happen. He was a big man with a walrus-style mustache and a lantern jaw. "Sir?"

"The enemy laid waste to KIC-36—and killed fifty of our men. Rather than give aid to the wounded, the bastards shot them. We're going to hunt the slimeballs down! I want the Komando combat-ready thirty minutes from now."

The exaggerations were intended to motivate the troops, and judging from the anger in Kurst's eyes, the strategy was working. "Yes, sir!"

Ottmar smiled grimly as the taskmaster departed. The Confeds might have some fancy armor, but they were burdened with hundreds of POWs, and a long way from Confederate lines. He and his Snakeheads were going to find the degenerates and make them sorry they'd ever been born.

* * *

The drugs were beginning to wear off, and Raynor was exhausted as the sun rose in the east and he guided the vulture out of a canyon and onto a flat plain. He'd been riding the hover-cycle for hours by then and felt like an old hand as he cut power and let the machine coast to a gentle stop. What had been a single road now split into three well-defined tracks.

Stiff fingers fumbled for the stimpack, found it, and slapped the device against the back of his neck. It buzzed softly. That meant it was empty, so Raynor threw it away. *Damn.* All the places where Moller had stuck needles into his body hurt like hell.

The saber rolled up to a point about twenty feet away and came to a stop. Tychus climbed out, eyed the sky, and lit a cigar. Puffs of smoke trailed behind him as he made his way over to the hover-cycle. Raynor, who had just taken a long pull from a water bottle, gargled and swallowed. "We're sitting ducks out here."

"Yup," Tychus acknowledged. "We sure as hell are. That's why Vanderspool wants us to find a defensible spot and hole up."

"What for?" Raynor demanded. "Why can't they send some dropships to pick us up here?"

"There's a shortage," Tychus answered laconically. "That's what Colonel Shit-for-brains claims anyway. We lost too many dropships last night and they have to bring some in from the north."

"Well, that's just wonderful," Raynor responded. "I guess I'd better go find a hole for us to crawl into."

"You do that," Tychus said agreeably. "And Jim . . ."

"Yeah?"

"Find it *soon*. Most of our vehicles are running on fumes."

Raynor swore, pulled a pair of goggles down over his eyes, and gunned the engines. The vulture fishtailed as it took off and raised a rooster tail as it sped west. Various rock formations could be seen in the distance, and Raynor was trying to figure out which one of them was closest when something caught his eye almost directly ahead. It was too symmetrical to be natural, yet so large he couldn't believe it was man-made until he topped a rise, and the entire machine came into view.

It was roughly the size of a thirty-story office tower laid on its side. And, judging from the enormous tracks that were partially buried in the sand, the enormous device was a so-called "mineral stripper," a mobile processor that could "eat" a fifty-foot-wide strip of ground as it crawled across the surface of a planet, extracting the minerals, and process them on board. Waste materials were fed out the back as trucks pulled up alongside to receive the ore and carry it away. The words RAF-

FIN BROTHERS MINING were printed along the stripper's rusty flank in letters twenty feet tall.

Judging from the damage that could be seen, and all of the sand that had accumulated around the machine's monstrous tracks, the processor had been bombed during the early stages of the wars and had been abandoned thereafter. Could they hide inside? And wait for help to arrive? Yes, there was plenty of metal to protect them, and the stripper was closer than the rock formations in the distance.

Raynor skidded to a stop, flicked a switch, and spoke into the mic. "Sierra-Nine to Sierra-Six. . . . Come to Daddy. I have it. Over."

The reply wasn't what he was expecting. *"Hit the throttle, Nine. . . . You have an inbound Hellhound at three o'clock!"*

Raynor was still in the process of absorbing the words as geysers of sand jumped into the air all around him and there was a sudden roar as the enemy fighter flashed overhead. Raynor gunned the engine and sent sand spewing in every direction as he took off. The vulture caught a large pocket of air as it passed over the top of a dune and pancaked in twenty feet beyond.

The impact nearly threw Raynor off the bike, but he managed to hang on as the hover-cycle began to regain its momentum, and the Hellhound circled back. The distance to the stripper had been halved by then—but Raynor knew that the pilot was going to get a second chance at him. So he cranked the handlebars to the left. That caused the vulture to turn in on the fighter and made the Kel-Morian's target that much smaller.

Since the vehicles were rushing at each other at a combined speed of more than three hundred miles per hour, the pilot had only seconds in which to score a kill. Raynor looked up, saw laser bolts coming straight at him, and marveled at how pretty the lights were as they plowed parallel furrows through the sand. A slight turn to the right was enough to steer the bike *between* the incoming beams as the Hellhound roared overhead.

That was Raynor's cue to execute a sharp turn to the right and make a run for the protection offered by the stripper. The rest of the convoy was halfway across the open area by that time, each vehicle throwing up its own plume of dust, as they raced toward safety. The only exceptions were the APCs, which sat side-by-side, roof-mounted double-barreled gauss cannons stuttering as they attempted to bring the Hellhound down.

Then a bus came too close to a low-lying rock formation, ran up onto the ledge, and flipped over! The vehicle skidded for fifty feet on its roof, wheels still spinning, before finally coming to a stop. POWs were just starting to crawl out through the windows when the Hellhound came back to strafe the wreckage. The bus burst into flames and a column of oily smoke boiled up into the sky as if to mark a funeral pyre.

It was a terrible loss, but one that gave the rest of the vehicles enough time to circle around both ends of the stripper and seek safety between the processor's mighty treads. It was darker in there, and cooler, too, as Tychus exited the saber to find Raynor waiting for him. "They know where we are now," Raynor said grimly. "Ground units are probably en route. Let's bring the APCs in to block both ends of this hulk."

It was a good idea, and Tychus was about to say as much, when an accelerated spike hit. The explosion wasn't that big by military standards, but sufficient to blow a huge divot out of the sand just inside the north entrance and cause Tychus to change his mind. "Get the POWs out of those vehicles!" he shouted. "See the stairs to either side? Take them up and put them at the very center of this thing. And do it yesterday!"

"Where the hell did that spike come from?" Raynor asked, as the rangers hurried to obey Tychus's orders.

"I don't know," Tychus answered grimly, as his cigar waggled up and down. "But I'll bet we're gonna find out."

Ottmar and his Snakeheads were sitting atop a low ridge that ran east to west across the plain.

The mineral stripper was clear to see about a mile ahead. Thanks to information provided by the Hellhound pilot, not to mention the thick black smoke, the fugitives had been easy to locate.

Ottmar panned the battlefield with his field goggles. Eight combat four-wheeled light attack vehicles (LAVs) led the charge. In keeping with the Komando's motto, *"Move fast and strike hard,"* each LAV was armed with a fixed gun and was large enough to carry two armored soldiers. The four-wheelers could travel at speeds up to sixty miles per hour over a reasonably flat surface. That made them perfect for scouting, quick raids, and rat hunts like this one.

Two sloths followed close behind. Repurposed to function as tanks, the sloths had once been huge earth movers to which large caliber cannons had been fitted in place of dozer blades, along with lighter slugthrowers for anti-personnel use. Metal plates had been welded all around the circumference of the machines and were angled wherever possible in order to deflect incoming projectiles.

The rest of the unit, including the command vehicle, the comm-truck, the supply hog, the fueler, and the men required to defend them were almost ten miles to the rear. Having lost their battle with the Hellhound, both of the captured APCs were burning. The fighter, which was running low on fuel, was on its way back to base.

As the tanks fired on the stripper, the resulting explosions were little more than tiny flashes of light against the machine's vast gray bulk. "Snake-One to all units. . . . Save your ammo," Ottmar ordered. "The Confeds are inside that monster by now. Over."

That was when the driver of the LAV to Ottmar's right jerked spastically and a distant crack was heard. Then, with a ponderous dignity, the Snakehead fell sideways onto the ground. A sniper had seen an open visor and taken his shot. The rats had teeth!

The number two man on the right-hand LAV was behind the controls by then as Ottmar twisted his throttle and sent his attack vehicle surging forward. The key was to get in under the beast, kill any guards who might be waiting there, and fight their way upward. A simple matter, really—and one he would take pleasure in.

Ward could see the oncoming LAVs and knew what they hoped to accomplish, as he left the shadows and lumbered out to stand at the very center of the huge opening. Quad rocket launchers sat atop Ward's squared-off shoulders, and a Kel-Morian gauss cannon was cradled in his arms. This was the moment he'd been waiting for, and there was a smile on his lips as targeting data scrolled across his HUD.

"Ward!" Tychus yelled over the comm. *"Get your dumb ass back over here! That's an order!"*

But Ward couldn't hear anything other than the sound of his wife calling their children in to dinner, and the music of their laughter, followed by a series of explosions as the Hellhounds bombed his village. He staggered as incoming fire sparkled against his armor, but was only marginally aware of the danger as he chose each target with care. Once the process was complete, Ward was careful to brace himself against what he knew was going to be a massive recoil. There was a satisfying whoosh as all eight of the rockets left their launchers at once, locked onto the heat generated by the targets they had been assigned to, and corkscrewed across the sky. The gauss cannon was up and firing by that time, an LAV exploded, and Ward gave thanks. He was a happy man.

Ottmar figured the man who stood legs apart at the very center of the opening was either very brave or very foolish—not that it made much difference, because in a moment he was going to be very dead!

Then he saw the flash of rockets being fired, the vapor trails they made, and knew what would happen next. There was little more than a couple of seconds in which to think about Hana, the children, and the brown lizard before a rocket blew

Foreman Kar Ottmar and the man seated behind him to bloody bits.

Not all of the eight rockets found their targets, but five of them did, and that was sufficient not only to blunt the Snakehead attack, but to leave the survivors without sufficient transportation.

Ryk Kydd, who was up on the processor's stern observation deck, could see the stranded KMs *and* the burning vehicles. He was very unforgiving. Three shots rang out—and three Kel-Morians fell.

But the sloths were still in commission, as were three LAVs, and they were damned hard to hit as thc four-wheelers wove in and out.

Ward was shooting at the sloths with the gauss cannon, but he was out of rockets, and it was a waste of time. But he stood there blasting away until Tychus dashed out into the opening and tackled him. Nobody other than Tychus would have been strong enough to snatch an armored man off his feet and push him to safety, even as the beneficiary of his kindness threatened to kill him.

Then the enemy was inside the tunnel as two four-wheelers entered, firing as they came. Two rangers threw up their hands and went down as a hail of spikes punched holes through their body armor.

But their short-lived success was over as

Raynor pulled out from behind a parked truck and followed the LAVs toward the other end of the tunnel and the daylight beyond. The vulture's grenade launcher made a steady chugging sound as it lobbed grenades straight ahead.

Raynor wasn't very skilled with the weapon since he'd never had an opportunity to fire one before, but it turned out that he didn't have to be, as one of the four-wheelers took a direct hit, and the second ran into a pair of explosions that sent it skidding out of control. Black smoke whipped past as the vulture carried him around the wreckage and out into the open area beyond.

Meanwhile, as the first sloth came to a halt beneath the stripper's massive bulk, Harnack was there to greet it. He was wearing goggles, and carrying a captured shotgun as he dropped onto the vehicle's rear deck from a catwalk above.

There was a loud clang as the top hatch opened and fell against steel. That was the moment when the Kel-Morian saw Harnack's face grinning down at him. Harnack's grenade fell inside, rattled as it fell into the compartment below, and wound up just a foot away from the reserve ammo locker.

Harnack jumped off and was fifty feet away by the time the ammo blew. The explosion also damaged the second sloth, which continued to shake convulsively as rounds cooked off inside the wreckage.

Only two of the LAVs were still operational at

that point, and both of them made a run for it, as half a dozen Avengers arrived on the scene and attacked them from the air. Both vehicles were destroyed in a matter of seconds.

Suddenly all sorts of orders were coming in as ten dropships appeared and began to land one after another. The first dropship to touch down disgorged eight armored soldiers, who immediately went to work rounding up the POWs.

Meanwhile, Tychus, Raynor, and Harnack began to make their way out from under the gigantic crawler. Moments later Kydd, Zander, Ward, and Doc fell in behind them. Together they walked out of the tunnel and into the sunlight beyond. The job was almost finished—but there was one more thing to do. Find the rest of the Kel-Morian attack group and kill them.

Thanks to the tracks the sloths and the LAVs had left behind, it wasn't all that difficult to find the rest of Foreman Ottmar's Komandos. The unit's support vehicles plus two LAVs had taken shelter under a protruding rock shelf where they would be in the shade and invisible from above.

It was a pretty good hiding place, all things considered, but not good enough to protect the KM soldiers from the heat-seeking missiles fired by a pair of Avengers, or the troops that landed shortly thereafter. The fueler was on fire, the comm-truck was badly damaged, and bodies lay scattered all about. "Check the bodies to make sure they're really dead," Tychus ordered. "And we *are* taking prisoners, so mind your manners."

Raynor could have remained on the drop-ship, but couldn't stand to sit there while the rest of the team hit the dirt. So he followed them into the shadow cast by the outcropping of rock, saw the undamaged command vehicle sitting off to one side, and drew his pistol.

The door was partially open, but he was careful to approach at an angle, so he could see inside. "Hello? Anybody there? If so, put your weapons down and come out with your hands on top of your head."

There was no response. So Raynor made use of the pistol barrel to push the door open, and took a moment to peer into the relative darkness, before climbing a set of fold-down stairs. It was hot inside the truck, *very* hot, and once Raynor was sure that the vehicle was empty of people, he wanted to bail out. But first there were some files to go through. The intel people would want to look at any reports, maps, or other official documents that were accessible.

Raynor had just opened a camo-covered briefcase, and was shoving files inside, when he came across a hand comp. A single touch was enough to turn the device on. The document that blossomed on the screen was a letter from one of the KMs to a woman named Hana. His wife? Yes, he thought so. But rather than the sort of letter that one might expect a soldier to write, Raynor found himself reading a story about a lizard. A tale clearly intended for the author's children.

Raynor scrolled to the bottom of the document, saw that the story was unfinished, and shook his head sadly. It was hard to believe that the man who had written the letter was all that different from the people Raynor served with every day. That wasn't what the government claimed, though. According to the Confederacy, *all* of the KMs were monsters. Brucker was—no doubt about that. But *this* guy? Raynor wasn't so sure.

He shoved the hand comp into the briefcase, followed by a personnel roster, both of which would be eagerly welcomed at Fort Howe.

While Raynor continued to fill the briefcase, a tiny brown head popped up from the boonie hat that was resting on a side shelf. After checking its immediate surroundings for signs of danger, a small lizard emerged and darted out of the hat. Its mottled body was motionless for a moment, as its tongue tasted the air, and its nearsighted eyes stared at the area directly in front of it.

Then the lizard was off, scurrying the length of the shelf to the point where it could jump down onto a toolbox, and from there to the floor. After that it was a short run to the open door, the fold-down stairs, and the hot sand that waited beyond.

CHAPTER TWENTY-FIVE

"They fell from the heavens, and they fought like hell to free the Confederate POWs held deep inside KM territory. No one else could have done it. No one else did. That's how the Heaven's Devils earned their name."

- Captain Clair Hobarth, decorated POW, in an interview with Max Speer
January 2489

FORT HOWE, ON THE PLANET TURAXIS II

It was late afternoon as a necklace of dropships snaked around Fort Howe, turned toward the south, and landed in quick succession. Moments later ramps went down, field ambulances raced out to meet the newly arrived dropships, and medical personnel rushed aboard. Not only were there wounded to care for, but POWs as well, some of whom were in very bad shape. Then and only then were the troops allowed to make their way down onto the tarmac.

Doc tried to convince Raynor to ride in an ambulance, but he refused, insisting that he be allowed to exit the aircraft with the rest of his platoon. Of the thirty-five soldiers who jumped over the Kel-Morian base, only seventeen were still alive and three of them were wounded. So the bedraggled group that followed Tychus across the concrete toward the buildings beyond wasn't much larger than a full-strength squad.

Two men were waiting in front of the nearest hangar. Both were dressed in civilian clothes but might as well have been wearing uniforms, because everything else about them was military, including their haircuts and erect postures. One was tall, the other was short, and he was the one who spoke. "Ark Bennet?" he inquired, as the group walked past. "We'd like to speak with you."

Kydd nearly fell for it. The only thing that saved him was the fact that he'd been using "Kydd" for so long that it took a second to process what the man had said. And that was sufficient time for his brain to kick in and override the natural tendency to say, "Yes."

Some of those around Kydd knew his true identity, of course—but a frown was sufficient to silence them. And by that time, the shorter of the two men had switched to a different tactic. "Private Kydd? My name is Corly. . . . And this is Sergeant Orin. We're with MSS and we'd like to talk to you."

"MSS" stood for the Military Security Service,

a group it was almost impossible to say "No" to. But before Kydd could reply, Tychus chose to intervene. "I don't know what this is about," the noncom said ominously, "but whatever it is can wait. We just came in out of the field. Of course you rear-echelon sons of bitches wouldn't know much about that, would you?"

When Sergeant Orin turned toward Tychus, his eyes were like blue lasers and his face was wooden. "Sergeant Corly has a medal of valor—and was wounded three times in the battle of Rork's Rift." He stepped closer until Tychus felt the agent's breath on his face. "You think we don't know what it feels like to put our lives on the line? To see our brothers and sisters get blown to pieces right in front of us? You watch your mouth, son, and pray you never turn up on my case list."

Kydd knew that a large handgun was probably responsible for the visible bulge under Orin's jacket. But Tychus was armed, too, and Kydd could see the pressure starting to build, as the noncom took a step forward. "You know where you can shove your case list, Sergeant. Or maybe I should do it for you."

Kydd hurried to get in between them. "No problem, Sarge. . . . I might as well get this over with. I'll see you back at the barracks."

Raynor nodded. "Come on, Tychus. . . . You can use your natural charm to get me some service at the infirmary."

Tychus glowered, but allowed himself to be steered away. That left Kydd with the MSS agents. Corly eyed the sniper's rifle. "Is that thing unloaded?"

Kydd nodded. "It is. . . . Would you like to check?"

"No," Corly replied. "That won't be necessary. Please accompany us to the command center. We have some questions to ask you—but the process won't take long. We'll have you back with your buddies shortly."

Was that true? Or an attempt to put his fears to rest? Kydd didn't know, not that it mattered, because the MSS agents would do whatever they wanted to do.

It was a short walk to the command center, through the entrance, and down a side hall to an office labeled MAINTENANCE OFFICER. Kydd felt an emptiness at the pit of his stomach. Because here, after all of the combat, was a different kind of battle. It was a stark choice. Did he want to go back to being Ark Bennet—son of privilege, a businessman, and head of an Old Family? Or did he want to be Ryk Kydd—soldier, sniper, and adventurer?

Orin opened the door to the empty office. A round table was positioned in front of a utilitarian desk covered with clutter. Corly gestured to one of four seats. "Please, sit down."

Kydd hesitated. This would be a crucial, life-defining decision—there was no turning back after this. What was the saying Raynor used every now and then? The one he always attributed to his father? *"You are who you choose to be."* Yeah, that was it. Kydd had always laughed off Raynor's attempts to impart his sentimental brand of wisdom—that kind of warmth was completely foreign to him. But somehow this one resonated with Kydd, even now, when his mind was filled with anxiety.

Both MSS agents were seated at the table by the time Kydd lowered himself into the steel chair. Corly eyed a viewscreen. "According to your P-1 file, you submitted affidavits claiming that your *real* name is Ark Bennet—and that you were snatched off the streets of Tarsonis by a rogue recruiter. Is that correct?"

Kydd took a slow, deep breath as he chose his next words. He thought about the former version of himself, the one that had gone for a stroll in the neighborhood called Hacker's Flat back on Tarsonis, and understood what he had been looking for back then. He'd been looking for a chance to live life outside of the obligations he'd been born to, beyond the cocoon of safety in which his family preferred to live, and earn a place in the world rather than simply inherit it.

"I filed affidavits in which I claimed to be Ark Bennet," Kydd admitted. "That much is true."

Corly raised an eyebrow. "And the claim itself? Is that true as well?"

"No," Kydd said, trying to appear remorseful as he looked down at the tabletop.

"So you lied to Major Macaby?"

Kydd looked straight into his interrogator's eyes. "Yes, sir." Kydd swallowed the lump in his throat. "I did." He shifted his eyes toward Orin.

There was a moment of silence as the MSS agents glanced at each other. It wasn't the response they'd been expecting.

Kydd's mind swirled with worry. *Did they believe him? Did they already know the truth? Was his father watching them right now?* He pretended to cough as he glanced around the room. If there was a camera, he couldn't see it.

Corly leaned forward. "Why did you lie?"

"Why? I wanted to get the hell out of the Marine Corps," Kydd replied matter-of-factly. He continued, gaining confidence as he spoke. "I'd heard that a rich kid was missing, and based on the description they gave of him, it sounded as though we have a similar appearance."

"Yes, there *is* an uncanny resemblance, Private." He paused for a moment as he examined Kydd's face. "Although you look leaner, tougher almost. So what changed?" he asked as he looked back at the screen. "Why are you coming clean now?"

"I've had time to think it through. I mean, how far would I get?" Kydd inquired cynically, as his eyes came back into contact with Corly's. "To

Tarsonis? Where the family would denounce me?" He laughed incredulously, for dramatic effect. "I mean, is the family still *looking* for this kid? How long's it been? Months?"

"There are quite a few bounty hunters out there trying to nab the hefty reward offered by the family. Damn shame we're not eligible for it, because Sergeant Orin and I are feeling pretty close to finding our man." Those words sent a chill down Kydd's spine. "So yes, even now, the search is still ongoing. We have nearly a hundred leads to comb through." He pressed some buttons on the terminal. "You may be surprised to learn that your profile was assigned a relatively low percentage rating for a match. But then again, Sergeant Orin and I know that the computers are programmed to assume that all of our military recruiters are law-abiding citizens."

Kydd felt relieved, but was careful to keep the emotion hidden.

"But," Corly continued, "allowing for the possibility that some recruiters *will* break the law to make quotas, we ran a retinal scan and compared it to the one the Bennets gave us." He looked squarely at Kydd. "You're a match, Private."

The floor seemed to drop out from under Kydd. He felt dizzy, nauseous. His voice quivered as he spoke. "Regardless of what you think," Kydd pleaded, "I'm in this for good, and you can't take that away from me. I have a great record, I'm the best at what I do, and my platoon needs me." He paused to muster his resources, which seemed to be fading. "Those men and women—those are my brothers and sisters out there." He punctuated his words by jutting his finger in the direction of the barracks. His eyes moistened. Embarrassed, he looked down at the table.

"What he says is true," Orin said calmly, as he spoke for the first time since they had entered the office. He twirled a wand stylus in his fingers. The larger sergeant's deep, resonant voice was a sharp contrast to Corly's. He had brown skin, and his piercing blue eyes had shifted to Corly by then. "He *does* have a helluva record—and he *is* a skilled sniper. In fact, the commanding officer of Firebase Zulu put him in for a medal."

That was news to Kydd. *A medal!* It was hard to believe. Here was further validation of what he already knew inside. He was good at something, and the military was his home.

"So, where does that leave us?" Corly asked.

Kydd's eyes shifted desperately between the two sergeants.

Orin was silent for a moment, and when the noncom spoke, his eyes were slightly out of focus as if seeing himself in another time and place. "Lying to get out of the Corps was wrong. But Private Kydd admits that—and all of us make mistakes. And sometimes, if we're real lucky, somebody cuts us some slack." He looked squarely at Kydd.

"You're a credit to the Confederacy, son, and you exemplify everything the marines stand for. Private Kydd, unless Sergeant Corly here disagrees, I believe you're free to go."

Kydd looked immediately at Corly, who nodded sagely and smiled. "You're a lifer, boy. Pure and simple." He pressed both hands on the table. "This case is closed."

The young soldier surprised everyone—himself included—by letting out an audible sigh of relief. He recovered quickly and was grinning from ear to ear as he stood up and shook hands with the men who saved Private Ryk Kydd.

Three days had passed since the raid on the Kel-Morian base, it was about 2000 hours, and the HTD was crawling with pilots, marines, and rangers. A lot of them went bar to bar up and down the main drag, looking for the perfect watering hole, but never finding it.

The single exception was Three Fingered Jack's, which was so packed that it was difficult to get in or out. A blue haze hovered over the tables, the buzz of conversation made it difficult to hear, and a live band added to the cacophony of sound. Raynor, Tychus, Harnack, Doc, Ward, and Kydd were seated at a large round table at the center of the room. Other members of the 321st were present as well, along with about fifty ex-POWs, and about half of the pilots who had rescued the whole bunch of them from the disputed zone. It was a very rowdy crowd.

But when a vehicle delivered Captain Hobarth and her medical aide out front, a path magically opened up before her, and everyone broke into applause as she shuffled back into the main room. Then, once she raised a skeletal hand, the noise died down, and it was Three Fingered Jack himself who handed the pilot a mic. "First," the captain said hoarsely, as she looked around the room. "I want to toast the brave soldiers who led this dangerous mission. Here's to our heroes, a group of fine men and women whose name shall be echoed for generations to come—our very own *Heaven's Devils*!"

The crowd cheered. By that time Speer's on-the-scene reporting had been seen throughout the Confederacy—and the entire crowd was familiar with the STM platoon's new nickname. Thunderous applause resonated throughout the room as everyone who wasn't already standing came to their feet and turned to face the table where the soldiers were seated. Tychus grinned broadly, Raynor looked embarrassed, Harnack struck a pose, Kydd gazed around in awe, Zander frowned disapprovingly, Ward stared at his hands, and Doc was too high to know what was going on.

Hobarth smiled, and when the noise dropped down, she spoke again. "Secondly, I want to thank the entire 321st Colonial Rangers Battalion for rescuing my brothers and sisters from KIC-36."

That provoked another round of clapping, as the entire battalion came in for some well-deserved recognition, and the Heaven's Devils joined in.

Hobarth nodded soberly as the noise died down. "Last, but not least," the officer said, as she extended her hand to accept a shot glass of Scotty Bolger's whiskey. "I would like to propose a toast. This is for the fine men and women who gave their lives for the Confederacy and their fellow soldiers. We shall hold them in our hearts and minds until the time comes to join them. Then, as now, we'll get drunk as hell! The next round is on me!"

The next couple of hours were a smoky, booze-drenched blur from which Raynor awoke to a buzzing sound, as a sharp object dragged across his arm. Then the worst of the pain went away as the bald man on the stool next to him swore and got up to take a fone call.

Raynor struggled to focus his eyes and get his bearings. He was surrounded by tiny drawings, no—tattoo designs. Thousands of them, laminated and tacked to the walls, corners blowing in the breeze created by a rusty fan.

Raynor had a vague memory of leaving Three Fingered Jack's with the rest of the squad and staggering down the main drag. He remembered stopping to take a piss on a brick building. And he remembered stumbling past neon lights into a doorway with Tychus's heavy arm slung around his shoulder.

"Ty-chus . . . Ty-chus . . . Ty-chus," Raynor called out in a singsongy voice. He heard a grunt originate from behind him. He followed the direction of the voice and saw that Tychus was laid out on a table, where a woman with bright blue hair was busy inking a new tat onto his sculpted abs. For his part the big man was puffing on a cigar while staring at the artist's cleavage.

Raynor got up, stumbled over to the table, and squinted at the design. It was blurry at first, but when the image rolled into focus, Raynor found himself looking at a winged skeleton. It was partially concealed by a hooded robe, and armed with an old-fashioned rotary machine gun. There was a mushroom-shaped cloud in the background, and the name HEAVEN'S DEVILS was spelled out on the banner over the skeleton's head. "I like that," Raynor said thickly. "I like that a lot."

"I sure hope so!" Ward yelled out, but Raynor didn't understand why.

"Mine's better," Doc said as she looked back over a bare shoulder. "Check it out." She was seated on a stool about ten feet away with a tattoo artist behind and to her left.

Raynor was proud of the way he was able to

cross the intervening section of floor without falling down. The tattoo artist smiled and moved to one side so he could see. As Raynor examined her shoulder tattoo, he realized that it was exactly like the one Tychus was getting except that the machine gun had been supplanted by a huge syringe and needle!

"Whaddya think?" Cassidy asked. "Cool, huh?"

"Very," Raynor replied airily. "It's just like Tychus's. Cute, very cute, you two." He waggled a finger at Doc and turned back to face Tychus, at which point he delivered a wink and a smile. "Matching tattoos, huh?"

Raynor heard laughter from all around the shop, and wondered what he was missing.

The bald man came to collect him. "Come on," he said. "We're about halfway through yours."

As the man led Raynor back to his table he realized that the Heaven's Devils had taken over the establishment and all of them were getting tattoos!

"Sit down, champ," the man said patiently. "And hold still."

Raynor heard more snickering from all around him. He laughed, too, not knowing why. "Yup, you got it." He closed his eyes and took a nap.

The tattoos took time, as did the enormous breakfast that followed, so it was about 0500 before the

Devils finally reentered the base and made their way back to the barracks. And that was where First Lieutenant Samantha Sanchez was waiting for them.

The officer had black hair worn in a buzz cut, a face that might have been pretty with a little bit of makeup, and a blocky body that was all muscle and no fat. Unlike Quigby, Sanchez wasn't insecure, didn't need to run her mouth, and, judging from her hands-on-hips stance, wasn't going to take crap from anybody. Not even Tychus, whom she chose to address first.

"Are you in charge of the first squad? I thought so. . . . My name is Sanchez. I want your people out front and ready to run the perimeter of the base at 0530. No excuses, no exceptions, and no bullshit. Do you scan me, Sergeant?"

Tychus had served under all sorts of officers during his years in the military and knew the real deal when he saw it. "Yes, ma'am," he replied. "Five by five."

"Good," Sanchez replied, as if she would have been surprised by any other response. "Maybe you've heard of a city called Polk's Pride. . . . It seems that the KMs have a strategic resources repository there. And we're going to be part of the effort to capture it. If we succeed it will shorten the war. Questions?"

Kydd raised a hand. "Didn't the first attack fail?"

Sanchez nodded. "That's right. . . . And the *second* attack failed, too. So we'll have our work cut out for us. Any more questions? No? Well, get your shit together. Because you'll be up to your asses in Kel-Morians a few days from now and I expect this platoon to do its part. That is all." Sanchez did an about-face and left.

Harnack watched her go. "So what was that about?"

Raynor was tired, sore, and sickeningly hung over. It took considerable effort to produce a smile. "That was her way of saying, 'howdy,' " Raynor replied weakly. "It was all stick and no carrot. Same way Tychus runs things."

Harnack shrugged. "Works for me. . . . I don't like vegetables." He grinned in response to his own joke and slapped a wobbly Raynor on the arm as they headed for the barracks.

"Ow! Watch it." Raynor's arm seared with pain, and as he walked, he lifted his sleeve to see if any of the swelling had gone down. He peeled back the gauze bandage. No such luck. The skeleton was plump and fleshy, and the HEAVEN'S DEVILS banner was three-dimensional. As if it had come to life.

CHAPTER TWENTY-SIX

". . . and here at the home offices, our own staff is experiencing a changing of the guard. Six members of the UNN executive board stepped down today, citing 'personal and professional differences with the current network philosophies.' This change was followed by two dozen layoffs as the UNN hierarchy went through what one shareholder called 'significant restructuring.' What this will mean for the media giant and its subsidiary stations is the subject of much debate."

Handy Anderson, *Evening Report* for UNN
February 2489

THE CITY OF POLK'S PRIDE,
ON THE PLANET TURAXIS II

Polk's Pride had once been the second largest city on Turaxis II, with a population of four million people and a thriving economy. Back before the wars, it had been famous for hundreds of man-made canals that not only gave the metropolis its special flavor, but fed barge traffic onto the heavily traveled river that meandered through the downtown area. In fact, the Paddick flowed for more than a thousand miles before eventually emptying into the planet's single ocean.

By now, all but a few hundred thousand of Polk's Pride's population had been forced out into the countryside, where dozens of refugee camps were set up to accommodate them, and the city was split in two. For the moment the area north of the Paddick River was in Kel-Morian hands—and the Confederacy controlled everything south of it. But that was subject to change as the battle for the city seesawed back and forth.

As a result of the ongoing conflict, a mile-wide swath of land along both sides of the river lay in ruins. Buildings had been bombed into rubble, streets were filled with fallen debris, and once-picturesque canals were blocked by half-submerged wrecks.

Along the banks of the river the remains of the city's once-graceful bridges could be seen. Each had been different, but beautiful in its own way, which was why they had been known as "The Seven Sisters."

All of them were lying in the river now. There was always less flow at that time of year, so that, combined with a drought up north, had caused the water level to drop to a record low. But occasionally a pile of debris would build up behind one of the spans, only to be broken by the weight of the water behind it, thereby releasing a momentary flood. And there, mixed in with all of the other trash that regularly came their way, the people who lived downstream would find hundreds of half-rotted bodies.

It was a public health problem, not to mention a gruesome sight, so they tried to sort them out at first. The idea being to bury Kel-Morians with Kel-Morians and Confederates with Confederates, both because it was assumed the opposing armies would want it that way, and as a sort of insurance policy—it wasn't clear which side was going to win and therefore be in charge. But as things turned out, there were far too many bodies for the civilians to deal with, which meant they were forced to inter the dead soldiers in mass graves.

Such was the landscape as Colonel Vanderspool led Lieutenant Sanchez and her platoon through the once thriving streets of south Polk's Pride to the edge of no-man's-land. The office tower that loomed above them was still largely intact even though Kel-Morian sloths located on the far side of the river routinely used it for target practice.

Broken glass crunched under Raynor's boots as Harnack said, "Whoa . . . check that out," and pointed upward. The back end of a Hellhound could be seen sticking out of an office on the fire-ravaged twenty-sixth floor. Raynor wondered if the dead pilot was still sitting in his cockpit or had been removed by a graves registration team.

There wasn't any power in the building, so they had to climb nine flights of stairs to reach Vanderspool's objective. Since the enemy was on the opposite side of the river, the men hadn't been required to wear full combat armor, so they were relying on their own strength. Tychus, who had never seen Vanderspool do much more than strut around Fort Howe, was surprised to learn that the officer could climb nine stories without breaking a sweat.

Finally, a fire door with the number 9 on it appeared, and Vanderspool led the platoon down a hall and into a trash-strewn office. A squad of marines was there waiting for them. When Master Sergeant Rockwell hollered, "Atten-hut!" all of them crashed to attention.

Rockwell was a man with whom Raynor and Tychus were well acquainted. As the battalion's senior NCO, Rockwell had a lot of power and liked to use it. And there was something about the Heaven's Devils that cracked him off, so his hobby was coming up with shit details for Tychus and the squad to take care of.

And now, as Rockwell's squad stood in perfect alignment, with their backs ramrod straight, they could have been awaiting inspection. That was over the top, even for marines, especially in a combat zone. And as Raynor examined them more closely, he saw that they all wore the same thousand-yard stares, perfect uniforms, and spit-shined boots. The whole thing made him uncomfortable.

"At ease," Vanderspool said, as if he were used to being received in that fashion. He gestured to the view. "Do you see the tower over there on top of the hill? The tall, skinny one?"

Raynor peered out the window to see the hillside across the river—a bleak, seemingly deserted cluster of buildings—upon which lay a tower surrounded by high walls.

"That comsat station marks the location of the Kel-Morian strategic resources repository," Vanderspool continued. "Down below it there is a network of tunnels and caves where stocks of rare minerals are stored. If we can capture or destroy the repository the KMs will have to shut down their factories north of the city, their military units will begin to run short of critical supplies within a matter of weeks, and we'll be able to push the bastards off Turaxis II! So this is a very important push."

The shattered windows offered Raynor an unobstructed view of no-man's-land, the much-abused river, and north Polk's Pride. Like the sky overhead, the area beyond the river was unrelievedly gray. A few buildings still stood. They looked like headstones in a sprawling graveyard. Thready columns of black smoke marked the spots where

Kel-Morian soldiers were camped in the ruins, or stubborn citizens eked out a bleak existence in spite of repeated efforts to force them out.

"The repository is our target," Vanderspool continued grimly. "But, as you can imagine, the structure is well protected. Which is why it's still vertical in spite of more than two dozen air strikes." At that point the officer handed his binoculars to Zander with an order to pass them around.

"You'll notice that the comsat station is surrounded by circular blast walls and protected by dozens of computer-controlled missile turrets. More than that, all of the approaches are defended by goliaths, regular comsat sweeps, and a squad of rippers. So getting inside won't be easy. Questions?"

"Yes, sir," Sanchez replied. "How large a force are we going to throw at the objective?"

"You won't be alone, of course," Vanderspool continued. "The entire battalion plus elements from other units will take part in the attack. Sergeant Rockwell's people are going in first. . . . That means the unit will probably suffer heavy casualties. But, no guts, no glory. Isn't that right, Sergeant?"

"Yes, sir!" Rockwell said emphatically. *"What's your mission, soldiers?"* he called out.

All of the rangers knew that the first people to go in stood a very high chance of getting killed, but if the marines realized that, there was no sign of it on their faces as they responded to the non-com. *"To die for the Confederacy!"*

That was when Raynor remembered the program Brucker had mentioned and realized something. . . . Judging from what Tychus had told him about Lassiter, and seeing the marines in front of him, he knew the Kel-Morian overseer was correct. Certain people were being brainwashed. What did they call it? Resocial something? Resocialized. That was it. No, *neurally* resocialized, and in considerable numbers, too. Was *that* what Raynor was supposed to be fighting for? A society in which citizens were transformed into flesh-and-blood robots?

"Sanchez, you and your platoon will advance immediately behind them. That's why you're here. As I said, this is not going to be easy, so that's why I've brought on the best of the best."

Raynor began to wonder. What was up with Vanderspool anyway? Was he trying to win the wars? Or make general in record time? Or was he simply determined to give the KMs a good whupping? There was no way to be sure as the tactical aspect of the briefing began. There was a lot for the platoon to learn—and only a few days in which to learn it. The clock was ticking.

It was raining. Not hard, but persistently, so that as Raynor stood at the edge of the roof of the building in which the battalion was temporarily headquartered, the lunch he had brought up from the field kitchen below was starting to get damp. But he didn't care. Because with the exception of four lookouts, two missile turrets, and the birds who wanted to share his food, the huge expanse of roof was a place where he could be alone for a few minutes. And even feel homesick if he wanted to.

Thirty minutes earlier he had placed a call to his parents on Shiloh. But then, even as the fone rang in his parents' house, he had broken the connection. Because up until that point in his life he had never lied to them. Not about anything important anyway. So what would he say if his mother answered? That he'd lost track of how many people he'd killed? That he and his friends had stolen government property and sold it? That the money he sent them hadn't been won playing cards? That he didn't trust his commanding officer? No, he couldn't tell his mother those things. And, if he *didn't* tell, he'd have to make up lies to cover up the truth. So it would be wrong either way.

"What the hell are you doing up here, jerk weed?" Tychus demanded, as a heavy hand fell on Raynor's shoulder. "We've been looking all over the place for you."

Raynor turned to see that Tychus had Kydd, Harnack, Ward, and Zander with him.

Raynor sighed. "I'm eating lunch . . . or trying to."

Tychus turned his face upward, blinked as the raindrops hit his eyes, and looked down again. "It's raining."

"Yes," Raynor replied irritably. "I noticed. Was there something you people wanted to see me about?"

"Yeah, there was," Tychus said, as he selected the larger half of the damp sandwich and took a bite. He was still chewing when he spoke. "The brass held a briefing for all of the junior officers and noncoms."

"And?"

"And the assault is gonna be a total bitch," Tychus said, as he eyed the other half of the sandwich. "They aren't saying how we're gonna cross the river, that's top secret, but it sounds like they're setting us up for an impossible mission." He finished the rest of the sandwich with one bite. "Rockwell's marines are gonna get massacred within seconds, you know that. And where does that leave us? Oh yeah, we'll be right there behind 'em."

"There's something going on with Rockwell's guys, I know it . . ." Kydd added darkly. "I think somebody's been messing with their heads."

"Yeah," Raynor said. "I think so, too. Brucker kept asking me questions about it. He called it 'neural resocialization.' Criminals are being experimented on at some facility—something about erasing their antisocial tendencies. He thinks a lot of them are serving in our armed forces."

"Holy shit," Harnack put in excitedly. "Remember the whackos on the *Hydrus*? The ones who tried to kick the crap out of us? Then, when we ran into them the night before graduation, they were like a bunch of schoolgirls. I bet they were resocialized."

"And then there's Sam Lassiter," Tychus added. "They had that lunatic locked in a steel box at MCF-R-156 *before* he shanked a sergeant with a fork! Then, I'm walking across Fort Howe, and there he is! Just as nice as you please . . . and when I asked him how he got out of the facility, he didn't even remember *being* there."

"Bingo," Zander said grimly. "It's all starting to make sense."

Raynor frowned. "So, what are you saying? That they're going to use Rockwell's troops as cannon fodder?"

"That's exactly what I'm saying," Tychus replied. "Once you cut through all the weasel-worded bullshit, it's obvious that those poor bastards'll be walking into a meat grinder. And guess how we're going to become the great war heroes of the Confederacy? By following those fools right into a bloodbath and donating our bodies for fish food and fertilizer."

"It's almost as if Vanderspool wants us to get killed," Ward observed.

Raynor opened the bag of chips and scattered them along the rail. Then, as the birds came fluttering in, he stood back to watch them peck at the unexpected bounty. "So, what's the solution?"

"I figure we should hang back, let the resocs die for the Confederacy, and live to fight another day," Tychus replied.

"They may be mind-zapped, but they aren't dogs," Raynor objected. "They're people, just like you and me."

"Are they?" Tychus inquired cynically. "You saw Rockwell's guys. I'm not so sure."

Raynor sighed. "If you're done eating my lunch, let's go inside. It's raining out here."

The cavernous high-speed tube station had once been the backbone of south Polk's Pride. It boasted twelve parallel arrival and departure stations, plus an equal number of tracks, all accessed by escalators and bridges. The walls were covered with colorful murals, each of which was a landscape inspired by a different region, all harkening back to the days before the fighting. And unlike what Doc had seen earlier that day, the underground facility was untouched by the wars except for the fact that more than a thousand troops were housed in the vast lobby, the arcades located to either side of it, and the tunnels themselves.

Cave-ins, both accidental and intentional,

meant that the underground tubes through which crowded trains once roared were silent now and home to nothing more than a few hardy eccentrics and a legion of flesh-eating rats. Animals that had grown fat on the dead bodies that littered the area bordering the river.

Cassidy shivered at the thought of them as she followed a frozen escalator down onto platform two, and from there out along an island of concrete toward the train that was parked next to it. A sign proclaimed that she was about to travel on the "Yellow Line," which, had it been operational, would have carried her to Picket, Traverston, Oakwood, and the suburbs beyond.

Because the city was so crowded, there weren't any open areas upon which a command center could be built. So Vanderspool had been forced to take up residence in the underground tube station.

A couple of marines were on sentry duty outside the train where his office was located. Cassidy immediately recognized them as belonging to the colonel's newly created "color guard." Though theoretically charged with protecting the battalion's colors in battle, that was a largely ceremonial function, and no longer relevant to the way battles were being fought.

No, the *real* function of the platoon-size unit was to serve as Vanderspool's personal bodyguards, both on and off the field of battle. And, judging from the intensity with which the men greeted her, the rumors were true. They were not only resocialized, they were willing converts, which was to say, fanatics. "Hold it right there," a weasel-faced corporal said, with one hand on his sidearm. "This is a restricted area."

"Yeah," Doc replied, "I know. My name is Cassidy. Colonel Vanderspool sent for me."

That was true, and a subject of some concern for the medic, since repeated trips to see Vanderspool would be noticed by Tychus and the rest. But only three days had passed since the battalion's arrival and there hadn't been any opportunity to set up an alternate system. "Scan her," the noncom instructed, as he examined his Handheld Personal Information-Gathering and Navigation Unit, otherwise known as a Pig.

The scanner flicked across Doc's eyes and she heard a soft *beep*. "Her name is Cassidy," the second marine said, "and she's a medic."

"Roger that," the corporal said evenly. Then, having turned his attention to Doc, his eyes narrowed. "You're two minutes late, Petty Officer Cassidy. You can do better. Perfection is within our grasp."

Doc eyed him emotionlessly. "Flick you, Corporal . . . *and* the private you rode in on."

The resoc shook his head sadly, apparently unable to understand why she was so hostile, and stood to one side as the medic brushed past him and entered the streamlined car beyond.

The car's interior was much as it had been before the wars, except for the fact that all of the seats had been torn out and replaced with mismatched office furniture salvaged from the surrounding office buildings. The same corporal who'd been in charge of Vanderspool's office back at Fort Howe looked up from a tidy desktop. She nodded politely. "Have a seat. . . . The colonel's meeting is running long. It should be over any minute now."

Cassidy shot the cutesy, pug-nosed girl a fake smile and sat down on one of two chairs. Unlike the last time she had met with Vanderspool, her crab supply was sufficient to get her through the next few days. Then, with the new stuff that she was about to receive, Doc figured she'd have some cushion. And that would feel good.

"You can enter now," the corporal said, as a well-dressed civilian left.

Cassidy said, "Thank you," and made her way along the left side of the car. More than half its width had been walled off to create an office for Vanderspool. The door consisted of a curtain that was pushed to one side. Doc knocked on a side window, heard Vanderspool say, "Come!" and entered a long, narrow space with an executive-style desk at one end of it.

She was about to come to attention but Vanderspool waved the formality off. The officer was in his military mode, as was apparent from the fact that he addressed her as "Cassidy," rather than "My dear."

"Have a seat, Cassidy," Vanderspool said, as he pointed at the chair in front of him. "I must say that I've been looking forward to this meeting. Having scanned all the after-action reports, I know Overseer Brucker was killed during the raid on KIC-36. What I don't know is *how* he died. Did his heart fail? That's what Sergeant Findlay told the debriefers. Or was there some other cause?"

Cassidy answered the question by giving Vanderspool a blow-by-blow account of Brucker's death, starting with the leg wound, and finishing with the words she had whispered into his ear. "Damn!" Vanderspool responded happily. "I love it! I assumed you'd have to shoot him. Could you tell if he understood?"

Doc nodded. "There's no doubt about it, sir. . . . His eyes bulged, and he tried to say something, just before his heart stopped."

"Then it *was* a heart attack," Vanderspool exclaimed. "Well done. . . . You saw those POWs. The bastard deserved it."

Cassidy had to agree, although the message she'd been asked to deliver to the dead man made Vanderspool's motive very clear—it wasn't a desire to seek revenge on behalf of the prisoners, but for himself. *Just how dirty* is *this guy?* she wondered. *Business deals with Kel-Morians, spying on his own battalion, resocialized marines popping up all over the goddamn place . . .*

"Here you go," Vanderspool said, as he opened

a drawer and withdrew a small metal box. "It's payday. But be careful," the officer added, as he pushed the container across the surface of the desk. "I wouldn't want you to die of an overdose."

"Thank you, sir," Doc said dryly, as she accepted the box and slipped it into a pocket. "Your concern is very touching."

"Watch your mouth, Cassidy," Vanderspool warned sternly. "And remember your place. You may be useful, but you're a crab junkie nonetheless, and a disposable one at that. Now, what else do you have for me?"

Doc's lips were suddenly dry and she ran her tongue across them. "It's about Private Kydd, sir."

Vanderspool frowned. "The sniper?"

"Yes, sir. The way I understand it, Kydd was at basic with Raynor and Harnack. Back then Kydd claimed to be a guy named Ark Bennet. According to the story he told people at the time, he was drugged and sold to a Marine Corps recruiter."

Vanderspool's eyebrows rose. "Did you say *Bennet*? As in *Bennet Industries*?"

"Yes, sir. I don't know anything about Bennet Industries—but I'm sure the name was Bennet. Anyway, when we came back from the raid on Brucker's base, two MSS agents were waiting to interview Kydd. And later, after he returned to the barracks, he told Tychus that the agents were checking to see if he was Bennet."

"And?"

"And he told them he wasn't," Cassidy continued. "Because somewhere along the line he changed his mind and wants to stay in the service."

"So he *is* Bennet?"

"That's what both Findlay and Raynor believe," Doc reported. "I wasn't sure whether the Kydd situation would be of interest to you. But I brought this along just in case."

So saying, Cassidy removed a plastic-encased slide from her shirt pocket and placed it on the surface of the desk.

Vanderspool eyed the object as Doc pushed it toward him. "What have we here?"

"That's a sample of Kydd's DNA," the medic replied simply. "I had to sample the entire squad in order to get it. They believe it's part of a routine medical test."

"You are a clever little bitch," Vanderspool said appreciatively. "Is there anything else?"

"I've noticed that he has a thing for Sanchez . . . follows her around like a puppy dog."

"Okay. The Kydd thing is intriguing though unimportant. Keep it to yourself, however. . . ." Vanderspool said, as he toyed with the test tube. "Dismissed."

Doc rose, did an about-face, and left the officer. The session had gone well, all things considered, and she felt relieved.

As Doc left the car she was shocked to see Tychus standing on the platform waiting for her! Did he suspect? No, judging from the big smile on his face, Tychus had other things on his mind. "Hey, babe," he said, as he draped a massive arm around her shoulders. "I heard you were here."

"Yeah," Doc replied. "You know how the personnel people are. . . . I had to sign some form or other . . . what a pain in the ass."

"And that's what I was thinking about," Tychus said with a wicked grin. "Not the pain . . . the other part. Or both. What would you say to a first class dinner at my place—and a roll in the hay to follow?"

Cassidy gave him a backhanded blow to the gut. It was like hitting a rock. That was one of the things she liked about Tychus. He was built, and in spite of what some people said, size matters. Or it did where she was concerned. So even if her relationship with Tychus wasn't entirely of her own choosing, it was often pleasurable, and absolutely necessary. Due to the wars, crab was almost impossible to buy on the street anymore. She felt a strong desire to touch the metal box through her clothing, to confirm that it was there, but managed not to do so. "You don't have a place," Cassidy temporized. "Other than your bivvy bag, that is."

"Oh, yes I do!" Tychus replied cheerfully. "Money talks. . . . I'm the proud owner of a utility closet. Complete with deep sink."

"We'll see how dinner goes," Doc said. "Who knows? If you chew with your mouth closed you might get lucky. And stop that. . . . How many times have I told you? Don't pat my ass in public!"

Tychus chuckled happily as he led her up a floor and through a confusing maze of hallways. Finally, having unlocked a door labeled MAINTENANCE, he stood to one side. As Doc entered the pitch-black, concrete room, Tychus aimed a flashlight at the mattress on the floor. "See?" Tychus said proudly, as he towed Cassidy over to the makeshift bed and pulled her down. "All the comforts of home."

As Doc knelt on the mattress she saw that a bottle of Tychus's favorite booze was sitting next to it. Normally her lover didn't go in for much foreplay, but rather than simply grab her the way he usually did, Tychus surprised Cassidy by producing a box and shoving it her way. "Happy birthday, sexy, I hope this is okay."

Doc stared in disbelief. Chocolates? Tychus wasn't the kind of guy who bought a girl chocolates. Was she totally wrong about him? About all of this? She was shocked by a sudden swell of emotion; at once she felt sad, guilty, and completely undeserving of Tychus's affection. Even so, she wrapped her arms around his neck. Not because she wanted to make love to him at that particular moment, but because of the tears that were trickling down her cheeks, and the opportunity to bury her face in his shoulder.

CHAPTER TWENTY-SEVEN

"Bein' a medic isn't too different from bein' a soldier. I just kill in reverse."

Petty Officer Third Class Lisa Cassidy, 321st
Colonial Rangers Battalion, in an interview on
Turaxis II
March 2489

THE CITY OF POLK'S PRIDE,
ON THE PLANET TURAXIS II

The factory and its adjoining machine shop were set up in the spacious maintenance facility where subway cars had been repaired back before the war. Tracks led into open bays that were now occupied by goliaths. The goliaths stood with cockpits open as pilots and technicians ran final checks, a power wrench screeched, and the bitter smell of ozone laced the air.

Further back, in the brightly lit room once occupied by workbenches, row upon row of CMC-

300 suits could be seen, all hanging from carefully aligned racks. It was 0214 hours, and the attack on the Kel-Morian repository was due to begin in less than two. There were plenty of jokes, and nearly nonstop banter, as the men and women of the 321st Colonial Rangers Battalion began to seal their suits.

But as Raynor stepped into his armor and went about the process of connecting the padlike interfaces to various parts of his body, he knew what the people around him were *really* thinking. *How many of us will be badly wounded? How many of us are going to die?* And most important, *Will I survive?*

Raynor's suit smelled of someone else's sweat, but as he examined the readouts on his HUD, all of them came up green. And that was what mattered most. Having jumped into Kel-Morian territory wearing an experimental hardskin, Raynor had a new appreciation for the tried and true.

The "experiment" could more or less have been considered a failure, as the High Command had discontinued Thunderstrike armor following several mishaps during field tests. Though he'd never admit it to Feek, who'd spent countless hours working on the armor, Raynor also had serious doubts about its usefulness in battle.

Needless to say, the project was put on the back burner, with the exception of the 230-XF, which was being converted into a non-jump "firebat" suit. Since the announcement, Harnack didn't let a day go by without asking Feek when his new suit would be ready.

Having sealed himself in, Raynor made his way over to a freestanding rack, selected the slab-sided gauss rifle that wore the same number his suit did, and took a look at the ammo indicator. It was full up.

From the rack it was a short trip to the table where a private was distributing extra ammo. Then, having completed all of his preparations, Raynor made his way over to the assembly area next to track two. Sanchez was already there with her visor open and a rifle slung over one shoulder. "Where's Findlay?" she asked.

Before Raynor could answer, Kydd sidled up beside him. "He's fondling his armor. I think he's in love with it."

Sanchez laughed, and when Raynor looked over at his friend, he noticed something that made him smile even more broadly. Kydd was gazing at Lieutenant Sanchez with worshipful eyes. Raynor wasn't surprised—she was a beautiful woman. Even her laugh had a musical quality. Raynor hoped he would get the chance to hear it again. Max Speer, who was wearing yellow armor with the word MEDIA stenciled across his chest plate, was present to capture the moment.

* * *

The battle began as most ground attacks do, with an air strike by a squadron of Avengers, followed by an artillery barrage from a dozen siege tanks. The shells rumbled ominously as they passed over south Polk's Pride to pound enemy held territory. And as the Confederate guns opened up, their crews immediately came under counterfire from the Kel-Morian side of the river.

Then, as the early morning darkness was torn asunder by flashes of light and the roll of artificial thunder, the *real* bloodletting began.

The first challenge Colonel Vanderspool faced was to get his troops across the river, a task two other officers had failed to accomplish. An attempt to use boats had been a complete failure. By the time the bargelike watercraft were launched, Kel-Morian artillery batteries had their range and cut them to pieces. It was said that the Paddick ran red with blood, as a battalion of bodies floated downstream, and thousands of rot birds swooped in to feast.

A plan to launch sections of a pontoon bridge upriver, ride them down, and hook them together at the last moment had proven to be equally disastrous when one of the modules ran afoul of a sunken bridge, and rendered the rest useless. It was a colossal screwup that left hundreds of Confed troops milling around waiting to be slaughtered by enemy air strikes and artillery fire.

So Vanderspool had come up with a *third* alternative. Something that had never been tried before. A strategy that was calculated to take advantage of the fact that the Paddick River was much shallower than usual.

The first person to witness Vanderspool's genius was a lowly Kel-Morian taskmaster named Evers who, along with his squad of outriders, was on a routine patrol when the air attacks and the artillery barrage began. So there he was, inside the gutted remains of a waterfront warehouse, waiting for the ground to stop shaking under his boots when a pair of softly glowing forms materialized from the ruins on the other side of the Paddick.

Evers thought their size, as well as the amount of heat they were generating, was consistent with that produced by Confederate goliaths, and his HUD confirmed the hypothesis. *Okay,* the taskmaster thought to himself, *all they can do is strut back and forth along the riverfront and take occasional potshots at us. What a waste. Our artillery will pound them flat in no time at all.*

Had it been daylight Evers would have known better, but it wasn't until the first goliaths entered the river that he realized the specially modified walkers were carrying something between them, and understood what the Confederates were up to. The goliaths were carrying sections of a pontoon bridge between them, and because of their height, would be able to *wade* across the Paddick!

Then, having created a span over which regular troops could cross, the combat walkers would switch to an offensive role and open fire on anyone who opposed them, thereby establishing a beachhead that would be very difficult to dislodge. That was important stuff, and Evers was just about to tell his superiors all about it when a Kel-Morian artillery shell fell short and landed directly on top of his position. He and his squad were decimated.

The resulting flash of light strobed the surface of the river, and two walkers could be seen, both almost fully submerged as they towed a section of bridge between them. Three minutes later they were ashore where they secured the section designated as "span one" to preselected anchor points. With that accomplished, they scanned the ruins for targets and began to kill everything warm enough to produce a heat signature. Meanwhile, the next pair of goliaths was hooking span two to span one.

That was when the Kel-Morian overseer in charge of north Polk's Pride was awoken from a deep sleep and given the news: The Confederates had thrown a bridge across the Paddick and walkers were already coming ashore. He swore, wondered how such a thing was possible, and whom he could blame.

Other than the goliath pilots and Max Speer, who insisted on dashing across first in order to get a shot of their arrival, a resoc named Sergeant Trent and his squad were the first people to cross the newly created bridge. Sanchez, Raynor, Tychus, Harnack, Kydd, Ward, Zander, and Doc followed immediately behind, just ahead of a full company of resocialized marines. They were to be followed by the rest of the ranger battalion, plus various auxiliary units, including a platoon of SCVs.

The comsat station and the repository were straight ahead. So even though the street that would take them there was heavily defended and preregistered by half a dozen sloths, Trent and his resocialized marines went right up the middle. Shells exploded all around them, two men fell within a matter of seconds, and the only reason the rest were able to continue forward was because the artillery barrage stopped suddenly and a squad of rippers threw themselves into the fray.

It was a desperate move. One that was intended to stall the invaders long enough to bring reinforcements up to block their advance. Raynor felt a rising sense of anger as the rippers killed Trent and the rest of his marines within a matter of seconds. Vanderspool had *known*, damn him—and sacrificed the resocs like pawns in a chess game.

Revenge came swiftly as a couple of goliaths came forward to destroy the rippers. Ward unleashed four of his eight heat-seeking missiles, and a series of eye-searing explosions strobed the surrounding buildings. "Follow me!" Sanchez yelled over the platoon frequency, as she led her troops forward.

Even as the Devils stepped over dead marines and plodded up the street firing as they went, *more* resocialized marines were surging forward, seemingly eager to enter the meat grinder up ahead. Raynor felt a surge of adrenaline as a ripper lurched out of a side street. Raynor brought the gauss rifle up and opened fire, knowing full well that the ensuing engagement would be more a matter of luck than skill since the two of them were evenly matched.

And Raynor was correct, because the 8mm spike that killed the Kel-Morian wasn't fired by Raynor. It was a ricochet that hit the plascrete in front of the enemy soldier, bounced upward, and punched its way through a weak spot in the jury-rigged armor into his helmet.

Raynor stepped over the armored body and followed Sanchez up the blood-splashed street. Resocialized marines were all around them as a Kel-Morian goliath emerged from a parking garage to confront them. But the towering machine was transformed into bloody sleet as Ward fired the rest of his missiles at the walker and it exploded.

Raynor felt pieces of the monster's neosteel skin rattle against the back of his hardskin as the Devils followed Sanchez into what had been a department store. They walked parallel to the sidewalk. The front of the building gave the Devils some momentary cover as two squads of marines charged straight up the middle of the street and were cut to bloody ribbons.

Raynor caught only glimpses of the slaughter through the store's blown-out windows, but the sight of it made him feel sick to his stomach. It had become clear that if it weren't for the resocs' mindless self-sacrifice, the assault would have stalled by then. The resocs were like robots who would take chances that regular troops wouldn't, charge no matter what the odds against them were, and die without complaint.

It was a moment he would never forget as the Devils were forced to leave the relative safety of the store through a window and reenter the street in front of a barricade. The KMs had made use of overturned vehicles, ribbon wire, and anything else they could lay their hands on to block the entire width of the street. About two dozen Kel-Morian regulars were concealed behind the obstacle, hosing the street with automatic fire, as both the marines and the Devils pounded their fortification.

But there were gaps between the cars, and holes in between the sheets of metal that bridged them, so Sanchez called Harnack forward. "See that gap?" she demanded. "The one next to the bus? Light 'em up."

Harnack's firebat suit was impervious to small-arms fire, so with Raynor and Tychus to guard both flanks, he was able to make his way up to the barricade and send a tongue of fire in through the gap. The bus caught fire, the gas stored in its tank exploded, and a hole appeared. The resocialized marines stormed through. Two of them went down, and it was necessary for Tychus to step on one of them to reach the other side.

Unfortunately, the next barrier was harder to overcome. Two sloths were positioned about a block away, and as the first barricade fell, both opened fire. "This way!" Sanchez shouted as she took a sudden left and led the team up a plascrete ramp and into a parking garage. The tanks were still firing at the marines and rangers as the group continued to climb.

Once they arrived on the roof it would have been a simple matter to cut across it and make the twelve-foot jump to the next building, had it not been for the Kel-Morian dropship that was sitting on top of the garage!

Even as the Confederates continued to charge forward, a group of unarmored Kel-Morian regulars spilled out of the dropship's belly and opened fire. Raynor saw their weapons sparkle and heard the insistent rattle of small-caliber bullets as they hit his armor, but really couldn't feel much.

A few of the enemy soldiers were armed with rocket launchers, however, and Raynor saw a bright flash as a ranger's legs were cut out from under him and his hardskin cauterized the bleeding stumps. He was screaming by then, but only until a noncom cut him out of the comm net, so that orders could be given.

Doc was there seconds later, kneeling in a pool of blood as she eyed the scanner in the palm of her hand. Thanks to a link with the suit's CPU she could see the patients' vital signs. She did the best she could to comfort the soldier, as she opened the safety clasps and applied plastiscab dressings to the raw stumps. Having treated such injuries before, she knew what was on the soldier's mind.

"Don't worry," Doc said kindly, as bullets whipped around her. "They missed your balls. We'll strap a pair of electro-mechanical sticks onto you, reprogram part of your brain, and voilà! You'll be good as new."

It looked as though the advance was about to stall out when Tychus shot two Kel-Morian regulars and got close enough to toss a grenade into one of the dropship's air intakes. The bomb exploded inside the starboard engine; it blew up, and a fuel tank went with it.

Sanchez yelled, "Duck!" and most people did, as a fireball floated up into the sky and the dropship's retros fired for the very last time. Then, having achieved an altitude of about six feet, the ship crashed onto the roof and broke into three large pieces. All of which continued to burn.

"That's what I'm talking about," Ward said contentedly. "Burn, you bastards."

Zander slipped a set of rockets into the empty launch tubes on Ward's shoulders. "I'm out of reloads," Zander said. "You only have four rockets left. Use them wisely."

"Roger that," Ward rumbled, as he hefted his gauss cannon. "Meet Mister Backup!"

Both men were overridden as Sanchez ran toward the edge of the roof. "This is Alpha-One-Six, follow me!" She was picking up speed, and about to jump the gap that separated the garage from the building next to it, when a sniper hidden somewhere in the densely packed buildings on the hill in front of them squeezed his trigger. The first bullet hit her visor. The second passed through her right eye. The officer took two additional steps, toppled forward, and fell straight down.

Tychus, who was second in command, swore as Sanchez disappeared between the two buildings. "Kydd!" he shouted, as the rest of the Devils sought cover. "Find that bastard and kill him!"

Kydd was already on the job. He was crouched behind the low wall that circled the roof, scanning the rampart-like blast walls on the hill. The acoustic targeting system built into his suit fed information to his HUD. The other sniper was somewhere on the hill, but he already knew that. The rifle, which was normally so heavy, seemed a good deal lighter now that he was wearing powered armor.

The sun was just starting to rise, so the eastern side of the comsat station was glazed with silvery light, and a dark shadow fell toward the west. Eventually the daylight would be helpful. But for the moment the overall light level was still relatively low, the effectiveness of Kydd's night vision equipment was starting to fade, and there were so many targets on the fortification it was impossible to know which one to shoot at. Assuming the enemy sniper was visible, that is—and odds were that he was too smart for that.

Making the situation worse was the fact that once Kydd fired at one Kel-Morian, the rest would seek cover. So what he needed to do was draw the other sniper out, get the sonofabitch to reveal himself, and take him out with the first shot. "This is Alpha-Two-Five," Kydd said into his comm unit. "I need someone to draw fire. Don't show yourself for long, though. . . . This guy is good."

Raynor was hidden behind the concrete structure that capped a set of stairs. He felt himself step out into the open, and wondered if the armor was making him foolishly overconfident. He experienced an enormous sense of relief when nothing happened, resolved to count to three before ducking into cover, and was on two when what felt like a sledgehammer struck his helmet. Raynor felt a brief moment of pain, followed by a long fall, and a sudden stop as his suit hit the ground. He heard Tychus shout, "Doc! Jim is down . . . Get your butt in gear, damn it!" Then he was gone.

Kydd was completely unaware that Raynor had been hit. All of his mental and physical energy was focused on locating and killing the Kel-Morian sniper who was concealed somewhere on the hillside in front of him. So when the enemy marksman fired, and Kydd saw the momentary wink of light that signaled a muzzle flash, he slipped into the fugue state he had first experienced on the firing range in boot camp. To him, it came easily, as though he had entered an alternate reality in which time slowed, enabling him to shift the crosshairs on his telescopic sight half an inch to the right, and consider the crosswind that could nudge the .50 caliber slug off course—all the while allowing for the chance that the fraction-of-a-second lag created by his armor could throw off his aim.

The rifle had an enlarged trigger guard, making it possible for armored fingers to access it. And the highly specialized weapon was equipped with a two-stage trigger. That meant once the trigger was activated, and the initial slack was taken out of the mechanism, only a very light touch would be required to drop the firing pin on the round in the chamber and send death spinning through the air.

So as the target began a slow-motion pullback, preparatory to disappearing altogether, Kydd applied the necessary amount of pressure and felt the trigger "break," as the first stage was released.

Then, having taken a deep breath and let it out, he ordered his right index finger to contract.

The report was muffled because of his helmet, and the recoil was negligible thanks to Kydd's hardskin. It was his duty to kill the Kel-Morian, but it was personal, too, because even though she was a few years older than he was, Kydd had developed feelings for Samantha Sanchez.

So as time jerked forward, and the heavy slug blew the top of the other sniper's head off, Kydd felt a primal sense of exultation. He could almost hear Sanchez say, *"Good shot, Private Kydd . . . okay, what are you people waiting for? An engraved invitation? We have a hill to climb."*

As he imagined her voice, a lump formed in his throat. He wished he'd had the guts to give her the chocolates he had purchased for her, rather than allowing Tychus to swipe them for Doc's birthday. He felt like such a coward.

"Nice shot, Kydd," Tychus said over the squad freq. "Okay, what are you jerk weeds waiting for? Let's jump that gap!"

Kydd broke cover and made his way forward. Tears were streaming down his cheeks and he was grateful that no one could see.

CHAPTER TWENTY-EIGHT

"They took the Kel-Morians by surprise and freed hundreds of Confederate POWs, and now the brave soldiers known as the Heaven's Devils have been sent to a new location. Security regulations prevent me from saying where they are, but you can be sure of one thing: the enemy will be sorry!"

Max Speer, from a dispatch filed somewhere on Turaxis II

THE CITY OF POLK'S PRIDE,
ON THE PLANET TURAXIS II

As Tychus led the Heaven's Devils onto the roof of the building beyond, and the rest of the company followed, Doc knelt next to Raynor. The bullet had cut a deep groove into the side of his helmet and a trickle of blood was leaking out of it. Cassidy thought Raynor was dead at first.

A servo whirred as Doc thumbed the external visor release button. It slid out of the way to reveal

Raynor's pale face. It appeared as though Raynor had turned his head, or moved just as the sniper fired, causing the round to bounce off the curvature of his helmet without penetrating it. Cassidy triggered the release on her right gauntlet so she could reach inside her patient's helmet—and pressed a finger against a point located just below his right earlobe and at the back of his jaw.

Raynor felt a sudden stab of pain and opened his eyes to find Doc peering down at him. "Damn," he said. "I'm alive."

"'Fraid so," Cassidy agreed.

"How bad is it?"

"I suspect you've got a scalp laceration," Doc replied clinically, as she stood. "But your blood pressure is normal, so it can wait. What the hell were you thinking anyway?"

Raynor reached up to take her hand. "I was thinking how lucky I was that the sniper wasn't going to shoot me," he said ruefully. "Damn, that hurts."

"You want some pain juice?"

"Hell no . . . the last time you did that I felt *too* happy. Let's go."

Having made the jump to the roof beyond, the Devils returned to street level *behind* the sloths. They were firing south at the resocialized marines and newly arrived rangers. All of whom were struggling to move up the street toward the hill and the repository deep inside of it. "Ward!" Tychus said, "Take those bastards out."

Ward braced himself, took careful aim, and fired a rocket. It hit the right-hand sloth low, in between its tracks. The resulting explosions lifted the machine a couple of inches up into the air, blew a hole in its vulnerable belly, and triggered a powerful secondary explosion. That blew the turret off and sent a gout of flames shooting straight upward.

The second sloth's turret was coming around by then, trying to find the new threat and kill it, but that opened it up to a ground attack by the resocialized marines. They swarmed through the barricade farther down the street and came forward firing handheld rocket launchers of their own. The sloth shook as it took a couple of hits, shuddered convulsively, and blew as one of the resocs threw a D-6 charge in under its belly. The resoc died in the resulting explosion, but that made no difference to his comrades, who charged forward and quickly caught up with the Devils.

Now the combined force was at the bottom of the hill and approaching the fortification's heavily defended main gate. It had taken a direct hit from a siege tank and consisted of little more than a crater surrounded by a collar of debris. A bloodied leg could be seen protruding from the dirt.

But that didn't mean the Kel-Morians were

going to let the invaders enter the repository unopposed. As the Devils and a force of resocs pushed up the slope and surged around both sides of the crater, a squad of Guild Guards was there to receive them. Suddenly, what had been an arm's-length conflict became extremely personal as the groups overran each other.

"To *me*!" Tychus shouted over the comm, as he fired his gauss rifle at point-blank range. It was important to form a phalanx that could produce massed fire and hold the real estate they'd been able to take.

The Devils were the first to respond as Ward, Zander, and Harnack came together to form a solid front. The rangers and marines hurried to realign themselves as Ward loosed his remaining missiles. The closely spaced explosions left ragged gaps in the enemy's ranks, but the battle was far from one-sided, as one of the guards fired his flamethrower and a ranger was engulfed in a fiery conflagration.

Retribution came swiftly. Because rather than charge the enemy with the others, Kydd had orders to hang back and choose his targets with care. So the man with the flamethrower blew up as a slug found a fuel tank and Harnack triggered his own weapon. "You bastards want to play?" he demanded angrily, as a gout of flame played across the guards in the Kel-Morian front line. "Well, let's fire it up!"

Tychus, meanwhile, had met his match. The KM taskmaster was as tall as he was, but not as broad in the chest, and armor clashed as they collided. They were so close together that neither man could use his rifle for anything other than a club, so both took swings at each other. As each man blocked the other's blows, they were forced to release their weapons and fight hand to hand.

It was a situation that favored the Kel-Morian, because the Guild Guards prided themselves on close-quarters combat while Confederate military forces spent precious little time on such training. So Tychus found himself being subjected to a well-executed leg-wheel hip-throw and a follow-up blow that dented his helmet. *Sweet mother of mercy,* Tychus thought to himself, *this bastard needs to die.*

But killing the other man wasn't going to be easy as Tychus attempted to roll away. The suit's backpack made that difficult as the Kel-Morian methodically kicked him in the side.

As Tychus came to rest on his back, and the exhaust from his backpack splashed the ground, he caught one of the huge boots and gave it a powerful twist to the right. That brought his opponent crashing down. Tychus was quick to follow up by rolling on top of the taskmaster and sitting astride the other man's chest.

Tychus felt for a grenade with one hand, found it, and thumbed the Kel-Morian's visor release with the other. It opened to reveal an unshaven face that was contorted into a fearsome grimace as the Kel-Morian struggled to buck his opponent off. "Sweet dreams, asshole," Tychus said as he armed the grenade, dropped it into the other man's helmet, and immediately rolled away.

Maybe, had there been a little more time and had the Kel-Morian been able to pull his gauntlets off quickly enough, he might have been able to reach down into the cavity next to his chin and remove the bomb before it went off. But such was not the case. There was a flash of light and a loud bang as the taskmaster's helmet exploded.

"Quit laying down on the job," Raynor said as he arrived on the scene and reached down to give his friend a hand.

"I thought you were dead," Tychus said as he came to his feet and bent to retrieve his rifle. "We were going to have a big party and everything."

"Sorry to disappoint you," Raynor replied dryly, as a marine lieutenant led a platoon of resocs across the body-strewn expanse of concrete toward the ramp beyond. "Maybe next time."

"Come on!" Ward shouted. "Today is the day! I can *feel* it!"

"The crazy sonofabitch is going to try and get himself killed!" Raynor exclaimed. "Come on!"

Max Speer grinned happily and continued to record the action as the Heaven's Devils chased after Ward up the ramp and into the meat grinder beyond.

* * *

Raynor hadn't traveled more than a hundred feet before his boots began to slip on the blood-slicked surface. Then it became necessary to climb over piles of bodies, as the twin-barreled gauss cannon on the landing above continued to roar, and spikes blew holes through both the living and the dead. One of the badly shot-up suits belonged to the lieutenant who had been leading the platoon. He lay with an arm outstretched, as if pointing the way.

It might have ended then and there. But the Heaven's Devils had a guardian angel looking out for them and his name was Ryk Kydd. So as Ward charged up the incline bellowing his rage, a piece of divine intervention was on the way. It was shaped like an armor-piercing round and smashed through the gunner's visor. As he fell over backward, the weapon ceased firing and tilted upward.

Another KM tried to take over, but Ward had arrived by then, and fired his gauss cannon from six feet away. A hail of spikes blew divots out of the Kel-Morian armor until one of them found a way in and bounced around for a second before running out of kinetic energy. Ward, who was surprised to be alive, paused. That gave the others a chance to catch up and hem him in.

Having arrived on the landing, Tychus and Raynor took the opportunity to eyeball the path ahead. It was a zigzag affair that switchbacked up the hill. That enabled the defenders to fire at the attackers not only head-on, but from above as well, which made for a deadly combination. The realization was punctuated by the flat crack of a high-powered rifle. From above, a figure threw up his hands and toppled down the hill. Kydd was still on the job.

"These people are starting to piss me off," Tychus said, as he let his rifle fall so he could free the gauss cannon from its tripod. That was when a fresh platoon of resocialized marines arrived from below. They were under the command of Master Sergeant Rockwell. As usual he was following rather than leading as he yelled at the top of his lungs. "Get up there, you jerks! Rip the bastards apart!"

Raynor threw up a hand and stepped out to block the way. "Hold on. . . . There's bound to be a gauss cannon on the next landing. Sergeant Findlay is going to take it out. Then you can advance."

"Ignore that command," Rockwell ordered sternly, as he arrived on the platform. "The platoon will advance! And that's an order."

With that the marines surged around Tychus and ran up the slope. A hail of spikes cut them down. "Stop!" Raynor shouted. "Wait, goddamn it!"

But it was too late. Struggle though they might, the marines didn't have a chance. But they were brave, or crazy, not that it made much difference. As the front ranks fell, those behind struggled forward, boots slipping as rivers of blood flowed downhill, desperately trying to achieve the goal that had been assigned to them.

Finally, after thirty seconds or so, the last marine fell. And that was when Rockwell spoke. Raynor realized that the noncom was still on the platform! "What a bunch of losers," Rockwell said disgustedly. "It makes you wonder what the Confederacy is coming to."

The haymaker started down around Raynor's knees, gathered force as it curved upward, and made contact with the lower part of Rockwell's helmet. It packed enough force to lift the noncom an inch off the pavement and throw him backward. He landed with a crash, skidded for three or four feet, and came to rest against the waist-high wall. "I'll have your ass for that!" Rockwell shouted from his position on the ground. "You're on report!"

"And you're an asshole," Raynor responded disgustedly, as he turned to follow Tychus upslope. "Not to mention a coward."

Logically enough the repository's overseer had sent all of his armored personnel down to the bottom of the hill in a vain attempt to stop the invaders at the main gate. So, as Tychus marched up the ramp firing the gauss cannon, the unarmored troops on the next landing were badly outmatched. Especially since each time someone tried to bring the weapon into action, Kydd killed them.

By that time the Devils were like a well-oiled machine, darting from position to position, always careful to cover one another before advancing further. So by the time the Devils arrived on the level area, there was little more than a pile of bodies waiting there to greet them. "One more stretch to go!" Raynor exclaimed, as another squad of resocialized marines brushed past.

"Poor bastards," Tychus said, as he dumped the gauss cannon in favor of a KM assault rifle. The reason for his disgust quickly became apparent as a Kel-Morian goliath appeared at the top of the ramp. Now it was impossible for the Devils to fire without hitting the resocs, and the marines paid a heavy price as the goliath opened fire on them. The cannon shells literally blew them apart, spraying both sides of the ramp with gore.

"Fall back!" Tychus shouted. "Ward! Can you take him out?"

"No, Sarge, my tubes are empty," the soldier replied as Zander dragged him back.

"Damn it," Tychus said, as the monster lumbered downhill and the Devils were forced to retreat.

As the walker arrived on the platform and swiveled toward them, it looked as though nothing less than a wholesale slaughter was about to ensue, until one of the dead bodies stood up!

Raynor immediately recognized the red armor and the distinctive tanks as belonging to Harnack! The Devil was behind the goliath and no more than ten feet away when he said, *"Surprise!"* and triggered the igniter. There was a loud whump as the flames hit the big machine, found their way into its power supply, and followed a fuel line to its source. The machine's pilot was just starting to react when the goliath came apart and the resulting boom echoed between the buildings of north Polk's Pride.

Doc was already in motion, with Max Speer only steps behind her, as pieces of debris floated down out of the sky and the black smoke began to clear. That was when they saw Harnack. The front surface of his suit had been blackened and his chest plate was cracked, but he was still vertical. "Damn!" Harnack said, as he reached up to remove his helmet. *"That was awesome!"*

"You are one crazy bastard," Tychus commented as he strode past. "Bail out of that suit. . . . It's toast."

Now that the goliath had been defeated, the trip up past the point where the resocs had been slaughtered was relatively easy. And once on top, where one of the comsat station's sturdy legs provided cover, it was possible to spread out and go after the rear-echelon types who had been ordered to take part in a last-ditch defense effort. "Time for some sweet talkin', boys," Tychus announced. "We gotta seduce these ladies outta their hiding spots."

A few chuckles, kissing noises, and *here, kitty kittys* crackled through the frequency as the Devils began to stalk their prey.

The KMs were crouched behind pieces of fanciful sculpture that harkened back to more peaceful times and were firing on anything that moved. Kydd thinned them out with a few shots while the rest of the Devils singled out their targets and took them down.

Just then a lieutenant arrived on the scene with some resocialized marines right behind him. He waved the troops forward. Two or three fell as grenades exploded among them, but most made it through and slaughtered the KM survivors with ruthless efficiency.

That cleared the way to the circular lobby directly below the comsat station's mast. The lifts would take them down into the maze of tunnels below, so Tychus waved the Devils forward, but was forced to stop when the lieutenant stepped out to block the way. "Hold it right there, Sergeant," the officer said evenly. "You will enter the elevators on my command."

Tychus frowned. "No offense, sir, but we have the bastards on the run. . . . Shouldn't we follow up?"

It was like talking to a rock. "We have our orders, and our orders are always correct," the resoc answered.

"He's one of Vanderspool's color guards,"

Raynor said quietly. "Which means the big cheese will arrive any second now." As if to confirm the connection, a loud roar was heard as a dropship flared in to land on the plaza beyond. And as a ramp dropped, the officer emerged. His armor was spotless. Having waited until the surrounding area was secure, Vanderspool was there to take part in the final assault, even if that gave the KMs more time to prepare.

The reason for the delay was apparent as Speer ran forward to document the colonel's arrival. "What an asshole," Tychus said to no one in particular.

"The sergeant will employ correct comm procedure," the lieutenant said primly, "and refrain from the use of profanity. Over."

Raynor thought about Sanchez, the resocialized marines, and all the others whose bodies lay like a bloody carpet between the river and the repository. An important objective had been taken. But at what price?

CHAPTER TWENTY-NINE

". . . so completely devastated by war, it's difficult to say whether the natural resources that initially drew settlers to Turaxis II were a blessing or a curse."

Historian Tannis Yard, in an excerpt from *The Guild Wars*

THE CITY OF POLK'S PRIDE,
ON THE PLANET TURAXIS II

The afternoon following the attack on the Kel-Morian repository the Confederates were still in the process of securing the repository and the area around it. A battalion of resocialized marines had been brought in to relieve the surviving members of the 321st. Clusters of them were sitting around the riverfront, shooting the breeze and waiting for a chance to cross the pontoon bridge into south Polk's Pride.

The span was too narrow to accommodate two-way traffic, so until such time as the second parallel bridge was completed, it was necessary to wait up to an hour before the MPs switched the flow from one direction to the other.

The members of the Heaven's Devils didn't care, though. It was early afternoon, the air was warm, and they were happy to sit around doing nothing as traffic rumbled over the bridge. The Devils had taken over what had once been a ground-floor office in a blown-out warehouse, and most of them had shed their suits. The single exception was Ward, who was waiting for Feek to run a diagnostic program on his armor. The rest of the Devils were lounging about as Speer strolled into the area.

There were warm greetings as everyone gathered around to say hello to the civilian a few of them regarded as an unofficial member of the squad. And that was when Speer urged the group to step outside the shattered building for a group vidsnap.

The Devils shuffled out and gathered in a loose formation, despite Speer's protests to "Move closer," "look alive," and "please, work with me, here!" They were worn out, beat up, and, though in high spirits, a couple of them still had no patience for the reporter. As they turned out to face the camera, Harnack insisted on holding his flamethrower, Zander thought it would be funny to light a cigar off of it, and Kydd hid most of his face under a boonie hat and a pair of mirrorshades.

Feek was there as well, perched on top of Ward's gauss cannon, right behind Raynor and a bare-chested Tychus. Doc, who was high on crab, sat off to the side. "Got it!" Speer said brightly as he took the shot. "I'll call it 'the Devils take a break.' Our viewers will love it. So, where are you headed next? Or is that classified?"

"Raynor's probably headed for a work camp," Tychus said, "since Sergeant Rockwell is going to press charges."

"And the rest of you?"

"Who the hell knows?" Tychus continued. "There's got to be some sort of shit detail they can give us."

Speer made a face. "Well, hang in there. . . . Perhaps we'll meet again."

Feek said his good-byes and both men left. A Klaxon sounded ten minutes later, traffic began to flow south across the bridge, and the Devils were free to follow. For others, millions of them, the wars continued.

MILITARY STOCKADE-7, WEST OF POLK'S PRIDE, ON THE PLANET TURAXIS II

Raynor's wrist and leg irons rattled noisily as he hobbled out of Barracks #2 and began to cross the barren yard. It was surrounded by one-story buildings that were all painted the same shade of puke green with wire mesh over their windows.

About three dozen other prisoners were out getting some sun, and a few hollered greetings as Raynor shuffled past. He waved with two linked hands in response.

The restraints were standard for anyone who was receiving a visitor. It wasn't that the stockade personnel believed prisoners would try to escape—the well-secured visitors' center made that very unlikely. No, they were intended to humiliate the prisoners, which was considered part of their punishment.

Raynor could just imagine his mother's face, seeing him shackled like that, and his father, wondering if he'd done his son a disservice by teaching him to stand up to bullies. Because in the real world, the rules were different—or at least that was what Raynor had come to find out. This wasn't some obnoxious kid cutting him off in traffic. This was real. Painfully and sickeningly real.

But Raynor wondered, should evil go unpunished just because it's wielded by someone in power? Was this one of those times that his dad had described to him, when you had to know "when to get involved and when to walk away"? Plenty of times during his sentence he had asked himself, if he had the chance to live that moment over again, would he still hit Rockwell? The answer was always the same, and no shackles or chains could ever change it.

A hard-eyed resocialized marine held up his

hand as Raynor approached the door. "Hold it right there, Private. . . . Let's have a look at those eyeballs."

Damn, Raynor thought to himself, *they're everywhere.*

In addition to being sentenced to thirty days in the stockade for striking Sergeant Rockwell, Raynor had been busted to private, and his pay had been docked as well. Now, after twenty-eight days in the slammer he was used to being scanned, and was careful not to blink as the guard flicked the pistol-shaped device from left to right. Because to blink, and possibly interrupt the scan, was to be defiant. And that could result in a loss of privileges, including the freedom to receive visitors.

"You may proceed," the marine said cheerfully, as he stepped to one side.

Chains rattled as Raynor was forced to hop up three stairs and open a metal door with both of his shackled hands. Once inside he hobbled across a mirror-bright floor to the check-in kiosk where a bored-looking corporal scanned him *again.*

Then, having been cleared, Raynor was sent to Booth #3 where Feek was waiting for him. All of the Devils had been by at various times, but Feek's visits had been the most frequent, because the civilian had the freedom to come and go as he pleased. "How ya doin'?" Feek asked. A plasteel barrier separated them, and, as usual, Feek had to kneel on his chair in order to speak through the metal grill.

"Good," Raynor lied. "Real good. I sure am itchin' to get back, though."

"I'll bet," Feek agreed. "The whole squad will be down in Darby two days from now. And Tychus talked your new platoon leader into letting you go, too. His name is Tyson and he *hates* Rockwell. So no problem there."

"That's great," Raynor said enthusiastically. "I could use some R and R. That's for sure."

Feek grinned understandingly. "I wish I could join you . . . but I'll be working overtime. A new shipment of suits came in and I've gotta get them up and running."

"And my suit?"

"It's black," Feek replied, "just like you asked for, with the skull on the visor. It looks so badass, man. Lieutenant Tyson will shit a brick when he sees it—but that's *your* problem."

"Roger that," Raynor agreed. "It's time those KM bastards know that death is coming for them."

"Maybe," Feek replied doubtfully. "Meanwhile, there's something else I need to tell you about. Something you should pass on to Tychus."

"Yeah? What's that?"

Feek looked left and right as if to assure himself that none of the other visitors were close enough to hear before making eye contact with Raynor. "Vanderspool sent a tech I had never met before down to run maintenance checks on about forty sets of armor—including all of the suits that belong to you guys."

"So?"

"That's *my* job. Why send a new guy? Unless somebody doesn't trust me.

"Once the tech left I went over the suits with a fine-tooth comb. And guess what? The sonofabitch installed kill switches in every hardskin."

Raynor frowned. "Kill switches?"

"Yeah," Feek replied. "Meaning remotely operated switches that would enable the colonel to trigger the emergency lockdown mode and freeze your suits."

Raynor gave a low whistle. "The rotten SOB."

"Exactly," the other man agreed. "So I cut the input circuits. Which means Vanderspool can push the button all day long and nothing will happen."

Raynor grinned. "How many beers do we owe you?"

Feek laughed. "Enough for me to swim in! You watch that bastard, Jim. You watch him real good. He's up to something and that's no lie."

The rest of the fifteen-minute-long visit was spent on more trivial matters, but when it came time for Raynor to hobble out into the prison yard, his mind went back to what Feek had told him. Vanderspool was up to something . . . but *what?*

THE CITY OF DARBY, ON THE PLANET TURAXIS II

The city of Darby was located seventy-five miles south of Polk's Pride, and because it had little to no strategic importance, was almost entirely untouched by the fighting. It was a picturesque place that occupied the western shore of a beautiful lake. It was fed by the Paddick River, which meant dead bodies were swept up in fishing nets from time to time, but the city was otherwise bright and cheerful, even at night when the citizens made use of flashlights to counter the mandatory blackout.

Having completed an uncomfortable truck ride down from Polk's Pride and checked into a so-called "military hotel," the Devils had agreed to go their separate ways during the first evening and gather the following night. Tychus, Doc, and Harnack were headed out to sample the city's nightlife, while Ward was intent on logging some extra rack time, and Kydd was determined to have what he called some "real food." That left Zander, who offered to accompany the sniper.

After obtaining the name of a good restaurant, Kydd and Zander ventured out onto a busy street. Both wore tasteful civvies, but no one who knew anything about the area would have mistaken them for locals.

Two moons were still up, so there was enough light to see by as the men left their hotel. They had obtained a map and flashlights for later from the concierge, but before they started on their way, Kydd and Zander paused for a moment to look out over the lake. Most of the city's homes were built on terraces carved out of a large hill, but at least a thousand were perched on pilings and sat directly above the water. Those structures, along with some of the businesses that served them, were connected by a maze of elevated bridges, walkways, and in some cases simple planks. That meant visitors had to be very careful not to get lost or fall into the cold waters below.

It was a possibility that Kydd kept firmly in mind as he and Zander followed the map down to the waterfront, out onto a pedestrian-only causeway, and into the Lakehome neighborhood. Charming homes stood side by side with shops as well as utilitarian buildings that served the city's extremely important fishing industry.

And farther out, where unobstructed views of the water were available, restaurant row was waiting to be explored. That's where the young men were headed, to an eatery that was supposed to be one of the best. In the meantime there were cute girls to look at, other soldiers to systematically ignore, and storefronts that sold things other than porno, tattoos, and trashy clothing. All of which was a change for Zander, who had been raised in a slum and was very conscious of his lower-class origins.

Kydd was aware that many of his childhood friends would have seen someone like Zander as "low class," but after months spent in the military, he no longer cared about such distinctions. Zander was a member of Heaven's Devils—and that was the only pedigree he had any interest in.

Still, Zander felt the first stirrings of doubt as they arrived in front of the restaurant called Waves, and made for the front door. "I don't know, Ryk," he said doubtfully, as a well-dressed couple entered in front of them. "Are you sure about this? What if I use the wrong fork or something?"

"Just do what I do," Kydd replied confidently. "But even if you make a mistake, who the hell cares? You're a Heaven's Devil! That's an accomplishment that none of the people in this restaurant can match."

Kydd's comments made Zander feel better, and he held his head high and shoulders back as they were shown into the dining room. It featured dozens of linen-covered tables, all of which looked out onto a marvelous view. Thousands of jewel fish rose to the surface each evening, and people never tired of looking at the fabulous wash of color generated by their red, green, and blue-tipped feelers.

The most prized seats were directly in front of an enormous window that looked out onto the lake. But such tables were reserved for VIPs, or those willing to slip the maitre d' some cash. So Kydd and Zander were shown to a small two-person table on the second tier next to the south wall. But the view was *still* incredible, and as Zander sat down, he knew he'd been correct to accompany Kydd. Because Zander had been to plenty of dives, but here was something completely different, and very special.

Neither one of them was familiar with the local cuisine, so they ordered "Wave Samplers" on the theory that they were sure to like at least part of what the restaurant had to offer. And, based on the deep-fried kitza appetizers that were forthcoming ten minutes later, they were in for a treat.

So there they were, enjoying mugs of locally brewed beer and delicious civilian food, when two men entered and were shown to the best table in the restaurant. A spot centered on the huge window and lit from above. Kydd's eyes were focused on the view beyond, so Zander was the one to take notice of the newcomers. "Holy crap, Ryk . . . Colonel Vanderspool just walked in!"

Kydd shifted his gaze, saw Vanderspool, and was about to say something snarky when the *other* man's face came into view. That was when Kydd's eyes widened and his jaw dropped. It couldn't be! Yet there he was, sitting no more than twenty-five feet away! Kydd immediately dropped his gaze down, propped an elbow on the tabletop, and lifted a hand to his forehead.

Zander saw Kydd's reaction and looked concerned. "Ryk? Are you okay? What's wrong?"

"I know the second man," Kydd said tightly, "although I'm surprised to see him here."

"Yeah?" Zander said. "Who is he?"

"His name is Errol Bennet," Kydd replied, "and he's my father."

The second course arrived, but the two soldiers didn't notice. Zander looked at the man in question and back again. "No way! That's terrific! Are you going to go over and say hello?"

"No," Kydd replied flatly. "Part of me wants to. . . . I admit that. But another part wants to know the answer to a very important question."

Zander's eyebrows rose. "Which is . . . ? "

"Why is my father on Turaxis II—having dinner with Colonel Vanderspool, who is a self-aggrandizing asshole, and almost certainly a thief?"

Zander shrugged philosophically. "Um, remember Fort Howe? And the load of jammers? We're still spending the money."

Kydd knew Zander was correct. It was hypocritical to accuse Vanderspool, and by implication his father, of crimes *he* had committed. But even so, he couldn't bring himself to stand up and cross what seemed like a vast chasm. He'd been living a lie for months now, but somewhere in the middle of it all, that lie had become reality. And there was Vanderspool to consider. . . . What would happen if Kydd walked up to them right then and there? It would be catastrophic! The truth regarding his identity would come out—and his father would insist that he leave the military.

Kydd felt a vague plan start to form in his mind. A childish scheme, really, that involved following his father back to wherever it was that he was staying, and a possible reunion without Vanderspool being present. He warned his dinner companion, and gave the other man a chance to bow out, but Zander shook his head. "Are you kidding? No way . . . I'll watch your six."

The two managed to enjoy the rest of their dinner, but Kydd never took his eyes off the pair.

Having already paid the rather extravagant bill, Kydd was ready when the two men rose from their table, paused to say something to the formally attired maître d', and left. It was easy to follow them out of the restaurant and down a darkened walkway.

But rather than head for the pedestrian causeway and the shoreline beyond, Vanderspool and Bennet turned in the opposite direction. Kydd was surprised to see that neither one of the men was accompanied by bodyguards, but supposed that was indicative of where they were, and the nature of their relationship.

Despite being off the beaten path, there was

still a bit of foot traffic. So Kydd and Zander were able to remain inconspicuous as they followed the two men to a low-slung building that had the name FISHCO painted on the side of it in big black letters. A boatyard was located right next door. There was the glow of what might have been floodlights from the water side of the structure, and based on the intermittent sound of power tools, it appeared that work was going to continue well into the night.

As the door to the FishCo building opened to let the men enter, a shaft of light shot out onto the walkway. Kydd caught sight of two Bennet family retainers and a couple of men who might have been resocialized marines dressed in civilian clothes.

What could that mean? Kydd wondered as he and Zander paused at the end of the boardwalk and pretended to look at the view. A throaty rumble was heard and a dimly lit wave skimmer appeared out of the darkness. It slowed as it passed under them, and Kydd could hear waves slapping against the pilings as the engine died.

Were more people arriving to meet with Vanderspool and his father? Or was that simply a fishing boat? Kydd had no way to know but was very curious. "Wait here," he said, as he turned to Zander. "I'm going to find out what's going on in there."

"Forget it," Zander responded. "I'm coming with you! Remember Firebase Zulu? I had your back then and I've got it now."

Kydd slapped the other man on his shoulder and smiled. "You're just as crazy as Harnack. You know that?"

Zander grinned. He was forced to speak loudly to be heard over the chatter of a power wrench. "Look who's talking! How are we going to get in?"

"Over there," Kydd replied. "See the outside stairs that lead up to the second floor? Maybe the door's unlocked."

That seemed unlikely, but Zander didn't have a better idea, and seconds later he was a few steps behind the sniper, tiptoeing up the wooden stairs to a landing and a weather-beaten door. It was, as Zander had expected it would be, firmly locked. "Damn!" Kydd whispered. "We're fekked."

"I have an idea," Zander replied. "Boost me up. . . . Maybe there's a way down from the roof."

Kydd looked up, judged that the roof was flat enough to stand on, and nodded. "Good idea . . . be careful, though. I know my father's people will be armed, and chances are Vanderspool's bodyguards are, too."

Zander nodded, put his right foot into the cradle that Kydd provided, and was ready when the larger man heaved him upward. There was a muted thump as Zander threw his forearms out onto the roof. Then, having brought a leg up and over, he disappeared from sight.

Three long minutes passed, and Kydd felt very exposed on the open stairway, as Zander did whatever he was doing. Finally, after what felt like an eternity, the other Devil was back, his head projecting out over the edge of the roof. "Ryk . . . there's a set of skylights. Half of them are propped open. I could hear them talking. Here . . . grab my belt."

The leather strap wasn't very long but Kydd was in good shape, and once he had hold of the belt, was able to pull himself up to the point where he could transfer his grip to the roof. Then, with help from Zander, Kydd scrambled onto the slanted surface. Thanks to a splash of light from the boatyard next door, he could see well enough.

Zander held a finger to his lips, motioned Kydd forward, and led him across the heat-absorbing roof to a row of partially opened skylights. Somebody was hammering on metal in the boatyard so there was very little chance of being heard.

The inside of the glass was painted in keeping with blackout regulations, but triangles of buttery light could be seen from the sides, and Kydd could hear the soft murmur of conversation emanating from below. Part of it anyway, until a chain hoist rattled momentarily and drowned everything out.

He knelt next to one of the openings, looked down through the gap, and realized that except for some side galleries the second floor was open. Judging from the hooks that were visible, plus a net that was stretched from one side to the other, the space was used to repair fishing gear. Three men were gathered directly below him, including his father, Vanderspool, and a man Kydd had never seen before. And it was he who was speaking. He had a deep, gravelly voice.

"I'm talking about a billion credits worth of ardeon crystals all headed for Port Horthra," he said. "That's where they will be uploaded to transports and shipped to a more secure planet for safekeeping."

"Except we plan to intercept them," Vanderspool put in smoothly, "and that's where Bennet Industries comes in. A Confederate task force is scheduled to drop into orbit three days from now. That will force your armored freighters and ore carriers to withdraw for a few days. At that point, a second-party ship contracted by Bennet Industries will take on a high-priority government cargo. One which my troops will guard." There was something else as well, but the words were lost as some sort of announcement was made over the PA system next door.

Kydd felt sick. He remembered the speech his father had made at the university the last time he saw him. About how profitable the wars were for the Confederacy. Now he knew why.

"Which raises a very important question," the KM official interjected. "After your troops hijack the crystals—what's to keep them from talking later on?"

"I have a plan for that," Vanderspool assured

him. "The raid will be conducted by the 1st platoon, Alpha Company, of the 321st Colonial Rangers Battalion. That includes the squad the press calls 'Heaven's Devils.' Once the operation is over I will send the survivors off to be resocialized."

The Kel-Morian chuckled appreciatively. "Perfect . . . no loose ends. I like it."

Kydd felt a heavy weight drop into the pit of his stomach. *Resocialized!* That was something that happened to other people. Like contracting a terrible disease—or taking a bullet in the head.

"So," the Kel-Morian continued, "we have one last thing to discuss, and that's the final split."

Vanderspool said something inaudible as a Klaxon sounded, and Bennet shrugged. "How about thirds? You deliver the crystals, the colonel hijacks them during what looks like a Confederate raid, and I take them off planet."

Kydd looked at Zander and back down again. Listening to the matter-of-fact way his father and the other men were preparing to steal valuable cargo and then brain-pan innocent soldiers made him sick to his stomach.

"That could work," Vanderspool allowed thoughtfully. He looked straight at Bennet. "But what if I could offer you compensation of another kind?"

Bennet looked skeptical. "Such as?"

Vanderspool smiled slowly. "I know where

your son, Ark, is, and in return for half of your cut, I'll put you in touch with him."

Kydd was shocked. How did Vanderspool know?

The offer was followed by a long moment of silence. And as the seconds ticked away Kydd felt his chest grow tight, so tight he could hardly breathe, as the head of the Bennet family took a moment to consider Vanderspool's proposal.

Kydd couldn't see any of their expressions from where he was, but he could imagine the slight widening of his father's eyes, and the man's otherwise impassive features. A face that even his mother admitted she couldn't scan clearly. "So he's in the military," Bennet concluded. "Somewhere on Turaxis II."

"I didn't say that," Vanderspool countered. "And it really doesn't matter. The question is do you *want* your son—or would you prefer to have the moncy?"

Kydd frowned and bit his lip as his father spoke. "Ark could have made contact with us and he chose not to. Clearly he doesn't care for us as we care for him. So wherever he is, he's going to have to learn to be a man on his own. You have nothing to offer. My share stands at thirty-three percent."

Kydd uttered a half-choked animal cry, but the sound was obscured by a loud ratcheting noise from next door, as Zander clapped a hand over his friend's mouth. Kydd tried to push him away. That was when Zander wrapped his arms around his friend and threw both of them into a combined roll. Four rotations later they fell into the stygian blackness. Kydd took a blow to the head as he fell past a protruding support beam, and heard the roar of a passing boat as he splashed into the lake. The water was very cold, and as Kydd sank, he hoped the bottom would rise to claim him.

CHAPTER THIRTY

"Citing the passage of time, and having received no new information regarding their son's tragic disappearance, Errol Bennet and his wife, Lisa, held a private memorial service for their son, Ark, who is presumed to have been murdered while on a walk in Tarsonis City."

Handy Anderson, *Evening Report* for UNN
March 2489

THE CITY OF DARBY,
ON THE PLANET TURAXIS II

Doc was naked and sitting astride Tychus as the knock came on the door. They were just back from a night on the town and were a little high. "Go away!" Tychus ordered in his best parade-ground voice, and reached up to cup Cassidy's breasts.

"It's Zander," a muffled voice said, from out in the hall. "We got trouble, Sarge . . . *big* trouble."

"Damn it to hell," Tychus said irritably, as Doc

swung a shapely leg over his torso. "What am I? A goddamned babysitter?"

Cassidy pouted as she pulled a blanket up around her shoulders. She poked her foot out and playfully traced Tychus's thigh with her big toe as he bent over to put on his boxers. With lightning speed, he reached out, wrapped one hand around both her ankles and began to tickle her feet, his favorite part of her. In a fit of screams and giggles, she squirmed around on the bed, kicking out at Tychus until he let go.

"You stay put," Tychus warned, pointing at Doc. "I'm not done with you."

Cassidy twisted herself back into the blanket and rolled onto her side, biting her lip and smiling up at Tychus. Her eyes were so glazed over from the drugs, it looked as though they were twinkling.

"This better be important," Tychus said, as he made his way toward the door. "Because if it isn't I'm going to rip your head off and use it as a spittoon." Tychus thumbed the lock, opened the door, and frowned.

Zander was not only soaking wet, but supporting Kydd, who had a gash on the side of his head.

"What the hell happened to you two?"

"Sorry, Sarge," Zander said apologetically, his eyes darting quickly from Tychus's scant clothing to the tousled bed behind him. "Hey, Doc," he said with a slight wave. The medic smiled and offered a half-assed salute.

"It's bad, Tychus," Zander continued in a hushed voice. "We overheard Vanderspool talking to Ryk's dad. We're talking Errol Bennet here—the head of an Old Family. They're planning some big heist, and we're right in the middle of it."

Tychus quickly ushered the guys into the room and glanced both ways to be sure the hallway was empty. He locked the door behind him. Zander wasn't one to exaggerate, so Tychus knew something serious had gone down.

"We fell into the lake," Zander continued. "Kydd has a gash on his head—he's bleeding, as you can see, and I didn't know where to take him. I don't know who else is in on this."

Tychus glanced at Kydd, who was trembling and drained of color, and seemed completely detached. "Hey, Doc! Get up," Tychus said gruffly. "You got a cut to tend to."

Doc was zoned out. Zander watched her slide off the bed and liked what he saw. But Tychus was right there so he had to avert his eyes as Cassidy rearranged the blanket prior to making her way over to a corner and rummaging through the pile of gear stored there. "Get him out of those wet clothes," she ordered. "And get some hot caff from room service."

Five minutes later a mostly clad Cassidy was there to clean Kydd's cut and apply a plastiscab bandage. "Sorry your scar won't be as ugly as the one Tychus has," she said, "but you can try again later."

Kydd's eyes were still a bit dull, but he wasn't shaking anymore, thanks to the bedspread that was wrapped around him. Room service arrived moments later, and if the bellman was surprised at the unusual scene inside, he showed no sign of it as Zander gave him a large tip.

Then, with both Zander and Kydd sipping hot drinks, it was time for them to share their story. Zander launched the narrative, but seconds later a heavyhearted Kydd began to chime in. Tychus grabbed a bottle of whiskey and dumped a generous dollop into Kydd's drink; the booze took effect quickly and Kydd's somber story soon transformed into an explosive, furious rant about his father. "The bastard disowned me," Kydd said bitterly. "*And* he totally sold me out! But that's not all. . . . He's part of a plot to make us steal a billion dollars' worth of ardeon crystals and then resocialize us! Turns out my father is a greedy scumbag! I'm going AWOL while I still can."

Tychus sat sprawled on a reclining chair, still clad in nothing more than a pair of boxers. "Like hell you will," he said, as he removed the stogie from his mouth long enough to blow some ashes off his massive chest. "You want to put it to the old man? Well, the best way to accomplish that is to take what he values the most . . . his money." He took a deep swig out of the bottle.

It took Kydd a moment to absorb what Tychus was saying, but once he understood, a smile appeared on his face. "I like it, Sarge!" he said. "I like it a lot."

"Good," Tychus said grimly. "When the hell is Jim getting here?"

"Tomorrow morning," Kydd replied. "And what about the rest of the squad?"

"I can see Harnack signing on to just about anything," Zander replied, "and Ward will agree so long as he gets to kill some Kel-Morians."

"All right, Zander, you be in charge of rounding everyone up. Once Jim arrives we'll bang out a plan," Tychus said. "It'll be fekkin' beautiful. Vanderspool won't know what hit him, and your pop'll be cryin' into his soup while we make off with his blood money." He looked back at Doc, who was propped against the headboard with her knees drawn up, her eyes focused on nothing in particular. He turned toward Zander and Kydd. "Now if you'll excuse us, gentlemen, please get the hell out of my room."

THE CITY OF DARBY,
ON THE PLANET TURAXIS II

It was approximately 0900, and a misty rain was falling, as Doc slipped out of the hotel and into a hovercab. She took a hit of crab to steady her nerves.

The Mondoro Hotel was located at the very top of the terraced hill, where its guests could enjoy sweeping views of the lake below. So it took a while for the cab to make its way to the top, where it settled in under a formal portico, and a uniformed doorman hurried out to greet Cassidy.

A couple of dozen steps took her through a pair of sliding glass doors and into a sumptuous lobby. It was decorated with Talvarian marble and beautifully upholstered furniture, all of which was positioned around a fountain and tiled pool.

House fones were positioned here and there, so Doc chose one next to a comfortable chair, and put the receiver to her ear. Once the operator responded, she asked to be connected with Colonel Vanderspool's room, and the fone started to ring a few seconds later. Her heart was pounding. It took the officer a long time to answer, and when he finally did, he sounded groggy. "Yes?"

"This is Petty Officer Third Class Cassidy," Doc said. "I'm down in the lobby."

A moment of silence passed before Vanderspool spoke again. He was clearly angry. "How the hell did you find me?"

"It wasn't hard," Cassidy answered honestly. "I went to the reception desk where I'm staying and asked the clerk for the name of the most expensive hotel in Darby."

Vanderspool swore. "Okay, damn it . . . what do you want? If you're out of crab that's too bad. Maybe you can steal some money from Findlay."

"No," Doc replied levelly, "I'm not out of crab.

And I don't plan to be out of crab ever again. I have some very valuable information, and I expect to be paid for it."

"Oh, really?" Vanderspool responded sarcastically. "What? You found out where Findlay keeps his cigars?"

"I know who you met with last night," Doc replied, suddenly breathless. "And I know what you plan to steal—and how you intend to do it."

There was a long pause before Vanderspool spoke. There was no sign of grogginess now. "I'm in room 804. Come on up." There was a loud click as the connection was broken.

Doc smiled thinly as she stood, paused to examine herself in a full-length mirror, and straightened her clothes. Then, having shakily applied some lip gloss, she made her way toward the elevators. Her knees felt weak, but she managed a steady stride.

As she walked, the image she'd been trying to avoid crept into her thoughts. Tychus—dead, disfigured, or worse, *resocialized*. As she entered the elevator, she shook the image out of her head and took another generous hit of crab. She felt for Tychus, in a primitive, selfish way—it felt good to be close to him at the end of the day. It made her feel less lonely.

But she knew Tychus would eventually dump her for someone else; they always did, and he, more than anyone, wasn't the kind of guy who would stick around. She had to think of herself this time, and she wanted to be on the winning team. Vanderspool had the military apparatus to secure a victory, and could pay her enough to keep a solid stash of crab for a long time to come.

But the rest of the guys . . . they were her comrades, and it pained her to think that she was sealing their fate. So she closed her eyes as the drug flooded her brain, and felt thankful that she didn't have to think at all.

SOMEWHERE OVER KEL-MORIAN–HELD TERRITORY, ON THE PLANET TURAXIS II

The dropship made a droning sound and threw a dark shadow down to caress the land below as it entered Kel-Morian-controlled airspace. It had been three days since Raynor was released from the stockade and had gone down to meet his friends in Darby. The news that Vanderspool planned to use Heaven's Devils to steal a load of ardeon crystals and resocialize them should have come as a tremendous shock. But after everything he'd been through, and in light of Vanderspool's efforts to have remote-controlled lockup switches installed in the unit's suits, Raynor was anything but surprised.

Nor had he offered any objections to the plan that Tychus put forward. Because with the exception of a scattering of officers like Sanchez, it was obvious that the entire command structure was made up of thieves who were working for thieves. And that was true of both sides of the conflict. So if there was a chance to steal from the thieves—then Raynor was happy to take part. *And* leave the military behind in the process.

All of the dropships were painted to look like Kel-Morian transports, and equipped with transponders and codes supplied by Vanderspool's Kel-Morian friend. Raynor knew he should be worried, because Tychus claimed the scheme was foolproof, and the other man was better known for impulsive reactions than carefully thought out plans. But Raynor had to admit that the scenario was pretty straightforward, and simple plans usually worked best.

Having used Tychus's connections to set up a sale of the ardeon crystals, all the Devils had to do was intervene at the right moment and load their ill-gotten loot onto one of the dropships. Then, rather than fly back to Confederate-held territory, they would put down in Free Port, a loosely governed city that sat astride the divide between Confederate and Kel-Morian territory. That was where the final transaction would take place.

Once in Free Port, and flush with money, it would be possible to take on new identities and book passage off planet. Not on a liner, since they didn't serve Turaxis II anymore, but on a freighter. According to Tychus there were always captains willing to make some extra money carrying passengers the owners weren't necessarily aware of.

Raynor's thoughts were interrupted as Tychus came shuffling down the center aisle. The noncom was wearing what appeared to be Kel-Morian armor and a shit-eating grin that was visible through an open visor. "So, soldier," he said in an attempt to imitate a gung-ho Quigby-type officer. "Are you ready to give your life for the Confederacy?"

"Yes, I am," Raynor grated. "Right after I give *yours*."

That got a laugh from those seated close enough to hear. "That's the spirit!" Tychus said cheerfully. "Your parents would be proud."

No they wouldn't, Raynor thought, as the dropship droned on. *They wouldn't even recognize what their son has become.*

The resocialized marines sat facing one another, eyes to the front, and backs to the bulkhead as the second dropship skimmed over the countryside below. Vanderspool sat just aft of the cockpit. It felt good to know that the marines would do whatever they were told without asking a single question. And if that meant they got killed, then so be it. Because they were criminals and sociopaths who had no place in decent society anyway.

As the pilot's voice sounded in his helmet and the ship began to circle Korsy's tiny starport,

Vanderspool was under no illusions. He and his troops would have to fight in order to take control of both the city and the train station. Fortunately the town wasn't that large and the opposition was going to consist of Kel-Morian guards who were paid to keep the local workers in line. The inhabitants were citizens of the Confederacy mostly, who had been captured when the KMs took over, and forced to work in factories and food processing plants.

But Vanderspool knew it would be a mistake to underestimate the Kel-Morians, who were bound to be well-armed. The key was to drop in unexpectedly, take their leadership out as quickly as possible, and hit the rest of them hard.

Such were Vanderspool's thoughts as the ship flared in for a landing and the ramp went down. He made eye contact with Lieutenant Fitz, the officer in command of the resocialized marines, and the other man nodded. His people were ready. All of them were equipped with black armor so that anyone who saw them would assume they were Kel-Morian troops.

Confident that everything was proceeding according to plan and that there weren't any hostile troops waiting for him below, Vanderspool made his way down the ramp and onto the tarmac. His visor was open so he could see the lead gray sky, the fuel tanks located a few hundred feet beyond the starport, and the factories beyond. Meanwhile, other dropships were landing farther out.

A jitney had pulled away from the low-lying terminal building and was coming out to meet him. That was to be expected, given the circumstances, and Vanderspool waited patiently as the vehicle drew up and two men hopped out. They wore black berets, mismatched uniforms, and symbols of rank Vanderspool had never seen before. Were they mercenaries? Or the equivalent of prison guards?

The one on the left was tall and thin. He had heavy brows, half-lidded eyes, and prominent cheekbones. The other man was of average height and equipped with a bulbous nose covered with a tracery of broken veins. And, judging from his expression, he was upset. "Who *are* you?" he demanded aggressively, as his eyes roamed Vanderspool's armor, searching for some sign of the Kel-Morian unit to which the visitor belonged. "Why wasn't I informed that you were coming?"

"My name is Stokes," the Confederate officer lied. "And you are?"

"Overseer Dankin," the man replied. "I am in charge of both the starport and the town of Korsy."

"Excellent," Vanderspool said cheerfully, as he brought a gauss pistol out from behind his back and shot Dankin between the eyes. "You're just the man I'm looking for."

The second Kel-Morian flinched as a look of surprise appeared on Dankin's face and he fell over backward. The flat crack of the report sent a flock of birds up off the starport's control tower, where they circled for a moment before landing again. The empty casing pinged as it bounced off the tarmac.

Vanderspool's pistol was aimed at the other man by then. The Kel-Morian's lips were moving but no sound came out. Vanderspool smiled engagingly. "I could use a guide. . . . Would you be interested in the job?"

The security officer nodded jerkily.

"Perfect," Vanderspool said. "Please be so kind as to surrender your sidearm and tell me all about the town of Korsy."

CHAPTER THIRTY-ONE

"Sometimes one rocket isn't enough to solve a problem. That's why I carry eight."

Private Connor Ward, heavy artillery, 321st Colonial Rangers Battalion, in an interview on Turaxis II
March 2489

THE TOWN OF KORSY,
ON THE PLANET TURAXIS II

In the wake of Lieutenant Sanchez's death Tychus had been named interim platoon leader, an unusual assignment for someone of his rank, but one he was happy with given what he knew to be Vanderspool's *real* plan for the Heaven's Devils. But Tychus had a plan of his own. One that would take care of Operation Early Retirement once and for all!

Sergeant Pinkham was in charge of the second squad. Both he and Tychus were about the same age, had the same larcenous instincts, and enjoyed a long-running love affair with Scotty Bolger's Old No. 8. So once the other noncom was given the opportunity to hear from both Kydd and Zander, he'd been quick to bring his people in on the counterplot, rather than face the prospect of resocialization.

As the 1st platoon left the dropship for the tarmac below, Tychus turned toward the front of the ship. The pilot had his helmet off and turned to look as the noncom stuck his head into the cockpit. "We're about to head out. Now, just to make sure you'll be here when we return, please remove the security lock-out from under the instrument panel and hand it over."

The pilot's face turned red, and he was just about to go off on the noncom, when Tychus frowned disapprovingly. "Sorry, sir . . . I don't have time to listen to your bullshit. Give me the lock-out or I'll kill you. And don't try to fake me out. I did my homework."

The pilot's face turned pale. He reached under the lower edge of the instrument panel and felt for the cylinder. Without the device it would be impossible to start the engines. Having found the lock-out, he gave it one turn to the right and felt it pop into his hand. An enormous gauntlet was waiting when he turned back. "Don't lose it," the pilot warned. "Because all of us will be stuck here if you do."

"Roger that," Tychus said approvingly, as he tucked the device away. "Now, unless I call you, stay off the comm. Private Haster is going to stay here and keep you company. Hand me your sidearm."

"This is entirely unnecessary," the pilot objected, as he complied with the noncom's instructions.

"I'm glad to hear it," Tychus replied. "I'll see you in a couple of hours."

Tychus gave the pistol to Haster, cautioned the private to stay alert, and made his way down the ramp to where the rest of the platoon was waiting. Vanderspool arrived seconds later in one of the sabers that had been unloaded from the third dropship. Vanderspool jumped out onto the tarmac. "Lieutenant Fitz and I will take the marines to the train station," Vanderspool said as he jumped onto the tarmac. "Your job is to sweep the west side of town, deal with any KMs you come across, and make sure the area is secure. Meet me at the lev station at 1330 hours and not a second later. Understood?"

"Sir, yes sir," Tychus replied.

"Good. You have a suit comm. . . . Use it if you need to. Execute."

Tychus saluted in the vain hope that an enemy sniper would see the gesture of respect and put a bullet through Vanderspool's visor. But nothing happened as he turned to rejoin his platoon.

Having assigned *all* of the vehicles to the re-socialized marines, Vanderspool, his Kel-Morian guide, and Lieutenant Fitz left the starport a few minutes later with a column of armored resocs double-timing along behind.

Tychus gave them a one-fingered salute as they left, waved his platoon forward, and led them west toward the low-slung food processing plants. The starport's comm tower was topped with an array of sensors, as were the metal masts that stood at regular intervals, so Tychus knew someone was watching as they crossed the parking lot. Would they send a force of soldiers out to meet him? Or had the loss of their commanding officer thrown the Kel-Morians into a state of confusion?

The answer came quickly as a door opened and half a dozen unarmored soldiers spilled out into the parking lot, firing their slugthrowers. Tychus didn't even slow down as the bullets pinged against his hardskin. He simply bowled two of the KMs over, knowing that the men behind him would handle the rest as he burst through the open door and entered the plant beyond.

The interior was lit by skylights, and there, under the cold gray light, hundreds of workers could be seen standing in front of long tables upon which all manner of produce was being sized and sorted. They had gaunt faces, and were dressed in little more than rags, as they turned to look at the invaders.

"You've been liberated!" Tychus announced via his external speakers, knowing that once the workers flooded into the streets it would make it that much harder for the Kel-Morians to reassert control of the town.

But the workers had been slaves for a long time, and rather than head for the exits, they remained right where they were. So Tychus fired a short burst through one of the skylights, saw them flinch as broken glass showered down on them, and felt a sense of satisfaction as the mad scramble to escape began.

Having cleared the processing plants, Tychus led his platoon south along the western security fence with plans to turn east to rendezvous with Vanderspool at the lev station. It was necessary to pause every once in a while to deal with pockets of resistance, but the Kel-Morian troops weren't equipped to handle combat-armored soldiers, and were quickly dealt with. Tychus didn't even break a sweat. "Maintain your intervals," he said. "Don't bunch up."

He took a hard left and began to follow one of the main streets east toward the railroad tracks. That was when three soldiers ran out into the street. Two opened up with assault weapons as the third fired a rocket launcher. The heat-seeking missile seemed to wobble slightly as it left the tube. Then it locked onto a target, drew a straight line to Sergeant Pinkham, and exploded on impact. The resulting boom echoed between the surrounding buildings as it sent pieces of armor and chunks of bloody flesh flying in every direction. Thanks to the space between them, none of the other soldiers suffered more than minor damage to their suits.

"Shoot them, goddamn it!" Tychus roared. "What are you waiting for?"

The man with the rocket launcher had less than three seconds to celebrate his kill before Kydd brought him down. Then Zander fired and a second KM fell. But the third turned, ran up a short flight of stairs, and pushed his way through a door.

Zander checked his ammo indicator, saw that he still had 357 spikes left, and followed the soldier up the stairs, through the door, and into a lobby. Two young women were huddled off to one side, sobbing, as Zander appeared. Even though Zander was small compared to his friends, he looked enormous in his armor, and they were clearly terrified when the blue giant paused to look down at them. A servo whirred as Zander's visor slid out of the way. He smiled reassuringly. "Don't cry. . . . I won't hurt you. What is this place?"

"I-i-i-t's a day care," the taller of the two women sobbed.

"Take a walk," Zander said kindly. "I'm going to kill the man who went inside."

They took off down the stairs.

Ward was there, right behind Zander, ready to back him up. "The bastard will be waiting for you."

"Yeah," Zander said, "I know." And with that he turned to push the door open. A small-caliber bullet hit Zander right in the middle of the chest as he entered the office. The soldier was standing in front of a desk holding a wailing toddler with one hand, and a pistol with the other. His rifle was slung across his back. The handgun came up so that it was pointed at the child. "Get out!" he snarled. "Get out or the kid dies."

Without a second's hesitation, Zander pulled the trigger and the gauss rifle jumped. It was pointed down, but not *all the way down,* and the guard screamed as the lower part of his left leg disappeared. The Kel-Morian fired reflexively, but the bullet missed the toddler's head by a fraction of an inch, and Zander was there to catch the child as the soldier fell. By then, he was rolling around on the floor trying to stop the bleeding with both hands.

Concerned as to what the toddler might see next, Zander held him so they could see each other through the open faceplate, and was rewarded with a big grin.

The screaming stopped when Ward kicked the soldier in the head. "Come on, Max. . . . We have to go."

"Yeah," Zander said, as he jiggled the toddler

up and down. "You go ahead. . . . These people need to haul ass while they can. I grew up in a place like this so I know how to get a lot of children from one place to the next. I'll get them started in the right direction and catch up with you in a few minutes."

Ward started to object, started to say that Tychus would be pissed, but the words died in his throat. He couldn't help but think of his own children—and the raid that killed them. "Okay, but you hurry . . . hear me?"

As Ward turned to leave, the toddler bopped Zander on the head with a tiny fist, and giggled.

Some of the Kel-Morians were still on the loose. Raynor knew that. But at least a couple dozen of the bastards had been dealt with—and he figured that was good enough for government work. So, cognizant of the time, he and Tychus led what remained of the shrinking command east toward the train station.

Half were on one side of the street, half on the other, their eyes roaming the storefronts opposite them, looking for any signs of resistance. There were open windows, and the occasional flash of a face, but no signs of opposition as they put the business district behind them and entered the industrial area beyond. The town was strangely quiet, as if holding its breath to see what would happen next. And that was a good question. What *would* happen next? Would the train arrive on time? Would they be able to get the drop on Vanderspool and his "brain-panned" marines? If not, a whole bunch of people were going to die.

A couple of the resocs were out on the platform in front of the train station, acting as lookouts. Their visors were open, and Raynor saw one of them murmur something into his comm unit before producing a generic resoc smile, which he directed at Tychus. "Good morning, Sergeant."

As Tychus led the others forward, Raynor wondered how the marine could say something over the comm without it coming in over the company freq. Unless the resocs were communicating with Vanderspool on a private push! And why would they want to do that unless . . .

Raynor wanted to say something, wanted to warn Tychus of possible trouble, but it was too late by then. The noncom had already pushed the door open and was inside the train station. The ceiling was low, rows of bench-style seats took up most of the waiting room, and the loading platform was visible beyond. "Well done," Vanderspool said expansively, as he came forward to meet them. "The train is due in ten minutes, and we're ready to receive it."

"Lieutenant Fitz," Vanderspool continued. "Please position Sergeant Findlay and his troops where you think they'll do the most good."

Raynor couldn't help but notice the way in which Fitz placed each member of Heaven's Devils up front, where they would not only be the first to make contact with the Kel-Morians, but would be caught in a crossfire if the resocs chose to fire on them from behind.

But, as the train appeared to the north and began to slow, there wasn't anything he could do but check his rifle and sweat into his hardskin. Stealing was a lot harder than he thought it would be.

Overseer Aaron Pax eyed his HUD as the high-speed lev train rounded a gentle curve and began to decelerate. Thanks to the counter located in the lower left-hand corner of his HUD, he knew that the maglev would arrive in one minute and thirty seconds.

Assuming that everything had gone well, Vanderspool and his troops would be in complete control of the town by that point and awaiting his arrival. Once the doors opened, they expected to board the train virtually unopposed, overcome a force of twenty unarmored troops, and steal forty chests of ardeon crystals worth one billion credits. Crystals that would be worth more, *much* more, when the war ended, as it would soon.

That's what Vanderspool and his troops were *expecting*. What would actually take place was quite different. Pax was still furious about the truck that had disappeared during the Fort Howe disaster. Vanderspool swore that someone else had taken it, but Pax never believed that. The Kel-Morian was buzzing with excitement. Revenge would be sweet.

Once the maglev came to a stop, and the Confederates came out to meet it, a platoon of carefully chosen rippers would attack them. Then, having been taken by surprise, the hijackers would be slaughtered.

Later, after the battle was over, Pax would claim that a small group of Confederates had been able to escape with the crystals. Would he be promoted in the wake of such a loss? No, but he wouldn't be punished either, because who could possibly anticipate such a daring raid?

Once the inevitable investigation was over, Pax would return to Korsy and retrieve the crystals from a hiding place that had already been prepared. Only two of the rippers knew about it, and once the treasure was safely hidden away, both of them were going to die. Later, in return for a larger cut, Errol Bennet had already agreed to spirit the treasure away.

It was a good plan—no, an *excellent* plan. What had been little more than a blur resolved itself into a security fence as the train continued to slow, with some globe-shaped fuel tanks beyond, and a succession of dreary buildings. The town of

Korsy certainly didn't *look* like much, but it was a very special place, or soon would be. The thought brought a smile to Pax's lips.

Vanderspool was keyed up as the Kel-Morian train came into sight and began to slow. Everything was going according to plan, and he was about to be very wealthy. "Okay," Vanderspool said over the scrambled command frequency. "Safeties off and stand by. And remember . . . take no prisoners. Over."

There was a series of clicks as both the Heaven's Devils and the resocialized marines acknowledged the order. The train produced a loud hissing noise as it came to a halt. Then the doors slid open, rippers surged out onto the platform, and the slaughter began.

"Bastards!" Vanderspool knew he'd been double-crossed the moment the first ripper appeared and Ward put a rocket into him. But Vanderspool wasn't about to give up as the enemy soldier exploded and showered the platform with bloody confetti. Not with one billion credits on the line.

"Fire!" Vanderspool yelled, as he pulled the trigger on his rifle and took a series of hits. Internal alarms sounded as spikes penetrated the outer layers of his armor and sent him stumbling backward.

Two or three rippers staggered as Tychus and a resocialized marine fired a flurry of gauss spikes. The KMs' patchwork armor held for a moment and then failed as a second volley cut them down. "Kill them!" Vanderspool shouted. "Kill *all* of them!"

Knowing that they'd be engaging in close quarters combat, about a third of the Kel-Morians had armed themselves with large-bore slugthrowers. The Confederate troops reeled under the impact of the Kel-Morian assault and were forced to give ground.

It could have been a rout. Would have been a rout. Except that was when Harnack stepped forward and, with no friendlies in the way, pulled the trigger on his igniter. There was a loud whump as a wave of fire washed across the oncoming rippers. Two of them began to beat at themselves in an attempt to extinguish the flames, and the rest of the KMs were unable to advance.

That was enough for the train's engineer, who took over from the computer that normally controlled the maglev. He released the brakes, pushed the throttle forward, and the badly scorched train pulled away from the station.

That left Pax and a group of rippers standing on the platform. But not for long, as Ward fired a cluster of rockets that threw the group back and off the edge. The train was gone by then, so they fell onto the tracks below.

Vanderspool shouted "No!" as the train continued to accelerate. "Stop!" But it was too late. One billion credits' worth of ardeon crystals were still aboard. His perfect plan had been transformed into a disaster, and odds were, Kel-Morian reinforcements were on their way, and might cut him off from the starport. For the first time in a long while, Vanderspool was truly frightened.

CHAPTER THIRTY-TWO

"In a stunning display of solidarity, representatives of the Confederacy have agreed to discuss the possibility of a ceasefire with their Kel-Morian counterparts as the first step in a process that could lead to peace talks."

Max Speer, *Special Evening Report from the Front Line* for UNN
April 2489

THE TOWN OF KORSY,
ON THE PLANET TURAXIS II

Vanderspool's mind was racing. It was difficult to part with the crystals, and the imaginary lifestyle he had created for himself, but Vanderspool was a realist. As such he knew how important it was to switch gears and recover as smoothly as he could.

He needed to get to the starport before KM reinforcements could arrive—but first there were the Heaven's Devils to deal with. Having lost a significant number of marines, he was no longer confident of his ability to take the misfits prisoner, so resocialization was out. The obvious solution was to kill them. And thanks to his foresight that would be easy.

So as Vanderspool turned away from the track and toward the troops on the platform, he brought out the special remote and pointed it at Tychus. There was only one button, and it was large enough to accommodate a massive thumb. Vanderspool pressed it and saw the indicator light glow green as all of the pre-equipped suits froze up.

That's how it was *supposed* to work at any rate, except that Tychus grinned evilly and shook his head in mock sympathy. His visor was open. "What's the problem, Colonel? Did something go wrong with your new toy?"

Vanderspool swore. Tychus knew about the kill switches! But that didn't matter, because the colonel had a backup plan. He made eye contact with Fitz, who threw an arm around Cassidy's chest as a corporal aimed a handgun at her face. She was wearing armor, but the pistol was only inches away, and would do the job.

Tychus, who was in the process of bringing his gauss rifle up, paused. Vanderspool smiled thinly. "So," he said harshly. "There *is* honor among thieves. But, just in case you have second thoughts about how valuable Doc Cassidy is to you, take a look around."

The Heaven's Devils and several members of the second squad had their backs to the door and were half-ringed by marines. That meant the resocs could fire without hitting one another—and that implied that the whole thing had been planned in advance. But why? Unless Vanderspool knew about the plan . . .

Vanderspool saw the look on Tychus's face and laughed. "Oh, my! If only you could see your expression right now! That's right, Sergeant Findlay. . . . Petty Officer Cassidy loves crab more than she loves you!"

Tychus stood stock-still for two agonizing seconds. Then, with a roar, he brought his rifle up and fired at Cassidy. But the spike went wide as Raynor jerked his friend back toward the door and shouted, "Light 'em up, Hank!"

Harnack pulled the trigger on his igniter and swept the flamethrower from left to right. That created a wall of flames that not only prevented the marines from advancing but made it difficult to see. They fired, but not very effectively, as the Devils backed out through the door. Harnack was the last one out, but even after he was clear Tychus continued to shoot through the opening, until Raynor shouted his name. Then, firing short, controlled bursts, he backed his way out to where the vehicles were waiting.

Harnack, Kydd, and members of the second squad were in possession of the first saber. The vehicle sat on big, knobby tires, and was large enough to haul four armored soldiers, but not much more. They had a gauss cannon trained on the door to the train station and were using it to keep Vanderspool and his resocialized marines penned up inside.

Raynor was at the wheel of the second saber waiting for Tychus and several other men who were clambering in. Zander arrived and shed his badly damaged hardskin before making for the third saber. He took the wheel as Ward sat down beside him.

There was a screech of tires as Harnack took off.

Raynor was right behind him, with Tychus riding shotgun, and a ranger on the saber's gauss cannon.

As Harnack prepared to turn right onto the street that led to the starport, a shriek sounded as a shell passed over their heads and landed to the north of them. The resulting explosion sent a column of debris surging into the air and shattered windows all around. It was Kydd who identified the nature of the threat and let the rest of them know where the shell had come from. "Kel-Morian sloths! Two of them! To the south!"

Raynor swore as he braked, skidded into the intersection, and turned his head to the left. That was when he saw two slab-sided sloths, as well as a mob of unarmored Kel-Morians sent to support them. Had the sloths been dispatched to cut them off from the starport? Yes, given where the shells were landing, that appeared to be the case.

"Go for them," Tychus ordered grimly. "Those cannons will be useless once we get in close."

Raynor wasn't so sure about that, since the rippers had been sent to prevent such a move, but gunned the engine anyway and sent the saber racing forward. One of the men in back was firing the gauss cannon by that time. The weapon was useless against the sloths but extremely effective where the KM ground forces were concerned. Half a dozen of them were cut to bloody ribbons as the heavy spikes tore them apart.

"Watch your field of fire!" Tychus warned, as Harnack's vehicle swerved in front of them and came dangerously close to being hit by the stream of deadly tracers.

Then the Devils were in close, firing every weapon they could bring to bear as knobby tires bounced over dead bodies, and Kel-Morians fell in a welter of blood.

Both sloths were equipped with secondary weapons, all of which were firing by then, but it was hard to hit the speedy sabers as they circled the slow-moving behemoths, looking for some sort of opening. But there wasn't any to be had, and the sabers were forced to retreat as the sloths continued their inexorable advance.

Meanwhile, Ward spoke over the squad freq as Zander braked to avoid a smoking shell crater. "Stop the car and let me out. . . . Maybe I can stop those things."

"Okay," Zander agreed. "But don't hang around to count your hits. I'll be waiting for you."

"Or maybe I'll be waiting for *you,*" Ward countered as the saber skidded to a stop. Then, before Zander could reply, Ward was on the pavement and headed for the middle of the street.

Raynor put his saber into a tight turn, braked, and saw what Ward was preparing to do. He shouted, *"No!"* as the sloth fired and a shell passed within a few feet of the other man's head.

But it was too late as Ward planted both feet, poured all of his concentration into the image on his HUD, and realized that the first sloth was shielding the second. That meant he couldn't fire on both. But he sure as hell could put a full load of rockets into the *first* machine and send the crew straight to hell!

Ward's tubes had been reloaded by that time. He braced himself and triggered all eight rockets at once, and was firing his gauss cannon when six of his projectiles hit. The leading edge of the first sloth was momentarily obscured as a series of explosions rippled across its bow. But that was where the sloth's armor was thickest. So there was a high probability that the machine would have survived all of the impacts had it not been for a stroke of luck.

Because as Ward fired at the sloth, it fired at him. And when the projectiles collided only inches in front of the machine's cannon, the force of the combined explosion was sufficient to blow the machine apart. A column of orange flame sent the turret straight up, a section of track flew off, and a secondary explosion sterilized the crew compartment.

Without the first sloth's bulk to shield him from the second machine, Ward was terribly exposed. Raynor saw the second sloth's cannon start to swing. *"Run!"* Raynor shouted. "Run, goddamn it!"

But Ward wasn't about to run as he opened fire with the gauss cannon. Time seemed to slow, and he could hear his children laughing, as he saw the muzzle flash. Then Ward was gone as a cannon shell struck the middle of his chest and his world exploded.

Unfortunately there was no time to mourn Ward's death as Kydd's voice was heard over the comm unit. "Tychus! Jim! We're taking fire from the east! Over."

Raynor took his foot off the brake, brought the

saber around, and saw that the sniper was correct. Vanderspool and his marines were advancing up the street, seeking cover wherever they could find it, and firing at targets of opportunity. "We have to reach the starport before they do," Tychus said over the comm. "Follow us!"

Raynor took off, and as Harnack pulled in behind the lead saber, he was careful to jink back and forth as cannon shells sent columns of debris soaring into the air. His windscreen shattered, there was a metallic clang as something landed in the cargo compartment, and Harnack swore.

Zander was in the last vehicle and still trying to process Ward's sudden death as he spotted one of the two young women he'd encountered earlier. She was alone, her dress was smeared with blood, and she was terrified—not to mention the fact that she was standing in the line of fire. Zander swore, stood on the brake, and turned to one of the men in back. "Take the wheel!" he shouted. "I'll catch up!"

The ranger was a member of the second squad. He nodded, jumped out, and was just about to get behind the wheel when a shell scored a direct hit on the saber and sent the shattered wreck tumbling end-for-end. Armored bodies flew through the air and fell like broken dolls.

Zander was twenty yards away by then, having dragged the woman off the street. He wanted to lead her to safety, but as the sloth rolled past and Vanderspool's troops rounded a corner, he knew his friends needed him. "Go to the west gate. Get out into the countryside and hide. It's your only chance. *Now go!*"

She mumbled something incoherent and took off erratically in the direction he'd indicated.

Zander turned back toward the street. Unfortunately it was too late. Vanderspool was there with his needle-gun already leveled. Zander was completely vulnerable—without his hardskin, the private was down to sweat-stained cammies.

Cassidy was present as well. Like Vanderspool she'd been forced to shuck her armor and stood with her medic bag slung over one shoulder. She tried to meet Zander's eyes but couldn't. She felt hollow inside, as if whatever remained of her inner being had been left at the lev station, where the final betrayal had taken place. Now, fully aware of what was about to happen, Cassidy began to shake. It was like going through withdrawal, only worse, because she knew that no amount of crab was going to make her feel better.

"Well, well," Vanderspool said, as he eyed the man in front of him. "Look what we have here."

Zander began to swing his weapon left, but knew there wasn't enough time, as Vanderspool fired. The first needle knocked Zander off his feet, the second smashed through his forehead, and the third was completely unnecessary.

* * *

There was a resounding *BOOM* as a stray shell hit one of the globular fuel tanks a city block east of the street the Devils were on. But rather than explode the way it was supposed to, the shell punched a hole in the 500,000-gallon container, which released a column of pinkish fuel. The high-octane portrenol shot straight out, splashed into the containment area that surrounded the tanks, and a lake began to form.

Meanwhile, as the sloth's foreman corrected his aim and sent a projectile screaming toward the starport beyond, Tychus was on the comm. *"We have to stop that thing before it can destroy the dropships. How 'bout it, Hank? Can you light that bastard up? Over."*

"Roger that," Harnack replied as he brought his saber to a shuddering halt.

In an attempt to distract the sloth's foreman and buy time for Harnack, Raynor sent his saber roaring forward, as one of his passengers fired the gauss cannon. The weapon clattered methodically, and sparks of light signaled a series of hits as the spikes punched a line of divots into the sloth's hull. But to no avail.

The saber passed within ten feet of the sloth's squared-off bow before entering a skidding turn. But the pass wasn't enough to prevent the sloth from firing another shell at the starport. And this one scored a direct hit.

There was an eye-searing flash of light as dropship number three exploded and chunks of the ship's fuselage soared high into the air, where they seemed to pause momentarily before cartwheeling down. "The sonofabitch has the range now," Tychus said grimly. "This ain't good."

And it *wasn't* good. A fact not lost on Harnack, who was lumbering forward. Would the sloth crew notice him as he came in from the side? Maybe . . . but Harnack figured they were focused on the starport as he approached the mountain of metal.

That was when Kydd saw that fuel was pouring out of the containment area and onto the street. Either the ditch was too shallow or someone had left one of the flood control gates open. Not that it made much difference since the result was the same. "Harnack!" Kydd shouted. *"Don't fire!"*

But Harnack was within range by then and completely unaware of the fuel that was flowing his way. There was the familiar click as he pulled the trigger and the igniter produced a spark. That was followed by a loud whump as a gout of flame shot forward to blister the sloth's paint job.

That got the crew's attention, and one of the treads stopped as the other continued to clank forward. So Harnack sent a tongue of fire in under the monster, because that's where it was most vulnerable. As the machine began to turn, he was forced to do likewise or be cut down by the sloth's forward-firing slugthrowers.

Kydd opened his mouth to yell again, but the river of fuel was lapping around Harnack's boots by then, and the result was inevitable. There was a thump as the high-octane liquid caught fire, wrapping both Harnack *and* the sloth in an inferno of red-orange flames.

Harnack tried to run but didn't get far. The scream was a long, lung-emptying sound that Kydd knew he would never forget as the rifle came up, and time slowed. Even though it seemed like an eternity, less than two seconds elapsed as the crosshairs settled over their target and the firing pin dropped. The butt kicked Kydd's shoulder, the slug hit Harnack in the head, and most of his brains flew sideways.

Then like a wax figure exposed to heat, Harnack began to melt, the sloth rolled over him, and the tanks on his back exploded. The result was a stupendous boom as the sixty-ton monster was transformed into a thousand pieces of metal confetti. It hissed as it fell into a lake of fire.

Kydd felt a lump form in the back of his throat as images of Harnack flickered through his mind. There were lots of them. Harnack laughing manically as he rolled around on the grass in front of the police station. Harnack attacking the rippers at Fort Howe. And most of all, Harnack standing next to the fallen goliath, just below the repository in Polk's Pride. He'd been like a brother. A crazy, "I don't give a shit" brother who had been brave to a fault. And he'd gone out the way he would want to go out. With a loud bang.

Suddenly Kydd knew what to say. Knew what would mean the most to his brother. "That was awesome, Hank. . . . That was fekking awesome."

"Sarge!" a voice said over the squad freq. *"This is Haster. . . . Transport three took a direct hit. . . . What the hell is going on? A civilian truck pulled up outside and I caught a glimpse of Colonel Vanderspool."*

"They must have captured it and circled around the east side of the fuel tanks," Raynor observed grimly.

"Raise the ramp," Tychus ordered tersely. "And don't allow anyone to enter. Not Vanderspool and not Cassidy. . . . Do you scan me? Over."

"Five by five, Sarge. Over."

"Good. We're on the way. Over."

There were only two sabers by that time. The one Raynor was driving, and a second vehicle, with Kydd at the wheel. The third transport was still burning, and a thick finger of black smoke rose to point at the sky as the sabers passed through an open gate. "Be ready, Jim," Tychus said, as he shoved a fresh magazine into his gauss rifle. "We could be outgunned."

Raynor could see the flatbed truck by then, as

well as the people who were spilling out the back, and knew the situation was serious. He knew Vanderspool would almost certainly destroy the first transport if he had the means to do so and escape in the second. Then, with no one left alive to contradict him, he'd be free to concoct whatever story he chose.

As Raynor brought the saber to a screeching halt, the scene that greeted him was considerably different from what he expected to see. Vanderspool was present all right, as was Doc—but both were prisoners.

Pax's helmet was missing, a bloodstained bandage was wrapped around his head, and the two rippers standing behind him were in equally bad shape. But the Kel-Morians were vertical, heavily armed, and definitely in control. At some point they had captured Vanderspool and Cassidy, loaded them onto a civilian truck, and circled around behind the storage tanks.

"Hold it right there," Pax said as Tychus swung his enormous feet out of the saber and stood up. "Drop your weapon or I'll shoot Colonel Vanderspool in the head."

Raynor had circled to the front of the saber by that time. Both Raynor and Tychus began to laugh as Vanderspool scowled. The sound was amplified, and boomed over the external speakers. "Be my guest," Tychus said coldly. "Do us all a favor and blow his fekkin' head off."

Pax looked at Tychus, saw the cold determination on his face, and knew the noncom was serious. "Your troops aren't very loyal, are they?" the Kel-Morian officer said disgustedly. "I should have known."

Having stopped the saber about five hundred yards away, Kydd was standing next to it, using the hood as a rest for his rifle. From that angle most of Pax's body was obscured by Vanderspool's. There was another option, however. Kydd adjusted his aim slightly, his finger took up the last bit of slack, and the rifle fired. Vanderspool's body jerked spasmodically as the heavy slug smashed through his shoulder and hit the man immediately behind him.

Blood sprayed the area as the bullet tore Pax's throat out and the other Kel-Morians opened fire. The result was nearly instantaneous as both Tychus and Raynor hosed them down with a hail of gauss spikes.

The enemy soldiers attempted to stand their ground, but one of them fell as Kydd fired on him, and the other staggered drunkenly as the incoming gauss spikes tore through his suit. Then he toppled over backward and skidded for a short distance before coming to a halt.

That was when Tychus realized that Cassidy had taken a spike through the chest at some point in the exchange of fire and was lying on her back looking up at the sky. He hurried to kneel next to her and placed a hand under her head. The liquid in her throat made a gargling sound as she spoke. "It wasn't personal. . . . It was never personal. You know that."

"Yeah," Tychus replied soberly. "I know."

Doc forced a smile, and was about to say something else, when her eyes went out of focus. She was gone.

Tychus swore, forced himself to rise, and took a look around. That was when his eyes came to rest on Vanderspool. The officer was on his knees, clutching the bloody mess that was his shoulder and sobbing loudly. "Please!" Vanderspool pleaded as he looked up. "I need a medic! I'll pay you!"

"Doc is dead," Tychus said flatly. "You killed her."

That wasn't true. Not that it mattered. Raynor stepped beside Tychus, looked down at Vanderspool, and felt the anger start to build inside him. Because there, kneeling in front of him, was the personification of everything he had come to hate. How many people had given their lives so that Vanderspool could line his pockets? Hundreds? *Thousands?* It was impossible to say. But one thing was for sure. . . . It was never going to happen again.

Kydd joined his brothers, rifle at his side, and the three men watched the colonel writhe in agony, his façade of power and strength shattered by his own greed.

"Your father wants to see you," Vanderspool pleaded to Kydd. "I know where he is. I'll take you there. Please, I'm in pain."

Kydd snorted and shook his head.

Pax's pistol was lying on the tarmac. Vanderspool made a grab for it and Raynor stepped on his hand. Flesh gave way, bones broke, and Vanderspool screamed.

"I can ease your pain, you piece of trash," Raynor growled as the skull on his visor whirred and his real face appeared. His voice was unnaturally cold, guttural. Seething with rage, Raynor brought the gauss rifle to bear. "Good-bye, asshole."

Vanderspool's eyes grew larger, he opened his mouth to say "No," and a single spike slammed into his chest. As the officer toppled over onto his side, Raynor felt his anger melt away, to be replaced by something else. Somehow, without intending to, he had become part of the very thing he despised. A universe in which the Old Families could take whatever they wanted, send brainpanned citizens out to fight interstellar wars, and kill with impunity. The realization was followed by a profound sense of shame—and a determination to be who he *wanted* to be. Or, in his father's words, the man he *chose* to be.

The three men stood there for a moment. The

area was completely silent except for the crackle of flames as they continued to devour the city—and the sudden whine of engines as Vanderspool's dropship prepared to lift without him. Tychus was the first to speak. "The Hellhounds will be here soon. We'd better get a move on."

The men turned toward the remaining dropship. Haster had dropped the ramp by then, and was waiting inside, as they began to make their way up. Tychus led the way, with Kydd right behind him. Raynor paused to take one last look at the city where so many of his friends had given their lives. *We weren't angels,* Raynor thought, *we were the Heaven's Devils. The best of the worst.*

The thought brought a nostalgic smile to Raynor's lips and it was still in place as the dropship took off and left the carnage behind. He was going AWOL, so *his* war was over, but he would never forget the friends who had fallen in the town of Korsy. Not ever.

ABOUT THE AUTHOR

William C. Dietz is the bestselling author of more than thirty novels, some of which have been translated into German, Russian, and Japanese. He grew up in the Seattle area, spent time with the Navy and Marine Corps as a medic, graduated from the University of Washington, lived in Africa for half a year, and has traveled to six continents.

Dietz has been employed as a surgical technician, college instructor, news writer, television producer, and director of public relations and marketing for an international telephone company. He is a member of the Science Fiction and Fantasy Writers of America, the Writer's Guild, and the International Association of Media Tie-In Writers.

He and his wife live near Gig Harbor in Washington State, where they enjoy traveling, kayaking, and not too surprisingly, reading books. For more information about William C. Dietz and his work, visit: williamcdietz.com.

STARCRAFT TIMELINE

c. 1500

A group of rogue protoss is exiled from the protoss homeworld of Aiur for refusing to join the Khala, a telepathic link shared by the entire race. These rogues, called the dark templar, ultimately settle on the planet of Shakuras. This split between the two protoss factions becomes known as the Discord.
(*StarCraft: Shadow Hunters*, book two of the Dark Templar Saga by Christie Golden)
(*StarCraft: Twilight*, book three of the Dark Templar Saga by Christie Golden)

1865

The dark templar Zeratul is born. He will later be instrumental in reconciling the severed halves of protoss society.
(*StarCraft: Twilight*, book three of the Dark Templar Saga by Christie Golden)
(*StarCraft: Queen of Blades* by Aaron Rosenberg)

2143

Tassadar is born. He will later be an executor of the Aiur protoss.
(*StarCraft: Twilight*, book three of the Dark Templar Saga by Christie Golden)
(*StarCraft: Queen of Blades* by Aaron Rosenberg)

c. 2259

Four supercarriers—the *Argo*, the *Sarengo*, the *Reagan*, and the *Nagglfar*—transporting convicts from Earth venture far beyond their intended destination and crash-land on planets in the Koprulu sector. The survivors settle on the planets Moria, Umoja, and Tarsonis, and build new societies that grow to encompass other planets.

2323

Having established colonies on other planets, Tarsonis becomes the capital of the Terran Confederacy, a powerful but increasingly oppressive government.

2460

Arcturus Mengsk is born. He is a member of one of the Confederacy's elite Old Families.
(*StarCraft: I, Mengsk* by Graham McNeill)
(*StarCraft: Liberty's Crusade* by Jeff Grubb)
(*StarCraft: Uprising* by Micky Neilson)

2464

Tychus Findlay is born. He will later become good friends with Jim Raynor during the Guild Wars.
(*StarCraft: Heaven's Devils* by William C. Dietz)

2470

Jim Raynor is born to Trace and Karol Raynor, farmers on the fringe world of Shiloh.
(*StarCraft: Heaven's Devils* by William C. Dietz)
(*StarCraft: Liberty's Crusade* by Jeff Grubb)

(*StarCraft: Queen of Blades* by Aaron Rosenberg)
(*StarCraft: Frontline*, volume 4, "Homecoming" by Chris Metzen and Hector Sevilla)
(*StarCraft* monthly comic #5–7 by Simon Furman and Federico Dallocchio)

2473

Sarah Kerrigan is born. She is a terran gifted with powerful psionic abilities.
(*StarCraft: Liberty's Crusade* by Jeff Grubb)
(*StarCraft: Uprising* by Micky Neilson)
(*StarCraft: Queen of Blades* by Aaron Rosenberg)
(StarCraft: the Dark Templar Saga by Christie Golden)

2478

Arcturus Mengsk graduates from the Styrling Academy and joins the Confederate Marine Corps against the wishes of his parents.
(*StarCraft: I, Mengsk* by Graham McNeill)

2485

In response to the Confederacy's underhanded appropriation of resources, the Morian Mining

Coalition and the Kelanis Shipping Guild join forces to create the Kel-Morian Combine. Their goal is to protect their lucrative mining operations and provide military aid to any mining guild oppressed by the Confederacy. Rising tensions between the Combine and the Confederacy lead to the outbreak of open warfare. This conflict comes to be known as the Guild Wars.
(*StarCraft: Heaven's Devils* by William C. Dietz)
(*StarCraft: I, Mengsk* by Graham McNeill)

2488–2489

Jim Raynor joins the Confederate Marine Corps and meets Tychus Findlay. In the later battles between the Confederacy and the Kel-Morian Combine, the 321st Colonial Rangers Battalion (whose membership includes Raynor and Findlay) comes to prominence for its expertise and bravado, earning it the nickname "Heaven's Devils."
(*StarCraft: Heaven's Devils* by William C. Dietz)

Jim Raynor meets fellow Confederate soldier Cole Hickson in a Kel-Morian prison camp. During this encounter, Hickson teaches Raynor how to resist and survive the Kel-Morians' brutal torture methods.

(*StarCraft: Heaven's Devils* by William C. Dietz)
(*StarCraft* monthly comic #6 by Simon Furman and Federico Dallocchio)

Toward the end of the Guild Wars, Jim Raynor and Tychus Findlay go AWOL from the Confederate military.

Arcturus Mengsk resigns from the Confederate military after achieving the rank of colonel. He then becomes a successful prospector in the galactic rim.
(*StarCraft: I, Mengsk* by Graham McNeill)

After nearly four years of war, the Confederacy "negotiates" peace with the Kel-Morian Combine, annexing almost all of the Combine's supporting mining guilds. Despite this massive setback, the Kel-Morian Combine is allowed to continue its existence and retain its autonomy.

Arcturus Mengsk's father, Confederate senator Angus Mengsk, declares the independence of Korhal IV, a core world of the Confederacy that has long been at odds with the government. In response, three Confederate ghosts—covert terran operatives possessing superhuman psionic powers enhanced by cutting-edge technology—assassinate Angus, his wife, and their young

daughter. Furious at the murder of his family, Arcturus takes command of the rebellion in Korhal and wages a guerilla war against the Confederacy.
(*StarCraft: I, Mengsk* by Graham McNeill)

2491

As a warning to other would-be separatists, the Confederacy unleashes a nuclear holocaust on Korhal IV, killing millions. In retaliation, Arcturus Mengsk names his rebel group the Sons of Korhal and intensifies his struggle against the Confederacy. During this time Arcturus liberates a Confederate ghost named Sarah Kerrigan, who later becomes his second-in-command.
(*StarCraft: Uprising* by Micky Neilson)

2495

Jim Raynor ends his outlaw years when his partner in crime, Tychus Findlay, is apprehended by authorities. Raynor starts a new life as a Confederate marshal on the planet Mar Sara.

2499–2500

Two alien threats appear in the Koprulu sector: the ruthless, highly adaptable zerg and the enigmatic protoss. In a seemingly unprovoked attack, the protoss incinerate the terran planet Chau Sara, drawing the ire of the Confederacy. Unbeknownst to most terrans, Chau Sara had become infested by the zerg, and the protoss carried out their attack in order to destroy the infestation. Other worlds, including the nearby planet Mar Sara, are also found to be infested by the zerg.
(*StarCraft: Liberty's Crusade* by Jeff Grubb)
(*StarCraft: Twilight*, book three of the Dark Templar Saga by Christie Golden)

On Mar Sara, the Confederacy imprisons Jim Raynor for destroying Backwater Station, a zerg-infested terran outpost. He is liberated soon after by Mengsk's rebel group, the Sons of Korhal.
(*StarCraft: Liberty's Crusade* by Jeff Grubb)

A Confederate marine named Ardo Melnikov finds himself embroiled in the conflict on Mar Sara. He suffers from painful memories of his former life on the planet Bountiful, but he soon discovers that there is a darker truth to his past.
(*StarCraft: Speed of Darkness* by Tracy Hickman)

Mar Sara suffers the same fate as Chau Sara and is incinerated by the protoss. Jim Raynor, Arcturus Mengsk, the Sons of Korhal, and some of the planet's residents manage to escape the destruction. (*StarCraft: Liberty's Crusade* by Jeff Grubb)

Feeling betrayed by the Confederacy, Jim Raynor joins the Sons of Korhal and meets Sarah Kerrigan. A Universal News Network (UNN) reporter, Michael Liberty, accompanies the rebel group to report on the chaos and counteract Confederate propaganda.
(*StarCraft: Liberty's Crusade* by Jeff Grubb)

A Confederate politician named Tamsen Cauley tasks the War Pigs—a covert military unit created to take on the Confederacy's dirtiest jobs—to assassinate Arcturus Mengsk. The attempt on Mengsk's life fails.
(*StarCraft* monthly comic #1 by Simon Furman and Federico Dallocchio)

November "Nova" Terra, a daughter of one of the Confederacy's powerful Old Families on Tarsonis, unleashes her latent psionic abilities after she telepathically feels her parents and brother being murdered. Once her terrifying power becomes known, the Confederacy hunts her down, intending to take advantage of her talents.
(*StarCraft: Ghost: Nova* by Keith R.A. DeCandido)

Arcturus Mengsk deploys a devastating weapon—the psi emitter—on the Confederate capital of Tarsonis. The device sends out amplified psionic signals and draws large numbers of zerg to the planet. Tarsonis falls soon after, and the loss of the capital proves to be a deathblow to the Confederacy.
(*StarCraft: Liberty's Crusade* by Jeff Grubb)

Arcturus Mengsk betrays Sarah Kerrigan and abandons her on Tarsonis as it is being overrun by zerg. Jim Raynor, who had developed a deep bond with Kerrigan, defects from the Sons of Korhal in fury and forms a rebel group that will come to be known as Raynor's Raiders. He soon discovers Kerrigan's true fate: instead of being killed by the zerg, she is transformed into a powerful being known as the Queen of Blades.
(*StarCraft: Liberty's Crusade* by Jeff Grubb)
(*StarCraft: Queen of Blades* by Aaron Rosenberg)

Michael Liberty leaves the Sons of Korhal along with Raynor after witnessing Mengsk's ruthlessness. Unwilling to become a propaganda tool, the reporter begins transmitting rogue news broadcasts that expose Mengsk's oppressive tactics.
(*StarCraft: Liberty's Crusade* by Jeff Grubb)
(*StarCraft: Queen of Blades* by Aaron Rosenberg)

Arcturus Mengsk declares himself emperor of the Terran Dominion, a new government that takes power over many of the terran planets in the Koprulu sector.
(*StarCraft: I, Mengsk* by Graham McNeill)

Dominion senator Corbin Phash discovers that his young son, Colin, can attract hordes of deadly zerg with his psionic abilities—a talent that the Dominion sees as a useful weapon.
(*StarCraft: Frontline*, volume 1, "Weapon of War" by Paul Benjamin, David Shramek, and Hector Sevilla)

On the fringe world of Bhekar Ro, terran, protoss, and zerg forces fight to claim a recently unearthed building belonging to the xel'naga, an ancient alien race that is thought to have influenced the evolution of the zerg and the protoss.
(*StarCraft: Shadow of the Xel'Naga* by Gabriel Mesta)

The supreme ruler of the zerg, the Overmind, discovers the location of the protoss homeworld of Aiur. The zerg invade the planet, but the heroic high templar Tassadar sacrifices himself to destroy the Overmind. However, much of Aiur is left in ruins, and the remaining Aiur protoss flee to the dark templar planet of Shakuras through a xel'naga warp gate. For the first time since the

dark templar were banished from Aiur, the two protoss societies are reunited.
(*StarCraft: Frontline*, volume 3, "Twilight Archon" by Ren Zatopek and Noel Rodriguez)
(*StarCraft: Queen of Blades* by Aaron Rosenberg)
(*StarCraft: Twilight*, book three of the Dark Templar Saga by Christie Golden)

The zerg pursue the refugees from the planet Aiur through the warp gate to Shakuras. Jim Raynor and his forces, who had become allies with Tassadar and the dark templar Zeratul, stay behind on Aiur in order to shut down the warp gate. Meanwhile, Zeratul and the protoss executor Artanis utilize the powers of an ancient xel'naga temple on Shakuras to purge the zerg that have already invaded the planet.

The United Earth Directorate (UED), having observed the conflict between the terrans, the zerg, and the protoss, arrives in the Koprulu sector from Earth in order to take control. To accomplish its goal, the UED captures a fledgling Overmind on the zerg-occupied planet of Char. The Queen of Blades, Mengsk, Raynor, and the protoss put aside their differences and work together in order to defeat the UED and the new Overmind. These unlikely allies manage to accomplish their goal, and after the death of the second Overmind, the Queen of

Blades attains control over all zerg in the Koprulu sector.

On an uncharted moon near Char, Zeratul encounters the terran Samir Duran, once an ally of the Queen of Blades. Zeratul discovers that Duran has successfully spliced together zerg and protoss DNA to create a hybrid, a creation that Duran ominously prophesizes will change the universe forever.

Arcturus Mengsk exterminates half of his ghost operatives to ensure loyalty among the former Confederate agents who have been integrated into the Dominion ghost program. Additionally, he establishes a new Ghost Academy on Ursa, a moon orbiting Korhal IV.
(*StarCraft: Shadow Hunters*, book two of the Dark Templar Saga by Christie Golden)

Corbin Phash sends his son, Colin, into hiding from the Dominion, whose agents are hunting down the young boy to exploit his psionic abilities. Corbin flees to the Umojan Protectorate, a terran government independent of the Dominion.
(*StarCraft: Frontline*, volume 3, "War-Torn" by Paul Benjamin, David Shramek, and Hector Sevilla)

The young Colin Phash is captured by the Dominion and sent to the Ghost Academy. Meanwhile, his father, Corbin, acts as a dissenting voice against the Dominion from the Umojan Protectorate. For his outspoken opposition, Corbin becomes the target of an assassination attempt.
(*StarCraft: Frontline*, volume 4, "Orientation" by Paul Benjamin, David Shramek, and Mel Joy San Juan)

2501

Nova Terra, having escaped the destruction of her homeworld, Tarsonis, trains alongside other gifted terrans and hones her psionic talents at the Ghost Academy.
(*StarCraft: Ghost: Nova* by Keith R.A. DeCandido)
(*StarCraft: Ghost Academy* volume 1 by Keith R.A. DeCandido and Fernando Heinz Furukawa)

2502

Arcturus Mengsk reaches out to his son, Valerian, who had grown up in the relative absence of his father. Intending for Valerian to continue the Mengsk dynasty, Arcturus recalls his own progression from an apathetic teenager to an emperor.
(*StarCraft: I, Mengsk* by Graham McNeill)

Reporter Kate Lockwell is embedded with Dominion troops to deliver patriotic pro-Dominion broadcasts to the Universal News Network. During her time with the soldiers, she encounters former UNN reporter Michael Liberty and discovers some of the darker truths beneath the Dominion's surface.
(*StarCraft: Frontline*, volume 2, "Newsworthy" by Grace Randolph and Nam Kim)

Tamsen Cauley plans to kill off the War Pigs—who are now disbanded—in order to cover up his previous attempt to assassinate Arcturus Mengsk. Before doing so, he gathers the War Pigs for a mission to kill Jim Raynor, an action that Cauley believes will win Mengsk's favor. One of the War Pigs sent on this mission, Cole Hickson, is the former Confederate soldier who helped Raynor survive the brutal Kel-Morian prison camp.
(*StarCraft* monthly comic #1 by Simon Furman and Federico Dallocchio)

Fighters from all three of the Koprulu sector's factions—terran, protoss, and zerg—vie for control over an ancient xel'naga temple on the planet Artika. Amid the violence, the combatants come to realize the individual motivations that have brought them to this chaotic battlefield.
(*StarCraft: Frontline*, volume 1, "Why We Fight" by Josh Elder and Ramanda Kamarga)

The Kel-Morian crew of *The Generous Profit* arrives on a desolate planet in hopes of finding something belonging to the planet's former inhabitants that is worth salvaging. As they sort through the ruins, the crew members discover the terrifying secret behind the planet's missing populace.
(*StarCraft: Frontline,* volume 2, "A Ghost Story" by Kieron Gillen and Hector Sevilla)

A team of protoss scientists experiments on a sample of zerg creep. However, the substance begins to affect the scientists strangely, eventually sending their minds spiraling downward into madness.
(*StarCraft: Frontline,* volume 2, "Creep" by Simon Furman and Tomás Aira)

A psychotic viking pilot, Captain Jon Dyre, attacks the innocent colonists of Ursa during a weapon demonstration. His former pupil, Wes Carter, confronts Dyre in order to end his crazed killing spree.
(*StarCraft: Frontline,* volume 1, "Heavy Armor, Part 1" by Simon Furman and Jesse Elliott)
(*StarCraft: Frontline,* volume 2, "Heavy Armor, Part 2" by Simon Furman and Jesse Elliott)

Sandin Forst, a skilled Thor pilot with two loyal partners, braves the ruins of a terran installation

on Mar Sara in order to infiltrate a hidden vault. After getting access to the facility, Forst realizes that the treasures he expected to find were never meant to be discovered.
(*StarCraft: Frontline*, volume 1, "Thundergod" by Richard A. Knaak and Naohiro Washio)

2503

Dominion scientists capture the praetor Muadun and conduct experiments to better understand the protoss' psionic gestalt—the Khala. Led by the twisted Dr. Stanley Burgess, these researchers violate every ethical code in their search for power.
(*StarCraft: Frontline*, volume 3, "Do No Harm" by Josh Elder and Ramanda Kamarga)

Archaeologist Jake Ramsey investigates a xel'naga temple, but things quickly spiral out of control when a protoss mystic known as a preserver merges with his mind. Afterward Jake is flooded with memories spanning protoss history.
(*StarCraft: Firstborn*, book one of the Dark Templar Saga by Christie Golden)

Jake Ramsey's adventure continues on the planet Aiur. Under the instructions of the protoss

preserver within his head, Jake explores the shadowy labyrinths beneath the planet's surface to locate a sacred crystal that might be instrumental in saving the universe.
(*StarCraft: Shadow Hunters*, book two of the Dark Templar Saga by Christie Golden)

Mysteriously some of the Dominion's highly trained ghosts begin to disappear. Nova Terra, now a graduate of the Ghost Academy, investigates the fate of the missing operatives and discovers a terrible secret.
(*StarCraft: Ghost: Spectres* by Keith R.A. DeCandido)

Jake Ramsey is separated from his bodyguard, Rosemary Dahl, after they flee Aiur through a xel'naga warp gate. Rosemary ends up alongside other refugee protoss on Shakuras, but Jake is nowhere to be found. Alone and running out of time, Jake searches for a way to separate the protoss preserver from his mind before they both die.
(*StarCraft: Twilight*, book three of the Dark Templar Saga by Christie Golden)

A team from the Moebius Foundation—a mysterious terran organization interested in alien artifacts—investigates a xel'naga structure in the far reaches of the Koprulu sector. During their

research the scientists uncover a dark force lurking in the ancient ruins.
(*StarCraft: Frontline,* volume 4, "Voice in the Darkness" by Josh Elder and Ramanda Kamarga)

Kern tries to start his life anew after a career as a Dominion reaper, a highly mobile shock trooper who was chemically altered to make himself more aggressive. But his troubled past proves harder to escape than he thought when a former comrade unexpectedly arrives at Kern's home.
(*StarCraft: Frontline,* volume 4, "Fear the Reaper" by David Gerrold and Ruben de Vela)

A nightclub singer named Starry Lace finds herself at the center of diplomatic intrigue between Dominion and Kel-Morian officials.
(*StarCraft: Frontline,* volume 3, "Last Call" by Grace Randolph and Seung-hui Kye)

2504

A world-weary Jim Raynor returns to Mar Sara and struggles with his own disillusionment.
(*StarCraft: Frontline,* volume 4, "Homecoming" by Chris Metzen and Hector Sevilla)

GLOSSARY

B-2 bag: A military field bag used to carry personal supplies.

Bivvy bag: A thin waterproof sack that can be used as a temporary shelter. (Short for "bivouac bag.")

Boonie hat: A soft, wide-brimmed military hat that is usually camouflaged.

Brass: High-ranking military officers.

Brig: A military prison.

Brig rats: Military personnel who are habitually sent to the brig.

Buck sergeant: A sergeant of the lowest rank in the military.

Cammies: Slang for "camouflage uniform."

Camo: Slang for "camouflage."

Civvies: Slang for "civilian clothing."

CMC: Abbreviation for "Confederate Marine Corps." This abbreviation is used in regard to powered combat armor. The version of the armor depends on the number accompanying "CMC" (e.g., 220, 225, 230, etc.).

CO: Abbreviation for "commanding officer."

Color guard: Soldiers who are tasked with carrying national and military-related flags during ceremonies.

Deass: Slang for "to exit or leave."

DI: Abbreviation for "drill instructor."

Dopp kit: A small toiletry bag used for storing men's grooming tools for travel.

Ground pounder: Slang for "ground-based military units."

Hardskin: Slang for "terran powered combat armor," such as the CMC-220.

HQ: Abbreviation for "headquarters."

HUD: Abbreviation for "heads-up display."

KIA: Abbreviation for "killed in action."

KIC: Abbreviation for "Kel-Morian internment camp." The number following "KIC" indicates the specific camp.

KM or KMs: Confederate slang for "Kel-Morian" or "Kel-Morians." (Noun and adjectival forms.)

LAV: Abbreviation for "light attack vehicle."

Lifer: An individual who plans to stay in the military and make a career of it.

M-1 bag: A military field bag used to carry medical supplies.

MP: Abbreviation for "military police."

MSS: Abbreviation for "Military Security Service."

P-1 file: A P-1, or Personnel 1 file, consists of a chronological record of a soldier's service in the military.

POW: Abbreviation for "prisoner of war."

R & R: Abbreviation for "rest and relaxation."

SCV: Abbreviation for "space construction vehicle."

Skalet: A domesticated farm animal that is similar to the cows of Earth.

STM: Abbreviation for "Special Tactics and Missions platoon."

UNN: Abbreviation for "Universal News Network."

WIA: Abbreviation for "wounded in action."